The Parchment

The Parchment

A Novel

Gerald T. McLaughlin

Lindisfarne Books

2005

Lindisfarne Books
400 Main Street
Great Barrington, MA 01230
www.lindisfarne.org

Library of Congress Cataloging-in-Publication Data

McLaughlin, Gerald T.

The parchment : a novel / by Gerald T. McLaughlin.

p. cm.

ISBN 1-58420-030-8

1. Manuscripts—Collectors and collecting—Fiction. 2. Church history—Sources—Fiction. 3. Vatican City—Fiction. 4. Catholics—Fiction. 5. Popes—Fiction. I. Title.

PS3613.C548P37 2005

813'.6 — dc22

2004023450

First edition, printed in the U.S.A.

10 9 8 7 6 5 4 3 2 1

Historical Background & Disclaimer

The story of *The Parchment* is played out against the Palais des Papes in Avignon, St. Peter's Basilica in Rome, the destruction of the Temple of Herod, and the Crusades. This story was not written as a work of history and should not be read as one. Although there is much history in it, historical accuracy has been sacrificed when necessary to the demands of the narrative drama. The characters depicted in this story are purely fictional. With the exception of historical figures, any similarity to actual individuals is coincidental.

Preface

"Latin American liberation theology, Catholic peace movements in the United States and Europe, ashram movements in India, and base groups in many countries in the Northern and Southern hemispheres are examples of how the catholicity of the Catholic Church is not just a principle of faith but a human reality which is lived out in practice."

— Hans Küng, The Catholic Church: A Short History.

"[O]ur Church is a faith institution. A home to Christ's people. It is not a criminal enterprise. It does not condone and cover up criminal activity. It does not follow a code of silence.... To resist grand jury subpoenas, to suppress the names of offending clerics, to deny, to obfuscate, to explain away; that is the model of a criminal organization, not my church."

— Governor Frank Keating, Letter of Resignation as Chair of Bishops Oversight Committee.

Dedication

This book is dedicated to my wife Irene. Writing a novel—particularly a first novel—is a lonely occupation. During the long hours, during the constant rewriting and sharpening of the story, there were times when I needed inspiration, times when I needed humor, times when I needed encouragement, and times when I needed a friendly hand on the shoulder. Irene was there during all these times. One could ask for little more.

The Parchment

Chapter 1

A CRISIS IN JERUSALEM

POISED TO SHOOT, the sniper crouched behind a concrete barrier. He kept the casement window of the church in his sights.

A man with an infrared sensor huddled next to him. "He's about ten yards from the window. He's on a cell phone."

The sniper whispered. "Is it him?"

A soldier with earphones nodded. "We have voice confirmation from central command. He drove the car at the Wailing Wall bombing."

"I have a clean shot. Should I take it?"

"Yes."

The sniper pulled the trigger. The crack of the rifle reverberated through the church square, sending a flock of pigeons flying into the sky.

At the report of the gun, Habib instinctively ducked behind the altar. He heard a cell phone clatter to the ground next to him. His brother Mahmood had slumped to the floor of the church. Blood foamed from his mouth.

One of the hostages ran over to help.

"I'm a doctor." He quickly checked the body. "The bullet went through his heart."

Enraged, Habib shoved the barrel of his pistol into the doctor's mouth.

"Son of a bitch. You're Jewish, aren't you? "

Yassir, the commander of the Hamas terrorists, quickly moved between them and pushed the gun aside. "Habib, stop it! The hostages aren't Jews.... Doctor, go back to your place."

Hamas's brutal car bombing near the Wailing Wall had set off another spiral of violent recriminations in Jerusalem. Within days of the bombing, Israeli soldiers closed the Al-Aqsa Mosque on the Temple Mount and arrested dozens of suspected Hamas militants. To force Israel to reopen the mosque and release their captives, Hamas notched up tensions further still. Gunmen stormed the Church of the Holy Sepulchre, the most sacred church in all of Christendom, capturing over a hundred Dutch pilgrims who had been worshipping at the Tomb of Christ when the raid occurred. The siege at the church was now in its fifth day, and conditions inside the building were becoming increasingly grim. Hostages huddled in frightened groups throughout the sanctuary. The only exercise permitted them were trips to the baptismal font, which now served as a lavatory. The Israeli army lit up the walls of the church with giant floodlights and played loud music to keep the terrorists from sleeping. The nightmare inside the church had already caused several hostages to succumb to depression and bouts of crying.

Yassir took Habib to the far end of the transept.

"Your brother knew the Israelis would kill him for his part in the bombing. Mahmood understood the risks. He died a martyr for Islam."

Habib glared at the commander. "The Israelis arrest our brothers and sisters. Their marksmen kill us. It is time to act, Yassir, not talk."

Stung by Habib's rebuke, Yassir stared for a moment at the door of the Basilica.

"Habib, give me your brother's cell phone."

Yassir dialed a number and waited. A voice came on the line.

Yassir spoke English with a slight accent. "Tell your Prime Minister we've been negotiating with words. Now he negotiates with bullets."

Yassir walked to where the doctor was sitting. Sunlight splashed color on the floor of the church.

"I'm going to release you, Doctor. The world must see that the hostages have not been harmed. Come with me to the entrance."

Yassir unlocked the metal bolt on the inside of the door.

"Put your hands above your head and walk slowly out into the square. The Israelis won't shoot."

The doctor stepped through the church door, arms raised high. He stood for a moment until his eyes adjusted to the bright light of the square.

An Israeli bullhorn crackled. "Walk straight ahead and keep your hands where we can see them."

Without warning, Yassir pulled out his pistol, took aim, and shot the doctor in the back. The doctor's body fell in a pool of blood in front of the church.

Yassir dialed the cell phone again.

"It's six o'clock in the morning. Unless the Al-Aqsa Mosque is reopened and our brothers released, we will start executing Christian hostages at noon tomorrow—thirty hours from now."

Yassir clicked off the cell phone and handed it back to Habib.

Outside, a stray dog poked curiously at the body of the doctor, but a shot from an Israeli marksman drove him away.

Cardinal Francesco Barbo, the Vatican secretary of state, was awakened at 5:30 in the morning and told of the shootings at the Sepulchre. Barbo quickly dressed and hurried to his office. Given what had happened at the church, Barbo knew he had to take charge personally of the Vatican's response.

The cardinal secretary of state was a tall, big-boned man with an aristocratic nose and dark silver hair. Although seventy years of age, Barbo's energy and stamina were legendary. He had risen through the Curial ranks with meteoric speed. Born into a middle-class family in Milan, he entered the priesthood when he was sixteen. From his earliest days in the seminary, Barbo was singled out to join the papal diplomatic corps. After finishing four years of study in Milan, he was invited to attend the Pontifical Ecclesiastical Academy—the Vatican school for diplomats. Then after two years, he was sent to the Jesuit-run Gregorian University for his theological training. At the "Greg," Barbo became fascinated with the Crusades—most particularly with the fabled Order of the Knights of the Temple of Solomon. Led by laymen, the Templars were a unique brotherhood of warriors, priests, monks, bankers, diplomats, and scientists. Barbo's doctoral dissertation—*Mixing the Secular and the Religious: The Knights of the Temple and Their Structure of Governance*—had won plaudits, both for the depth of its research and the incisiveness of its analysis.

Barbo's advancement in the Vatican diplomatic corps was assured when he was sent to earn a doctoral degree at the Woodrow Wilson School for Diplomacy at Princeton University. While at Princeton, Barbo was asked to give a series of guest lectures on Church history at Harvard's John F. Kennedy School of Government. Barbo possessed a first-class mind and an acerbic wit. The cardinal spoke six languages fluently and was comfortable in four more. Little passed him by without notice and, once noticed, little was ever forgotten. When he was named cardinal, the Latin coat of arms he chose read *Fides et Utilitas*—"Faith and Pragmatism."

Father Enrico Alessandri, the cardinal's chief of staff, stood in the corridor outside Barbo's office. Although he had spent the night monitoring events in Jerusalem, the thirty-two-year-old Alessandri showed no sign of fatigue. Lean and muscular from years of soccer playing, Alessandri's starched Roman collar and pressed cassock gave him a clean, almost scrubbed look.

"Your Eminence, our nuncio in Israel, Archbishop Finnergan, called. The Israelis have retrieved the body of the doctor. It is being flown to the Netherlands for burial."

"'This has been a sad day for everyone, but that is good news, Enrico. Have there been any further communications from inside?"

A secretary, her eyes bloodshot from lack of sleep, stuck her head into the hallway. "Your Eminence, I'm sorry to interrupt but the Holy Father is on your line."

Barbo strode quickly to his desk. The cardinal waved a handful of staff members out of his office so he could speak privately with the pontiff.

"Francesco." There were traces of sleep in Pope Benedict's voice. "The Israeli Prime Minister just called. The terrorists inside the church have issued an ultimatum; they will start executing hostages in thirty hours unless Israel gives in to their demands."

Barbo clenched his teeth in anger. "Holy Father, the Israeli sniper was the cause of this. The Israelis must take steps to defuse the situation."

"The prime minister understands that. He's willing to reopen the mosque and release the Hamas militants they recently arrested. But he refuses to free the gunmen inside the church. The Israelis believe they were behind the Wailing Wall bombing." Pope Benedict was silent for a moment. "Francesco, send Archbishop Finnergan into the Sepulchre to talk to the Hamas commander. It might help calm matters."

"Holy Father, Finnergan grew up on the streets of Belfast. Sometimes he forgets he's a papal nuncio and tries to negotiate with his fists."

"That's why he's the right person to deal with Hamas. He can't be intimidated." There was a resolve in the pope's voice that Barbo had not heard for several months. "What is Washington saying to the Israelis?"

Barbo fingered through a pile of emails on his desk. "Washington's trying to persuade the Israelis to let the gunmen go free, but the Americans are meeting resistance. The Israelis have told Washington they cannot do it politically."

A familiar voice suddenly came on the line. It was Sister Consuela, the pope's housekeeper. "Your Eminence, the Holy Father is exhausted. I must cut the conversation short—it could excite him too much."

"I understand, Consuela. I'll keep the Holy Father informed of developments."

The phone clicked off. Barbo walked to the window and looked up at the papal quarters. The solitary light in the pope's bedroom went dark.

Chapter II

THE REWARDS OF SCHOLARSHIP

PROFESSOR JANE MICHELLINI walked across the reading room in the Vatican Apostolic Library to where her colleague James Bielgard sat facing a pile of manuscripts.

"Don't forget, we've got to put in an appearance at the director's office today or our library clearances will expire. We don't want to lose access to the uncatalogued manuscripts."

Preoccupied, Bielgard barely heard what Michellini said. "Holy shit! I don't believe this." Bielgard's voice ricocheted around the room.

An elderly priest examining an illuminated Bible glared impatiently at Michellini and Bielgard.

"Jim, be quiet. If there are complaints, the library could revoke our privileges."

"Look at this! It appears to be a Jewish census record, Jane. Your Hebrew is better than mine."

Michellini lifted the manuscript from the table and read it. After a minute, she pulled a chair up to the desk, sat down, and studied it more carefully. Bielgard nervously tapped his walking stick on the library floor.

After several minutes of concentration, Michellini stood up and stared at Bielgard with a stunned look on her face. "Where in God's name did you find this?"

"Upstairs in a chest filled with twelfth-century documents from the Knights of the Temple."

Distracted by the nervous tapping of Bielgard's cane, the priest slammed his hands on the table and angrily motioned for a library attendant to carry the illuminated Bible into an adjourning reading room.

At sixty, James Bielgard, the Robert M. Kevin Professor of Medieval History at the University of Michigan, was a tall avuncular looking man, with a high forehead and a thin aquiline nose. With his inexhaustible collection of bow ties, Bielgard cultivated a flamboyant image among his academic colleagues. He admitted to a close friend, however, that the walking stick he carried with him at all times was an affectation, not a medical necessity. A brilliant and entertaining lecturer, Bielgard's classes at the university were always over-subscribed. Some students thought Bielgard's intellectual pretense bordered on the humorous. Amused, they would organize a weekly lottery. Whoever guessed how often Bielgard would cite his own publications won twenty dollars.

Jane Michellini, an arrestingly beautiful woman, was an associate professor of European History at Bard College in New York. Unlike Bielgard, her former teacher and mentor, Michellini was a stylish dresser, sporting a trademark red and gold scarf that set off her long black hair. Her concentration and focus were legendary. She was reputed once to have sat reading manuscripts for three consecutive days in the Huntington Library in Pasadena, California, with virtually no food or drink.

A few years earlier, Michellini and Bielgard had coauthored a biography of Eleanor of Aquitaine, which had won the coveted United States Historical Association Prize for Medieval History. The decision to award the prize to the two American scholars, however, was not a simple one. A French colleague had accused Bielgard and Michellini of plagiarizing several pages from his article on Eleanor's relationship with her son, King John of England. In a close vote, a jury of historians exonerated Bielgard and Michellini on the plagiarism charge but warned them about "failures in appropriate citation." They hoped their second collaborative effort, tentatively entitled "Jihad in the Middle Ages," would be as critically acclaimed as the Eleanor biography but with less controversy. Initially, at least, they had every cause for optimism. After two unsuccessful attempts, they had finally been given access to the library's uncatalogued manuscript collection. Bielgard attributed the access to their perseverance; Michellini, to a phone call from the White House Press Secretary, who coincidentally had been Michellini's former roommate at Mount Holyoke College.

Standing up from the table, Michellini motioned Bielgard to follow her out of the reading room. The two professors found a quiet corner in the coffee bar.

"God, Jim. If this parchment is authentic, it dwarfs the discovery of the Dead Sea Scrolls. Think of the recognition we'll get. The Vatican Library should call a press conference."

"Forget the library! We found the manuscript, not them."

Michellini glanced at Bielgard with a puzzled look. "What does that mean?"

"I'm not sure—let me think. The parchment is uncataloged. We could smuggle it out of here and sell it to a collector."

"Right, and get caught like Robert McNabb."

The McNabb affair had sent tremors through the library world. A frequent researcher at the Vatican Library, retired Iowa State University Professor Robert McNabb had removed illuminated pages from the Vatican Library's fourteenth-century manuscript collection and offered them for sale to wealthy collectors.

Bielgard thought for a moment as he absentmindedly fingered his cane. "We're in a different position from McNabb. We don't have to approach collectors. The Catholic Church will pay a fortune to get this back."

Michellini frowned at Bielgard as her mind raced through the implications of his words. "Are you suggesting we blackmail the Vatican?"

"It's a possibility."

"Well, count me out. I went along with your scheme on the Eleanor biography. I barely got out of that with my reputation."

A bell sounded, and the public address system announced that the library would close in ten minutes.

"Jane, we can talk about this later. Please do me a favor and renew my library clearances. I'm covered with dust from handling these manuscripts. I've got to wash up. I'll meet you at the exit."

"Okay."

Michellini returned to the reading room, picked up her laptop, and walked toward the down staircase. At the director's office on the ground floor, she filled out the necessary paperwork to renew library clearances for herself and Bielgard. As she was paying the renewal fees, she saw Bielgard hurrying down the library staircase, waving his cane. Without warning, he slipped on the bottom step and fell on the ground. Several security officers ran over to help him up.

"Grazie. It was this damned walking stick. I tripped over it."

Michellini took Bielgard's arm as they left the library.

"Jim, I'll treat you to a cab back to the hotel. You really took a spill in there."

At nine o'clock in the morning, a panel truck drove up to the entrance of the Church of the Holy Sepulchre. Archbishop Michael Finnergan, the papal nuncio to Israel, climbed out of the truck and, along with three priests, carried food and medical supplies into the church. A camera crew from the Al-Jazeera news agency accompanied them.

"Who's in charge here?"

"I am." Yassir lifted his machine gun menacingly and walked up to Finnergan.

"I would like to talk to the hostages and hear their confessions. You've endangered their lives."

"No tricks!"

"I give you my word as a priest."

Yassir pointed with his gun. "Go ahead. Make it fast."

Finnergan took a white stole out of his pocket and walked over to a group of hostages. Brandishing his automatic rifle, a gunman stepped in front of him.

"I'm a Palestinian Christian, Monsignor. Hear my confession first." Finnergan knew that the Palestinian was baiting him for the sake of the Al-Jazeera cameramen.

"I will not administer the sacrament to someone who threatens the lives of defenseless people. Find forgiveness somewhere else."

The Palestinian pushed Finnergan back with the butt of his rifle. For a long moment, Finnergan stood stock-still. Then his Irish temper exploded. He clenched his right fist and hit the Palestinian hard in the stomach. The gunman doubled over, his rifle falling to the floor.

"You son of a bitch." The Palestinian picked up the rifle and raised it to shoot.

A special BBC report from the Church of the Holy Sepulchre flashed on the television screen in Cardinal Barbo's office. Barbo slammed his fist on the desk as he watched the live Al-Jazeera footage of Finnergan's encounter with the Hamas gunman. Barbo was furious with himself. He should have objected more strenuously to Pope Benedict's decision to send Finnergan into the Sepulchre. Finnergan had problems keeping his temper in check. Still a part of Barbo had to admire the Irish archbishop; it took guts to confront an armed terrorist with only his bare hands.

Barbo turned the television off and buzzed for his chief of staff, Father Alessandri.

"Enrico, I want Finnergan on a plane for Rome immediately. It's an order. Tell him to lease a private jet if he has to. Get the rest of our Middle Eastern nuncios back here as well—Kennedy, Viret, all of them. I want them sitting in my conference room at eight o'clock tonight."

"Yes, Your Eminence."

Barbo checked his watch. If they stuck to their deadline, the Hamas gunmen would begin executing their prisoners in approximately twenty-seven hours.

When the two professors returned to their hotel, Bielgard invited Michellini to his room for a drink.

Michellini sat down on the couch and kicked off her shoes. "You're certainly in a good mood, considering your fall."

"I was lucky." Bielgard opened the minibar and poured two scotches. He handed one to Michellini. "I want to talk to you about the parchment we found. It'll make us rich."

Michellini took a few sips of scotch but said nothing. The wail of a police siren passed under the hotel window. Michellini got up from the couch to see what had happened. When the sound of the siren had trailed off into the night, she picked up her belongings and walked to the door of Bielgard's room.

"Thanks for the drink, Jim, but I'm tired."

"Jane, won't you at least hear me out on this?"

"You play things too close to the line, Jim. I'm showing the manuscript to the director tomorrow. We'll get credit in the academic world for discovering it. I could end up at Harvard before this is all over."

"Jane, just give me another minute, that's all—please."

"If it's so important to you, Jim, I'll give you your damned minute but nothing more." Michellini reluctantly sat back down on the couch. "The clock's ticking."

Bielgard gulped down his scotch and poured himself another. "Think practically, Jane. You have young children. The money you could get from the Vatican would let your kids go to the best schools—get a real start in life."

"I'm an academic, Jim, not an extortionist. I wouldn't know how to bribe the Vatican even if I wanted to."

Bielgard rubbed the silver handle of his cane as if he were polishing it. "It's simple."

Michellini laughed aloud. "As simple as your plagiarism scheme with the Eleanor of Aquitaine biography! You were so sure that a general footnote would let us use those verbatim quotes."

"I promise you, we won't get close to this one. We'll hire someone to approach the Vatican for us. There's no way they won't buy it. There's too much at stake."

Michellini rolled her eyes in exasperation. "For starters, how are you going to get the parchment out of the library? Since McNabb walked out with those texts, they've tightened security. You'd get caught."

"If they've tightened security, it's not obvious to me. You can still smuggle almost anything out of there if you set your mind to it."

Michellini frowned. "How can you say that? They only let you take a notebook or a laptop into the reading rooms."

"And a cane." Bielgard unscrewed the silver handle of his walking stick and removed the parchment scroll.

"How in the world...?"

Bielgard smiled. "It was easy. While I was in the washroom, I took the scroll, rolled it up, and slid it inside the cane."

Michellini jumped up and slapped Bielgard hard across the face. "You son of a bitch. Your fall was staged."

"Yes." Bielgard grinned. "The security guards were so concerned that I might have been injured that they forgot to check the cane."

Michellini sat down again and considered this turn of affairs. She leaned forward and looked squarely at Bielgard. "You really think we can blackmail the Vatican and get away with it?"

"Yes, I do. It simply means finding the right person—someone who knows what really goes on in that *sanctum sanctorum.*"

"And, of course, you know that person?"

Bielgard looked at Michellini impishly. "As a matter of fact I do. Last year, a publishing friend got into trouble with the Italian tax authorities. He was advised to hire a well-connected lawyer here in Rome named Pietro Visconti. The lawyer made a few phone calls, and that was that. How about the three of us having dinner at Tre Amici in Piazza Margana?"

Michellini hesitated. "I don't know, Jim. I...."

"If you're still uncomfortable after we talk with Visconti, I promise I'll drop the whole idea."

Michellini shrugged. "I guess a dinner can't hurt."

Bielgard poured Michellini another scotch. "Good, Visconti has already phoned for reservations this evening."

After Alessandri had left to summon the nuncios to Rome, a phone call came in on Barbo's private line. The cardinal recognized a familiar voice.

"John, we should meet face to face.... Yes, I know the place. I can be there in an hour."

Cardinal Barbo walked quickly along Via Rafaello. Shopkeepers were hosing down the street before the start of business. The smell of the water washing the dust from the street reminded Barbo of his childhood in Milan. Every morning except Sunday, his father would rise early and wash the street in front of the family bookstore. He would always say: "The entrance to a bookstore is the door to learning. It must be kept spotless."

A dark green Mercedes Benz was parked in front of a neighborhood trattoria. The secretary of state opened the car door and slipped into the passenger seat. A man about sixty years of age with thick curly hair and wire-rimmed glasses sat across from Barbo in the driver's seat. There was a tremor in the man's left hand from the early onset of Parkinson's disease.

"You have some explaining to do, John." Barbo looked impatiently at the man sitting next to him.

"About the sniper?"

"Yes. How could Washington let Israel do that?"

"Francesco, it's not like turning a spigot on and off. We don't control the Israelis that way."

Barbo had met John Vincent thirty years before when Barbo was a young monsignor in the Vatican Secretariat of State, and Vincent, the deputy section chief of the CIA in Rome. They had become close friends during the years when President Reagan and Pope John Paul II had worked together to topple the Communist regime in Poland.

"The president has squeezed the Israelis as much as he can over the gunmen in the church. The Israelis want five of them but they'll let the rest go free—on condition that they leave the Middle East. Can the Vatican arrange safe havens for them?" From years of habit, Vincent looked reflexively in the rear view mirror.

"I'm sure we can. But I'm afraid Hamas won't accept the offer. They'll never agree to turn over five of their men to the Israelis. The president is going to have to call the prime minister again."

Vincent pounded his fists on the steering wheel. "Look, Francesco, I told you the president pushed the Israelis as far as he could. He can't perform miracles like your boss."

Barbo smiled. "It's not a miracle we need, John. It's some bare-knuckled politics—the kind Reagan knew how to play. The Israelis must need something from the Americans."

Vincent glared at his old friend. "I'll go back to the White House again, but the president won't be pleased. Can I tell them that the Vatican secretary of state says it's okay to bribe the Israelis?"

Barbo grinned. "If it means saving lives, yes, by all means."

Vincent sat quietly for a moment. "Despite all this, Francesco, the president wants you to know how much he appreciates the Vatican's help trying to resolve this crisis."

Barbo was puzzled at the president's comment. "What did Washington expect, John? The hostages are fellow Christians. The Holy See will do whatever it can to get them out of there safely. Think of the consequences if Israel storms the most sacred church in all of Christendom."

"Don't take me there, Francesco. By the way, it wasn't just the Israeli sniper who almost derailed negotiations. What about your papal nuncio Finnergan? Have you seen the Al-Jazeera broadcast?"

Barbo tensed. "You won't hear from Archbishop Finnergan again." The cardinal checked his watch. "Twenty-six hours to go."

The two men shook hands. As Barbo opened the front door to get out of the car, Vincent handed him a piece of paper. "Francesco, here's the cell phone number of the Hamas commander in the Church of the Holy Sepulchre. Maybe the Vatican can get him to extend the thirty-hour ultimatum."

Chapter III

A Meeting of Nuncios

Lightning flared in the evening sky behind St. Peter's Basilica. The silhouette of the cupola appeared and disappeared with each flash. As he walked across St. Peter's Square, the secretary of state saw none of this. His mind was focused on the Hamas ultimatum in Jerusalem and his upcoming meeting with Finnergan and the other papal nuncios.

As cardinal secretary of state, Barbo oversaw a far-flung network of diplomatic missions. The Vatican posted a nuncio or ambassador to each nation that recognized the sovereignty of the Holy See. Although Vatican nuncios received high marks for their professionalism, Barbo had become increasingly upset with their handling of the crisis in the Church of the Holy Sepulchre. What infuriated him most was the nuncios' failure to coordinate their press releases and statements with his office in Rome. On top of that, of course, was Archbishop Finnergan's conduct inside the church. His drubbing of the Palestinian gunman was being played and replayed on news channels worldwide. Fox News called the archbishop "courageous" and compared his striking the terrorist to Christ's driving the moneylenders out of the Temple. CNN and most European news media, however, reported the incident as a confirmation of the Vatican's tilt toward Israel in the crisis.

As he neared the entrance to the Apostolic Palace, the cardinal's cell phone rang.

It was Sister Consuela, the pope's housekeeper. "Consuela, how is the Holy Father doing?... Of course I can. I'll be there in five minutes."

As the secretary of state entered the vestibule of the Apostolic Palace, a Swiss Guard snapped to attention. Barbo had never completely rid himself of the notion that, with their striped uniforms and plumed helmets, the Swiss Guards were tourist attractions—there to provide a colorful addition to innumerable snapshots. He knew better, of course. Each of the guards had been trained in the most sophisticated antiterrorist and crowd-control techniques.

Once inside, Barbo passed through the metal detector and hurried to the palace stairway. The cardinal's ring and pectoral cross set off the alarm. A Swiss Guard raced over and disabled the machine.

"Eminence, I'm sorry. I didn't see who it was."

Climbing the stairs, the cardinal noticed a painting hanging in the stairwell. Although he had passed it a thousand times, Barbo had never given it much thought. The painting showed Mary at the foot of the Cross holding the body of her crucified son. This was not a humble, idealized Mary staring up resignedly to heaven. This was a human Mary—a mother angry with God for requiring the death of her only child—a defiant Mary who could no longer utter the words, "Thy will be done." The people of Rome say that the death of a child orphans a mother. The cardinal could see the look of emptiness in Mary's face. Without her son, she would walk the roads of Palestine alone.

When he reached the landing on the third floor, Barbo knocked at Pope Benedict's private apartment. Sister Consuela came to the door.

"Ah, Your Eminence, the Holy Father must have asked for you ten times in the last hour. He has been pacing up and down and refuses to take his pills."

The pope sat on the side of his bed in bathrobe and slippers. Sister Consuela had already turned down the sheets for the night and adjusted the air-conditioning. Three white pills and a glass of water stood on the pope's night table.

Cardinal Barbo walked over to the pope and kissed his ring.

When Benedict recognized who it was, he jumped up from the bed.

"Francesco, how are the hostages doing?"

"Conditions inside the church are deteriorating rapidly, Holy Father. In sixteen hours, Hamas will start executing hostages."

The pope began to pace up and down the room.

"Your Holiness, take your medicine."

"No. The pills make me groggy. What about the nuncios, are they here?"

"Yes, I'm on my way to the meeting."

The pope looked at his Secretary of State. "Finnergan behaved disgracefully at the Sepulchre. And the rest of them—don't they understand that at times like this, you keep quiet. The last thing you do is issue a press release."

"Holy Father, don't upset yourself. The negotiations are still proceeding. Washington has pressured Israel to agree to arrest only five of the gunmen. The Americans have asked us to use our good offices to find safe havens for the remaining twelve. I have called several prime ministers myself."

"Why didn't you use the nuncios?"

"You once told me, Your Holiness, if you need a coordinated plan, do it yourself. Our nuncios are fond of telling me they play as a team. If they are a team, then they play by a strange set of rules. They tackle their captain instead of their opponents."

The pope smiled at his secretary of state. "You were always a good student, Francesco. How many nations have agreed to take some of the gunmen?"

"Italy, Spain and the Netherlands have each agreed to take three. Portugal is still considering the request."

"The Netherlands should take more." The pope looked angry. "After all, it's their countrymen whose lives are at stake."

"The Dutch prime minister assured me privately he would take more if it meant ending the crisis. He knows two of the hostages personally."

The Dutch prime minister's private assurance seemed to calm the pontiff. "So if Washington can persuade the Israelis to free the last five gunmen, the siege is over."

"Yes, *if* Washington can persuade the Israelis. But no matter what happens, Holy Father, the president is grateful for what the Holy See is doing to help. It's the right time to approach him on your initiative."

"You were going to give me a short list of possible envoys to present my initiative to the president."

"It should be on your desk, Holy Father." Barbo found the list under a pile of unread documents.

"The Secretariat has vetted three names. I ruled out two—Abbot Maloof and Cardinal Verebrand. Even though he's an Arab, Maloof doesn't have a red hat. You know how important titles are to the Palestinians. Verebrand, on the other hand, has the title but I'm afraid the Israelis will veto him because his uncle was an officer in the SS."

"'That is true. Who else do you have?"

"Cardinal Jean Calvaux. He's lived in the Middle East, speaks Arabic, and comes from an old French aristocratic background."

"He's a Montelambert. I forgot that."

"He comes without any obvious baggage. What's more he's a new face. He may add some excitement to the process."

"Calvaux is a good choice. I will speak to him myself."

"But your health, Holy Father. Are you well enough to meet with him?"

"Yes I am."

"Are you taking your medicine?"

"Only when Sister Consuela forces me to."

"You must take it, Your Holiness."

Barbo picked up the three pills on the night table and handed them to the pontiff. Begrudgingly the pope took a drink of water and swallowed them.

"Francesco, I know what's coming. This morning I forgot where I left my breviary. Sister Consuela told me where it was but within a couple of minutes, I'd forgotten what she told me. It will be more and more like this."

"Holy Father, God has taken your health for some purpose."

Pope Benedict paused for a moment as if he were looking at the dark road that lay ahead of him.

"How long have we been friends, Francesco?"

Barbo looked affectionately at the Holy Father. "You taught me theology at the seminary."

"Then I must have told you the story about Thomas Aquinas's last words."

"If you did, I don't remember it." Barbo lied. He had heard the story many times before but he could not deprive the pope of his obvious pleasure in retelling it.

"It's rather amazing. One day, as the great theologian took communion, he fell to the ground. When he got up, he said 'All I have written is straw.' He rarely spoke after that."

"Did Aquinas suffer from Alzheimer's, Holy Father?"

"I prefer to think it was something else. After pushing reason to its limits, Aquinas had a direct experience of God—like Moses in the Sinai or Ezekiel."

"And that beggared all he had written."

"Yes. Perhaps Jesus is giving me the same chance—to experience him in a place beyond human understanding."

Barbo touched the pope gently on the arm. "But your work for peace in the Holy Land will never be considered straw."

Pope Benedict smiled. "Straw can make bricks and bricks can build bridges. Maybe my initiative will help rebuild trust in the region. You have been my strong right arm on so many things. Help me this one last time."

Barbo's eyes filled with emotion. "You need not ask me that."

The cardinal walked over to a phone on the pope's bedstead and dialed the Vatican switchboard operator.

"This is the Secretary of State. Please get me Cardinal Calvaux in Marseilles." Barbo looked at the Holy Father. The two friends knew the significance of the call.

"This is Cardinal Francesco Barbo calling from Rome. The Holy Father wishes to speak with Cardinal Calvaux."

Barbo could hear frantic whispers at the other end of the phone. Finally a man's voice came on the line.

"This is Monsignor Rosuet, the vicar general of the diocese. Cardinal Calvaux is at City Hall. The Mayor is hosting a trade delegation from Sicily. I will try to patch him in on his cell phone?"

Several minutes later Cardinal Calvaux came on the line. Barbo handed the receiver to Pope Benedict.

"Jean?"

"Holy Father, it's good to hear your voice."

"Thank you. I feel remiss. Marseilles is so close but I have never come to pray in your cathedral."

"We will be blessed if you would come."

"Perhaps some day soon. But right now, Jean, I must ask you to travel to Rome. There's a matter that I would like to discuss with you. It's urgent."

"I can be there tomorrow."

"Good! Cardinal Barbo will join us for our meeting. In the meantime, watch out for your Sicilian guests. They know how to tempt even a Prince of the Church."

Cardinal Calvaux laughed. "Yes, they do appreciate how expensive it is to run a diocese. They have even offered to build the archdiocese a new cathedral."

The pope put down the receiver.

"Francesco, Calvaux will be here tomorrow. The peace initiative has begun."

Barbo kissed the pope's ring and turned to leave. "The nuncios are waiting in my conference room."

"One thing more, Francesco." The pontiff hesitated as if debating whether to raise the issue. "Will Finnergan be at the nuncios' meeting?"

"Yes, he will."

"Remember he was my choice to send into the church. Don't be too hard on him. God can sometimes work in strange ways."

Cardinal Barbo walked down the stairs to the conference room adjacent to his office. When he opened the door, the group rose from their seats. As secretary of state, the cardinal was head of the Vatican government and second to the pope in the Church's hierarchy.

"Please, keep your seats. Thank you all for flying in on such short notice."

The door to the conference room suddenly flew open and a perspiring archbishop Paul Kennedy, papal nuncio in Amman, Jordan, entered. A chain-smoker, Kennedy was out of breath from climbing the stairs to the second-floor landing.

"I'm sorry, Your Eminence, I missed my connection in Tel Aviv."

"Take a seat, Paul." There was an edge to Barbo's voice.

A place had been kept open for Kennedy between Archbishop Finnergan and the Vatican nuncio to Egypt, Archbishop Eugenio Rontalvi. Although Church protocol did not require it, seating at nuncios' meetings went according to strict hierarchical rank, with archbishops at the head of the table, followed by bishops, and finally by monsignori. Seeking to emphasize equality among nuncios, Barbo had discouraged the practice. He soon realized, however, that this was a battle he would not win.

"Your Eminence, before we begin, could I ask a rather undiplomatic question?" With his expressionless face and coal black eyes, there was a hint of the Inquisition about Archbishop Eugenio Rontalvi.

"Of course, Eugenio."

"How is the Holy Father's health? He hasn't said Sunday Mass in St. Peter's for two weeks."

Barbo sensed that the question came from the group.

"The pope is preoccupied with the crisis in the Middle East, Eugenio. You know how hard he has worked to bring peace to the Holy Land."

"Your Eminence," Archbishop Paul Kennedy spoke, "please tell the Holy Father to slow down a little. We don't want a conclave in the near future."

"Paul, you go and tell the pope to work less. He will smile and thank you for your concern and. . . ."

Kennedy smiled. "And keep on working."

"Exactly. Now, gentlemen, to the matter at hand." Barbo's tone of voice made it clear that there would be no more discussion of the pope's health.

Several nuncios glanced at one another. Barbo had nimbly evaded the question.

"If I may be blunt, gentlemen, our diplomatic efforts in the Hamas crisis have made us look foolish." There was steel in Barbo's voice.

Barbo stared at Finnergan. The Irish archbishop sat stone-faced, his eyes fixed on a crucifix that hung over the entrance door. Perspiration glistened on his brow.

"I will speak with Archbishop Finnergan privately about the incident in the Church of the Holy Sepulchre. Let us focus now on the immediate concern. Over one hundred hostages are still in the church. Hamas has threatened to start executing them at noon tomorrow."

"Your Eminence, let me open the discussion." The speaker was Monsignor Albert Goethals, the apostolic delegate to the Palestinian Authority. Goethals' mellifluous voice annoyed Barbo—it made him appear more intelligent than he really was. "In my view, the Israelis will reopen the Al-Aqsa Mosque and let the suspected Hamas militants go free. The stumbling block will be the gunmen in the church. The Israelis have evidence that this group was involved in the bombing at the Wailing Wall. The incident shocked the country to the core. It limits the Israeli government's latitude for negotiating."

Finnergan nodded in agreement. "Monsignor Goethals is right. Israel won't let the terrorists in the church be flown to safety. When the opportunity presents itself, they'll go in and get them."

Barbo interrupted. "According to American sources, the Israelis have agreed to free twelve of the seventeen terrorists. But I'm afraid there won't be a deal unless all of them are freed."

Bishop Jacques Viret, the nuncio to Iraq, nodded his head in agreement. "His Eminence is right. Hamas loves death more than the Israelis love life. The terrorists will die rather than surrender even one of their men to the Israelis."

"That's a pretty grim assessment, Jacques." Finnergan spoke gruffly to his fellow nuncio.

"But a realistic one," Viret replied.

Goethals broke into the conversation. "Of course, we wouldn't be in this crisis if Israel had agreed to create a Palestinian state on the West Bank and close their settlements there."

Finnergan pounded his fist on the table. "You can't just close the settlements, Goethals. People live there."

The secretary of state pushed his seat back from the conference table and stood up impatiently.

"Gentlemen, lives hang in the balance in the Church of the Holy Sepulchre. We are here to get the hostages out alive—not to debate what might have been done to avert the crisis."

Cardinal Barbo's cell phone rang. As he listened, blood drained from his face.

"Yes, Holy Father. I will tell them."

Barbo clicked off the phone and reached for a glass of water. Viret noticed that the cardinal's hands were shaking.

"Gentlemen, the Holy Father has been informed there's been a sarin gas attack in Eilat—over a hundred Israelis have been admitted to hospitals—including many children."

Bishop Viret finally broke the silence. "Chemical weapons—God help us!"

Stunned by the news, Barbo walked out of the room.

Chapter IV

PIETRO VISCONTI

BIELGARD AND MICHELLINI **motioned the cab** driver to stop at the bottom of the Capitoline steps. They crossed the busy Via di San Marco and walked down Via Piacenza to the Piazza Margana. When they reached the Piazza, Bielgard saw Pietro Visconti sitting at a table outside Tre Amici Restaurant. Next to him sat a diminutive man.

"Visconti is here already."

"I'm nervous, Jim." Michellini clutched a large briefcase tightly in her hand.

"It's only a dinner."

"There is no such a thing as 'only a dinner.' Once you start a process, events sometimes have a way of getting away from you."

"Ah! Professor Bielgard." Visconti hurried over to greet his guests. "Your phone call intrigued me. I took the liberty of inviting Professor Baldini from the University of Rome to join us. He is an expert on the dating of Hebrew manuscripts."

Baldini got up from the table and bowed stiffly to Bielgard and Michellini.

"Jim, you warned me that your colleague Professor Michellini was a formidable scholar but you never told me that she was so beautiful." Always a master of the courtly gesture, Visconti took Michellini's hand and kissed it. "But come; why are we all standing?" Visconti's face was framed with smiles. "I've ordered some antipasti and a bottle of Tre Amici's best Tignanello."

Carlo Visconti had the dark good looks of an Italian movie idol. Born into a poor Roman family, he had learned the rules of survival on the streets of Rome. Visconti studied law at the City

University and quickly gained notoriety as a shrewd and tough-minded negotiator. He had a reputation not only for brokering deals which others thought impossible, but also for his discretion. If a deal unraveled, one thing was certain—nothing would ever be traced back to Visconti or to one of his clients. Through his wife's family, Visconti was also reputed to have strong ties to the Mafia. There was sentiment among some that Visconti's father-in-law was the *capo regime* in Rome. Whether true or not, one thing was undeniable. Visconti had friends at all levels of Italian society. He was the consummate fixer—the person to hire for very private matters where there could be no scandal and, of course, no press coverage.

"I'm fascinated by this census record you discovered in the Vatican Library. Show it to Professor Baldini."

Professor Michellini opened her briefcase and carefully unrolled an ancient piece of parchment and laid it flat on the table.

Baldini put on a pair of wire-rimmed glasses and bent over the document. After he studied it for several minutes, he looked up from the text.

"Remarkable—truly remarkable." Baldini sat silent for a moment as if savoring the suspense of what he was about to say. "This census record notes that Yeshua of Nazareth and Mary from the village of Magdala were married in the Hebrew year 3791. A son named David was born to them during the following year and a daughter named Tamar the year after that."

"Is the census record authentic?" Visconti was impatient for the answer.

"It has very distinctive writing. There's a superscript on one of the prongs of the letter *shin*. I have never seen a superscript like this except in first-century Hebrew manuscripts. A forger would have to be pretty sophisticated to get the *shin* right."

"So it's real?" Bielgard almost bolted out of his seat.

"You are a historian, Professor Bielgard." There was a scolding tone to Baldini's voice. "I would have to take it for carbon dating to be sure."

Visconti interrupted. "How long would carbon dating take?"

"Normally three weeks, but if I pay our lab technicians to work through the night, I could have preliminary results by early afternoon tomorrow."

"Pay what you have to, Baldini. Do the test as quickly as possible. Even preliminary results would be helpful."

"Just wait a moment!" Michellini scowled. "I signed on for a dinner. Now we're talking carbon testing."

Bielgard patted Michellini on the arm. "Jane has some misgivings about this, Pietro. But I'm sure she'll trust her old mentor a little while longer."

Professor Baldini carefully scrutinized the parchment. "I must take a small piece for testing. Perhaps from here where there's no lettering?"

Bielgard looked at Michellini. "What do you say, Jane?"

Michellini stood up from the table and gathered her belongings. "Let him take what he needs. It's only carbon dating—right Jim?"

Cardinal Barbo had hardly fallen to sleep after the nuncios' meeting when the phone rang in his apartment. The alarm clock said it was 3 A.M. The secretary of state was accustomed to late-night phone calls from around the world, but he sensed that this call was different.

"Your Eminence, come quickly!" The voice was Sister Consuela's. "The pope is not well."

Cardinal Barbo hurried to the Holy Father's apartment. Sister Consuela led him into the bedroom. Barbo's heart fell when he saw Benedict. His hair disheveled, the pope sat in a chair staring vacantly out a casement window. His breviary lay open on his lap but it was upside down.

"The Swiss Guard found him wandering in the corridor. He kept asking the guard how many hours until the hostages would be shot." Sister Consuela brushed a tear from her eye. "When I put the Holy Father back in bed, he immediately jumped up again and opened his birdcage. You know how he adores those two finches. Well, he ran around the bedroom chasing after them. He knocked over a vase and a lamp. When he couldn't catch them, he looked bewildered and sat down on the bed. I gave him his breviary. It calmed him until I could get the birds back in the cage."

The cardinal walked over to the Holy Father and spoke quietly. "Benedict, do you hear me? It's Francesco."

The pope turned his eyes in the direction of Barbo's voice but seemed not to recognize who was talking to him.

There was a knock on the door. Doctor Roger Hendricks, a specialist in neurological disorders at the Mayo Clinic, hurried into the room. During the past several months, Hendricks had commuted to Rome regularly to monitor the pope's condition. Hendricks sat on the bed next to the pope and directed a small light into his eyes. Putting down the light, Hendricks examined the pope's arm and leg flexibility.

Hendricks asked Sister Consuela to stand in front of the pope.

"Who is this, Holy Father?"

The pope looked at his housekeeper without any sign of recognition.

"Francesco, you asked me to tell you when it was time to have the conversation. I'm afraid now is the time."

The cardinal and doctor walked to the corner of the pope's bedroom, leaving Sister Consuela to minister to Benedict's needs.

Hendricks poured himself a glass of water. "Your Eminence, these bouts of memory loss are becoming more frequent. The pope's Alzheimer's is not going to get any better."

Barbo stared hard at Hendricks. "Weren't the drugs you prescribed slowing the progression of the disease?"

"Yes, but they've stopped working."

"Sometimes, Benedict refuses to take the medicine you prescribed."

"Francesco, I wish it were just a question of a stubborn patient. The pills are no longer effective. There's nothing else to try."

Barbo fingered his pectoral cross. "You know where all this leads?"

Hendricks nodded. "Yes, I do. But that's the Church's decision, not mine."

"I must be sure, Roger."

"I'll have the pope's medical records faxed anonymously from the Mayo Clinic to two colleagues—Doctor Johan Bentzel at the Royal Karolinska Institute in Stockholm and Doctor Henri Souvenne in Montreal. Maybe they'll have some additional thoughts, but I'm not hopeful."

Barbo sat for a moment looking across the room to where the Holy Father sat. "Roger, get their opinions. So much hinges on the medical prognosis."

"Who would administer the Church if Pope Benedict were required to abdicate?"

"Cardinal Agostino Marini—the pope appointed him the camerlengo."

"The camerlengo?"

Barbo smiled. "Roger, I guess you haven't been around the Vatican long enough to have heard about the camerlengo?"

"I guess not."

"The camerlengo administers the day-to-day operations of the Church when there is no pope. If there's no encouragement from your colleagues in Stockholm and Montreal, I will inform Cardinal Marini about the pope's condition."

"I'll have the medical records sent immediately." Doctor Hendricks stood up and left the papal apartment.

Barbo looked at his watch. It was five in the morning. If Hamas carried out its ultimatum, the first executions would begin in seven hours.

At precisely 1:30 P.M., Professor Baldini was ushered into Pietro Visconti's office. Professors Bielgard and Michellini sat nervously on a couch under a picture of Visconti walking arm in arm with the prime minister and the president of the republic.

"Well, Baldini? What does the carbon dating say?"

Baldini took out his note pad. "Preliminary results date the parchment to the first century."

"First century, where?"

"First-century Palestine. I asked a colleague to perform a pollen test. He found several microscopic spores characteristic of plant growth in Palestine."

"Thank you, Professor." Visconti handed Baldini an envelope. "Take this for your efforts."

When Baldini had left the room, Bielgard turned to Visconti.

"Pietro, how much would the Vatican pay for this?"

Visconti thought for a moment. "Ten million euros would be a good place to start discussions."

Bielgard leaned closer to Visconti. "Would you approach the Vatican on our behalf?"

"Yes."

"And your fee?"

Visconti smiled. "We'll talk about it at a later date."

"Wait a minute!" Michellini started to put the parchment back in her briefcase. "First, it was dinner, then carbon dating, now extortion—events are moving ahead a little too fast for me."

"Pure and simple, Pietro, Jane is worried that we'll get caught."

Visconti stared at Michellini with a bemused look. "The Vatican is a multinational corporation and acts accordingly. It'll pay handsomely to keep this document from its shareholders. I assure you, there will be no police involvement. Trust me."

"Mr. Visconti, could Jim and I step out of your office for a moment."

"Of course. Use the conference room across the hall."

When they entered the room, Michellini exploded. "Don't try to make me out as the frightened academic. I told you what I want out of this—peer recognition. I want heads to turn when I enter the room. I want them to say that woman over there is Jane Michellini from Bard College. She discovered the Jesus-Magdalene parchment. Now she's at Harvard!"

"Recognition doesn't pay college tuitions, Jane. I'll take the money every time."

"I'll agree to let Visconti approach the Vatican to explore their level of interest and report back to us. Then we'll see."

"You're making the right decision, Jane. Let's talk some more with Visconti."

Cardinal Barbo sat at his desk, staring at his watch. In just over an hour, Hamas's threatened executions would begin.

Alessandri buzzed on the intercom. "The Portuguese prime minister is on line two, Your Eminence."

Barbo anxiously picked up the phone. "Isabella, thanks for calling me back so promptly."

"I wish I had better news. My staff tells me that taking these Hamas terrorists will give our anti-immigrant party here the opening they need to pillory me. The election polls are very close."

"Thanks for trying, Isabella. Sometimes you must say 'no,' even to the Holy Father."

"Please express my best wishes to His Holiness."

"In all this talk of Hamas and hostages, I forgot to tell you some good news. Both you and Grand Duchess Charlotte of Luxembourg have been nominated to receive the Golden Rose. As you know, it is conferred only on women heads of state who have demonstrated their devotion to the Church."

There was silence on the phone.

"I'm flattered. The Golden Rose has not been awarded in decades."

"Not since 1956. But the Holy Father believes that you and the Grand Duchess are deserving candidates. It will be difficult for the Holy Father to choose which of you has most helped the Church."

"I hope the Vatican realizes just how good you are, Francesco. How many Palestinians must I take to stay in the running?"

"Three."

"And what have you asked of the Grand Duchess?"

"The Church has many needs, Isabella."

"I guess I'll have to live with some extra political risk. Portugal will take your three Palestinians."

Barbo had hardly time to enjoy his success, when Alessandri buzzed again on the intercom.

"There's someone named John on line three. He won't give his full name. He says he's an old friend of yours."

"Put him through."

Barbo waited impatiently for Vincent to come on the line. "John, Portugal will take three. The Dutch Prime Minister promised that he would take more if it put an end to the crisis. If the Israelis will let the remaining five gunmen go, I think the crisis is over."

"I'm afraid they won't, Francesco. The Israelis just told Washington that all negotiations over the hostages in the church are off. They're furious over Eilat. They're threatening to invade the church no matter what the cost in lives."

"John, that cell phone number you gave me. I never used it. Stay on the line."

Barbo dialed the number of the Hamas commander in the church.

After three rings, someone picked up the receiver. "This is Cardinal Barbo, the secretary of state of the Vatican. Let me speak to your commander." Barbo could hear several men arguing in Arabic. Finally a man who spoke English took the receiver.

"What do you want?"

"Time," answered Barbo. "We are trying to convince the Israeli authorities to let all of you leave the country safely."

"The ultimatum stands." The man's voice was as hard as flint.

"The hostages are innocent pilgrims. They have done you no harm. Allah is a merciful God."

The speaker paused. Barbo heard him shout in Arabic to someone else in the church. The two men talked for several minutes. Finally the speaker returned to his conversation with Barbo. "Does this priest Finnergan work for you?"

Barbo was taken aback by the question. "Yes, Archbishop Finnergan is our nuncio."

"I admire his courage. He risked his life for strangers. I will give you another day but no more. And no tricks from the Jews."

Barbo pushed the button to reconnect Vincent. "John, they'll hold off until noon tomorrow because of the courage Finnergan displayed in the church. Contact Washington and tell them they have more time to persuade Israel to change its mind and let all the terrorists go."

"I'll tell the president, but after Eilat I think we have run out of leverage."

"Gentlemen, Hamas will extend the deadline for another twenty-four hours." There was loud applause from the nuncios when Barbo made the announcement. "That's the good news. The bad news is that the Israelis have withdrawn from negotiations because of Eilat. They're threatening to invade the church."

Archbishop Finnergan stood up. "Your Eminence, let me try to speak with the Israeli Prime Minister."

Goethals snapped at Finnergan. "With all due respect, Your Excellency, we can't be seen begging the Israelis."

"Goethals, I'd beg the devil if it meant saving the lives of innocent people."

"You're a diplomat, Archbishop Finnergan. We can't take sides."

Finnergan's eyes flashed with anger. "Go to hell with all your diplomatic niceties."

Goethals jumped up from his seat and glared at the Irish prelate. "Most Irishmen can tell a man to go to hell and still have him enjoy the journey. Somehow Archbishop Finnergan never inherited that skill. Whatever politeness he learned must have been in the back alleys of Belfast."

Barbo stood up from his chair slowly and deliberately as if to emphasize his impatience with the bickering in the room.

"Archbishop Finnergan, call the Israelis. I'm expected at a reception in honor of the president of the republic at the Quirinal Palace. Archbishop Kennedy, will you chair the meeting in my absence?"

"Of course, Your Eminence."

As Cardinal Barbo climbed the grand staircase of the Quirinal, steel-helmeted guards dressed in red and blue uniforms snapped to attention. After he had greeted the president of the republic and the

Italian prime minister in the grand salon of the palace, Barbo saw Pietro Visconti coming toward him.

"Could I have a moment with you, Eminenza?"

"Of course, Signor Visconti."

"It is too noisy here. Perhaps we could step out on the balcony?"

"As you wish, Pietro."

When they found a quiet spot on the terrace, Visconti handed Barbo an envelope. "Before I forget, one of my clients wishes to have Masses said in honor of his parents. I assume, Eminenza, you can make the necessary arrangements."

Barbo opened the envelope. "Of course I can, but this is too much, Pietro"

"My client is a generous man. Use the rest to help the poor in Rome."

Barbo thanked Visconti and tucked the envelope in the pocket of his cassock.

"Eminenza, I have been asked to approach the Church on a matter of some delicacy."

"My chief of staff, I'm sure can handle it. You know Father Alessandri, of course."

"Yes, but this matter requires your personal attention."

Barbo shrugged. "Come to my office today at five o'clock. I'm sure Alessandri can fit you in."

As they rejoined the reception in the grand salon, Barbo was surprised to see Hans Cardinal Diefenbacher among the guests. A Jesuit, Diefenbacher was archbishop of Durban and primate of South Africa. Jailed for his opposition to apartheid, Diefenbacher had recently become a passionate advocate of a decentralized Church. In a recent article in the Jesuit weekly, *America,* Diefenbacher had floated the idea of sharing the pope's spiritual authority with the Eastern Rite patriarchs and giving national bishops' conferences a much wider role in Church governance. Some suspected that what Diefenbacher really wanted was virtual autonomy for national churches, with the pope acting simply as a unifying symbol of faith and belief. "If Diefenbacher were ever elected pope," Alessandri joked after reading the *America* article, "he would give away so much of his authority that he would have little to do. I guess he could wander about Rome in the morning shaking hands and in the afternoon passing out holy cards."

"Hans, it is good to see you. You know, of course, Pietro Visconti."

"Yes, of course. We had dinner with mutual friends the last time I was in Italy."

"What brings you to Rome, Hans?" Barbo noticed that Diefenbacher wore no pectoral cross or other sign of his rank in the Church.

"It's my five-year *ad limina* visit." Diefenbacher looked at Visconti and rolled his eyes in mock aggravation. "Every five years, the Congregation for the Doctrine of the Faith sifts through a bishop's statements on faith and morals to see if he's still orthodox. I have passed the test, but just barely. My interrogators looked concerned." Diefenbacher made a dismissive gesture. "I'm now waiting for my audience with the Holy Father."

Visconti bowed to the two cardinals. "If you would excuse me. I'll let you two catch up on Church politics. Until this afternoon, Cardinal Barbo."

"Yes, at five."

As Visconti left, Diefenbacher took a glass of champagne from a passing waiter. "Francesco, be honest with me. I have not been able to schedule an audience with the Holy Father for two weeks. How is the pope's health?"

From years of diplomatic training, Barbo was skilled at answering one question by asking another. "If you were ultimately responsible for getting the hostages out of the Church of the Holy Sepulchre, Hans, wouldn't you be preoccupied? The pontiff thinks of nothing else."

A photographer pushed his way through the crowded salon and approached the cardinals for a picture.

Diefenbacher looked uncomfortable. "Not with this in my hand." He gave his glass to a waiter. "Some in my diocese would not approve."

As the picture was taken, there was a flourish of trumpets and the president of Italy stepped up to the podium to speak. The two cardinals turned their attention to the president's remarks.

When Barbo returned from the luncheon reception at the Quirinal Palace, Roger Hendricks was waiting in his outer office.

"Francesco, bad news."

"What?"

"I faxed the pope's medical records to Bentzel and Souvenne and asked for an immediate response. I told them the patient was the CEO of a multinational corporation."

"And?" Barbo tensed.

"They both think that, given the patient's failure to respond to medication, his pace of deterioration will increase rapidly. Like me, they think the pressure of the office may be speeding his deterioration."

"We've tried to relieve Benedict of most of his day-to-day papal responsibilities."

"But you can't relieve him of everything, Francesco. This Hamas crisis is literally killing him."

"So the three of you agree that staying in office worsens his condition."

"Yes. Stress has a known synergistic effect on Alzheimer's."

For a moment, Barbo stared at a silver icon of Jesus the Pantocrator that hung on the wall behind his desk. Barbo always drew strength from Jesus' eyes—strong but compassionate.

"Thank you, Roger."

When Hendricks left, Barbo buried his face in his hands. As the highest ranked churchman after the pope, the secretary of state would have a decisive say in whether the pope would have to abdicate.

Alessandri knocked softly at the door.

"I'm sorry Your Eminence but Signor Visconti is here with two American professors. He has no appointment."

"See if you can handle the matter, Enrico."

"I tried to, but Signor Visconti insists on seeing you. He said he spoke to you at the reception."

Barbo felt the envelope in his pocket. Given the generosity of Visconti's clients, Barbo knew he would have to go through with the meeting. At least, he would keep the meeting short.

"Show them in."

When Visconti and the two professors entered his office, Barbo waved them to a seating area to the right of his desk.

"Eminenza, thank you for squeezing us into your busy schedule. Let me introduce you to Professor Bielgard from the University of Michigan and Professor Michellini from Bard College in New York."

"I am honored. Your biography of Eleanor of Aquitaine was superb. How can I help you? Pietro, you told me there was a matter of some delicacy."

"Yes, Eminenza."

Visconti removed a document from his briefcase.

"Eminenza, this is a photocopy of a Jewish census record. Although I know you read Hebrew, I have prepared an Italian translation of the original."

Visconti stood up and laid the photocopy and translation in front of the cardinal.

"Eminenza, I think you will find this manuscript troubling."

Barbo's face grew pale as he read down the document. "Where did you get this?"

"It's a photocopy of a document from the Vatican Library, Eminenza. The original was in a pile of Templar records from the twelfth century. I don't think it's been read in centuries."

Barbo looked at Visconti. "Well if the original is from the Vatican Library, then give it to me. I'll see that it gets back into the right hands."

Visconti stood up and walked to a window overlooking St. Peter's Square. "The worshippers down there live such simple lives. For us life is not so simple."

"What do you mean, Visconti?"

"You know as well as I that this census record contains information that could be damaging to the Catholic Church."

Barbo made a dismissive gesture. "I doubt it. Most of these discoveries turn out to be forgeries, as I'm sure this one is."

"Eminenza, this is not just another 'Da Vinci code' puzzle. It is a very straightforward document that simply states the facts. The parchment is authentic. Professor Baldini from the University of Rome has carbon dated it."

Barbo fingered his pectoral cross. "Look, Visconti. I'm busy. What do you want?"

Visconti smiled. "Like you, my clients wish to see the document get into the right hands. Still they are academics—and poorly paid at that."

Barbo stood up from his desk. "Don't toy with me. What's your price for the original?"

Bielgard interrupted Visconti. "Ten million euros—and in cash."

The cardinal's eyes grew cold. "You realize that I could have the three of you arrested for blackmailing the Vatican."

Bielgard responded caustically. "You could but you won't. We've obviously taken precautions."

Barbo walked toward the door to his office. "I've dealt with extortionists before, Professor Bielgard. It's one of the more distasteful aspects of being Vatican secretary of state. An expert from the Vatican Library will have to look at it and do whatever testing he feels necessary."

Visconti bowed to the cardinal. "My clients have no objection."

"I will telephone you as soon as I have made arrangements with the library. Now if you would excuse me, Father Alessandri will see you out."

Barbo paced angrily around his office. The Middle East and Benedict's health required immediate attention. Now this manuscript appears. He had to take the blackmail seriously. Visconti was too clever to become involved in a hoax.

Barbo buzzed for Alessandri.

"Enrico, have Bishop Renini come to my office at once."

Ten minutes later, Alessandri escorted the director of the Vatican Library into the cardinal's office. Barbo handed Renini the photocopy of the parchment.

"This translation goes along with it. Read the document and tell me what you think."

The Bishop perused the Hebrew carefully, occasionally looking at the translation.

"Your Eminence, this must be someone's idea of a tasteless joke."

"Two of your visiting scholars—professors Bielgard and Michellini—claim they found the original among some uncatalogued Templar documents in the Vatican Library. Check through all our databases and see if anything like this is listed in the collection. Have your staff look through the uncatalogued documents as well. They may discover something relevant."

"A thorough search of the uncatalogued collection would take weeks, Your Eminence."

"Do what you can."

Barbo thought for a moment. "Will a search of the Vatican Library databases pick up items in the archives of the Palais des Papes in Avignon?"

"No our files are not linked."

"Alessandri, get Bishop Pellent on the speakerphone."

In a matter of minutes, the director of the papal archives in Avignon came on the line.

"Your Excellency, this is Cardinal Barbo. Bishop Renini from the Vatican Library is here with me on the speaker phone."

"How can I help you, Your Eminence?" Pellet's Italian was heavily accented by his native Flemish.

"A first-century Hebrew census record has been found in a chest full of Templar manuscripts in the Vatican Library. Finding it with Templar documents may or may not be coincidental. I understand that the databases for the Vatican Library and the Palais des Papes are not linked."

Pellent sounded nervous speaking to the Secretary of State. "That's right, Your Eminence."

"Then I need you to run a search for any reference to this census record in your archives at the Palais. Bishop Renini is running a similar search here in the Vatican Library."

"Fax the text and I'll start immediately, Your Eminence."

"Pellent, if you discover anything, send it to me immediately." The cardinal paused for a moment and addressed both librarians "These searches must be conducted in absolute secrecy. Administer an oath of silence to both your staffs."

As Cardinal Barbo clicked off the speakerphone, Bishop Renini stood up to leave. "Is there anything else, Your Eminence?"

Barbo thought for a moment. "There is one thing. Could you send me several reference books on the Templars and a general history of medieval France?"

"Should I include a copy of your dissertation?"

"Yes, bring that, too."

Visconti hailed a taxi at the top of the Via della Conciliazione.

"That was easy." Michellini smiled at Visconti and Bielgard.

Visconti was silent for a moment. "Perhaps too easy. Barbo is shrewd. He may try to take the parchment from you. Where is it?"

Bielgard answered. "Right now it's in my room at the hotel."

"Put it in a bank vault for safe keeping." Visconti's voice left no room for debate.

As they were about to get into the taxi, Visconti's cell phone rang.

"Hello ... Ah Baldini ... at Tre Amici? ... Let me ask."

Visconti pushed the hold button on his cell phone. "Baldini would like to test the manuscript for salt residue. He suggests meeting for a late dinner tonight at Tre Amici. He can do the test at the restaurant."

Bielgard frowned. "Baldini said he had finished testing the parchment. Why the change?"

"He apologizes. He didn't have the necessary chemicals yesterday to do the test. There is a high alkaline content in parchment from the Holy Land. If the document you found has a high salt residue, it would further corroborate its authenticity."

Michellini nodded to Visconti. "Don't worry about Jim. We'll bring the parchment to Tre Amici at 10 o'clock."

Finnergan rang Cardinal Barbo's office late that evening. His voice sounded tired. "Your Eminence, the Israeli Prime Minister will not release the last five gunmen. He's under tremendous pressure from the extreme right wing. They want him to avenge Eilat. He appreciates the extra negotiating time, but he can't make any more concessions. Letting all the Hamas terrorists walk out of the Sepulchre free men is politically out of the question. I'm sorry, Your Eminence. I tried."

Barbo was disappointed but not surprised by what Finnergan said. "Then it's up to the Americans. They have one more day to find some way to convince the Israelis."

Bielgard and Michellini arrived at Tre Amici Restaurant ten minutes early. Visconti was already talking to the captain. When he saw the two professors, Visconti hurried over to greet them. Michellini nervously gripped her briefcase.

"Ah, my friends—the corner table is ours."

As they sat down, a waiter appeared from inside the restaurant with a plate of steaming pasta and a bottle of Bardolino.

Visconti signaled the waiter to pour the wine.

"Unfortunately, I have some bad news. Professor Baldini called on my cell phone with his apologies. His youngest son was taken to the hospital—a car accident. We'll have to meet with Baldini tomorrow."

"Tomorrow! When?" Bielgard was visibly roiled by the change in plans.

"Baldini suggested eleven in the morning at my office. In the meantime, let's enjoy a good meal and good wine. I have asked the waiter to order for us."

After their meal, the waiter brought espresso and biscotti. Bielgard and Michellini soon made their excuses and stood up to leave. Visconti also rose to his feet but did not leave the table. "My cell phone is full of unreturned calls. I will have another espresso and answer them. Until tomorrow at eleven."

As Bielgard and Michellini left the restaurant, Visconti nodded to two men at a nearby table. They followed the Americans along Via Piacenza to Via di San Marco. As the professors tried to hail a cab on the busy thoroughfare, Visconti's men walked up to them. One grabbed Bielgard. The other shoved Michellini and pulled at the briefcase in her hand. Her high heel shoes caught in the pavement and still grasping the briefcase, she tumbled to the ground. When her assailant reached down for the bag, Michellini kicked him in the groin. While he was doubled over in pain, Michellini struggled to get up. The second assailant, who had thrown Bielgard to the ground, grabbed Michellini's arm and twisted it behind her back. She screamed in pain and dropped the briefcase. One of the men picked it up, and they disappeared into the crowd.

The assault had occurred so quickly that, by the time Bielgard understood what had happened, Michellini was already on her feet. "I'm okay, Jim. Get those bastards."

Dodging through traffic, Bielgard ran after the two assailants. Michellini followed him out into the thoroughfare. Motorists slammed on their brakes to avoid hitting them. A panel truck swerved to the right, careening into several cars. Drivers jumped out of their vehicles and started shouting. The ground was strewn with glass from shattered headlights. A student carefully maneuvered his Vespa through the angry crowd. Without looking in his side-view mirror, a burly taxi driver pushed open his door and hit the passing Vespa.

The cab driver got out of the taxi with a conciliatory look on his face. "It was an accident. Troppo traffico."

"Cornuto!" The student growled back the insult.

"Figlio di puttana!" The taxi driver could not resist responding in kind. Angered by the suggestion that his mother was a prostitute, the student kicked the door of the taxi.

The cab driver exploded with rage. Grabbing the student around the neck, the driver pummeled him on the head. As others joined in, Bielgard and Michellini reached the far side of Via di San Marco. They spotted the two assailants running toward a parked Alfa Romeo. The driver of the car pulled out from the curb and the assailants jumped in. As the car picked up speed, Bielgard threw his walking stick at the windshield and jumped spread-eagle onto the hood. Unable to find a grip, he lost his balance and rolled to the ground. The driver slammed on the brakes but not fast enough to avoid hitting Bielgard. He then put the car into reverse to avoid rolling over Bielgard's body. He did not see Michellini rush over to help her injured colleague. Shifting the Alfa Romeo into third gear, the driver floored the gas pedal. Suddenly, he saw Michellini kneeling on the ground and swerved to avoid hitting her. It was too late. The right fender of the car struck her full force.

Pedestrians poured into the street—some tried to help Bielgard and Michellini—others tried to stop the Alfa Romeo. Gunning the accelerator, the driver sped off, weaving furiously through the stalled traffic. Within seconds, the taillights of the Alfa Romeo disappeared down a narrow street.

Detective Giorgio Cameri from the Rome Police Department took a phone call at 11:45 P.M. It was a report of an accident on Via di San Marco. Two Americans had been injured, but the details were sketchy.

Normally a detective would not be sent to investigate a car accident unless there were fatalities. But as a favor, Cameri thought the captain might give him this assignment. It was almost midnight, and Via di San Marco was on his way home. After he had finished the investigation, he could leave early and fill out the necessary paperwork at home.

Cameri walked over to the captain's desk.

"I'll take this accident on Via di San Marco. Two Americans have been injured."

The captain smiled. "There must be a vehicular homicide before a detective can go out on the investigation. You know that as well as I do, Giorgio."

"Come on, Captain. I've been working lots of overtime lately."

"Okay, go ahead. Remember you owe me one."

The first ambulance arrived with two police cars. A surgeon jumped out of the ambulance and ran over to the bodies lying on the street. Detective Cameri followed her.

The surgeon attended Bielgard first, searching for a heartbeat.

"Blood pressure's falling." The surgeon pushed hard on Bielgard's chest with her hands. "He's going." The doctor shouted to the paramedic. "Get a defibrillator." The doctor hit hard on Bielgard's chest a second time. Cameri saw Bielgard's lips move.

"Doctor, he's trying to say something."

The surgeon put her ear next to his lips.

A shudder ran through Bielgard's body.

"He's seizing." The doctor gave Bielgard a shock from the defibrillator. "Damn it! No pulse."

The surgeon jumped up and ran to Michellini.

"What did he say?"

"'Barbo—Francesco Barbo.' Detective, get these people out of the way. I've got to work on the woman here in the street or she'll die, too."

Cameri pushed back the crowd of onlookers. The surgeon hooked Michellini to an intravenous injection and strapped an oxygen mask over her face.

"Get the tent up. Hurry!"

The paramedic pulled a large canvas bag from inside the ambulance and quickly assembled a tent in the street. Cameri and the paramedic gently lifted Michellini onto a stretcher and carried her inside the canvas flaps of the emergency enclosure.

"Shine the headlights into the tent. I've got to do a tracheotomy right now."

Cameri maneuvered the ambulance so its headlights illuminated the inside of the emergency tent.

A second ambulance arrived. Two paramedics lifted Bielgard's body onto a gurney and wheeled it to the back of the vehicle. When Bielgard's body was securely racked, the ambulance moved off through the crowd. The wail of the departing ambulance was soon lost in the sounds of Rome.

Traffic on Via di San Marco edged around the tent as drivers' heads craned from car windows to get a closer look at what had happened. Behind the canvas walls of the tent, the doctor and paramedic fought to save Michellini's life. In the muted light, their moving shadows reminded bystanders of ministering angels.

After Bishop Renini left Barbo's office, the secretary of state asked Alessandri to brief him on the diplomatic mail that had been received during the past several days. Events in the Middle East had so preoccupied Barbo that he had been unable to focus on developments elsewhere in the world. As Alessandri worked his way through the dispatches, Barbo stared absentmindedly at his television monitor. A picture of an emergency tent and several ambulances suddenly flashed across the screen. The cardinal turned up the volume.

"This is *Telegiornale's* Giorgio Cucchi reporting live from Via di San Marco, the site of a fatal accident this evening. Two Americans were struck by a black Alfa Romeo as they ran across the busy thoroughfare."

Split-screen photos of the professors flashed on the television monitor.

"Professor James Bielgard, a historian from the University of Michigan, died at the scene of the accident. His colleague from Bard College in New York, Professor Jane Michellini, was seriously injured. As you can see behind me, doctors have set up an emergency facility on the Via di San Marco in an attempt to stabilize her condition."

Alessandri put down the dispatches in his hand. "My God, Your Eminence, it's the two professors who were in your office earlier today. I recognize the woman."

The *Telegiornale* reporter paused for a moment and adjusted his earphone.

"We have just learned that Professor Michellini will be moved to Gemelli Hospital. Her condition is described as critical. We have also been informed that Professors Bielgard and Michellini were visiting scholars at the Vatican Library."

The cardinal shifted uncomfortably in his chair as he switched off the television monitor. "Call Gemelli Hospital, Enrico. Make sure Professor Michellini gets the best medical care available."

"Of course, Your Eminence. Do you wish to finish the dispatches?"

"Not now. We'll do the rest tomorrow."

Once Alessandri had left the room, Barbo hastily dialed a number on his cell phone.

"Visconti?"

There was a long pause at the other end of the phone.

"Ah, Eminenza, I didn't recognize your voice."

"One of your clients is dead and the other seriously injured. I assume you will return the parchment to its rightful owner, the Church."

"We must meet."

Barbo played nervously with a pencil. "Why?"

"There are matters still to be discussed with respect to the ownership of the manuscript. Perhaps we could meet tomorrow night in Trastevere, in Piazza Santa Maria."

"Not tomorrow night, Visconti. Now!"

"As you wish, Eminenza. The restaurants in Trastevere stay open late. Let me suggest La Cappella Sistina just off the piazza. One of my clients owns it. I'll bring a good bottle of Tuscan wine—perhaps a Tignanello."

"I know the restaurant." Barbo looked at his desk clock. "It's almost eleven o'clock now. I'll be there in half an hour."

Barbo hurried back to his apartment on Via Mascherino just outside the Vatican walls. Searching through his wardrobe, he chose a gray blazer, a dark blue turtleneck and khaki pants. Dining in Trastevere was casual. The last thing Barbo wanted was for some paparazzo to photograph his meeting with Visconti.

Chapter V

AN ENCOUNTER WITH EVIL

VISCONTI WAS ALREADY standing outside La Cappella Sistina when Barbo pulled up in a taxi. Punctuality was one of Visconti's trademarks.

"Ah, Eminenza, it is good to see you." Visconti's face was framed with smiles. "Come, join me. I'll have the Tignanello opened."

The two men entered the restaurant. Visconti signaled the captain. "Mario, open the wine and bring some prosciutto and melon. His Eminence may be hungry."

Barbo sat impatiently while the wine was uncorked and Visconti tasted the vintage. A tray of prosciutto and melon was brought to the table.

"I assume you'll return the census record to the Vatican Library."

"Ah the Hebrew parchment! You know Professor Baldini carbon dated it for me. There's no doubt it's from the first century."

"If you wish a small finder's fee for retrieving the manuscript," Barbo declared, "that can be arranged."

"Patience, Eminenza. Let me finish. When the conclave opens, the parchment could be a powerful weapon in the hands of your colleague from South Africa, Hans Cardinal Diefenbacher, and his liberal supporters. It would advance their agenda for approving married and women priests."

"You're posturing, Visconti. The parchment will naturally have some symbolic effect, but nothing more. As for Diefenbacher, for years he's been campaigning to become Pope Benedict's successor. I'm not worried."

"You should be worried," exclaimed Visconti. "Diefenbacher will stop at nothing to get what he wants. He has an agenda for restructuring the Church."

"An agenda that's too radical for most Catholics. Let's not waste each other's time, Visconti. How much do you want for the parchment?'

"It's not a question of money. It's a question of relationships." Visconti poured more Tignanello into Barbo's glass. "There are many situations where our institutions could support each other with very practical assistance."

Barbo looked contemptuously at Visconti. "I can hardly imagine one."

"The Church preaches against my clients in Sicily and throughout the Mezzogiorno. Priests tell the people to vote against candidates we support. My clients are good Catholics. Their children are baptized in the Church, they marry in the Church, and they die in the Church. They do not wish to hear themselves condemned from the pulpit."

Barbo became impatient. "So you want the Church to become less aggressive in condemning extortion, prostitution, and drug dealing?"

Visconti nodded his head. "The Church's rhetoric could be moderated."

"I'm sure that this isn't the only price for the manuscript."

Visconti grinned. "On occasion, there might be ways that my organization could help direct the energies of the Church."

"Get to the point, Visconti!"

"At the moment there's an opening in Turin for an antiterrorism prosecutor. It's an important post and needs a man or woman of unimpeachable credentials. Signor Rospalli would make an excellent choice. He has demonstrated great courage and ability as the organized crime prosecutor in Palermo."

"Yes, I know Rospalli." Barbo could sense what was coming.

"If the Church were to suggest to the interior minister that Rospalli should be given the position in Turin...."

Barbo finished the sentence. "...the Mafia would be rid of a thorn in its side."

"Perhaps, but Italy would also get an effective antiterrorism prosecutor."

"So the price of the parchment is silence from the pulpit on your activities and a new post for Rospalli?"

"And one thing more, Eminenza. I understand the Vatican Bank receives contributions from all over the world to the Peter's Pence collection."

"Yes. The proceeds of the collection support many Vatican charities."

"In the last year, transferring money from our operations in Latin America to Italy has become problematic. The Americans are carefully monitoring international bank transfers."

Barbo seethed. "So you want to use Church accounts in Latin America to transfer money to the Peter's Pence fund here in Italy."

"Yes. When the money reaches the Vatican, it will be transferred to various corporations here in Italy. Financial transfers made by the Church are not closely monitored by the Italian government."

"In essence, Visconti, you want the Church to help you with your money laundering schemes?"

"You forget one thing, Eminenza. Money from what you contemptuously call laundering schemes already supports many Church programs. When it comes to accepting donations, some of your colleagues are less scrupulous than you are."

Barbo slowly stood up from the table. Although angry, years of diplomatic training had taught the cardinal to mask his true feelings. "You will hear from me, Visconti."

The cardinal turned and left the restaurant.

Detective Giorgio Cameri was annoyed with himself. He should never have volunteered to investigate the car accident on Via di San Marco. A routine car accident would normally have taken him fifteen minutes to investigate, but this accident was far from routine. Still something told him that this might become an important case. An American professor had been killed and another seriously injured. Given that there was a vehicular homicide, Cameri knew it would be more prudent to return to his office to dictate the required reports than it would be to dictate them at home.

From the outset Cameri sensed that the theft of Michellini's briefcase was not the random act of petty thieves. Everything pointed to the work of professionals—the well-dressed assailants, the Alfa Romeo parked across the street, the quick getaway from the scene of the accident. What intrigued Cameri most about the case were Bielgard's dying words spoken to the doctor. Why did Bielgard whisper the name of the Vatican secretary of state? He toyed with the idea of including Barbo's name in the accident report but thought better of it. A reference to a prominent Vatican official in a police report would be a red flag. The investigation would be taken away from him and become lost in the bureaucracy.

Cameri's office phone rang as he was completing his accident reports.

"Giorgio, this is Mario Esposito—the captain at La Cappella Sistina in Trastevere."

"Eh, Mario."

"Stop by for a drink on your way home. Something interesting happened tonight."

"I'll be there."

Since his earliest years on the Rome police force, Cameri had cultivated the friendship of wine stewards, waiters, and bartenders. He was always willing to help with a favor—fixing a parking ticket, keeping a son out of jail, stopping a too-ardent courtship of a daughter. Favors given led to favors returned. Over time Cameri built up an impressive network that kept him apprised of what was happening in the city.

Cameri left his office at almost 2 A.M. and took a taxi to La Capella Sistina.

"Mario, how's your beautiful daughter?"

"She's getting married. He's a nice boy. You know how much we are in your debt, Gio." Mario poured Cameri some grappa.

"That's in the past, Mario. What happened here tonight?"

"You know Pietro Visconti?" Mario spoke sotto voce to the detective.

"What policeman doesn't? He knows everyone and has his finger in everything."

"Well, tonight he met with Cardinal Francesco Barbo."

"The Vatican secretary of state?"

"Yes, they sat over there at the corner table. The cardinal came late and spent about twenty minutes with Visconti. When they left, both were upset."

"What makes you say that?"

"They left behind a three-hundred-euro bottle of Tignanello."

Cameri walked up the flight of stairs to his apartment. Pouring himself another grappa, he turned on his computer and ran a Google search for the name "Francesco Barbo." He stared at a picture of Barbo receiving his cardinal's biretta from Pope Benedict. Barbo's name had come up a second time tonight. Better than most of his colleagues, Cameri had good intuition. Tonight it told him that Visconti and Barbo were linked to the incident on Via di San Marco.

When he left La Capella Sistina, Barbo decided to walk back to the Vatican over the Janiculum Hill. Although it was late, he had a lot to think about.

Barbo was not naïve. He knew the release of the parchment would have an explosive effect on the Catholic laity—but in varying ways. Those in Europe and North America, chafing under Vatican secretiveness and medievalism, would see the parchment as a support for radical change in Church policy. On the other hand, Catholics who lived in Asia, Africa, and Latin America, where the traditions of the Church were still deeply woven into local cultures, would be scandalized. They light candles before their santos and believe in the devil, in miracles, and in the healing power of relics. These Catholics would not accept the idea that Jesus was married—let alone to a reformed prostitute. If the parchment were released, many of these more traditional Catholics would desert the Church.

As for Diefenbacher, Barbo doubted the parchment would enhance his chances of being elected pope. The archbishop of Durban was simply too controversial in his views to persuade two-thirds of the electors plus one to vote for him. He had strong backing from liberal European and American electors, but little support anywhere else.

But there was a more serious problem that worried Barbo—apostolic succession. When he was growing up in Milan, there was never any expectation that he would take over his father's bookshop. In today's world, children routinely have careers separate from those of their fathers. But that was not true in earlier cultures. In first-century Palestine, the children of rabbis themselves became rabbis and assumed the leadership of their fathers' congregations. Jewish culture, therefore, would have expected that, if Jesus had borne a son, his son would have taken over the leadership of his followers. But until the appearance of this Jewish census record, there was no credible evidence that Jesus had male offspring. Only the Gospel of Philip—a Gnostic text not included in the Christian canon of the New Testament—makes passing reference to a divine bloodline.

In his Gospel, Philip, one of the Twelve, calls the Magdalene the person whom Jesus loved above all His disciples, someone whom he often kissed on the lips—a sign of intimacy. At the end of his Gospel, Philip speaks enigmatically of the Son of Man and the Son of the Son of Man—presumably a reference to a male offspring of Jesus and the Magdalene. Scholars have never paid much attention to Philip's reference because of a lack of corroboration. But now the Magdalene parchment could provide that corroboration. It intimates that Jesus and the Magdalene gave birth to a son—the Son of the Son of Man as Philip calls him. In Jewish tradition this child, not Peter, would have been expected to lead Jesus' followers. The references in the New Testament to Jesus' making Peter the rock on which he would build his Church might have been a later emendation justifying what in fact happened rather than what Jesus wanted.

The possibility that Jesus wished leadership in his Church to pass down through his own bloodline rather than through apostolic succession would be a major distraction in the next conclave. Even if it were true, there was no remedy. It would be impossible to trace Jesus' bloodline through two thousand years of history. In the midst of such turmoil, however, there would be an army of Judases who would come forward seeking to manipulate and destabilize the Church. There was a risk that all of the good that the Church had stood for would be forgotten. In a real sense, the next conclave could very well be the last.

As he approached Ponte Sant'Angelo, Cardinal Barbo saw the dome of St. Peter's looming ahead. He felt a sudden chill from the Tiber. He could sense a presence moving in the dark waters. As he looked down into the river, the presence was rising to the surface. At first it looked like the face of a young child. But as Barbo watched, the face grew old, and a malevolent smile formed on its lips. He smelled a fetid, almost putrid odor coming from the water and recoiled in terror. When he looked again, he saw the papal crown materialize on the figure's head.

Barbo hurried across the bridge. He knew who it was in the river—it was the Trickster, the Master of Lies. From his seminary days, Barbo believed that Satan was as real as God himself. The eternal struggle between Good and Evil takes place every day in thousands of conversations and in thousands of decisions. Barbo had an intuition that this Magdalene scroll was somehow part of that eternal struggle. If the parchment were made public, the Trickster would go about in the guise of a scholar or journalist, sowing confusion and deceit, chipping away at the legitimacy of the apostolic succession of the papacy.

By the time he reached St. Peter's Square, Barbo was wide awake. He decided to go back to his office to read the books he had asked for. When he opened the outer door to his office suite, Father Alessandri was still working at his desk.

"Enrico, did Renini send the books I asked for?"

"Yes, they're on your desk. Renini included a biography of Philip IV of France, even though you didn't ask for it."

"Good." Barbo glanced at his watch. "It's after two o'clock in the morning, Enrico. This is your second night without sleep. Go to bed."

Barbo entered his office and hung his blazer on the back of a chair. Pouring himself a glass of water, the cardinal did a quick inventory of the books that Renini had left for him—a biography of Philip IV of France, a history of medieval France, and several reference books on the Templars, including his own dissertation. Barbo smiled as he thumbed through a volume about the founding of the Order of the Temple. He remembered using the book to write his doctoral dissertation on the Templars. He was embarrassed to see how many pages he had left dog-eared. Barbo's father had admonished him not to damage books this way, but these paternal admonitions fell on deaf ears. Turning to the last page of the book, Barbo found a Latin epigram he had copied from the Roman poet Horace. *Et mihi res, non me rebus, subjungere conor.* "I try to suit life to myself, not myself to life." The epigram reminded Barbo of the idealism and sense of purpose he felt as a young seminarian. Little of those feelings had survived the successes and honors of his life. Idealism and a sense of purpose may be things you experience perfectly only once and then feel their loss forever, he thought.

Alessandri brought a tray into Barbo's office. "You might like some espresso and dolci."

"Thank you, Enrico." Barbo continued to page through the books on his desk.

Alessandri turned to leave. When he was halfway out the door, the cardinal looked up. "Enrico, do you believe in the devil?"

"Not if you mean the one with horns and a pitchfork."

Barbo smiled. "I forgot. The devil of old has been relegated to the basement along with our childhood toys. What about evil? Do you believe that there's a force capable of destroying the Church?"

"Yes, if you put it that way, Eminence."

Barbo looked at Alessandri. "I felt the reality of that evil tonight, Enrico—on Ponte Sant'Angelo. What frightened me was how chillingly close it felt."

Several hours later, having read a history of medieval France, Barbo yawned. He opened a balcony window to let in some fresh air. The first glimmers of dawn had begun to brighten the ancient facades of the city. Seeing the light of the morning drive off the darkness of night always comforted Barbo. God performs his greatest miracle every day, he thought, but few take the time to witness it.

Someone tapped lightly on the door.

"Come in, Sister Fiorina." From the lateness of the hour, the cardinal assumed it was the housekeeper here to vacuum the floor and tidy up his desk. Instead, a Swiss Guard stuck his head into Barbo's office.

"Eminence. You have a visitor."

"At five in the morning?"

"Yes. He says you're expecting him."

Barbo was curious. "Show him in."

A tall thin man carrying an overnight bag entered Barbo's office. For a moment, Barbo stared vacantly at his early morning visitor.

"Jean Calvaux! My mind was elsewhere. I apologize—I didn't recognize you."

Calvaux smiled. "Without a red hat, a cardinal is indistinguishable from the rest of mankind."

"Come, sit down. I didn't expect you so early." Barbo moved some books off his office couch.

"My brother volunteered the use of his company's Lear jet. I arrived here much faster than I expected." Calvaux put down his overnight bag and fell back onto Barbo's couch. "How are the hostages doing?"

"There have been no reports for several hours. If Israel will agree to free all the terrorists, the crisis would be over. We've pushed the Israelis as far as we can. It's up to the Americans now."

"How much time is left before Hamas starts executing the hostages?"

"Seven hours."

Calvaux paused for a moment. "And why does the Holy Father wish to see me?"

"I'll let His Holiness tell you himself. You know it's a coincidence that you should be here in my office. Tonight I've been reading a history of medieval France, and your family's name is mentioned prominently in several places."

"Yes, during the twelfth century, the Montelamberts became vassals of the Duke of Provence and were given seisin over the castle of Cours-des-Trois. There's even a legend associated with the Montelamberts. As I'm sure you can appreciate, Francesco, there's nothing better than a family legend to increase notoriety."

"What's the legend? This history I'm reading makes no mention of it."

"During the Crusades, an ancestor, Gerard de Montelambert, is said to have discovered a cave where in 70 AD Jewish priests had hidden sacred vessels and census records from the Temple of Herod. They were put there to keep them from being destroyed by the Romans."

"Census records?" A chill ran through Barbo's body.

"Yes. Historically, Jews have always kept meticulous records of births and marriages, because it proves who they are as a people."

"I want to hear the legend."

"Perhaps there will be time after meeting with the Holy Father."

"We'll make the time." Barbo looked at his watch. "It's almost five thirty. You must be exhausted. Let's find you a room in our new Vatican hotel, the Domus Sanctae Marthae."

"Thank you, Francesco. The Domus has turned out to be a boon for visiting prelates like me."

Barbo picked up the phone. "Not only that, Jean, it will also make the next conclave easier for all of us."

"No more cots outside the Sistine Chapel?"

"No more cots."

Calvaux smiled. "Too bad, though. The cots usually made for a short conclave."

Cardinal Barbo awoke with a start. Sister Fiorina was standing over him.

"Eminence, it is time to go home." She handed him a towel and an enamel basin of cold water.

"Thank you, Sister." Barbo splashed the cold water on his face.

Fiorina organized the piles of correspondence that lay scattered around Barbo's office. She took the history of medieval France from the cardinal's lap and laid it on his desk. "No more reading, Eminence. Your eyes are bloodshot—as red as your zucchetto."

"I will go home after I say Mass for Pope Benedict."

Fiorina threw up her hands in exasperation. "Do they make every Prince of the Church as stubborn as you?"

Barbo climbed the staircase to the pope's apartment. A rather animated Sister Consuela met him at the door.

"Your Eminence, you must talk some sense into the Holy Father. He has dressed himself and wants to go to St. Peter's tomb under the Basilica. It is too dangerous for him."

The pontiff's eyes lit up when he saw Barbo.

"Francesco, Sister Consuela won't let me go by myself. Maybe she'll relent if I'm accompanied by the cardinal secretary of state."

Barbo knew it was unwise to incur Sister Consuela's wrath. "Holy Father, it is difficult for men our age to climb down to the tomb."

The pontiff rummaged through a drawer in his desk. "Francesco, with your right arm and this flashlight, we should do fine."

Sister Consuela continued to hold her ground. "One of the Swiss Guards should accompany you."

Pope Benedict shook his head impatiently. "No, Sister Consuela, I want a private audience with St. Peter. I'll allow Francesco to come but no one else."

Consuela knew when she was defeated. She looked plaintively at Barbo. "Your Eminence, you must watch his every step. The Holy Father is unsure on his feet."

Barbo took Sister Consuela's hand. "I'll walk ahead of him so he won't fall."

The two men climbed down a winding staircase under the Basilica. At the bottom of the staircase was an ancient necropolis that had been excavated in the 1950s during the pontificate of Pope Pius XII. At the far end of the necropolis was a tomb that archaeologists believe to be the burial place of St. Peter.

The lights had long since been turned off, so the pope shone the flashlight on the tomb. "When I have a difficult decision to make, I often come here and speak to Peter. We have a good relationship." Barbo saw tears well up in Benedict's eyes. "Francesco, pray with me."

The two men, pope and cardinal, knelt on the ground and recited the fifteen decades of the Rosary, each focusing on some aspect of the life of Christ and Mary His mother. When they had finished, Benedict stood up and looked at Barbo.

"Francesco, leave me alone for a few minutes. I have something to tell Peter." Barbo saw Benedict place his hand on Peter's tomb and kiss the stone. After a few minutes, the Holy Father walked back to where Barbo was standing. The pope put his hand on Barbo's shoulder. "Francesco, I have decided to abdicate my position as Supreme Pontiff of the Catholic Church. It must be done quickly. Help me see this through."

"Holiness, I understand your fear of Alzheimer's, but there must be another way."

"Francesco, we have been friends for many years. You know as well as I there is no other way. My bouts of forgetfulness will grow longer and increasingly severe. Peter has given me the strength to make the decision."

"Please reconsider, Holy Father. Your abdication would be unprecedented."

"Perhaps in modern times but we both know Celestine V abdicated in 1294. He simply couldn't govern the Church."

"Yes, but Dante put him in hell for what he did."

"Dante's assessment was not the final word. Ten years after his abdication, the Church canonized Celestine. His feast day is May nineteenth."

"But your abdication will create dissension in the Church."

"No more so than my death, Francesco."

"Who is ready to take your place?"

"Perhaps it will be you, Francesco."

Barbo's face grew pale.

Shaken by Pope Benedict's decision to abdicate, Barbo returned to his apartment. After showering and putting on a change of clothes, he called Cardinal Calvaux in the Domus Sanctae Marthae.

"I hope you had a chance to get some sleep, Jean."

"Yes, I did. When is my audience with Pope Benedict?"

"The Holy Father will not be able to see you today as he had planned. Perhaps you could join me for breakfast. I'd like to hear about your family legend."

"My pleasure."

"There's a wonderful pasticceria near Borgo Santo Spirito. It opens early to accommodate the clerical traffic. Come to my office at eight thirty."

Cardinal Barbo was a frequent customer at Pasticceria di San Paolo. Before the two cardinals were seated, a splendid array of brioche and pastries magically appeared on the table.

"Try the pastries. They rival those made in your country, Jean."

Calvaux put his hands in the air defensively. "I'll stick with toast and jam."

"I understand you went to the Gregorian University for theology."

"Yes, the Jesuits were superb teachers."

"And your dissertation was on the massacre of the Cathars at Montsegur?"

Calvaux was impressed that Barbo had gone to the trouble of studying his resume. "Yes, it's left me with a passion for fourteenth-century French history."

"It's curious. My dissertation at the 'Greg' was on the Knights Templar."

Calvaux signaled the waiter for another espresso. "Both groups got pretty shabby treatment from the papacy and the French monarchy."

"We have some time, Jean. Tell me your family legend."

"About Gerard de Montelambert?"

"Yes and his discovery of the census records."

Calvaux thought for a moment. "The Montelambert legend actually begins centuries before Gerard was born. It starts in first-century Palestine with one of our ancestors—a wine merchant from Gaul named Evardus."

Barbo leaned forward and cupped his chin in his right hand. "Start where you will, Jean."

Chapter VI

THE DEATH OF A RABBI

Titus Flavius Sabinus, son of the Roman Emperor Vespasian and commander of the Roman Legions in Asia, stood on the Mount of Olives looking out over the Valley of the Kedron to the walls of Jerusalem. At thirty-one, Titus was in the prime of his life. Although shorter than the average Roman, he was a feared opponent, whether on the battlefield or in the gladiatorial arena. With his brawny arms and broad shoulders, he could crack the neck of a man like a dried twig. With his olive complexion and curly hair, Titus exuded the animal magnetism of a stallion in search of a female to mount. Women found him irresistible. He reciprocated with feats of sexual prowess that exhausted even the most lecherous courtesan. Titus boasted that during one imperial banquet, he seduced the wives of four Senators and then took to bed his lover—a sixteen-year-old male slave. "The people call me a god. They want to see me act like one. The great Alexander could not have done better."

Titus's prowess was not confined to the bedroom. He was a shrewd and cunning negotiator, with an instinctive sense of timing. He knew exactly when to act and when to hold back. His resourcefulness had recently been proven to his father. While Vespasian was commander of the legions of Asia and Titus was his second in command, a disastrous fire broke out in Rome. Although Emperor Nero accused a religious sect called Christians of starting the conflagration, the Senate blamed Nero. Convinced that the emperor had caused the fire, three officers of the Praetorian Guard—the troops assigned to protect Rome—broke into Nero's bed chamber, pulled him off his wife and stabbed him repeatedly in the chest. Nero's murder set off an immediate struggle for power, one group in the Senate vying against another. As the military force closest to

Rome, the Praetorian Guard had much to say in choosing the next emperor. When no senatorial faction could win the Guard's allegiance, however, the governor of Spain, Servius Galba, proclaimed himself emperor and marched on Rome to claim the prize. The Praetorian Guard put up no resistance.

Once Galba had solidified his power, he wasted no time in summoning Vespasian to Italy. "Having the general who commands our legions in Asia come to Rome," Galba wrote, "would be a sign of unity in the Empire."

When Galba's letter arrived, Vespasian read it and handed it to Titus. "Galba must take me for a fool. If I return to Rome, he will have me killed. I am his only rival."

"Father, send me in your place."

"What excuse would I give Galba for sending you?"

Titus thought for a moment. "The Jews are your excuse. They defeated the Twelfth Legion and captured its eagles. Until the Jews are crushed and the eagles restored to Rome, you cannot leave Palestine."

"But if you take my place, he will kill you."

"When you fear the lion, Father, you are careful not to harm the cub. Killing me would only lead to war, and at the moment that is the last thing Galba wants. No, he will accept my vows of loyalty—particularly when I wrap them in flights of birds and showers of meteors."

"What do you mean?"

"Galba is no fool, but he is superstitious. Let me invent a dream, Father. One night while asleep, you saw a golden eagle land on the steps of the Capitoline Hill. The eagle slowly scratched the letter 'G' on the ground. When you awoke, you consulted your soothsayers. The dream, they said, foretold that Galba would become emperor and that his reign would usher in a second golden age for the empire."

"Who would believe such a ridiculous story?" asked Vespasian.

Titus pulled a sheet over his shoulders and ran around his father's tent flapping his arms like a bird. "Galba would. He believes that birds bring messages from the gods."

"Titus, I am glad you are my son and not my enemy. Go to Rome and tell Galba about my dream."

Titus bowed to his father. "The next time you are called to Rome, Father, it will be as emperor."

Titus traveled to Italy in April of the year 69 A.D. Although initially suspicious of his adversary's son, Galba was gradually won over by Titus's charm and diplomatic skills. But there was a side to Titus that Galba did not see. Although he would praise and flatter Galba during the day, Titus sowed seeds of discontent at night. At dinners with prominent members of the senate, he would hint that Galba was thinking of disbanding that institution. When drinking in out-of-the-way tavernas with officers of the Praetorian Guard, he would toast his father's loyalty to the gods of Rome. Galba, he said, had failed to worship at the Temple of Jupiter when he had first entered Rome at the head of his legions.

After four months as emperor, Galba made a fatal mistake. To flatter his vanity, he decreed that all senators should bow their heads before addressing him. In full view of a horrified senate, Aurelius Minicius, a curmudgeonly old senator, furious at Galba's high-handedness, stabbed the emperor through the heart. A rumor quickly spread that the night before the murder, Titus had been seen leaving Minicius's house with the commander of the Praetorian Guard. Within hours after Galba's death, the Praetorian Guard hailed Vespasian as the new emperor. A day later, Aurelius Minicius's body was found in a ditch along the road to the seaport of Ostia.

When he returned to Italy in September of 69, Vespasian sent Titus to command the Roman legions in Asia. Titus's first priority was to complete what his father had begun—the suppression of the Hebrew insurgency in Palestine. Vespasian had already pacified Galilee using the tactics he understood best. Towns and villages were reduced to rubble, and Galilean men, women, and children were butchered by the thousands. Vespasian's legionnaires joked that the only peace he knew was the peace of the grave. Adopting his father's brutal tactics, Titus moved south through Samaria and Judea, systematically destroying everything in his path.

Despite his well-trained army, however, Titus did not underestimate the Hebrews. Several years before, Jewish zealots had ambushed his father's army as Vespasian marched on the Judean town of Emmaus. In the ambush, Hebrew partisans slaughtered more than five thousand Roman soldiers and captured the eagles of the Twelfth Legion. To lose a legion's battle standards brings not only shame and ignominy on a Roman general but on his family as well. A day hardly passed when Titus did not dream of recapturing the eagles and returning them triumphantly to his father in Rome. On a more selfish note—with his support among the Praetorian Guards, returning the eagles of the Twelfth Legion to Rome would almost certainly cement Titus's claim to be emperor after his father's death. A new imperial dynasty would be born that would rival that of Caesar Augustus and his descendants.

In February of the year 70, Titus reached the gates of Jerusalem, the holy city of the Jews and the last stronghold of Hebrew resistance in Palestine. For six long months, his army laid siege to the city. Although the Jews fought bravely, the Roman juggernaut was unstoppable. The Eighth Legion had breached the outermost wall of Jerusalem a month earlier, and now the battering rams of the Tenth Legion were about to do the same to the inner wall. Once that wall was breached, all that remained in Jewish hands was the Temple Mount—the plateau on which King Herod had rebuilt the ancient Temple of Solomon. The prize that had eluded Titus for so long was about to be his.

The strokes of the goldsmith's hammer rang out through the night. "Give me the eagles, Avram."

The young apprentice nervously handed the goldsmith the battle standards of the Twelfth Legion. With one blow of his hammer, the goldsmith broke the eagle off the first standard. With another blow, he snapped the Senatorial symbol—the letters "SPQR"—off the top of the second. Almost matter-of-factly, he threw the gold emblems into a clay bowl and, with iron pincers, placed the bowl inside the glowing kiln. When the gold had melted, the goldsmith poured the molten liquid into a clay mold in the shape of a menorah.

"Avram, run to the temple and ask the high priest to bring the original. We must compare the two." The young boy sped off into the darkness.

The air in the sanctuary was incandescent. David ben Hochba, the commander of the Jewish Sicarii, or Knife Wielders, could feel Yahweh's presence in every part of the room. He watched the high priest Hezekiah lift the branched candlestick off the altar and wrap it in his shawl. Yahweh, the God of Abraham, Isaac, and Jacob, had commanded the Jewish people to fashion the golden menorah as a sign of their fidelity to him. The menorah had been with them on their wanderings in the Sinai and during their exile in Babylon. When they returned from exile, Yahweh had ordered the Jews to place the menorah on the altar of the sanctuary—a location it had never left until tonight.

Ben Hochba followed the high priest out of the sanctuary. The menorah was the last of the temple vessels to be copied. Forging the copy of the menorah from the eagles of the Twelfth Legion had been ben Hochba's idea. As a soldier, he knew that the Romans would appreciate the ingenuity of the substitution. When they thought they were desecrating the temple vessels, the Romans would be desecrating the eagles of their own Twelfth Legion.

When the high priest arrived at the goldsmith's kiln, he set the menorah next to the clay mold. The mold was cracked open and the copy of the menorah taken out. The high priest compared the replica with the original.

"Goldsmith, I commend you. No one could tell them apart."

The high priest handed the original menorah to ben Hochba.

"David, take it through the tunnel tonight. I will put the copy back on the altar in the sanctuary."

The high priest turned to a tall rabbi who stood next to him. "Rabbi Yohannen, what about the temple records?"

"These are the last, Hezekiah. They are from the time Caiphas was high priest and Pontius Pilate, the Roman procurator. They cover Barrabas's revolt and the cults of Jesus the Nazarene and John the Baptizer."

Ben Hochba looked angrily at Yohannen. "Rabbi, a Sicarius will gladly risk his life to smuggle the temple vessels out of Jerusalem. They link us to our past in the Sinai and in Babylon. But these lists of births and marriages! Of what use are they to anyone?"

"Yahweh has made a covenant with us, David. We are His chosen people. These records of births and marriages show who we are as a people."

Ben Hochba shrugged in exasperation.

Ben Hochba and Zacharias, the deputy commander of the Sicarii, crawled through the tunnel that led from the Temple Mount under the northern walls of Jerusalem. After emerging from the passageway, the two partisans hurried to the northeast to find the Jericho road.

Ben Hochba stopped when they reached the road. He listened for a moment and whispered to Zacharias in a warning voice. "Hide behind these rocks. Soldiers are coming."

A Roman patrol walked along the road. A young Jewish boy, his hands tied behind his back, was being pulled behind them with a rope. A legionnaire stopped to adjust his sandal.

"Better a Hebrew girl than this circumcised boy."

"Maybe we will capture one tomorrow. But for tonight's pleasure, the boy will have to do." The infantrymen laughed as they continued along the road.

When he heard the bantering of the soldiers, Zacharias became furious and pulled out his knife. Ben Hochba put his hand on Zacharias's arm.

"There are too many of them. We must go to the cave."

When the patrol had passed, the two Sicarii followed the Jericho road until they reached the Oasis of the Red Waters. The oasis was empty – eerily so. For fear of encountering Roman patrols, they stayed hidden in the oasis during daylight. As it grew dark, ben Hochba and Zacharias left the oasis and continued along the road to Jericho. After several hours of walking, the outline of three hills began to appear on the right side of the road.

"Here we are, Zacharias."

The two men climbed up the middle hill until they reached a narrow path that wound its way around a stone outcropping. They walked along the path until they saw the cave.

Lighting a torch, ben Hochba and Zacharias entered the dark passageway. At the sound of the two men, thousands of bats stirred on the ceiling.

"They will not bother us, Zacharias. They fear the light."

A large pile of rocks lay on the ground about twenty paces inside the cave. After removing their shoulder bags, the two Sicarii lifted the rocks off the pile. Underneath the rocks was a wooden plank covering a large pit. Ben Hochba held the torch low to the ground while Zacharias pushed the plank aside. Surprised by the light, a lizard scampered out of the hole. Zacharias reached down into the opening and laid the menorah and census records next to the other items already in the pit. Zacharias pushed the wooden plank back over the opening.

Ben Hochba put out the torch. "We have finished what we came to do. Yahweh is blessed."

The two men left the cave and followed the road back to the Oasis of the Red Waters.

It was an hour after dawn when ben Hochba and Zacharias reached the oasis again. Roman supply wagons had stopped at the well to take on water. The two partisans watched from the reeds until the carts rumbled off toward Jerusalem.

"There may be more Romans, Zacharias. Get some sleep. I will stand guard."

The day passed uneventfully. The only visitors to the Oasis were a group of Samaritans. They stopped at the well to draw water and quickly moved on. When the sun began to set, ben Hochba woke his companion. "We must leave soon. You know you will die if you return to Jerusalem."

"Yes."

"You could escape to Jericho and save your life."

"Without my family, what would I live for?"

Ben Hochba put an approving hand on Zacharias's shoulder. "We must reach Jerusalem by dawn."

A tribune rode up the Mount of Olives to where Titus and several of his commanders were watching the battle.

"Will the Hebrews surrender? We have the Temple Mount surrounded."

"They will not, Imperator. They would rather die for their God than submit to our yoke."

"Then they will have their wish! What do they call this God of theirs?"

"Yahweh."

"I will show these Jews how much Rome fears him. Tribune, when do these Hebrews make sacrifice to this Yahweh?"

"On the day they call the Sabbath—the seventh day of the week."

"When is their next Sabbath?"

"In five days."

"Good. The day before their next Sabbath, bring me twenty prisoners—men, women, and children. I will prepare a little entertainment for these Jews."

"Imperator, in the Hebrew language, *chai* is the word both for life and for the number eighteen. Because of its association with life, the Jews revere the number eighteen as a symbol of life."

"Do they? I will show them how wrong they are. Eighteen prisoners will do as well as twenty."

Titus lifted the naked woman off the ground and began to rape her. He groaned with delight as the slave bit hard into his shoulder. He grew even more passionate seeing her mixture of shame and horror at his rough treatment. This was his way with women, and he was well known for his shows of sexual inventiveness and debauchery. "You rode her well, Imperator." Several of his legion commanders laughed as they applauded their leader. An exhibitionist, Titus derived intense gratification from having others witness his sexual prowess.

"Sigidius, I am told you have a special talent in these matters. Take this slave and entertain me."

"Majesty, you have exhausted the woman. Bring me someone else."

"Centurion, find another slave for Sigidius."

A slender green-eyed girl was quickly brought into the tent. Sigidius ordered her tied down to a stake in the floor. Sigidius gave a harsh laugh and told her, "Now we will give you everything you want." Cheering loudly, the other commanders formed a line to have their turn with the woman.

After a while, Titus noticed one of his most trusted commanders sitting off by himself. "Varro, get on line or you will miss Sigidius's entertainment."

"Imperator, I need the quiet of my tent for such matters."

"Varro, you served my father well for over thirty years. If you do not like Sigidius's entertainment, I have prepared one that I hope will be more to your liking."

A servant quietly entered the tent and whispered in Titus's ear.

"My banquet is ready." Throwing on a toga, Titus led his commanders into a nearby tent where a sumptuous feast of desert quail and wild pig had been prepared. For those who preferred fish, the banquet master offered caviar and dried sturgeon from the Caspian Sea. When the main course was ended, brass trays piled high with crimson fruit and green grapes were set before the guests.

Titus rose from his couch. "The fruit may be too bitter for some of you. If so. . . ." Titus clapped his hands gleefully. A naked slave girl, her body painted with red sugar, walked into the tent. "Rub your fruit on her body. It will sweeten the taste." Titus laughed. "Sigidius, you try her first. You always appreciate exotic pleasures."

At the end of the meal, Titus shouted for quiet.

"Commanders, come with me. I wish to introduce you to some special guests—eighteen of them to be exact. I have saved my best wine so I can include them in the festivities. They wait for us on the west rim of the hill."

There was an audible gasp when the commanders saw the entertainment that Titus had prepared. Eighteen Jewish prisoners had been hung on crosses along the rim of the Mount of Olives. Titus proudly strutted along the line of crosses with his hands clasped behind his back.

"Varro, I left it up to my tribunes to choose the victims. I must commend them—they made excellent choices. Look carefully at this woman, for example—she is pregnant. And the boy next to her, he looks no more than seven. Maybe they should have crucified an old Jewish hag. I am told the Jews revere their elders. What do you think, my old friend?"

"The tribunes selected well, Imperator. An old woman would have died too quickly." Varro kept his eyes fixed to the ground. Even for an infantry commander hardened by years of battle, the sight of women and children hanging on crosses revolted him.

"You are right, Varro. These Jews deserve slow deaths."

When he had come to the end of the line of crosses, Titus shouted to his servants. "Bring the wine. We must toast our neighbors on the Temple Mount."

"But Imperator. . . ."

"Yes, Sigidius?"

"It is too dark here. The Jews will not see our toast."

"You are right, Sigidius. It is too dark here."

Titus signaled to a centurion to bring a torch.

Rabbi Yohannen and David ben Hochba stood at the edge of the Temple Mount looking across to the Roman encampment. They saw a light move across the Mount of Olives.

"What is that, David?" The rabbi's eyes had grown dim with age.

"I do not know. It looks like the Romans are setting a tree on fire."

"They may be preparing for an attack."

Ben Hochba shook his head. "No Rabbi. The Romans know how to be patient. Before they attack, they make their enemies fear their power."

"Look, David, now there are more fires—two, three, four. The Romans seem to light them along the ridge of the Mount of Olives."

A hot breeze blew across the Valley of the Kedron from the Mount of Olives, bringing with it the smell of burning flesh. Yohannen turned away in horror. "They burn our kinsmen on crosses. There are eighteen fires. The Romans mock our belief in life."

Crying out like a wounded lion, Ben Hochba lifted his sword to the sky.

"Yahweh, for what the Romans do to Your people, smite these idolators with Your right hand."

In the morning, the Hebrews saw eighteen charred skeletons hanging from crosses. Titus was right. For those who stood on the Temple Mount that day, the number eighteen would never again be a symbol of life.

In the Temple, the High Priest opened to the Book of Lamentations. "Darkness covers the earth and thick clouds cover Thy people; but upon you, Zion, the Lord shines, and over you appears his glory." When the High Priest finished reading the words of the prophets, tears were streaming down his face.

As the morning wore on, crows began to gather for their grisly feast.

David ben Hochba crept up the Mount of Olives with five of his Sicarii. The partisans hid behind some rocks near the edge of the Roman camp. As expected, the Romans had posted guards along the line of crosses.

"We must kill the sentries." Ben Hochba unsheathed his dagger.

"David, the Romans have cleared a perimeter around the camp. Getting close to the sentries will not be easy."

"I grew up playing here, Zacharias. I know every rock and tree on this hill. There is a culvert that will take us around to the back of where the sentries stand guard. Follow me."

After dropping into the culvert, the Sicarii crept to within hearing distance of the sentries.

Suddenly ben Hochba signaled his men to lie flat on the ground. The sound of footsteps came along the culvert.

A man spoke to the sentries in Latin. "There is no moon tonight. Have there been problems?"

"No. General."

Ben Hochba looked over the edge of the culvert. A white haired man stood talking to the sentries. Ben Hochba ducked back down into the culvert and spoke quietly, "It is Aemilius Varro—Titus's most trusted commander."

Ben Hochba picked up a stone and threw it over the heads of the sentries. Momentarily distracted by the sound, the legionnaires turned their backs on the Sicarii. The partisans slipped out of the culvert, and ben Hochba whispered to his men. "Kill the others. Leave Varro to me!"

Before the Romans understood what was happening, the partisans were behind them. Ben Hochba grabbed Varro by the hair and pulled back his head. With one motion, he slit the general's throat from ear to ear. Wiping the blood from his dagger, Ben Hochba pointed toward the crosses. "Cut down our kinsmen before the Romans come looking for Varro."

The Sicarii worked quickly. They stacked up rocks like a ladder and gently lifted each body down from a cross. Several Sicarii wept softly as they brought down the charred body of a friend or a neighbor. When the eighteen corpses lay on the ground, ben Hochba laid a small stone on each body as a symbolic burial and recited the beginning verses of the Kaddish. "'Sanctified be the name of God throughout the world, which he has created according to his will.' We have buried our kinsmen according to the laws of Moses and Jacob. The rest of you go back to the Temple Mount. I will come right behind you."

Ben Hochba ran back to the sentry outpost. Varro lay face down on the ground. The Sicarius hacked off Varro's head. Crawling up to the edge of the Roman encampment, ben Hochba jumped to his feet and hurled the bloody projectile at the closest tent.

A centurion rushed outside to see what had hit the tent. When he looked down at the ground, he saw Varro's dead eyes staring up at him. The centurion pulled off his robe and covered the gruesome sight.

Titus was quickly summoned to the tent. Seeing Varro's head made the blood drain from Titus's face. "Search every inch of this hill. Find who did this. He will curse the day he was born."

In a fit of rage, Titus summoned his commanders. "Prepare the plans for the final assault. Varro was a second father to me. I will avenge his murder."

David ben Hochba hid in a small cave in the wall of the culvert. When the Romans gave up searching for Varro's executioner, ben Hochba crawled down the side of the Mount of Olives and returned to the Temple Mount before dawn.

The next day, under Titus's command, the Roman army began a full-scale assault on the Temple Mount. At dawn, the Tenth Legion struck from the north and the Eighth from the east.

Ben Hochba and Zacharias watched as the legionnaires formed their ranks at the base of the escarpment. Weeks before, the Sicarii had destroyed the only road to the top of the plateau. To capture the Temple, the Roman infantry would have to climb up the sides of the cliff. As the heavily armed infantrymen tried to get footholds in the rock, the limestone broke off under their feet. Zacharias laughed as he saw legionnaire after legionnaire lose his balance and slide down the side of the escarpment. "The brittleness of the limestone proves to be our best weapon. With the road gone, Titus has no choice but to send his men up the sides of the cliff."

"Don't be fooled, Zacharias." Ben Hochba's voice was somber. "This is all a diversion. It is staged like a spectacle in the Roman Coliseum."

"What do you mean?"

"Titus is too good a general to launch a frontal assault up the sides of the Temple Mount. There would be too many casualties. He is planning a surprise for us."

As the two men talked, a loud cry went up from behind them.

"The Romans are on the Temple Mount."

Incredulous, David and Zacharias looked over their shoulders. Roman light infantry were coming over the southern rim of the escarpment. Zacharias unsheathed his sword. "No army has ever scaled the south face. The Romans must have wings."

Ben Hochba shouted at his friend. "Wings or not, they must be driven off the Temple Mount."

Zacharias with a contingent of Sicarii behind him ran across the plateau to where the Romans were forming ranks. The sheer ferocity of the partisans' attack caught the Romans by surprise. Although the legionnaires fought bravely to keep a foothold on the plateau, they were pushed back to the edge of the escarpment. As the Roman perimeter shrank, Sicarii tackled legionnaires with their bare hands and jumped over the cliff, pulling them with them.

Black smoke now suddenly came billowing up from inside the Temple. When the Sicarii had attacked the legionnaires on the south rim, the Roman engineers pushed their catapults into range. After winching them back for loading, the engineers shot flaming balls of pitch at the Temple.

At the sight of the Temple in flames, the Sicarii threw down their weapons and ran to put out the fire.

"Stop them, Zacharias. The Romans must be driven off the Mount. The priests can contain the fire."

"They will not listen. The Temple is the center of their lives."

Once the Sicarii had deserted the battlefield, the legionnaires had time to regroup. The partisans' attack had decimated the Roman ranks but had not succeeded in pushing them off the plateau. More and more legionnaires reached the top of the Mount. When he saw the Romans hoist a battering ram over the south rim, Ben Hochba knew that the Temple could not be saved.

The shofar sounded. It was a signal that the Romans were on the Temple Mount. There was little time left.

When they heard the sound of the ram's horn, David and Zacharias ran to the easternmost courtyard where the women and children had gathered for safety. When they saw the Sicarii enter the courtyard, the women wailed and hugged their children. Everyone knew what had to be done. Tears rolled down David's face, as he walked to where his wife Miriam and three-year old son Nathan sat. When Nathan saw his father, he ran to him and started rummaging through his pocket.

"Abba, you promised me a present if I was good."

David threw his son up into the air as he did every day when he came home. When he put the child down, he pulled a brightly colored stone from his pocket. "I did not forget, Nathan."

Miriam embraced her husband for the last time.

"Be brave, Miriam. This is the life we have chosen."

"When it is over, David, put Nathan's hand in mine. He may be frightened when he sees Yahweh."

Zacharias stood behind Miriam and unsheathed his knife. He looked at David and hesitated.

"It must be done, Zacharias."

As he held his wife and son close, there was a flash of steel. David felt their bodies tighten and then go limp in his arms. He gently laid Miriam and Nathan on the ground and placed a stone on each of their bodies. As he brushed aside a lock of hair from his son's forehead, he put Nathan's tiny hand in his mother's.

His robe wet with the blood of his family, David walked mournfully to where Zacharias stood. The dead lay all around them. For a second the two men's eyes locked. Zacharias covered his wife's face as David took out his dagger. It was over in a second. Zacharias gently lowered his wife's body to the ground and closed her eyes with his hand.

A Roman tribune rode up to Titus as he watched the battle from the Mount of Olives. "There is still resistance, Imperator. The Jews fight so that you will not set foot in their Holy of Holies."

"They are brave, these Jewish dogs. I will honor their wish. I will not set my foot in their holy place."

When Rabbi Yohannen heard the sound of the shofer, he hurried to the sanctuary. High Priest Hezekiah was waiting for him. The priest took out a copper scroll from the folds of his robe.

"Yohannen, here is the map to the cave and a list of what we have buried there. Show it to the chief rabbis of Jaffa and Antioch so they will know what we have done."

"Hezekiah, the plan must be changed. Roman soldiers are everywhere. If David and I are captured trying to escape through the tunnel, Titus will have the scroll. All our planning will have been for nothing."

"What else can we do?" The High Priest asked Yohannen.

"Bury the scroll under the Temple. If David and I escape Jerusalem, we will not need the scroll to speak with the rabbis."

"And if you are captured?"

"Yahweh has made an everlasting covenant with the Jewish people. We must trust in Him, just as our fathers Moses and Jacob did. The scroll will be discovered according to Yahweh's plan."

"Where will you bury it?" asked Hezechiah.

"The Romans mocked our belief in life when they crucified eighteen of our people. We must reaffirm that belief, or our covenant with Yahweh will be at an end. Ben Hochba has hollowed out a stone under the Holies of Holies and marked it with the '*chai.*' I will put the scroll inside it. Someone with the eyes to see will find it."

"Who will have the eyes to see?"

"That will be Yahweh's decision."

Hezekiah looked off into the distance as if searching for guidance.

"Do as you must, Yohannen. We have no choice but to trust in Yahweh."

Rabbi Yohannen and Ben Hochba hurried down a staircase behind the sanctuary. After several minutes, the staircase flattened into level ground.

"Here it is, Rabbi." Ben Hochba pointed to a small *"chai"* chiseled into the face of an oblong stone along the right wall of the passageway. Ben Hochba took out his knife and pried the stone loose. The center of the stone had been hollowed into a cavity.

"Rabbi, put the scroll inside the stone. I will seal it up."

Yohannen touched the scroll to his forehead and laid it reverentially in the hollow cavity. Ben Hochba quickly took a rock plug and, like a vintner re-corking a wine bottle, pushed the plug into the hole in the stone. Once he was satisfied that the plug fit tightly, ben Hochba pushed the stone back into its place in the wall.

The sound of fighting could be heard in the courtyard directly above them. Ben Hochba pointed down the passageway. "Rabbi, we must escape through the tunnel before the Romans find us."

The two men hastened along the passageway until they came to a small stream that flowed under the Temple Mount. Once they had crossed the rivulet, ben Hochba counted off thirty paces. A flat slab of stone lay on the ground. Ben Hochba whispered to the Rabbi. "Help me move it."

The Sicarius and the rabbi pushed the stone slab aside, revealing a dark hole underneath. The clanging of Roman armor was heard coming down the staircase.

Ben Hochba motioned Yohannen to enter the tunnel. "Rabbi, you must go alone. The Romans are too close. I will push the slab back in place."

Yohannen knew that ben Hochba was right. As the Rabbi climbed down into the tunnel, ben Hochba handed Yohannen a small Star of David. "May Yahweh walk beside you." Their eyes brimming with emotion, the two men embraced. The Rabbi turned and disappeared into the tunnel.

Once the slab had been pushed back over the tunnel entrance, ben Hochba unsheathed his sword and ran back toward the staircase. The sound of Roman armor grew closer. When he came to the edge of the rivulet, ben Hochba stood and waited for the Roman legionnaires.

Titus rode across the plateau to Herod's Temple. "Tribune, show me this place the Jews call their Holy of Holies."

"There, Imperator." The Tribune pointed to an open door at the far end of the courtyard.

Titus rode slowly up to the door. He stopped for a moment and peered inside. Smoke from the burning roof of the Temple filled the room. With a loud cry, Titus spurred his horse through the entrance way. From out of the smoke, the robed figure of the high priest Hezekiah ran out in front of Titus's horse.

"Heathen! You desecrate this holy place. No Gentile can enter Yahweh's sanctuary." With both his hands, Hezekiah held the Torah high above his head like some Old Testament prophet. Frightened by the sudden appearance of the high priest, Titus's horse reared up and struck Hezekiah with his front hooves. The Torah fell from the priest's hands. As Hezekiah bent down to pick it up, Titus drove his short sword into the priest's back.

"Take your book and read it to this God of yours."

Titus saw several gold vessels on the altar. He spurred his horse up the altar steps. Unsure of its footing, the horse defecated on the floor. Titus reached out with his hand and took the gold menorah from the altar.

The sight of their commander riding his horse out of the Jew's holiest place electrified the legionnaires. They began rhythmically striking their swords against their shields as a sign of their approval.

"I kept my promise to these dogs," Titus shouted. "I did not set foot in their holy place. And my horse left a gift for their god. I took this branched candlestick as a fair exchange."

The thunder of swords striking shields grew deafening. The story of Titus's desecration of the Jewish Temple would be retold around Roman campfires for many years to come.

When the last pockets of Jewish resistance had been eradicated, Titus sent word for his commanders to meet him at the foot of the Temple Mount.

"Tribune, have you found the eagles?"

"No, Imperator. The Jews must have hidden them outside the city."

Titus' eyes flashed with anger. "Spare me your speculation, Tribune. Find the eagles. Hack the limbs off some of these Jews. They will tell you where they have hidden them."

"We have captured one of the Sicarii. He will know where the standards of the legion are hidden."

"Bring him here."

Ben Hochba was pushed to the ground in front of Titus.

"If you want me to spare your people, Jew, tell me where you have hidden the eagles of the Twelfth Legion?"

"You have the eagles already, heathen."

Titus smiled contemptuously at ben Hochba. "If I do, where are they?"

"In the menorah you stole from the Temple. I told your favorite commander Varro all about it. Ask him."

Enraged at the mention of Varro's name, Titus jumped off his horse and stabbed ben Hochba through the heart.

"Cut this Jew into pieces and feed him to the dogs. How many prisoners have we taken, Tribune?"

"Thousands, Imperator."

"Kill them all."

The Tribune looked at Titus. "Even the women and children?"

"Yes, and when you have done that, flatten Jerusalem. Leave it a pile of rubble."

"As you command, Majesty."

"I want even the desert rats to avoid this place."

Titus Flavius Sabinus wheeled his horse about and galloped back to the Roman encampment.

After crawling on hands and knees for several hours, Yohannen felt a hot breeze blowing on his face. He knew he was coming to the end of the tunnel. Several cubits ahead of him, he saw a glimmer of light. Pushing aside some underbrush, Yohannen observed a stony field in front him. The stones were hot from the blistering Judean sun. In the distance, he could see Roman patrols rounding up the Jews trying to escape from the city. With Roman soldiers on all sides, Yohannen realized it would be foolhardy to search for the Jaffa road in broad daylight.

As darkness fell, Roman soldiers still scoured the countryside looking for escaping Jews. Several patrols passed dangerously close to the tunnel entrance. Yohannen realized he had little choice but to stay hidden in the passageway during the night. By morning, however, Yohannen knew he had to risk capture in order to find water. His lips had become cracked from the intense heat and lack of moisture. The rabbi remembered there was a small well two leagues west along the Jaffa road. Barring no encounters with Roman patrols, Yohannen estimated he could reach the well by midday.

When the old rabbi emerged from the tunnel, the punishing heat of the desert made him lightheaded. For a moment, he sat down on the ground, afraid of losing consciousness. A bloated horse lay on the ground near him. The smell of carrion was overpowering. When he tried to stand, the rabbi twisted his ankle and fell back on the ground. Exhausted, he crawled toward some bushes by the side of the road. They would at least provide him shade. But before he could reach them, the rabbi lapsed into unconsciousness.

The next thing Yohannen heard was a voice saying "Old man, drink some water." Yohannen slowly opened his eyes. A stranger was standing over him holding a small cup. "You are weak, old man. You must get out of the sun."

The rabbi tried to push the man away.

"Don't worry! I'm not one of Titus's soldiers. I will not harm you."

When the rabbi realized the man was not a Roman, he took a drink from the cup. The man picked Yohannen up and carried him to a small pool of shade by the side of the road.

"My name is Evardus — a merchant from Gaul. I follow the way of Christ."

The rabbi tried to speak but the words would not come. He gestured for the merchant to come closer. Evardus bent down and put his ear near the old man's lips.

"The sacred vessels and records of my people are in a cave—buried in a cave."

"Where, old man?"

"There's a copper scroll—it is under the Holy of Holies." The rabbi's voice was no more than a faint whisper. "You must find it."

"Where under the Holy of Holies?"

"You must find it, you must—the scroll—it's in the 'stone of life.'"

"'In the stone of life.' What do you mean?"

The rabbi looked desperately at Evardus. He choked and gasped for air. "You are the only one who knows. Tell the Chief Rabbi in Jaffa and. . . ."

Yohannen said no more. The merchant gently laid the old man's head back on the road. Rabbi Yohannen was dead.

After burying the old rabbi near the place where he died, Evardus continued on his journey to the port of Jaffa. About an hour later, a company of Roman cavalry came thundering down the Jaffa Road behind him. As they came closer, Evardus knew it would be better to dismount from his horse and show no sign of nervousness. When the Roman soldiers rode up to him, a centurion signaled them to stop. The officer climbed off his horse and unsheathed his sword.

"Who are you?"

"Evardus. A wine merchant."

"You are not a Jew?" The point of the Roman's sword touched Evardus' throat.

"I am a Roman citizen from Gaul."

Not convinced that Evardus was telling the truth, the centurion continued to point his sword at Evardus's throat. "Why were you in Jerusalem?"

"I was not in Jerusalem. For the last week, I have been with Titus's quaestors selling wine to your army. I travel to Jaffa where my ship is moored."

"You have a ship in Jaffa?"

Evardus nodded his head. "Yes, I sail to Sicily tomorrow."

The centurian growled, "Why to Sicily?"

"I will buy more wine in Syracuse."

The Roman roared with laughter. "Syracuse is full of thieves. They flourish there like rats. I should know—I was born there."

"You are wrong, Centurion. These thieves live in Syracuse only during the day—at night they sleep in Gaul."

Amused by Evardus's quick wit, the centurion sheathed his sword. "Thieves do business with thieves. That will always be the way of the world."

Remounting his horse, the centurion motioned Evardus to follow behind the troop.

"Ride to Jaffa with us. If you have a ship in the harbor as you say, my soldiers will sample your wines and you will go free. But if you have lied to us, my sword will quickly find its way to your heart."

Evardus climbed on his horse and followed the Roman cavalry as they rode west along the road to Jaffa.

The Roman centurion belched as he drank the last casket of Evardus's wine. He staggered up and urinated over the side of the vessel.

"Wine merchant, I wish you could make more wine from this sea water. Some Jew claimed he could."

"Yes, his name was Jesus. They call his followers Christians."

"Ah! Now I remember. Nero used them as entertainment in the Coliseum. Jews, Christians—Palestine seems to breed strange beliefs."

Dusk was settling as Evardus walked along the narrow street looking for the house of the physician Timothy. A man appeared out of the shadows and greeted him.

"*Pax tibi,* my friend."

Evardus recognized the Christian greeting. He responded. "*Dominus resurrexit.*"

The man did not answer. For a minute Evardus thought he might have given the wrong response. "Who are you looking for?"

"The physician Timothy."

The man motioned for Evardus to follow him. "Come with me. We must be careful tonight."

"Why?" asked Evardus.

"Bartholomew, one of Jesus' Twelve, is with us."

When Evardus entered the house, Timothy's wife came over to greet him. She pointed to a tall man standing in the middle of the atrium. "Bartholomew is distributing the Eucharist." The Apostle offered bread to each person in the room. A woman followed Bartholomew carrying a cup of wine. When they reached Evardus, the wine merchant took a small piece of the unleavened bread and drank from the cup.

The Eucharist over, Timothy's wife brought Evardus to meet Bartholomew.

The Apostle's eyes were riveting. "I understand you have recently come from Jerusalem."

"Yes. Titus has destroyed the temple and massacred Jews by the thousands."

"The Emperor Nero martyred Peter and Paul. Now Titus has desecrated the Temple where Jesus preached. These are difficult days for those of us who follow the Master."

"Bartholomew, on the Jaffa road I found an old rabbi lying on the ground. He told me that a copper scroll had been buried under the Temple. He asked if I would carry word of the scroll to the Chief Rabbi of Jaffa."

Timothy's wife stared at Evardus with a rueful look. "The Chief Rabbi was crucified by the Romans two weeks ago. His body was left to rot on the cross as a reminder of the price of rebellion."

"Evardus, Roman spies are everywhere." Bartholomew put an avuncular hand on Evardus's shoulder. "Delivering a message to the Jews will endanger Timothy and the rest of your brothers and sisters here in Jaffa. If you are seen with the Jews, they will take you for one of them. The Romans do not understand that we follow Jesus, not Moses. Forget this copper scroll. Return to Gaul and spread the gospel of Our Lord and Savior."

Evardus took Bartholomew's admonition to heart. He left Jaffa and sailed to Sicily as planned. When he returned to his farm in Gaul, Evardus transcribed all he had seen and heard about the destruction of the Jewish temple and about Rabbi Yohannen and the copper scroll.

Nine years later Titus's father, the Emperor Vespasian, died from mysterious causes. The Praetorian Guard immediately proclaimed Titus as the new emperor. Fearing reprisals, the senate quickly approved the choice.

After two years, however, Titus, too, succumbed to a mysterious illness. Rumors of poisoning spread throughout Rome. Some claimed that a Jewish slave girl had brought him wine just minutes before he died. Those less partial to rumors believed that Titus had died from wounds received in the gladiatorial arena. One senator, however, voiced publicly what most would say only privately. Titus, the senator said, had died from too much fighting, too much drinking, and too much licentiousness.

Under pressure from the Roman legions, the senate ordered a magnificent arch built in the Forum in Titus's honor. Years later when he visited Rome, Evardus marveled at the friezes over the entrance to the arch. They showed Titus triumphantly carrying the Jewish menorah through the streets of Rome and laying it before the feet of Vespasian.

Barbo motioned the waiter to bring another espresso. "A fascinating story, Jean."

"Yes, it is."

"But how does Gerard de Montelambert fit into all of this?"

Calvaux looked at Barbo. "During the Crusades, Gerard went to Jerusalem and found Yohannen's scroll."

Cardinal Barbo's cell phone suddenly rang. "I apologize, Jean." He walked out to the street in front of the pasticceria. "Yes, Enrico, what is it?"

"There's a Detective Cameri from the Rome police here in your office. He won't tell me why he wants to see you."

"I'll be there shortly." Barbo clicked off the cell phone and went back inside the pasticceria.

"Jean, I must go back to my office."

"When there's time, you'll find Gerard's story as absorbing as Evardus's—perhaps more so because of your interest in the Templars. Gerard became a member of the order and was an eyewitness to their suppression by Pope Clement V."

"Walk back with me to my office. Do you know when the Templars were founded?"

"Wasn't it in 1118?"

"That's the official date but there's more to it than that. I'll give you a précis of the first chapter of my dissertation."

"Please do."

"The history of the Templars actually begins in Clermont Ferrand in November of 1095."

Chapter VII

A SPEECH IN CLERMONT FERRAND

THE FOREST PATH opened into a green valley with vineyards stretching out as far as the eye could see. The cold rain could not dampen the child's excitement. Seven-year-old Hugh des Payens scurried among the wagons and carts, playing hide-and-seek with his village friends. His mother had told him they were going to Clermont Ferrand to see the pope.

Hugh learned who the pope was from his older brother. The pope, his brother told him, was a very holy man. More important, he was also a magician. He always dressed in white and wore a conical-shaped hat on his head. With his wand, the pope could cure blindness and grow back a missing arm or leg. Hugh knew that his brother had to be right—it explained why there were so many old and sick people in the crowd. It also explained why several children were carrying sick pets in their arms.

As the path bent to the east, Hugh could see a vast assembly gathered in a meadow just to the east of Clermont Ferrand. A raised altar had been built in the center of the field.

"Is that where we are going, Mother—is that where the pope is?"

"Yes, he will stand on the altar and speak to us. We must pick a good spot so we can see him."

Hugh suddenly felt grown-up. He was determined to find his mother not just a good place to see the pope but the best place. Dodging through the crowd, he pulled his embarrassed mother behind him. Suddenly, Hugh heard a far-off cry: "The pope is coming." Jumping up from their seats on the ground, people surged forward to touch the pope and receive his blessing. Hugh and his mother had their pick of spaces on the grass. The seven-year old felt proud that he was able to do this for his mother. He knew what seeing the pope meant to her.

As the cheering came closer, a cold, tingling sensation ran down Hugh's spine. His heart pounded. He had never experienced anything like this before. Caught up in the excitement, some farmhands standing nearby tossed their caps in the air like schoolboys. Hugh marveled at how high some of the men could pitch them. He wanted to join the toss but knew he would not be able to throw his cap half as high as the others. One of the farmhands saw Hugh's hesitation. "Just throw it—it does not matter how high it goes. It is in honor of Pope Urban. Every hat goes high enough." Hugh pulled off his cap and made the toss. His cap hardly went above his head. Hugh tossed it again; this time it went higher than before. Again and again he tossed it, each time trying to touch the sky. On all sides, caps flew up to the heavens like prayers in honor of the pope.

A long procession of prelates and clergy ascended the steps to the altar platform. Everywhere Hugh looked there was a rainbow of colors. Befitting their status as Princes of the Church, cardinals stood next to the altar dressed in their bright scarlet robes; behind them were rows of purple-clad bishops and monsignori, and back farther still, a sea of white-surpliced priests. As if to frame the picture in darker shades, hooded monks dressed in black and brown robes lined the edges of the altar platform. Nobility from the neighboring regions of France sat on benches facing the altar—each prominently displaying his rank.

As the procession ended, Hugh jumped up and down, trying to see the pope. A solitary figure climbed the steps of the altar platform. When the crowd saw him, they began to cheer and clap their hands. Hugh knew instinctively that this man must be the pope. Still he was puzzled. This man wore a golden robe embroidered with silver threads, not the white garments Hugh's brother had predicted. While he did wear a conical-shaped hat, the man carried a shepherd's staff instead of a magician's wand. Without a wand, how could this man be a magician and without being a magician, how could he be the pope? Hugh had no answer to his questions. He decided to wait and see what would happen.

A hush fell over the vast assembly as the pope walked to the top step of the altar and sat on a carved wood throne. At a signal from a priest, several cardinals and bishops ascended the steps and prostrated themselves before the pope. After the cardinals and bishops had returned to their places, a group of nobles came forward and repeated the ritual. Hugh's mother whispered in his ear: "They do it as a sign of obedience to Pope Urban."

Once the homages had ended, Hugh saw the pope rise from the throne and hand his staff to a priest standing next to him. For a moment, Hugh became excited—perhaps now the pope would take a wand and perform magic for the vast crowd. To Hugh's disappointment, however, the pope did nothing of the kind. Instead he came down the steps of the altar and walked to the edge of the platform. He raised his hands to signal the crowd to be silent. Standing on the edge of the platform, Pope Urban towered over the crowd of the faithful like a giant elm towers over the forest that surrounds it.

"In the Year of the Incarnation of our Lord 1095, I—Urban, Bishop of Rome and Servant of the Servants of God—stand humbly before you. Today, God calls all of us to a great purpose. The Tomb of Christ is in Saracen hands. As Christians, we are summoned to redeem it, to liberate the place where our Lord and Savior died at the hands of the Jews. We are summoned also to redeem from the Saracen the relics of the holy martyrs and saints who died for Christ. To these great matters, God calls each and every one of us—the knight from Burgundy, the serf from England, the priest from Navarre, the merchant from Visby. Christians of Europe, embrace the Cross as your symbol. March to Jerusalem to do God's will. Rescue the holy places from the Saracen. Bring back the relics of our holy martyrs and saints. If a Crusader sets out on this sacred journey and makes a true and perfect act of contrition, all punishment for his sins will be remitted."

Hugh was not prepared for what happened next. The pope walked back to the altar and genuflected before a golden box that had been placed in front of the tabernacle.

"What is in the box, Mother?"

"Relics of Jesus."

Urban lifted the reliquary box high above his head and turned back and faced the multitude in front of him. At that moment, a shaft of light broke through the overcast sky and shone directly on the pope. "Behold a relic of the True Cross on which our Lord and Savior died to save us from sin." At the sight of the most sacred relic in all of Christendom, the crowd gasped audibly. Sensing the electricity of the moment, the pope cried out in a loud voice: "Christians, march to Jerusalem and free the Tomb of Christ."

Hugh did not know from where the cry originated. Some say it came from an old beggar who sat far back in the crowd. Others say it came from one of God's angels who was seen in the heavens. No matter! As Pope Urban stood holding the relic of the True Cross, someone cried out in a loud voice: "God Wills It!" The cry was first taken up by ten of the faithful, then by a hundred, then by thousands. It was an indescribable moment.

Hugh's mother grasped her son tightly as the roar of the crowd grew deafening. "God Wills It!" "God Wills It!" On an impulse, Hugh broke free from his mother and ran toward the altar platform. He dodged several soldiers and bounded up the steps two at a time. When he reached the top step, Hugh paused; his legs felt numb. The cries of "God Wills It" stopped as all eyes became fixed on the small child standing before Pope Urban.

"Holy Father," Hugh blurted out the words. "Let me go to Palestine to free the Tomb of Christ."

Urban smiled and put a hand on Hugh's shoulder. "You are too young, my son, but you can go when you are older."

Urban took a small gold cross from around his neck and put it in Hugh's hand. Then as if he had been his natural father, the pope lifted Hugh high up above his head and proclaimed in a loud voice, "Here is the first to respond to God's call."

The shouts of "God Wills It" started up again louder than before. As Urban put Hugh down, a bishop whispered in the pontiff's ear. "It's time, Holiness. The crowd may grow unruly." The pope nodded. Walking to the front of the altar platform, Urban lifted his right arm and imparted his papal blessing. *"In Nomine Patris, et Filii, et Spiritus Sancti."* The words of the benediction echoed across the meadow. Taking his staff, the pope descended the platform.

As he looked at the vast crowd spread out beneath him, Hugh stood at the portal to another world. He had experienced God's irresistible call to service. He made a promise that, when he was older, he would answer Pope Urban's call. He would go to the Holy Land and rescue the Tomb of Christ from the Saracen. As a light rain began to fall, Hugh wept.

Calvaux and Barbo stopped outside the entrance to the Apostolic Palace.

Barbo smiled. "That's the end of chapter one of my dissertation on the Templars."

"So years later, to fulfill his childhood promise, Hugh des Payens founded the Templars."

"Yes."

Calvaux thought for a moment. "There's a contradiction in all this. Urban's desire to free the Holy Land caused the death and enslavement of thousands. Hugh's plan to create an order of monks resulted in the creation of the best fighting force of the Middle Ages."

"Come to my office at four o'clock this afternoon. I want to hear your views on the Middle East."

"I am not an expert on the Middle East, Francesco."

Barbo smiled at Calvaux. "Jean, you are too self-effacing. You've lived in Egypt, speak fluent Arabic, and lead a diocese with a large Middle Eastern population."

"But what about my audience with His Holiness?"

"Come to my office at four, Jean."

Chapter VIII

TANGLED LOGIC

FATHER ALESSANDRI ESCORTED Detective Cameri into Cardinal Barbo's office. The secretary of state rose to greet his visitor.

"Signor Cameri, it is not often that I receive a visit from the Rome Police Department. How can I help you?" Barbo motioned Cameri to a seat in front of the cardinal's desk.

"Your Eminence, thank you for seeing me without an appointment. You must be so busy."

Instinctively, Barbo sensed that Cameri was not someone to take lightly. "How can I help you, Detective?"

"There was an automobile accident on Via di San Marco last night. An American professor was killed and another taken to Gemelli Hospital in critical condition."

Cardinal Barbo shrugged his shoulders. "I saw something on the television about it."

"Your name came up in the course of the investigation."

Barbo looked quizzically at Cameri. "I don't understand."

"Before he died, Professor Bielgard whispered your name to the doctor who was treating him."

Barbo sipped some water from a glass on his desk. "I imagine that's possible. Professor Bielgard had been in my office several days ago."

"Why was that?" Cameri's voice hardened.

"He and his colleague … what was her name?"

"Jane Michellini."

"Yes. They had discovered some manuscripts relating to the abdication of Pope Celestine V in 1294. I thanked them for the manuscripts and that was that."

Cameri continued his questioning. "Were they trying to sell them to you?"

"No. The manuscripts were from the Vatican Library. We do not buy our own property. Now if you will excuse me." The cardinal stood up from his chair signaling that the meeting was over.

Cameri slowly gathered up his papers "If Professor Bielgard had spoken to you about Celestine V, why would he repeat your name as he was dying? It makes no sense."

"Detective Cameri, as a priest, I often see things that do not make sense. Men say many things during their last moments." Barbo walked toward the door. "Leave your business card with Father Alessandri. If I think of anything more, I'll have Alessandri call."

"Just one more question, Your Eminence."

Barbo turned to Cameri with an annoyed look. "And what is that?"

"Do you know Pietro Visconti?"

"Yes." Barbo was taken aback by the question

"You had dinner with him last night."

"Yes."

"Everyone knows who's on his client list. We have police files on most of them. Don't you think it strange that a Prince of the Church would be seen dining with such a man?"

Barbo shot an angry look at Cameri. "I doubt you have files on his client Fiat or Banca di Roma. Signor Visconti generously supports many Vatican charities. Now if you would excuse me, Signor Cameri. Father Alessandri will see you out."

Cameri bowed stiffly to Barbo.

"In the future, Signor Cameri, any request to see a member of the Curia should be made to the Office of Vatican Security through your government's Ministry of the Interior. Sometimes the Rome Police forget that the Holy See is a sovereign nation.

Cardinal Calvaux spent a good part of the afternoon in the Domus corresponding with his diocese by email. At 3:15, he logged off the internet to prepare for his four o'clock meeting with Barbo.

He threw cold water on his face and put on his gold pectoral cross over his cassock. He debated wearing his cardinal's sash or fascia. Although the sash was uncomfortable, Calvaux knew that there would be disapproving looks from some of his fellow cardinals if he did not wear it. Ecclesiastical dress in the Vatican was more formal than in Marseilles.

When he stepped off the elevator into the lobby of the Domus, Calvaux noticed a large crowd gathered around a television monitor at the front desk. The concierge frantically motioned the cardinal to join them.

"Your Eminence, the Israelis are attacking the Church of the Holy Sepulchre. There are rumors of heavy casualties." Calvaux reflexively made the sign of the cross. He dropped his briefcase on a chair in the lobby and dashed out of the Domus. He sprinted across St. Peter's Square and pushed through the metal detector at the entrance to the Apostolic Palace. Bounding up the palace stairs three at a time, he startled a group of nuns on their way to lunch. Breathless, Calvaux burst into Alessandri's office.

"The Israelis are invading the Church of the Holy Sepulchre. Does Cardinal Barbo know?"

"Yes, we've gotten scores of phone calls. Cardinal Barbo is in his office. He's expecting you."

When Calvaux opened the door, the secretary of state was standing in front of a television set. "The BBC is about to broadcast live, Jean. Washington couldn't dissuade the Israelis from going in." As Barbo spoke, the television monitor flashed to Jerusalem.

"This is Liam Stewart from BBC News, near the Church of the Holy Sepulchre. At the moment, I'm standing on a rooftop about three hundred yards from where the fighting is still raging. I cannot let the contradiction pass. Men and women are dying here, near the spot where Christians believe Jesus rose from the dead."

The reporter was handed a note. "One of our cameramen has managed to get out of the church with some footage. The BBC warns its viewers that the pictures are graphic."

Barbo and Calvaux stood transfixed by what they saw. Israeli soldiers, their faces covered with gas masks, were pulling hostages along the floor toward the door of the Church. In the distance, the sound of gunfire erupted as ghostlike figures appeared and disappeared into clouds of smoke.

A desperate cry came from near the high altar. The cameramen zoomed in on a Hamas gunman standing over a woman and two children.

"No, I beg of you—not my boys!" The woman grappled to take a pistol out of the man's hand. The gunman pushed the woman aside and shot the children at point blank range. When the mother fell over the bodies of her sons, the gunman took aim and shot her in the back.

Barbo slammed his fist on the desk, knocking a picture of his parents to the floor. "Damn it. Maybe Finnergan was right. In the face of inhumanity like this. . . ." He angrily switched off the television.

"Jean, sit down for a minute."

Barbo walked over and closed the door to his office. "The pope wants what I tell you to be kept in the strictest confidence."

"I understand."

Barbo paused for a moment and looked at Calvaux. "You know how engaged the Holy Father has been in searching for peace in the Middle East."

"Yes, I know."

Warming to the subject, Barbo began to pace around his office. "The Holy Father has often said that the key to peace in the Middle East is investment and economic development. He's hoping to propose a new initiative. For want of a better name, he calls it 'A Covenant for Peace.'"

Calvaux looked skeptically at the secretary of state. "After what we just saw, you're not going to find many investors."

"Jean, the pope has spoken privately to the CEOs of several multinational pharmaceutical companies. With some prodding, they have formed a consortium to build three world-class hospitals in East Jerusalem."

"That's wonderful news. Who will staff them?"

Barbo picked up a fax on his desk and handed it to Calvaux. "Initially, Doctors Without Borders has agreed to recruit whatever medical personnel are needed."

"What do you mean 'initially'?"

"Hopefully the hospitals will develop research centers. Once that happens, there will be no problem recruiting quality staff."

"Three hospitals will not solve the problems of the Middle East."

"There is more to the pope's initiative, Jean." Barbo handed Calvaux a second fax. "As you can see, last week Credit Mobilier agreed to relocate its claims department to Jerusalem. This move alone will create hundreds of new jobs. And don't forget the oil companies. A group of them have agreed to consider moving some of their satellite operations to East Jerusalem."

Calvaux scanned the fax from Credit Mobilier. "The pope must be pleased."

"Yes but his eyes have been on an even greater prize."

"What?" Calvaux unconsciously moved his chair closer to Barbo as if the two men were about to share some conspiracy.

"He has talked with the secretary general about opening some UN programs in the city. UNESCO, in fact, is considering establishing five technical schools there. True, there's no commitment yet but talks are ongoing. If the UN agrees to this, it would be a dramatic gesture by the world community."

Calvaux looked unconvinced. "Won't some members of the Security Council object to putting any UN facility in Israel?"

"They will consent, as long as the facility is built in East Jerusalem."

"And what commitment will the Church make?"

Barbo chose his words carefully. "The Holy Father has something dramatic in mind, but he has not shared it with me. All he will say is that the Church's contribution will bring a sense of coherence and purpose to the rest of the projects."

"Won't the Israelis stop the pope's initiative in its tracks? They won't want to see too many resources going into East Jerusalem."

"That's where the United States comes in." Barbo looked Calvaux in the eye. "You must convince the president to pressure Israel to allow the pope's initiative to go forward."

"You want me to convince the president!" Calvaux scowled as if Barbo had made him the butt of a tasteless joke.

"Jean, the Holy Father wants this initiative to be handled outside diplomatic channels. He wants you to serve as his private envoy to the White House. If the president agrees to support the economic initiative, then His Holiness wants you to go to Tel Aviv and Ramallah to present it to the Israelis and the Palestinians."

Calvaux realized Barbo was not being facetious. "Francesco. I have no training in diplomacy. It would be like sending a sailor to fly an airplane."

"You have the qualities the Holy Father wants—intelligence, knowledge of the area, and a new face."

Calvaux stammered. "I must speak with the pope—I'm not the right person for this."

"You can't—not today."

"Well then, tomorrow."

"Not tomorrow either."

"You're hiding something from me, Francesco."

"Jean, the Holy Father is suffering from Alzheimer's disease."

Calvaux slumped back in his chair, dumbstruck. "You're serious, aren't you?"

"Completely."

Calvaux did not move for several minutes. "Who knows about Pope Benedict's condition?"

"Four people—Sister Consuela, the pope's physician Dr. Hendricks, Father Alessandri, and myself. You're the fifth. The Holy Father needs your help."

Calvaux took out a handkerchief and wiped his forehead. "How can I refuse?"

"Good. The president is returning to the United States today from a NATO meeting in Brussels. He's agreed to land Air Force One briefly at Brise Norton, a Royal Air Force Base outside London at about eleven o'clock tonight to meet with a papal envoy. He will give us only fifteen minutes of his time. Once you've been briefed, there's a plane ready to take you to the meeting."

"Make your briefing as detailed as possible."

"Don't worry. It will bc."

That evening, the secretary of state accompanied Calvaux to Leonardo da Vinci Airport. The VIP lounge was crowded with executives waiting for flights. Barbo and Calvaux sat unobtrusively in a distant corner but not unobtrusively enough for one portly Italian businessman. When he saw the two prelates, he deliberately sat down across from them and picked up a discarded newspaper. When Barbo and Calvaux lowered their voices, the businessman stood up and moved closer. Unsure of what to do, Barbo suggested that they speak in Latin. Outwitted, the businessman got up and walked to the bar where he ordered a glass of wine.

Calvaux smiled. "That's a trick I must remember."

Barbo looked around the lounge to assure himself that there were no more eavesdroppers. "After our discussion this morning, Jean, your trip to see the president is almost ironic."

Calvaux looked puzzled. "What do you mean?"

"Like your ancestor Gerard de Montelambert, you are embarking on a crusade—but a crusade whose aim is to bring peace to the Holy Land, not kill Muslims."

Calvaux signaled a waiter to bring an espresso. "Speaking of the Crusades, Francesco, I wanted to ask you a question about the Templars. They were originally founded both as a military and as a religious order, weren't they?"

"Yes—St. Bernard justified allowing Templar monks to kill non-Christians by adopting double-effect theory."

"Yes, I remember Bernard made much of the distinction between the killing of evil, 'malicide,' and the killing of a human being, 'homicide.'"

Barbo turned in his seat. "Once you accept Bernard's distinction, it all follows logically. Satan brought evil into the world and placed it in the bodies of non-Christians. When a monk killed a non-Christian, it was 'malicide,' because his primary intent was to kill this evil. The death of the individual Saracen or Jew was the unintended consequence of destroying the evil and therefore was not sinful. But if a monk killed a Christian, that would be 'homicide' and sinful."

Calvaux smiled. "As long as you intend to do good, you can accept any evil as an unintended consequence of your good intent. No matter how I try, I cannot envision Jesus preaching the 'Parable of Unintended Consequences.' You can justify almost anything with that tangled logic."

Barbo nodded his head. "Double-effect theory reads well in a theological textbook, but it's not much help when making tough moral choices."

"Let me ask you something, Francesco. Suppose you were offered a large sum of money to help the poor in your diocese but the offer had certain conditions attached to it. Would you take the money?"

"I see your interest in double-effect theory is more than theoretical. I would have to look carefully at the conditions—would they cause a disproportionate amount of evil or. . . ."

A stewardess interrupted the two cardinals.

"Cardinal Calvaux, your plane is at the gate."

Calvaux finished his espresso and picked up his attaché case. The stewardess escorted the churchmen through the airport concourse to a private gate where Calvaux's plane waited. Barbo and Calvaux shook hands.

"Jean, we can finish the conversation about double-effect theory when you get back. In the meantime, I'll pray for your success with the president."

As the stewardess closed the door of the plane behind Calvaux, the pilot turned on the engines. The plane pushed back from the gate. Barbo noted it was precisely eight o'clock. Calvaux should reach Brise Norton by ten thirty—half an hour before Air Force One was due to arrive.

When Barbo returned to his office in the Apostolic Palace, Bishop Renini was waiting for him in the reception area. The Bishop held tightly to his brief case.

"Your Eminence, I have a preliminary report on the Magdalene parchment."

"Come into my office." Barbo signaled Alessandri to join them. "What did you find, Renini?"

The bishop walked over to Barbo's conference table and opened his brief case. "A member of the library staff discovered this—in a cabinet drawer no less." Renini took out a yellowed document that had been placed inside a plastic folder. "This doesn't specifically mention a bloodline from the Magdalene but. . . ."

Barbo grew impatient. "What does it say?"

"It's a letter from the grand master of the Templars, Jacques de Molay, to someone named Gerard de Montelambert."

"Gerard de Montelambert!" Barbo was stunned.

"We think he was also a Templar."

Barbo could hardly contain his excitement. "Read the letter, Renini."

"It's only a few lines. 'Gerard, the Hebrew manuscript is in your safekeeping. Hide it well. Someday the world may come to learn whether there is a divine bloodline.'"

Barbo knew instinctively that this letter and the legend of the Montelamberts were somehow linked. For the second time in two days, Barbo felt the closeness of evil. Last night as he walked over Ponte Sant'Angelo, Barbo had seen the Trickster in the dark waters of the Tiber. Tonight he felt him staring out from the words of this letter. But this time Barbo was not frightened. On the contrary, he felt strangely alive and emboldened as if the Holy Spirit were calling him to some undisclosed task.

"Did you find anything else in the library?"

"No, but Bishop Pellent called me from Avignon. His computers are down. He'll work as fast as he can once everything is up and running."

"Remind Pellent that whatever he finds should be sent to me immediately."

Chapter ix

GERARD DE MONTELAMBERT

THE MEETING BETWEEN the president and Cardinal Calvaux had gone on twenty minutes longer than scheduled.

The president's chief of staff paced up and down outside the stateroom where the two men were meeting. Finally he knocked softly on the door. "Mr. President, we must be on our way. They're waiting for us in Washington."

The door opened, and the president and Calvaux emerged from the stateroom.

"Your Eminence, I apologize. My staff keeps me on schedule—too much so sometimes." There was a hint of impatience in the president's voice.

The president ushered Cardinal Calvaux to the door of Air Force One. A light rain was falling as the two men shook hands.

"Tell Pope Benedict, the First Lady and I are looking for some excuse to come visit him. Perhaps tonight we've found one."

"His Holiness would be pleased if you would come."

A Marine sergeant opened an umbrella and escorted Calvaux down the wet boarding ramp to the tarmac. As Calvaux watched from the ground, the door of Air Force One slowly closed and the ramp pulled back from the aircraft. Two secret service agents walked around the plane with flashlights doing a final check of the tires and the landing gear. Lights flashing, the president's plane taxied out to the runway. Just then two Royal Air Force jets streaked overhead, waiting to accompany the president's plane out of English air space. Air Force One was soon in the air, and a member of the president's security detail drove Calvaux to his plane.

Exiting the car, the cardinal stopped for a moment before boarding and dialed his cell phone. "Francesco, I just left our friend."

Over the years, Calvaux had learned never to trust the privacy of cell phones.

"What was his reaction to the initiative?"

"Positive—up to a point. Let's talk when I get back to Rome."

Calveaux's plane landed at Leonardo da Vinci Airport about 2 A.M. The cardinal was waved through customs and driven immediately to the Apostolic Palace. A Swiss Guard brought him to Barbo's office.

"You look exhausted, Jean. Can I offer you something?"

Calvaux took off his Roman collar. "Cognac would be nice."

Barbo opened a cupboard under one of his bookcases and took out two snifters. He poured the liquor liberally into both and handed one to Calvaux.

"So the president is positive up to a point. I didn't like the 'up to a point.'"

Calvaux swirled the cognac in the bottom of the snifter. "He has conditions for his support. First, the president wants the Vatican, not Washington, to brief Israel and the Palestinians on the details of the initiative. He doesn't want it to look like its coming from the Americans."

"That's reasonable. The president isn't a risk-taker."

"Once both sides are fully briefed, the president will speak with the Israeli Prime Minister and ask him not to dismiss the pope's initiative out of hand."

Barbo leaned forward. "Ask or tell?"

"He said 'ask.'"

Disappointed, Barbo sat back in his chair. "And his second condition?"

Calvaux consulted some notes in his briefcase. "He wants the pope to invite the world's major religious leaders—the Eastern Patriarchs, the Dalai Lama, the Sheik of Al Azhar, the Chief Rabbi of Israel—to join him in Jerusalem to pray on the Temple Mount. At the same time, the president will invite heads of state to come to Jerusalem as well. He hopes that the sight of religious leaders of all faiths praying alongside the world's government leaders may trigger an irresistible momentum for peace."

Barbo shrugged his shoulders. "The president is looking for a media event to end all media events."

"Will it be difficult for Pope Benedict to travel to Jerusalem in his present condition?"

"Yes, but it may not be totally out of the question. Anyway, we must tell him. He'll have to make the ultimate decision."

Barbo stood up and poured more cognac into Calvaux's snifter.

"Jean, my office has pending another matter of great importance to the Church. Strange as it may seem, your family history may have some bearing on it."

"How?"

"You told me how one of your ancestors, Gerard de Montelambert, discovered Jewish records that were hidden from the Romans during the first century."

"Yes, it's a fascinating story."

"I know it is late but could you tell me more about this Gerard. You said he was a Templar."

"Yes, he was."

"Push, Mistress, push." The midwife put her hand up the birth canal. "Push harder. I do not feel the child."

"Midwife, the contractions have stopped."

Thunder rumbled outside the window of the Marquise's bedchamber.

"You must expel the child or you will die."

The Marquise cried out in pain as she tried to resume pushing. "The child will not come. Bring my husband."

A servant girl ran to the great hall of the manor house. She spoke nervously to the Marquis. "My Lord, your wife cannot deliver the child."

The Marquis pushed past the girl and hurried to his wife's bedchamber.

"My Lord, take me into the chapel." The Marquise looked imploringly at her husband.

The Marquis lifted his wife out of bed and carried her into the small chapel that adjoined her bedchamber. When he set her down in front of the altar, the Marquise put her finger to her husband's lips as if anticipating an objection.

"You must leave, My Lord."

The Marquis left the chapel and paced nervously outside. Their first child had been a girl and the Marquis had prayed that this child would be the male heir he so desperately wanted. Now for this to happen!

A loud cry of pain sounded from the chapel. When the Marquis ran inside, his wife was smiling.

"The contractions have started again. I made a promise to the Virgin. She will give us our child."

And so, Gerard de Montelambert was born. The village of Cours-des-Trois—the ancestral home of the Montelamberts in the foothills of the Pyrenees—celebrated the birth of the Marquis's heir for three days. Although the Marquis asked numerous times, Gerard's mother would not tell her husband what promise she had made the Virgin. She would keep this a secret for two decades.

From his earliest years, Gerard de Montelambert displayed a fearsome courage that bordered on recklessness. Villagers told the story of how at twelve years of age, Gerard saved his younger sister Annette's life. The girl was trapped on the roof of a burning cowshed. Gerard doused blankets in a cistern of water and climbed up on the roof. Although the smoke blinded his eyes, Gerard could hear Annette crying. Stretching out his hand in the direction of her voice, Gerard managed to find her in the smoke. Throwing the wet blankets over both of them, he led her to the edge of the roof. A wagon full of straw was wheeled to the side of the shed.

Gerard listened to the voices below. "Push the wagon farther to the right."

When the wagon was moved, Gerard shouted to his sister. "Jump, Annette."

The girl stood paralyzed, refusing to leap into the smoke.

Gerard put his arm around his sister's waist and pulled her with him off the roof. Brother and sister landed safely in the wagon. Despite poultices from several doctors, however, it was two months before Gerard's eyesight returned. His sister Annette was less fortunate. She suffered severe burns on her right leg that stayed with her all her life.

When he learned what had happened, the village priest told the Marquise. "God has destined your son for great things."

Gerard grew tall and slender like a cypress tree. His dark brown hair and olive complexion reflected the rich soil of Provence. Gerard's mother insisted that he go to an abbey in a nearby town to learn to read the Scriptures in Hebrew and Latin. His father attended to his secular education. As the future lord of Cours-des-Trois, Gerard was taught how to plant and harvest crops, how to measure land by metes and bounds, and how to carry out the duties expected of someone of his station.

On Gerard's sixteenth birthday, his father summoned him to the great hall of the manor house. The Marquis's younger brother, Gerard's Uncle Edouard, was also there.

"Gerard, today you are old enough to begin learning the skills of a knight. Your Uncle Edouard has agreed to take on this responsibility. Your uncle was a Templar and fought in Palestine."

"Until a Saracen lance pierced my armor. The tip of the lance is still in my side. But that is in the past."

Edouard opened a locked casket and carefully took out an ancient parchment scroll. "Your grandfather showed this manuscript to your father and me on our sixteenth birthdays. It has been passed down through the Montelambert family for over a thousand years. It was written by one of our ancestors—a wine merchant named Evardus."

Edouard carefully handed the ancient manuscript to Gerard.

"Your mother tells me you learned to read Latin at the abbey. You should be able to understand it."

The young boy held the parchment up to the light. "It talks about the destruction of the Jewish temple in Jerusalem—about the things Evardus saw and heard."

"Read on."

"It mentions a Jewish rabbi whom Evardus met along the road to Jaffa. Before he died, the rabbi told Evardus about a copper scroll buried in 'the stone of life' under the Holy of Holies. The rest of the writing is faded—all I can make out are the words 'vessels and records of the Jewish people.'"

His father spoke. "Gerard, since the Crusades began, many of our family have gone to Jerusalem and searched for this scroll. None have found it."

"Why did you not go to Palestine, Father?"

A resigned look passed over the Marquis's face. "I was the oldest son. It was my duty to become lord of Cours-des-Trois."

Edouard stared at his brother reproachfully. "If you had wanted to, Brother, you could have left the bailiff in charge of the manor."

The Marquis slammed his hand on the table. "Edouard, please not in front of Gerard."

"Uncle, when you went to Outremer, the land beyond the sea, did you search for the scroll?"

"Yes—until the Saracen's lance cut short my efforts. Maybe it will be your destiny to find the scroll, Gerard."

The Marquis looked angrily at his brother.

"Edouard, enough of this. Remember Gerard is the heir to Cours-des-Trois. His responsibility lies here, not in Palestine."

Edouard began to train Gerard on the very next day. "Before you pick up a sword, Gerard, you must learn about your body—how far it can run, how much it can carry, how long it can fast, how high it can jump."

Edouard looked at the sky. "The day grows colder. Put on your heaviest cloak and stand outside the manor house for an hour."

When the hour was over, Gerard came inside, trembling with cold.

"Do it again, Gerard, only this time stand in the middle of your clothes."

"What do you mean?"

"Pull your body into yourself. Create a space between you and your clothes. The space will keep you warm."

After Gerard stood for another hour, he was not trembling.

"You have learned an important lesson about your body. It can be ruled by the mind."

Edouard created a daily exercise regimen for his nephew. Gerard would run three leagues, then carry heavy stones from one place to another and finally scale the wall that circled the manor house. Once a week, Edouard would add another component to the regimen. Gerard would be required to swim back and forth across the treacherous currents of the Durand River for two hours.

After three months, Edouard abruptly changed the daily routine.

"Gerard, you have learned what your body can endure. Now you must learn to sharpen your senses. For that, we must go into the forest."

On one day, Edouard would teach Gerard how to tell time from the position of the sun; on the next, how to live off the forest plants; on another, how to understand the behavior of animals.

One Sunday after Mass, Edouard took Gerard aside and handed him a silver coin. "Give this coin to your father's bailiff if he can find your hiding place."

Gerard warmed to the game. There was a grove of elm trees along the forest road where as a child Gerard had often hidden from his sisters. He climbed the tallest tree and waited. Several hours later, he heard the hoof beats of a horse. Someone dismounted and walked into the grove. Gerard saw the bailiff staring up at him.

"Have I earned the coin, my young master?"

Gerard told Edouard what had happened.

"Give the bailiff another coin if he can find you again. This time sit in the town square in front of the church."

Gerard followed Edouard's instructions. He spent the day talking with his friends in the town square. The bailiff never found him. When Gerard told Edouard what had happened the second time, his uncle smiled at his nephew's look of amazement. "Gerard, what do you learn from being discovered in the forest but not in the village square?"

Gerard thought for a moment. "Sometimes the best place to hide is in the sunlight."

When rain kept them out of the forest, Edouard would take Gerard into the stable.

"Gerard, when you jumped off the burning roof with your sister, the smoke made it impossible for you to see. What did you do?"

"I listened instead. The voices of the townspeople guided me to the wagon."

Edouard handed his nephew a blindfold. "Put this on and try to dodge my blows."

Edouard picked up a stave and hit Gerard on the back of his legs.

"You can learn to hear the blow coming, Gerard. Listen for it. Hear through your other senses." Although there were many nights when Gerard went to bed with bruises on his shins, he gradually learned a remarkable lesson—all the senses are interconnected. One can learn to hear colors and taste shapes.

After a year of training his mind and body, Edouard finally permitted Gerard to begin practicing with the sword and lance. From the very first drill, Edouard could see that Gerard possessed formidable talents. His foot movements were balletic; his thrusts and parries never left him off balance; and his instincts were unerring.

Late one November day after sword practice, Gerard shouted to Edouard. "Throw an apple in the air." The apple was hardly out of Edouard's hand before Gerard had cut it in half with one stroke of his sword.

Edouard smiled. "Now it is time to begin the last and most important part of your training. I will teach you a skill I learned as a Templar."

"What is that?"

"To talk to animals."

Gerard laughed. "Uncle, do not joke with me."

"It is no joke."

Every day, Edouard took Gerard into a dark room in the manor house where they sat without speaking for hours at a time. "To keep your mind from wandering, Gerard, concentrate on the word Outremer—first on the whole word and then on its parts." At first Gerard chafed at the monotony of these long periods of enforced silence. No matter how much he complained, however, Edouard would not vary the daily routine. "Gerard, just as the senses are interconnected, so too are all parts of God's creation. To hear their voices, you must learn to empty your mind."

"I cannot do it, Uncle. My thoughts keep coming back."

"Don't be discouraged. Focus on the word Outremer. Say it over and over again."

One day when Gerard accompanied his mother on a trip to a neighboring village, a raven landed on a nearby tree. He hopped from branch to branch and cawed raucously as Gerard and his mother rode up to the tree.

The Marquise smiled. "I think we are disturbing his nest."

Gerard stopped his horse and grabbed hold of his mother's reins. "Mother, we must go back. There is a fire ahead of us."

The Marquise shook her head. "There is no fire, Gerard. You are imagining things."

"No, I'm not. The raven told me."

Just then the acrid smell of smoke blew through the trees. Gerard and his mother hurried back to Cours-des-Trois. When the Marquise told Edouard what had happened, he grinned. On that day Edouard went to the manor house to speak with his brother the Marquis.

"I can teach Gerard nothing more. He fights with the cunning and determination of a young Hannibal. If you block his way, he circles around you; if you cut off his retreat, he charges you full tilt. It is as if God were training Gerard for some special purpose."

"I feel this too, Edouard."

On his twentieth birthday, Gerard entered the parish church of Cours-des-Trois to take the solemn oath of knighthood. He walked to the baptismal font where the bishop poured water over his head, as a reminder of his baptism. Accompanied by the bishop and his Uncle Edouard, Gerard processed down the center aisle of the church. At the foot of the altar, assisted by his two sisters, Gerard put on a white mantle marked front and back with a red cross. The white mantle symbolized a knight's purity, and the red cross the knight's willingness to suffer and die for Christ. After putting on the mantle, Gerard stood solemnly before the bishop and recited the words of his oath.

Then while everyone in the church watched, Gerard turned and knelt before his father and mother. The Marquis touched the blade of his sword to Gerard's shoulders. "My son, today you have taken the oath of a knight. It is an oath to follow the way of the Cross."

Gerard's father pointed to a large painting of the Crucifixion that hung over the altar of the chapel. "The cross has two bars — the vertical bar symbolizes spiritual life, and the horizontal bar temporal life. Jesus died at the place where the two bars meet. His death reminds us that if we wish to follow him, we must balance body and soul and live at the place where they intersect."

When the ceremony was over, Edouard motioned his nephew aside. "Gerard, take this coin. It bears the image of Hannibal. The Carthaginian was the master of surprise."

"Surprise turns one knight into ten and two into fifty. You taught me this lesson many times."

"Remember the lesson whenever you see the coin."

The day after his ceremony of knighthood, the Marquis asked Gerard to walk with him around the manor house.

"Gerard, your mother and I have looked forward to the day of your knighthood for many years. You have made us very proud. But now I must speak to you about other matters. The Montelamberts have been vassals of the Duke of Provence for many years. Every year, Cour-des-Trois must provide the duke with fifty cartloads of wheat and ten cattle. When there is war, the duke requires the village to pay scutage for twenty soldiers."

"Do not all the landholders in Provence pay similar duties to the duke?"

"Yes. But I am growing old. The doctors say I have a lump in my stomach. Neither leeches nor purgatives will shrink it. Your mother has become concerned. You must take over running the manor. When I die, you will become the Marquis of Cours-des-Trois."

"I cannot do what you ask, Father."

The Marquis looked stunned. "What do you mean, Gerard?"

"I must go on Crusade. Edouard thinks that it is my destiny to discover the copper scroll."

"Edouard has filled your head with nonsense. As my younger brother, he could go to Palestine because he was not heir to the Montelambert lands. But like me, Gerard, you are the heir to Cours-des-Trois—your duty lies here at the manor house, not in Jerusalem."

"I cannot do what you wish, Father."

"If you leave, who will take care of your mother and sisters?"

"Annette wishes to enter the convent, and Catherine is soon to be betrothed. They will not live on the manor."

"And your mother?"

"The rules of vassalage will allow her to stay here in the manor house until she dies."

"You would forfeit your inheritance to go on crusade?"

"I cannot betray myself, Father."

"But you would betray those who love you most. Leave me, Gerard."

"Father, I. . . ."

"Leave me!"

Gerard's mother found her husband sitting alone in the chapel. "My Lord, we have been married for almost thirty years. I have always obeyed you and never opposed your wishes. But I have spoken with our son and cannot support you on this. Gerard must go to Jerusalem. It is the promise I made to the Virgin."

The Marquis stared nervously at his wife.

"What do you mean?"

"The night when he was born—I never told you what happened in the chapel."

"No, you always refused."

"I knew Gerard was dying in my womb. I begged the Virgin Mother to save him. As I prayed, I felt her presence all around me. There was a whisper—'Your child will live, but he must follow the destiny that God has prepared for him. Promise me that.' I said 'yes.'"

"But Cours-des-Trois needs Gerard. He is its rightful heir."

"God needs him more. We have been blessed with Gerard for twenty years. Now he is in the hands of God. Your brother Edouard is a good man. He can carry on the Montelambert name here at Cours-des-Trois."

Chapter x

THE CRUSADER'S ROAD

THE DAY OF Gerard's departure was a sad one in the village. After Mass, the Marquis took Gerard into the great hall of the manor. "You will take the overland route to Palestine?"

"Yes. Knights from all over France and the Rhineland are gathering in Metz. The caravan will leave in mid-September. Edouard will accompany me as far as Burgundy."

"The Montelambert name is well-known in many parts of Europe. Take this letter of introduction with you, Gerard. It may be helpful."

The Marquis stood up slowly from his chair and kissed his son on both cheeks. "It is time, Gerard. You must move the cross."

Gerard lifted the large crucifix from its place on the altar and followed the curé and his parents out into the town square of Cours-des-Trois. There was an ancient tradition in the town; whenever the Marquis departed to go to war, he would carry the cross from the village church and place it outside in the square. When he arrived back in Cours-des-Trois, the Marquis returned the cross to its proper place on the altar. Gerard's father ordered that the cross be moved from the church to the village square in honor of his son's departure for the Holy Land. Once the cross was placed in the square, Gerard embraced his parents and his sisters.

The Marquise caressed Gerard's cheek and handed him a small piece of parchment.

"When you reach Jerusalem, put this into a crack in the walls of the Holy City. It is your family's blessings for you. When you stand before the Holy City, we will be praying at your side."

Holding back his tears, Gerard pushed the parchment into his pocket and quickly mounted his horse. The Marquise stretched her arms up to kiss her son one last time.

"Follow your destiny, Gerard. God has chosen you for a special purpose."

Gerard and his uncle left Cours-des-Trois and rode north for several hours until they reached the town of Ventoux. As the road bent into town, Edouard looked puzzled. He motioned Gerard to slow his horse to a pace.

"Something is wrong. The streets are usually filled on market day."

When they reached the town square, an unruly mob had gathered on the steps of the church. At first, neither Gerard nor Edouard understood what was happening. Then they saw a man and a young girl kneeling on the top step of the church. The girl was little more than ten years of age. Both had Stars of David sewn onto the backs of their garments.

"What are they doing to the Jews?" Gerard questioned a teenage boy standing near him.

"Their heads will be cut off. The Jews kidnapped a Christian baby and ate her flesh. An old woman saw them do it."

"Do you believe such a story?"

"It is not a story! It is the truth."

"The truth!"

"Yes, the town elders investigated—they found the bones." The boy twisted his lip in a sneer. "We do not have to go to Palestine to find Christ's enemies."

A priest emerged from the darkness of the church. A burly man carrying an axe followed him. The priest blessed the axe and then intoned the words *Libera nos a perfidis Judaeis.* The executioner walked over to where the Jews were kneeling on thc ground. The mob jeered and howled in delight. When he saw the executioner's axe, the old man begged for mercy.

"Spare my granddaughter. She is innocent."

The priest looked at the old Jew.

"Confess what you have done."

"I took the child and ate her flesh. I did it alone. My granddaughter is innocent."

The piteous words of the old man only made the mob howl and jeer the louder.

"Call on your God Jehovah to save your granddaughter."

Gerard drew his sword. The coin Edouard had given him rolled to the ground.

As he bent down to pick it up, Gerard caught his Uncle looking at him. "Gerard, remember surprise turns one man into ten."

"And two into fifty."

Brandishing his sword, Gerard spurred his horse to a gallop and rode headlong into the mob. Edouard followed close behind him, striking his sword on his shield. Given the suddenness of the attack, the mob parted like the waters of the Red Sea. When he reached the steps of the church, Gerard jumped off his horse and put his sword to the priest's throat.

"Order the executioner to throw down his axe or the crown of martyrdom awaits you."

"Please, Sir, I beg of you. You are a Christian knight. I am a good priest. Do not hurt me."

"Then do what I say! Tell the executioner to put down the axe."

Cringing with fear, the priest looked imploringly at the executioner.

"In the name of Saint Michael, François, do what the knight says or he will kill me."

The executioner threw the axe to the ground.

Edouard rode to the rear of the church and returned with two horses. "Priest, come with us until we are safely out of Ventoux. Ride with the child. Feeling her heart beat like a Christian's might teach you tolerance."

Keeping his sword drawn, Gerard climbed on his horse and led the others out of Ventoux. When they were a day's journey from the town, Gerard and Edouard left the village priest and the two Jews and continued on toward Burgundy. Weeks later Gerard could still see the look of hatred in the villagers' eyes.

Edouard embraced his nephew at the Burgundian border. "I have something for you. Gerard. I had a scribe copy it."

Edouard handed Gerard a piece of parchment. Gerard's eyes lit up with excitement. "It is Evardus's chronicle."

"Yes, Gerard. Take it with you to Jerusalem. The ruins of Herod's Temple are spread over many hectares. No one person can possibly search the length and breadth of them. Read Evardus's words, and search for the copper scroll through the eyes of faith. It is the only way."

The caravan to the Holy Land was scheduled to leave Metz on the Feast of the Exaltation of the Holy Cross—the day on which Constantine's mother, Saint Helena, discovered Jesus' Cross in Jerusalem. The task of organizing the convoy fell to the papal legate, Fulk de Teent, Bishop of Namur. Fulk's first act was to appoint a governing council made up of ranking nobility. The council designated the area north and west of the City as pilgrim campsites. During the weeks before departure, itinerant preachers had traveled the countryside proclaiming the spiritual rewards of pilgrimage. "Jesus said to sell everything and follow Him. This is the way to salvation." The response was overwhelming. Families, some with newborn infants in their arms, clogged the roads to Metz intent on joining the caravan to Jerusalem.

The council reserved the large meadow area to the east of the city for the nobility and their entourages. Never before had Gerard seen so many soldiers gathered in one place. Knights rode about the meadow with pennants flying from their lances. Sergeants, squires, and common foot soldiers competed with one another in swordsmanship and feats of strength. Only the archers seemed content to sit quietly on the ground oiling their bows and fashioning their arrows. Occasionally several knights of the Temple would ride through the campsite like princes from a far-off realm.

Bishop Fulk designated the area to the south of the city as a depot for provisioning the crusade. Under his watchful eye, physicians, coopers, wainwrights, blacksmiths—tradesmen of all sorts—were recruited to join the crusade. On most days, Fulk would stand with the muleteers as they chose beasts of burden to pull the supply wagons. Fulk decided the particularly sensitive issues himself. When a question arose over the number of prostitutes that would be allowed to join the cavalcade, Fulk decided on fifty. Before he made the decision, however, Fulk sought the advice of the harlot Marguerite. Tall and buxom with henna-dyed hair, Marguerite was well known in the brothels of Metz. Her high-spirited ways made her the subject of gossip even among the clergy. Charmed that a person as important as Bishop Fulk would ask her advice on the number of prostitutes to recruit for the journey, Marguerite immediately signed on to go herself. "It is time that I seek forgiveness for my sins," she told Fulk. "But with your approval, I would like to postpone total repentance until I reach Palestine. It would be wrong to overlook the needs of some of the younger crusaders during the journey. Of course, Your Excellency is always welcome in my tent."

On the morning of departure, the knights attended a Mass in the Cathedral. "Today you begin your long journey to Outremer, the land beyond the sea," the Archbishop of Metz thundered from the pulpit. "To shed the blood of the infidel is no sin. If anyone fights against you, they fight against Jesus Christ."

When the Mass was over, the archbishop stood on the steps of the Metz Cathedral and granted a papal indulgence to all in the cavalcade. Anyone who died on the road to Palestine would have punishment for his sins remitted and be admitted directly into heaven. As she walked past the archbishop, even Marguerite was overcome by emotion. She made the sign of the cross and received the indulgence. Fortified by the promise of salvation, Marguerite and the thousands who accompanied her marched out of Metz amidst a sea of flags and pennants.

The first two weeks of the journey passed uneventfully. When the cavalcade crossed into Serbian territory at Belgrade, however, fortunes changed. Torrential rains mired many of the supply wagons in mud. To move them to drier land, the wagons had to be emptied of their loads. A cooper devised an ingenious method of keeping the food and wine safe from vermin. He built a wooden platform and laid it on top of a tree trunk. The provisions of food and wine were moved from the wagons to the platform. Although rodents could climb up the tree trunk, they could not walk upside down to reach the edge of the platform. The crusaders were confident that their supplies would be safe until the wagons could be hauled out of the mud.

The night after the provisions had been loaded onto the platform, Gerard was awakened by a dull thud. Instinctively, he ran toward the platform. A dense mist lay over the ground making it difficult to see. When he reached the platform, Gerard's worst fears were confirmed. The platform had been shoved off the trunk, spilling food and wine on the ground. Rats were already enjoying their unexpected banquet.

"Rats are attacking the food." Gerard's alarm roused the camp. Soldiers and pilgrims picked up whatever weapon they could find and hurried to the platform. No matter how many rats were killed, more appeared. The food would have been totally devoured had it not been for the quick-wittedness of Marguerite and several other prostitutes. They gathered brush and built a circle of fire around what was left of the food. Afraid of the light, the rats retreated back into the forest.

Dawn revealed the full extent of the damage. More than half of the provisions had been eaten or otherwise spoiled. The morning also brought an even more serious problem than loss of food. In the struggle to save the provisions, several pilgrims had been bitten by rats. Fear of the plague spread through the caravan. After consulting with several physicians, Fulk ordered those who had been bitten to leave the caravan. Despite the scarcity of food, however, the bishop provided them with a week's provisions.

As the caravan marched deeper into Serbia, the provisions had to be rationed, which inevitably led to dissension and challenges to Fulk's authority. Against the bishop's commands, rogue bands of knights looted Serbian farms in the nearby countryside. Skirmishes between Serbs and knights were becoming increasingly commonplace. On many mornings, the decapitated torso of a knight or the burnt body of a Serbian farmer would be found lying by the side of the road. Things did not improve when they reached Thrace. In response to urgent pleas from Fulk, the Byzantine Emperor ordered the local populace to provide food for the caravan. The imperial commands, however, were largely ignored. Petitions to the local Orthodox Church also fell on deaf ears. Many in the caravan were reduced to eating grass and the roots of trees. Finally, after weeks of near starvation, the remains of the caravan—which had so proudly left Metz just months before—reached the Bosporus. On the horizon could be seen the spires of Constantinople, Constantine's City, the capital of the Byzantine Empire, and the richest city in Christendom.

Never had Gerard seen anything so majestic as the walls of Constantinople. Seventy feet in height, the stone bastions were three times taller than the walls of Cours-des-Trois. As he walked through the wide thoroughfares of the city, Gerard was awestruck by what he saw—crowds cheering their favorite horse in the Hippodrome; wealthy merchants in long silk robes, parading through Constantine's Forum; the Imperial Palace with its hundreds of rooms and chapels glimmering in the afternoon sun.

But for Gerard all the wonders of the city paled in comparison with Santa Sophia, the great Basilica of Holy Wisdom and the largest church in Christendom. On one of his many visits to the church, Gerard watched a frightened woman running out through the great bronze doors.

When she saw Gerard, the woman ran over to him and grabbed hold of his arm.

"Do not go in there. The dome is so high it will collapse on you."

Gerard recognized the woman—it was Marguerite from the caravan. "The church was built over 700 years ago." Gerard spoke to the woman soothingly. "There is nothing to be afraid of. Come back inside with me."

The woman clutched Gerard's robe tightly as he led her back through the doors of the church. The inside of the basilica was ablaze with color. Light poured into the church through forty stained-glass windows that ringed the base of the cupola. Marguerite stretched out her hand to touch the colored light. She moved her hand playfully from color to color. Slowly she released her grip on Gerard's arm.

Gerard prodded her encouragingly. "Look up at the ceiling. It will not fall on you."

Marguerite shook her head. "I cannot."

"Try to do it."

Slowly the woman lifted her eyes. She marveled at the wonders that she saw.

Gerard and Marguerite arranged to meet at Santa Sophia the next day. Gerard showed her the treasury of the basilica, where many of the most sacred relics of Christendom were displayed. As they walked through the rooms, Gerard showed Marguerite the nails that had pierced the hands and feet of Christ on the Cross, a vial of the Virgin's milk, and the coenaculum, the table from which Jesus ate his last meal with the disciples.

"Was Jesus married?" Marguerite asked.

"No, but why do you ask?"

"Because he had no family to help him through his pain and suffering."

"His disciples were his family."

"They deserted him at the Cross."

"Yes—only his mother, Mary Magdalene, and a few other women stood with him to the end."

"Who was this woman you call the Magdalene?"

After camping for two weeks outside the walls of Constantinople, Gerard and his companions crossed to the Asiatic side of the Bosporus. What lay ahead of them was the vast Anatolian plain, which stretched across Armenia and Cilicia. Day in and day out, they marched through a barren and trackless wilderness where land and sky seemed to merge into an endless space. The Seljuk Turks who ruled the area rarely attacked caravans. They understood that the

Anatolian plain itself was a far more potent weapon than their cavalry.

As the weeks progressed, the sheer monotony and sameness of the landscape brought depression to many. One crusader joked with Gerard. "A skirmish or two would be preferable to this interminable quiet." Convinced that they would never reach Jerusalem alive, several bands of pilgrims returned to Constantinople.

When the caravan finally reached the Seljuk town of Zanasra at the base of the Taurus Mountains, the mood abruptly changed. If all went as planned, on the following day they would pass through the Cilician Gates and arrive in Tarsus, the city of St. Paul. A day's journey after that and they would be in northern Palestine.

No sooner had the caravan bivouacked outside Zanasra, than a group of Turkish women visited the campsite. Angry at the competition, Marguerite and some other prostitutes from the caravan pelted the women with stones and excrement. Several of the Seljuk women were injured and one knocked unconscious Despite the tension earlier in the day, a band of knights rode into Zanasra after dark in search of pleasure. After drinking too much arak, they broke into Turkish homes in search of women. By dawn of the following morning, three of those who had gone into the town had not returned. A party of armed knights rode into Zanasra looking for their comrades. Inquiries were met with sullen glances and insolent looks. Angered by the hostility of the villagers, the knights took hostages and returned to their camp.

When there was still no word about the missing men on the second morning, Fulk decided to split the convoy into two groups. A contingent of heavily armed knights would remain outside Zanasra and continue the search for their missing companions. The greater part of the caravan would take what was left of the supply wagons and proceed through the Cilician Gates to Tarsus. Lots were drawn, and Gerard was chosen to join those going to Tarsus.

The climb through the Cilician Gates was difficult. Gerard quickly understood why the mountain pass was often referred to as the "Gates of Judas." Mountains dark with pine forests stood on all sides like gloomy sentinels warning travelers to turn back. The wind blew down the mountain defiles with such intensity that several muleteers were pushed off the path and fell to their death. As the crusaders climbed higher, ice formed on the ground, forcing those on horseback to dismount or risk sliding to their death down the sides of the gorge.

After a day of climbing, the advance patrol, commanded by Gerard, reached the top of the mountain pass. Three figures stood menacingly in the center of the road. There was an awkwardness about them, as if they belonged to a different world.

A knight cautioned Gerard. "We must not go forward. Spirits haunt these passes."

"These are not spirits. I fear they are all too real."

Gerard spurred his horse ahead. The mutilated bodies of the three missing knights from Zanasra stood propped up with twine and pieces of wood—their arms cut off and their testicles pushed into their mouths.

Gerard rode back down the mountain pass with news of the gruesome discovery. A meeting of crusaders was hastily assembled. Several knights, including Gerard, argued for restraint—in a few days, they would be entering the Holy Land. A crusader's hand should not be caked with innocent blood. A young knight from Orleans, however, expressed the sentiment of the majority. "The villagers did not just kill our friends; they butchered them. Our comrades must be avenged."

That night, the crusaders put Zanasra to the torch and slaughtered its inhabitants.

When the caravan reached the port of Tortosa, Gerard fell gravely ill with dysentery. For six days he lay delirious in a hospital run by the Knights of St. John. Despite angry stares, the harlot Marguerite insisted on nursing Gerard back to health. She bathed him to bring down his fevers and held him in her arms when he shivered from the cold. After she was assured that Gerard was out of danger, Marguerite left for Jerusalem with the caravan.

When he recovered, Gerard was advised to travel the rest of the way to Jaffa by ship. He visited the Templar commanderie in Tortosa to learn when he would be able to find space on a vessel sailing down the coast. The Templar commanderie was a large castle-like structure that dominated the port's entrance. As Gerard arrived at the front courtyard, a group of men were unloading bales of cloth and sacks of what looked like pieces of yellow rock.

Gerard stopped one of the workmen. "Who is in charge here?"

"Brother Michael. He is inside. You could not miss him even if you tried."

As Gerard walked to the door of the commanderie, he was confronted by what could only be described as an elemental force of nature. Standing in the doorway with arms folded was a giant of a man, rough-hewn with large callused hands and pockmarked skin. A cloth patch covered his left eye. Gerard knew that it would be foolish to try to push past him.

"Are you Brother Michael?"

As if he found Gerard's question irritating, the man answered brusquely: "Why are you here?"

Gerard handed the man the letter that his father had given him.

Brother Michael read the letter very slowly—a little too slowly, Gerard thought. After several minutes, the monk looked up with an embarrassed expression on his face. "I learned to read when I joined the Templars but thanks to a Saracen arrow in my eye, reading is not easy for me."

Brother Michael looked down at the letter a second time. "Ah, now I understand. It says your name is Gerard de Montelambert."

"Yes."

"Good French stock that! And it says here you are traveling to Jerusalem. Hold out your hand for a moment."

Brother Michael rolled up his right sleeve. "Feel how tough my skin is. If you are not careful, my young Montelambert, in two weeks' time, the Judean sun will dry your skin into leather like mine."

Brother Michael's laugh sounded like the roar of a lion. "Now to get you to Jerusalem."

The Templar pointed to a door at the eastern end of the courtyard. "Come with me to the treasury."

Brother Michael led Gerard into an airless room piled high with dusty forms and documents. Pushing some papers aside, he motioned Gerard to sit across from him. Within the hour, the necessary travel arrangements had been completed.

"Tomorrow you sail to Jaffa on one of our vessels called the *Madeleine.* From there you will join a Templar convoy going overland to Jerusalem. Now, for the financial arrangements—pay the cost of your trip all the way to Jerusalem. It is easiest." The Templar took Gerard's money and after a quick calculation, handed him a parchment voucher.

"What is this?" asked Gerard.

"A record of your deposit and current expenses," answered Brother Michael. "In Jerusalem, we will refund whatever is left on the voucher. It is our system."

"You have no guard outside the treasury."

Brother Michael looked amused. "A Templar does not steal money."

Gerard and Brother Michael left the treasury and walked into the sunlight of the courtyard. Men were still unloading cloth and bales of the yellow rock into a storeroom.

"What do you call the cloth?" Gerard asked. "It reminds me of gossamer?"

"Ah—the cloth. Here we call it gauze. They say it is made in the town of Gaza in the Sinai. And the yellow rock, have you ever tasted it?"

"No."

"Try some." Brother Michael broke off a small piece and handed it to Gerard. "The Saracens call it candy. Let it dissolve in your mouth."

The candy had a deliciously sweet taste; it reminded Gerard of the taste of cherries in late summer. "This candy is for the saints in heaven. How can the infidel make something so delicious?"

"A Saracen may not believe in Jesus Christ, but he is still a human being. You have much to learn in Palestine, my young Montelambert."

That night Gerard could not sleep. The thought of finally reaching Jerusalem made his heart pound with anticipation. Leaving the commanderie, he walked along the wharves of the Tortosa harbor. One large, triple-masted galley caught his attention. The ship loomed out of the water like a behemoth. As he stood admiring it, an Italian merchant walked over to him.

"It is a Venetian ship. We sail for Jaffa in two days. For a fee you can come with us."

"No, but thank you. I go tomorrow to Jaffa on a Templar ship."

"A Templar ship!" The man's voice could not conceal his contempt. "These Templars pretend they are monks but they all have the same bone between their legs like the rest of us. They rape woman and bugger young boys on their ships."

Later that night when he returned to the commanderie, Gerard repeated to Brother Michael what the man had said.

At the sound of the word Venetian, the old Templar spat on the ground in disgust.

"The Venetian scum hate the Templars."

"Why?" asked Gerard.

"Because our ships take business from them," answered Brother Michael. "Pilgrims prefer to travel to the Holy Land on one of our vessels. There have been too many stories about the Italians."

"What stories?" Gerard could not contain his curiosity.

"The Italians sell young boys and girls to slave traders. During a storm last year, Genoese merchants threw pilgrims overboard to protect their cargo. A piece of brocade is more valuable to them than the life of a pilgrim."

"But the Venetians accuse the Templars of pretending to be holy." Gerard could see Brother Michael becoming angry. "They say the Templars perform indecent acts with women and young boys."

Brother Michael exploded. "Greed makes the Venetians say these things. The pope needs their ships to transport his spoils back to Rome. For doing that, the pope gives them a third of his booty. We Templars give them nothing."

"Ah," Gerard chuckled, "business has made you implacable enemies."

"The Italians will suffer damnation—all of them."

"Unless St. Peter will take a bribe," retorted Gerard.

The Templar ship, the *Madeleine,* lifted anchor and sailed out of the port of Tortosa. Gerard held tightly to the rails as the ship rolled in the swells of the outgoing tide. As he looked up to the heavens, Gerard saw that dawn was pushing Cassiopeia out of the northern sky. The surface of the water flashed silver as schools of flying fish leapt high into the air—heralds announcing the arrival of a new day. As Gerard marveled at what he saw, two dolphins broke the surface of the water.

The captain of the *Madeleine* stood behind Gerard. "The Romans believed that dolphins were sacred to the sea god Neptune. They also believed that dolphins could move a ship more swiftly over the water."

A loud sound from below deck interrupted the captain. "It is the horses. The rolling of the ship frightens them. They need stable footing."

"Where are you taking them?"

"To Jaffa. The order trains horses in Provence and ferries them to our commanderies in Palestine."

Another crack sounded.

The captain looked concerned. "I had better go below. A horse can kick a hole in the side of a ship."

Gerard stood alone on the deck. The sails lofted in the wind as if fighting over which way to go. As he looked up, Gerard saw Beauseant, the black-and-white standard of the Order of the Temple, unfurl in the wind. The standard pointed the *Madeleine* south toward Jerusalem and Gerard's destiny.

Next morning, Gerard could hardly control his excitement. He was sure that he could see a faint line of gold separating the sea and the sky. It had to be Jaffa. Gerard ran in search of the captain.

"Jaffa is still a good half day away, my impatient friend. Most likely what you see is a sandstorm that has blown out to sea."

"No, Captain, the line is growing more and more distinct. I am sure of it." The captain started to laugh at Gerard's persistence, when two gulls appeared in the distance. The captain hurried below and returned with a small brass tube.

"The Saracens use these. They call them telescopes—they enlarge what you see." The Captain pointed the tube toward the horizon and looked into it. As he adjusted the distance, a sheepish look came over his face. "It is Jaffa." Shrugging his shoulders, the captain looked at Gerard. "Maybe the Romans were right about dolphins. But they must have worked night and day to get us here so fast."

As the *Madeleine* anchored in the harbor, Arab dhows with long frontal bowsprits ferried produce from ships moored in the harbor to shorefront markets. As the sails of the *Madeleine* were furled, Gerard waited impatiently to disembark. Ever since he was a young child, his mother had told him stories about the Holy Land—about Jesus and his Virgin Mother, about St. Peter and Saint Stephen. Now he was about to set foot in Outremer, the land where they had lived and preached. Gerard had always dreamed of this day. He wept openly.

When he disembarked from The Madeleine, crowds of pilgrims seeking lodging in Jaffa swept Gerard along. Thankfully, Brother Michael had given Gerard instructions on how to find the Templar commanderie in the city. "Look for the tower of the Monastery of Saint Catherine. Our building is within its shadow." When Gerard arrived at the commanderie, a group of Arab boys stood in the courtyard grooming horses. They must be the ones that came on the *Madeleine,* thought Gerard. An old Templar knight hobbled about the courtyard barking out instructions. His face was creased and fissured like a walnut shell. Gerard remembered Brother Michael's warning about the ravages of the Judean sun.

Gerard walked over to the Templar. "Sir, do you have a space for the night?"

The old man made a dismissive gesture toward Gerard. "There are no beds. Come back tomorrow."

Gerard took out the Templar voucher given him in Tortosa and handed it to the old man. "Ah, you have a voucher. That makes things easier. There are a few places left." The Templar pointed to a small building at the far end of the courtyard. "There's a place there—take it. It will be cooler during the night."

"When does the next pilgrim caravan leave for Jerusalem?"

"Early tomorrow."

"Is there still room?"

The Templar smiled. "There are over six hundred pilgrims now. One more hardly matters. Just show your voucher."

When Gerard left the commanderie, it was four hours after midday. There was enough time to buy a horse and some loose-fitting clothing for the journey. Despite an occasional breeze from the Mediterranean, Jaffa was brutally hot. Gerard knew that the desert road to Jerusalem would be hotter still.

Chapter XI

Outremer

THE BELLS OF St. Catherine's Monastery tolled three o'clock in the morning. Gerard left the commanderie and walked to the eastern gate of Jaffa, where the caravan was scheduled to assemble. A large crowd of pilgrims had already gathered for the trip. Hovering around the fringes of the crowd were vendors hawking food and drink. Gerard looked on in amusement as an old man swung his walking stick at a particularly determined vendor. As he watched the old man, he felt someone tugging on his sleeve. It was a young girl no more than six years of age.

"Please, sir, a few copper coins for bread and tea." Pitying the child, Gerard took some coins from his pocket. At the sight of money, several more children materialized out of nowhere. They circled around Gerard like a swarm of bees.

One of the children, a scrawny boy, pulled at Gerard's cloak. "Sir, these stones are from the Tomb of Christ."

A second boy grabbed his scrawny friend by the hair. "He lies! They are just ordinary stones—but this piece of wood is from the True Cross of our Savior Jesus." At the name of Jesus, the child blessed himself in mock solemnity.

Another said, "These bones are relics of St. Veronica—the woman who wiped blood from Jesus' face with her veil."

"And I suppose you have a piece of the veil as well?" asked Gerard.

The child responded. "I do not but my friend Jusef has half of it."

Gerard laughed at the utter brazenness of the child. As the pushing and shoving continued, Gerard became exasperated and pretending to be angry, drew his sword. The children scattered in all directions.

Free of the children, Gerard walked to the farthest end of the campground where there was a line of mule teams hitched to wagons. For a price, sick or elderly pilgrims could travel to the Holy City in more comfort. More affluent pilgrims could hire horse-drawn carriages with stretched canvas to block the sun and woven mats to cushion the jolts in the road. Many of the more self-righteous pilgrims grumbled when they saw these horse-drawn carriages. Jesus had entered Jerusalem on a donkey, and they believed it sacrilegious for a Christian to enter Jerusalem on any other beast of burden.

As the bells for matins rang in St. Catherine's Monastery, three horsemen rode out through the east gate of Jaffa. When the crowd saw they were Templars, the people grew silent. One of the horsemen spoke to the assembly. His deep voice boomed through the darkness.

"The caravan leaves within the hour. By midday, we will reach the Oasis of Bletheres. You will find ample water and shade there. We start again when the day becomes cooler." The Templar sat silent for a moment, as if underscoring the importance of what he was about to say. "Every day, pilgrims are robbed and killed along the road we are about to take. The Saracen devils have a favorite pastime—before they kill a Christian, they cut off a limb, usually the right arm. If you value your life, stay close to the caravan. Elderly and sick pilgrims are the easiest targets. So, muleteers, keep up with the rest of us. I want all of you to be able to shake hands with St. Peter at the gates of heaven."

When the Templars finally gave the signal to begin, a wave of emotion swept over the pilgrims. Shouting "God wills it," a priest ran to the front of the procession. Many joined in and the chant echoed out into the desert. As the morning progressed, children found it increasingly difficult to contain their exuberance. Whenever a village appeared, one of the children would run up to a Templar and ask if it was Jerusalem. For his part, Gerard spent most of the first day staring at the countryside. The strange textures and colors of the desert fascinated him. Provence, where he had been born and raised, was a land of green forests and lush fields, a land where the hills were lined with well-tended orchards. The desert was stark and monochromatic, a land of hypnotic and ever-changing shapes—a place where one's soul focuses on God without the distraction of color and topography.

When he awoke on the morning of the second day, Gerard became caught up in the excitement. Barring a change in the weather, the caravan would reach Jerusalem before the end of the day. Gerard began to daydream. He wondered what the holy places would look like. How wide was the River Jordan? Was the House of Lazarus still standing? Where did Mary learn that she was with child? Preoccupied by his thoughts, Gerard did not notice when a large contingent of Saracen cavalry appeared from behind a ridge to the east of the caravan. The Templars stopped the convoy. Squinting into the sun, Gerard counted over two hundred Saracen horsemen deployed along the top of the ridge. Many had fitted arrows to their bows.

One of the Templars rode over to Gerard.

"We need your help, Montelambert. Ride along the western side of the convoy. Keep the pilgrims calm. The Saracens should leave us alone."

Two Templars trotted slowly out toward the line of Muslim horsemen. A Saracen carrying a green flag waited for the Templars at the foot of the ridge. The Templars and the Saracen embraced each other and spoke for several minutes in Arabic. Finally the Saracen wheeled his stallion about and rode back to his comrades. Moments later, the Saracens turned away from the caravan and rode down the back slope of the ridge. When the Templars returned to the convoy, one of them shouted, "We can move on; they will not harm us."

Gerard was amazed by what he had just seen. He rode over to the Templar who had asked for his help. "Why did you embrace that heathen?"

"It is a Saracen custom for men to embrace. It shows that you are not carrying weapons. We told them that this is a pilgrim caravan, and that was that. Saracens have learned to trust the word of a Templar."

A pilgrim who was out ahead of the caravan climbed to the top of a steep hill. When he reached the summit, Gerard saw him fall on his knees. Pointing his finger off in the distance, the pilgrim began to shout aloud. "There it is! Jerusalem! The Holy City! I can see it!" Tears welled up in his eyes as he began to sing a hymn to Mary, the Mother of God. The man's singing electrified the caravan. Throwing aside whatever belongings they carried, men and women streamed wildly up the hill.

Gerard rode over to one of the Templars. "Is the sun playing tricks with the man's eyes?"

"No. Pilgrims call this place Montjoie. From here, when the sand does not blow, you can see Jerusalem."

Gerard jumped off his horse and clambered up the side of the hill behind the others. In every pilgrim's mind there exists an imaginary Jerusalem—an idealized place where the Son of God lived and died. What Gerard saw that day from Montjoie beggared his imagination. Shimmering magically in the afternoon sun was a city of turquoise domes and golden crosses. As he stood looking at the distant Jerusalem, Gerard knew that destiny had brought him here.

The first sight of Jerusalem affected each pilgrim in a different way. After months of traveling, most wanted to be left alone with their innermost thoughts and emotions. Others sought to share the excitement and joy they felt. Like children, they danced around in circles, embracing and kissing anyone in sight. One man stripped naked and rolled head over heels down the side of Montjoie. Although each pilgrim reacted differently, there was one bond they all shared in common. They were devout Christians who had risked their lives to come to Jerusalem to experience the closeness of Christ. What sustained them through their long and dangerous pilgrimage was not theology or the promise of papal indulgences, but the dream of worshipping at the place where Jesus had died and risen from the dead. Now they were almost there.

Without warning, an elderly German pilgrim struggled to his feet and threw off his cloak. "I must pray at the Tomb of Christ—I must go, I have not much time." Before anyone could stop him, the old man started to hobble down Montjoie toward the City. The fervor of the old pilgrim struck a deep chord in the hearts of others in the caravan. As if some floodgate had opened, groups of pilgrims began to follow the old man down the side of the hill. As the number of pilgrims grew, a Templar rode after them.

"Jerusalem is over four leagues away," the Templar shouted. "You have no water. In this heat, you will not get halfway there." The Templars' stark warning went largely ignored. Even Gerard paid no heed to it as he ran wildly down the side of Montjoie.

After running for half a league, the old German pilgrim staggered and collapsed on the sand. His breathing became labored as though a heavy stone had been laid on his chest. He cried out for water. Minutes later, a second pilgrim collapsed on the ground, then a third and a fourth. They all stretched out their hands and begged for water.

Without stopping to help, Gerard ran past the old German and the other pilgrims who lay on the ground. The city, like a siren, pulled Gerard irresistibly toward it. Nothing else seemed to matter except reaching the walls of Jerusalem. The glare from the sun made it difficult to see the ground ahead of him. Gerard tripped over a rock and fell on his knees He stood and stumbled again, this time falling face down on the ground. Wiping the sand from his eyes and mouth, Gerard struggled back up. Twenty meters more and he fell a third time. He lay on the ground exhausted, gasping for breath.

Then Gerard heard the voice—it came from somewhere deep inside of him. "Have faith, Gerard. Jesus fell three times on His way to Golgotha." As he lay on the burning sand, a shape began to materialize in front of him. A nimbus of bright light surrounded it. Gerard blinked, his eyes convinced that what he was seeing was an illusion. But the figure gradually grew larger and more distinct. He heard the sound of hoofbeats and could see a rider wearing the familiar red cross of a Templar. When he reached Gerard, the Templar jumped off his horse and pulled a goatskin bag from his saddle. Water poured into Gerard's mouth. When Gerard had drunk his fill, the Templar rode off to help other pilgrims who had collapsed on the ground. Soon more Templars rode out from Jerusalem with water. Despite their efforts, however, dehydration took the lives of five pilgrims. Like Moses and the Promised Land, God had allowed them to see Jerusalem but not enter it.

His strength renewed, Gerard stumbled ahead. The battlements of Jerusalem lay only half a league away. With one final burst of energy, he reached the city's walls. Gerard fell to his knees sobbing, his leg cramping with pain. Holding out his hand, Gerard gently caressed each stone as if it were a precious relic. He took the piece of parchment his mother had given him and pushed it into a crack in the city wall. He could hear his mother's voice whispering in his ear. "Gerard, your destiny lies here in Jerusalem. Follow God's plan." A door blew open in his mind. He pulled out from under his shirt the copy of Evardus's chronicle that Edouard had given him. Was it his destiny to find the copper scroll?

The gates of Jerusalem were closed from sunset until sunrise. As the evening shadows began to lengthen, crowds of late-arriving pilgrims hurried to reach the city before the gates were shut. Somewhere amidst these throngs, Gerard heard pilgrims singing a hymn he had learned as a child. "God is my shepherd and my staff," it began. The music reached out to Gerard like an encouraging hand. When he joined in the singing, Gerard felt the oneness that unites all Christians. Drawing strength from the faith of those around him, he steadied himself and staggered toward the gate of the Holy City.

At the Damascus Gate, a merchant caravan arriving from Antioch was given priority in entering the city. Gerard stared curiously at a long line of camels carrying woven rugs from Azerbaijan and Tabriz. The animals passed before Gerard like disembodied spirits, their padded feet making no sound on the desert floor. Behind the camels rode wealthy Saracen merchants on magnificent white stallions. As a sign of wealth and position, one of the merchants carried a hooded falcon on his arm. What amazed Gerard most, however, were the Numidian bearers—each one tall and regal in bearing and each capable of balancing double his body weight on his head. Absorbed by the spectacle of the caravan, Gerard did not notice the swarm of vendors busily seeking customers before the Damascus Gate was closed.

A short, unpleasant looking man accosted Gerard. "For three copper coins, I'll sell you a piece of John the Baptist's staff and take you to the place on the River Jordon where John baptized Jesus."

"I'll take you there for only two coins." The second man grabbed Gerard's arm and held it tightly. "And I'll add a stop at the house of Joseph of Arimathea for no extra charge."

Gerard pushed the two men away only to have a portly Lebanese merchant shove a vial of perfume under his nose. "Buy it for your wife." Gerard shook his head but the merchant was persistent, pulling out of his pocket a small packet of tea from Persia. "She may prefer instead this aphrodisiac." Gerard shook his head again. Undaunted, the merchant put the tea in Gerard's hand and waited to be paid. Gerard threw the tea on the ground and kicked the merchant as he bent to pick it up.

The haggling frenzy outside the Damascus Gate was suddenly interrupted by shouts of pain. Off in the distance, Gerard saw a line of pilgrims approaching the city. Each carried a heavy wooden cross on his back.

"Who are they?" Gerard asked a well-dressed man standing next to him.

"You have never seen a procession of contrition before? These pilgrims are called *flagellantes* because they mortify their bodies with whips and carry crosses into Jerusalem as a sign of their sinfulness."

As they drew near to the Damascus Gate, the flagellantes lay down their crosses. They knelt on the ground and, in loud voices, recited their sins—fornication, robbery, and sodomy, to name a few. As they confessed their sins, they untied ropes from around their waists. Begging God for forgiveness, the flagellantes whipped themselves on their backs and legs. The blows came faster and faster.

"See the red stripes on their backs." The man pointed to three penitents who had collapsed to the ground. "They have fainted from loss of blood. Their scourges contain pieces of metal." Gerard was revolted by what he saw.

When the last of the caravan had passed through the Damascus Gate, the pilgrims surged forward to enter the city. Gerard's heart pounded with pent-up emotion as the excited crowds carried him along. Passing through the gate was a triumphal moment for Gerard. God had called him to Jerusalem, and now he had answered his call. *"Domine Non Sum Dignus"*— "Lord I am not worthy." Gerard recited the ancient Latin prayer as he stepped over the threshold of the Holy City.

The Damascus Gate opened into a warren of narrow streets and alleyways. From the faces of those he encountered, Gerard could sense conflict and division. A Jew with dangling phylacteries stared sullenly at a Saracen fingering his worry beads. A white-robed Dominican glared at a Byzantine priest with the beard of an Assyrian king. An Arab woman, her eyes squinting from under her galabeya, muttered obscenities at a passing Christian knight.

Exhausted, Gerard walked a few more streets into the city, but had to stop and regain his strength. He sat down against the wall of a house and started to fall asleep. A familiar voice startled him.

"So my nursing skills were successful, Gerard de Montelambert."

Looking up, he saw Marguerite bending over him. "Do you have lodging in the city?" she asked.

"No," answered Gerard.

"Come with me then. I have quarters not far from here."

Outside Marguerite's house, an old man sat under an awning dreamily pulling on a water pipe. The old man motioned for Gerard to inhale the vapors.

Marguerite smiled. "He wants you to take the pipe. He will be insulted if you refuse his hospitality."

Gerard sat down next to the old man and inhaled deeply. A burning sensation in his lungs made Gerard choke and gasp for air.

Marguerite laughed. "Opium is to be inhaled slowly. The drug is like a woman. It prefers to be handled gently."

His face flushed with embarrassment, Gerard inhaled the pipe again. This time a warm and sensuous feeling coursed through his body.

When he entered the house, Marguerite saw that Gerard was limping. "Gerard, you are in pain. Let me ask one of the women to bathe you. The opium and the warm water will soothe you."

Gerard smiled. "I thought you came to Jerusalem to change your life."

Marguerite looked indignant. "I have. A young monk helps me with my daily prayers. He has even taught me some Latin."

"And what have you taught him?"

"A few things." Marguerite patted her strong buttocks. "Sit down, Gerard. Let me find someone to massage you."

Minutes later a tall Ethiopian woman entered the room. Her black hair cascaded down her back to her waist.

The women's voice was like honey. "Marguerite has sent me to bathe you."

The woman filled a large copper basin with warm water. With a piece of pumice stone, she scrubbed the dirt off Gerard's body. When she had dried Gerard, the woman poured oil in stripes across his back and massaged his neck and shoulders. "The oil is made from the leaves of the acacia plant. It will take away your pain." She gently rubbed more of the oil down Gerard's spine and lower back. The touch of her hands felt sensuous. The woman massaged his buttocks and moved her hands slowly to his thighs. She laughed when she saw his awkwardness. "You must take more opium."

The old man had come into the house. He handed the pipe to Gerard.

"This is my first time with a woman."

She smiled. "Ah! Your first time! Then you have much to learn. When you are invited to a banquet, you must savor the food bite by bite. You do not tear at it like some wild animal. Hunger is best satisfied when the food is digested slowly. The same is true of desire. To satisfy a woman, you must linger over her body."

As the woman spoke, she loosened her robe.

The next afternoon, Gerard left the woman's bed chamber. He heard her giggling with a new client in the next room. Although the woman was a prostitute, he could not forget the smell of her body and the pleasure of her touch. Gerard now understood the meaning of passion and desire. And jealousy!

A knight directed Gerard to a nearby barracks that catered to French knights. After securing lodging, he walked to the Church of the Holy Sepulchre and knelt before the Tomb of Christ. He felt soiled by what he had done last night. His lust for the woman had won out over his self-control. Jesus must have enjoyed the company of women. The Gospels show instances of that. Somehow, however, Jesus had learned to overcome His desire for sexual intimacy. Gerard knew he must learn to do the same.

While returning to his barracks several days after arriving in the city, Gerard passed near the Golden Gate, where Jesus entered Jerusalem triumphantly on Palm Sunday. A man who sat in the street called out to him.

"Please, sir, a few coins?" From his accent, Gerard knew the man was Provençal. "The Saracens raped and killed my wife. They robbed me of all I had and left me for dead. A pilgrim found me and saved my life."

"You look fit enough. We can always use able-bodied men in our regiment. Come with me."

"I cannot go."

"Why not?"

"Because of this. . . ." The man lifted his cloak. His right arm was gone. "The Saracens cut it off. They do it so a Christian cannot make the Sign of the Cross."

"Where did this happen?"

"On the desert road from Jaffa. Saracens are everywhere. They are butchers."

Gerard gave the beggar the coins he had in his pocket.

That night Gerard de Montelambert could not sleep. The sight of the beggar haunted him. He wondered if the Saracens had laughed as they severed the man's arm. By morning, Gerard had made up his mind what he would do. The Templars were seeking temporary recruits to increase the number of patrols escorting pilgrims between Jaffa and Jerusalem. Gerard agreed to a four-month commitment.

In Tortosa, Brother Michael had warned Gerard of the hostility between the Venetian and Genoese merchants and the Order of the Temple. Gerard quickly learned, however, that in Latin Palestine hostility and rivalry among Christian factions were not the exception but the rule. It was safer, the Templars would say, to trust the word of a Saracen than the word of a Christian. On the long patrols through the desert, Gerard came to admire the discipline and training of the Templars, but it was their devotional practices that most impressed him. He noticed how two Templars always ate from the same bowl. When he asked the reason, a Templar gave Gerard an uncomprehending look. "To guard against secret abstinence, of course. To praise God, many of our brothers would eat too little."

When his tour of duty was over, Gerard asked that he be admitted to full membership in the order. Gerard had no way of knowing that his request had set in motion a series of events that would result in tragedy both for him and for the Order of the Temple.

A *turab* blew through Jerusalem the night of Gerard's initiation into the Order of the Temple. Legend had it that the hot winds of the *turab* blow dust into one's heart, making it difficult to judge right from wrong.

Several hours after dark, the Templars stationed in Jerusalem filed into the dimly lit chapel adjacent to their commanderie. Gerard and three other initiates walked behind the others. The flickering candles on the altar cast eerie shadows on the chapel walls. Gerard wondered if the shadows belonged to long-dead Templars returning to help regenerate the order.

Gerard's thoughts were interrupted by the arrival of the seneschal of the order, a brooding hulk of a man with broad shoulders and protruding eyes. A curl in his lip left him with a permanent sneer. The seneschal administered the lands of the order and was responsible for its myriad financial interests. Behind the seneschal walked Jacques de Molay, the grand master of the order. Unlike the seneschal, de Molay was not a prepossessing man. He was short and wiry with thinning gray hair and beard. But while he did not display a commanding physical presence, de Molay did radiate a sense of inner conviction and integrity that was easily felt. But it was de Molay's eyes that caught Gerard's attention. A mixture of all the colors of the rainbow, they could probe deep into the darkest corners of one's soul.

The seneschal motioned for the Templars and the initiates to be seated. For several minutes, the congregation sat in silence. Finally the seneschal stood up and signaled the initiates to approach the foot of the altar. He took a thurible and incensed Gerard and the three other initiates. A cloud of smoke filled the church.

When the senechal put down the thurible, the grand master ascended to the top step of the altar and sat on a wooden chair. One by one, the initiates walked up the steps and knelt before de Molay to profess their vows. When it was his turn, Gerard walked nervously up the steps. As he knelt before the grand master, a strange feeling came over him — a feeling of intimacy, of personal communion — that somehow their two destinies were linked. Gerard did not know then just how inextricably bound their destinies would become.

The grand master's voice interrupted Gerard's thoughts. "Why do you come before me, Gerard de Montelambert?"

"To ask that I be initiated into the Order of the Poor Knights of Jesus Christ."

"Then pronounce your vows before all in this chapel. Gerard de Montelambert, do you vow that henceforth, all the days of your life, you will obey the Bishop of Rome and the Grand Master of the Order of the Temple in all earthly and spiritual matters, so that you may better serve our Lord and Savior Jesus Christ?"

"Yes, Grand Master, if it pleases God."

"Do you vow that henceforth, all the days of your life, you will live chastely in your body, denying yourself carnal relations with women so that you may better serve our Lord and Savior Jesus Christ?"

For a moment Gerard remembered the prostitute who had bathed him near the Jaffa Gate. "Yes, Grand Master, if it pleases God."

"Do you vow that henceforth, all the days of your life, you will live without property and will protect and defend Christian pilgrims who travel the roads of Palestine?"

"Yes, if it pleases God."

After the final vow had been taken, de Molay recited the paternoster and anointed Gerard's forehead, eyes, and hands with holy oil.

"Gerard de Montelambert, this anointing is a sign that you have become a member of the Order of the Temple. We promise you the food and water and the poor clothing of the order, and much pain and suffering."

When the initiation ritual was over, the assembled Templars rose from their seats and began to recite a strange litany.

"Listen to the words of Jesus.

"I am the light to one who seeks the path.

"I am the mirror to one who looks deeply.

"I am the door to one who seeks entry.

"I am the road to one who journeys far.

"I am the food to one who hungers.

"I am the healing to one who is mortally wounded.

"I am the clothing to one who is naked."

When the Templars had finished, the grand master continued reciting the litany.

"I am the ineffable one.

"I am the one who is beyond comprehension.

"I am not who I appear to be.

"When you come, then will you understand who I am."

The grand master's words confused Gerard. "I am not who I appear to be. When you come, then will you understand who I am." It must be a riddle, Gerard thought — but how was it to be unraveled? Did the words refer to Jesus? Jesus was beyond knowing — beyond understanding. Everything said about him is a metaphor. Jesus was fully God, but he was also fully a man. He lived and died here in Palestine. If Jesus was not what he appeared to be, then who was he?

During his first months as a Templar, Gerard mainly accompanied pilgrim convoys traveling back and forth along the Jaffa-Jerusalem road. On several occasions, Gerard was assigned to ride on special assignments — twice to Acre and once to the Templar Castle at Mount Pellerin.

As Easter grew close, attacks by Muslim bandits became more frequent and more daring. On the Wednesday of Holy Week, a large pilgrim caravan was attacked within sight of the walls of Jerusalem. The Muslim bandits captured a group of children who had been sent by the Bishop of Jaffa to sing at the Easter Mass in the Church of the Holy Sepulchre. The capture of the children's chorus shocked Jerusalem. A combined force of Templars and Knights of St. John rode out in pursuit.

The Muslim bandits were tracked to a rocky canyon north of the town of Bethany. The Saracens outnumbered the Templars several times over. While the size of the Saracen force was its greatest strength, it also proved to be its greatest weakness. Confident that the crusaders would not pursue so large a force, the Saracens violated two fundamental principles of desert warfare; they unsaddled their horses for the night and they allowed them to graze some distance from their tents.

The commander of the pursuing force divided the knights into two groups. The first group — mostly Knights of St. John — attacked the sentries and drove the horses into the desert. When the Saracens saw what had happened, they abandoned their camp and ran out into the desert to retrieve their horses. A second group of knights — mostly Templars under Gerard's command — disguised themselves as Saracens. They stole quietly into the camp and freed the children. Once the children were safe, Gerard ordered his men to shed their disguises and kill as many of the bandits as could be found. The Patriarch of Jerusalem personally thanked Gerard for his valor in freeing the children's choir.

The priest stood at the pulpit. "We celebrate today the feast of John the Baptist, he who prepared the way for the Lord. The two men must have shared deep bonds of friendship and trust. In a very real sense, John's beheading marked the beginning of Jesus' ministry. Today we pray that John will guide us as we seek God's truth."

Gerard's mouth was dry from nervousness. He had asked to speak with the grand master after Mass. Because of the feast day, however, the liturgy was taking longer than Gerard had expected.

When the Mass had finally ended, Gerard genuflected before the altar and walked outside. By custom the grand master was the last to leave the chapel. Gerard waited anxiously in the courtyard. Although it was only an hour after sunrise, the heat had already begun to make distant objects shimmer and appear unreal and impermanent. Gerard was glad that he had not been chosen to ride patrol today.

When Jacques de Molay finally emerged from the chapel, he squinted for a moment until his eyes adjusted to the sunlight.

"Grand Master, I asked to speak with you. It will only take a moment."

"Yes, Montelambert. We can talk better in my quarters."

Gerard followed de Molay through the courtyard and into a fortress-like building that housed records and documents concerning Templar properties in Palestine. The grand master's quarters were cool and spacious. Except for a large cross, the walls were bare.

Walking over to a wooden table, the grand master poured two cups of water. "The sun is hot already." He handed Gerard one of the cups.

"Thank you."

The grand master sat at his desk. "Why did you ask to see me?"

"Five years ago on my sixteenth birthday, my Uncle told me a legend that has been passed down in our family for centuries."

The grand master looked amused. "I am surprised at you, Gerard. Every day, I am besieged with reports of wondrous apparitions, discoveries of sacred relics, and yes, family legends. A Templar should be skeptical of such matters — not bring them to the grand master of the order."

"The legend of the Montelamberts is not about apparitions or relics," answered Gerard. "It is a story about the Jewish people and the Romans who conquered them."

"If you must, Gerard, tell me this family legend of yours." The grand master looked impatiently at Gerard.

"When Herod's Temple was besieged by the Romans, one of my ancestors, a merchant named Evardus, was selling wine to the Roman army. After concluding his business, Evardus left the Roman camp and rode west to the port of Jaffa. As a Christian, Evardus could not bring himself to witness the slaughter of the Jews who remained on the Temple Mount. After a time, he came upon an old rabbi lying unconscious in the road. When Evardus revived him, the rabbi told Evardus a strange tale."

The grand master poured Gerard another cup of water.

"The rabbi said that a copper scroll lay buried under Herod's Temple — in the 'stone of life.' The rabbi whispered something more, but Evardus could barely hear it. All the merchant could make out were the words 'vessels and records of the Jewish people.' When he returned to Gaul, Evardus wrote down all he had seen of the Roman siege and what the rabbi had told him."

De Molay smiled. "Ah, now I see. You wish permission to search for the copper scroll."

"Yes. When she could not deliver me, my mother promised the Virgin Mary that if I lived, she would see to it that I followed the destiny God had provided for me. I believe that God has destined me to find the copper scroll. The ruins of Herod's Temple are close by the Templar barracks. Let me try, Grand Master."

De Molay frowned. "During the pain of childbirth, it is easy for a woman to suppose that statues talk. Forget this silliness that you are destined to find this scroll."

"My father once explained to me the meaning of the two bars on the Cross. One points up to God and the heavenly Jerusalem, while the other parallels the ground and this earthly Jerusalem. I know that I must balance the two."

"Your father is a wise man, Gerard. But balancing the two Jerusalems is sometimes a difficult thing to do."

"I realize that."

"If I give you permission to search for this scroll, I know you will do your utmost to find it. But I am not sure that giving you permission is the best thing either for you or for the order."

"I know that I can keep this balance."

Jacques de Molay was silent for a moment. "I often rode into battle with your Uncle Edouard. Because of my admiration for him, I will give you permission — but only on one condition."

"What is that, Grand Master?"

"Your first responsibility must always be to the order and to your fellow Templars. You must shoulder your normal patrol duties and whatever else is required of you. This is the condition."

"I will not abuse your trust."

"Well, then, let us see if this legend of the Montelamberts has any substance to it."

Chapter XII

THE COPPER SCROLL

EDOUARD WAS RIGHT. As Gerard stood before the ruins of Herod's Temple, he realized that no one person would ever be able to search through this vast and bewildering subterranean world and discover something so small as a scroll. The only clue was that the scroll was buried in the 'stone of life' under the Holy of Holies. Yet the Romans had so devastated the Temple in 70 A.D. that it was virtually impossible to trace the original boundaries of the Sanctuary.

After hours of walking through endless corridors, however, Gerard noticed something peculiar. Regardless of which direction he took, he invariably found himself back at one particular passageway. Gerard saw that the floor of the passageway had been worn smooth from heavy use. In his mind, the condition of the passageway floor could be a clue of sorts. Once the Temple caught fire, the Jews would have had little time to bury the scroll. Most likely they would have hidden it quickly in an easily accessible place.

Gerard lit a torch and began to examine the stones along the walls of the passageway. After weeks of painstaking work, he discovered a stone marked with the faint outline of what appeared to be a *chai,* the Hebrew character for "eighteen." At the abbey, Gerard had learned that in Hebrew *chai* also meant "life." Because of its association with life, the Jewish people believed that the number eighteen had a mystical significance. Edouard had told Gerard to search for the scroll through the eyes of faith. When the Rabbi said the scroll was buried in the "stone of life," could he have meant that the scroll was hidden in a stone marked with a *"chai"?* With his knife, Gerard pried the stone loose from its place in the passageway wall. As he was lowering it to the ground, the stone slipped out of his arms. It struck the ground with a crack and split apart, revealing a small wooden box sealed with red wax. Gerard's body tensed as he broke the seal. Inside was the copper scroll that had been buried by Rabbi Yohannen more than a thousand years earlier.

The grand master was incredulous as Gerard handed him the copper scroll. "How did you find it?" he asked.

"Through the eyes of faith," Gerard responded.

"What does it say?" There was excitement in de Molay's voice.

"It is written in Hebrew, Grand Master." The sound of a Templar patrol returning from the Jaffa road could be heard in the distance.

De Molay handed the scroll back to Gerard. "Translate it for me!"

Gerard held the scroll near a candle. "'Five leagues to the northeast from the Oasis of the Red Waters stand three hills. Near the top of the middle hill is a cave.'"

Gerard's eyes opened wide. "Of course! This is what the rabbi meant!"

"What are you saying?" The grand master looked puzzled.

"According to Evardus, Grand Master, the old rabbi said something about 'vessels and parchments of the Jewish people.' The scroll says the Jews concealed their Temple vessels and records in the cave to keep them from being desecrated by the Romans."

"Incredible!"

Gerard looked at the scroll a second time. "The cave is five leagues northeast of the Oasis of the Red Waters. Where is this oasis?"

The grand master frowned. "I have never heard of it. There are no red waters in the Judean desert, Gerard."

Several days later, Gerard passed the place where Simon of Cyrene helped carry Jesus' cross. He heard a muffled cry and saw a knight hitting a young girl with his open hand. Gerard ran over and pulled the girl away.

"Stop hitting her. She is only a child!"

"This Christ-killer tried to cheat me. Stay out of this, Templar."

Emboldened by Gerard's presence, the girl blurted out, "You are wrong, sir. The ointment cost four copper coins, not three."

"Liar! You said three."

Knowing the fate of a stubborn Jew in a Christian world, the girl shrugged. "Take it then for three."

"Not before I leave a few more welts on your body."

Gerard drew his sword. "The child offers you the ointment at your price. Take it. It was a misunderstanding."

"Since when does a Templar take the part of a Jew?"

Gerard pulled the girl behind him for protection.

Unsure of what to do, the knight glared angrily at Gerard. Finally, picking up the ointment, he threw the three coins in the street and stormed off.

"Thank you, sir. Most Christians would not have stopped to help a Jew. You have done so twice."

"Twice?"

"You do not recognize me? I am the child from Ventoux. Come into my grandfather's shop. He will wish to thank you."

Together, they walked down a dusty side street and arrived in front of a small shop. Gerard bent under an arched door and entered a small, dimly lit room. The air smelled of cloves and cinnamon. An old man sat on the dirt floor grinding leaves in a brass pestle. His face was covered with a thin white film like a mask. Gerard sensed immediately that God lived in this place.

"Abba, we have a guest. It is the crusader from Ventoux. He protected me from a Christian knight in the street."

The old man looked up from his grinding. "My eyes are weak. Please come closer."

Gerard sat on the ground next to the old man.

"*Shema Israel!* You are the young knight from Ventoux." Tears began to stream down the man's face. "The Scriptures say that one who protects a member of a family becomes himself a member of that family. You must accept a gift."

Gerard shook his head. "I want nothing."

The old man pleaded. "You would dishonor me if you did not accept something. Perhaps some incense." The old man opened a jar and poured out a gray powder. "This incense is made from plants grown only in the Oasis of the Red Waters."

Gerard's body tensed. "What do you mean—the Oasis of the Red Waters?"

The old man looked apologetic. "I am sorry. I should have said the Oasis of Khan Hathrur. In Biblical times, the priests and rabbis often referred to the place as the Oasis of the Red Waters."

"Why did they call it that?" Gerard could hardly contain his excitement.

"Jews on their way to Jerusalem for the Sabbath would stop at the oasis to make an animal sacrifice to Yahweh. The ritual washing of the hands in the water of the oasis gave it its ancient name."

His heart pounding, Gerard thanked the old Jew for the incense and ran back to his quarters. He found a map of Palestine; the Oasis of Khan Hathrur was clearly marked. He traced his finger north-eastward from the oasis. There was only one road. The cave had to be somewhere along the road to Jericho!

Jacques de Molay was stunned by what Gerard told him. "Go to the cave, Gerard, but keep your destination secret. Tomorrow I ride north to the port of Acre. Sultan Hassan has gathered an army in Damascus and moves west into Christian Palestine. I will add you to my entourage. You have gone to Acre twice before, so it will not arouse suspicion. After we have left Jerusalem, break off from my party and ride east to the oasis."

The next morning before first light, Gerard joined the grand master's retinue and rode out from Jerusalem toward Acre. After half a league, Gerard turned to the northeast along the Jericho road. When he reached the Oasis of Khan Hathrur, dusk was settling over the desert. Gerard decided to spend the night there and search for the cave in the morning. Although the night would be cold, the trees of the oasis would provide shelter from the wind.

That night the desert sky was ablaze with stars. God had sprinkled them randomly across the sky like a farmer throws seeds across a field. As he gazed at the heavens, Gerard felt the immensity of the Judean wilderness that surrounded him. He understood why prophets and hermits had sought out the stillness of this harsh and barren land. The more inhospitable the landscape, thought Gerard, the more frequent a revelation of the Divine. The clicking of the grasshoppers lulled Gerard to sleep. As he slept, Gerard de Montelambert imagined all who had slept at the oasis before him.

"Excuse me, Jean." Barbo interrupted Calvaux's story as he searched for a book on his desk. "Wasn't it near the Oasis of Khan Hathrur that the Good Samaritan saved the Jew who had been robbed and beaten by thieves?"

Calvaux nodded. "Yes, it's ironic isn't it?"

"What do you mean 'ironic'?" asked Barbo.

"The Jews hid their wealth from the gentiles close by the place where a gentile opened his purse for a Jew."

Barbo reflected on what Calvaux said. "Today there is an even greater irony. Jews and Muslims kill one another on the very ground where Jesus preached peace."

At dawn Gerard ate some dried figs that he had brought from the Templar refectory. After rereading the copper scroll, he continued riding toward Jericho. The chill of the early morning soon gave way to the daytime heat. Except for the occasional pilgrim returning from Jericho, the road was deathly still. After several hours of riding, the road curved sharply to the north and descended into a dry wadi. Squinting into the sun, Gerard saw several sheep grazing on clumps of grass in the dry riverbed. A young shepherd sat on a flat stone idly watching them.

Gerard called out to the boy. "Shepherd, the sun is hot. You must know where there is shade."

The boy nodded. "There is a cave nearby but I am afraid to go there. People have heard children crying."

Gerard persisted. "How far away is the cave?"

"Not far. It is in the three hills."

"Three hills?" Gerard's heart skipped a beat. He reached into his pocket and took out two copper coins. "These coins are yours if you take me to this cave."

The boy shook his head from side to side. "No. The place is dangerous even for a Templar."

Gerard took another coin from his pocket. "Now there are three coins in my hand. Take them—they will pay for a new cloak."

The boy grabbed the coins from Gerard's hand.

Gerard smiled. "Now take me to the cave."

The shepherd climbed onto the back of Gerard's horse. "The three hills are just beyond this riverbed. The cave is in the center hill."

After a short walk, Gerard followed the shepherd up a steep path that wound its way to the top of the bluff. The boy stopped at a large stone outcropping about three-quarters of the way up the path. "The cave is behind here, "said the shepherd. He led Gerard down a narrow defile that snaked its way behind the outcropping.

"There it is." The boy pointed to a dark opening in the hillside.

Gerard could not mask his excitement. Shouting aloud, he tousled the shepherd's hair and pushed some extra coins into his pocket. The boy scrambled back up the defile, frightened that Gerard's shouts would awaken the spirits in the cave.

Gerard peered into the opening. Although sunlight slanted into the entrance, he could only see a few paces in front of him. To keep himself from tripping, Gerard put his hand against one of the walls of the cave. When his eyes adjusted to the darkness, he took a few cautious steps forward. As he walked farther into the cave, he saw what looked like a rock pile a few cubits in front of him. A lump grew in Gerard's throat. He furiously threw stones off the pile. Under the stones lay a large wooden plank. When he lifted up the plank, there was a dark pit—too dark to see what was in it. Gerard was tempted to put his hand into the hole but quickly thought better of it. What if a snake or desert scorpion had made its home there! He needed to find a torch.

Gerard ran down the hill to where he had tethered his horse. He tore a piece of cloth from an old blanket and wrapped the cloth around a dried branch he found nearby. Taking a flint and some tinder from his saddlebag, he ran back up the hill. Striking the flint, Gerard lit his makeshift torch and reentered the cave. With a deep breath, he thrust the torch into the hole. Gerard gasped in disbelief. Priceless menorahs and golden candlesticks from the Temple of Herod flashed in the torchlight. Behind them stacked neatly in rows were parchment scrolls—each tied with a leather band. Gerard lifted several of them out of the pit. He carefully untied them afraid that they might crumble in his hand. Gerard could see that the scrolls were written in Hebrew and contained lists of births, deaths, and marriages. They must be census records, Gerard surmised.

By now, it had grown hot in the cave. Gerard decided not to risk taking any of the gold artifacts back to Jerusalem without an escort. But he would take one of the scrolls. The most recent one was dated in the Hebrew year 3791. Gerard did a quick calculation—the year 3791 in the Jewish calendar would be roughly 30 A.D. in the Julian calendar. He would take this one to show the grand master. As he started to re-tie the leather thong around the scroll, a scorpion ran out from the pit. Gerard jumped back to avoid being stung and in the process dropped the scroll. He was relieved to see that the fall had not damaged the parchment. Picking it up again, he glanced inadvertently at some lines of text near the bottom of the scroll. The muscles in Gerard's face grew taut. The dim light in the cave must be playing tricks with his eyes, he thought. He took the parchment out into the sunlight. No, his eyes had not deceived him. He knew now that he must bring this scroll to the grand master at once. After replacing the planks and stones over the artifacts and remaining scrolls, Gerard quickly left the cave. With the parchment in his saddlebag, he rode into the desert.

For Gerard, it would be a long and troubled ride back to Jerusalem.

Chapter XIII

SULTAN HASSAN

When Gerard reached Jerusalem, he was shocked at what he found. The city he had left only a week before had been calm; the city to which he now returned was in chaos. Sultan Hassan had done the unexpected. Instead of attacking Acre, he had turned his army south and moved to within a day's march of Jerusalem. The Templars and the other crusader garrisons were strengthening Jerusalem's walls in anticipation of a long siege. Gerard learned, to his dismay, that de Molay had not returned to the city. When Hassan's cavalry had cut the road between Jerusalem and Acre, de Molay had set sail for Cyprus in the hope of gathering a force of crusaders to help lift the impending siege.

Gerard knew what he must do. The parchment had to be taken out of Jerusalem immediately and brought safely to Cyprus. Ships would still be available in Jaffa, but not for much longer. Riding to the seacoast, however, would be dangerous. Although the Sultan's army was still a day's march away, Saracen horsemen would most likely be patrolling the road between Jerusalem and Jaffa.

Gerard made up his mind to leave Jerusalem the night after he had arrived back in the city. Earlier in the day, he had volunteered to take Templar horses to graze outside the city. When it was time to return, Gerard left his own horse tethered in a secluded spot near the Jaffa gate. No one would notice that one horse was missing—at least not until the muster for morning patrols.

Just after midnight, Gerard slipped out of the Templar barracks. A curfew had been imposed in the city, leaving the streets deserted. Keeping in the shadows, Gerard carefully made his way to the western wall near the Jaffa gate. Two sentries stood talking on the battlements. Since the day Hassan's army began moving toward Jerusalem, lookouts had been posted at frequent intervals along the city's fortifications. Gerard waited impatiently for the lookouts to move on. When they did, he scaled the inside wall and fastened a rope around a stone parapet in the battlements. Tying the other end of the rope around his waist, he let himself down the outside of the wall. Once on the ground, he found his way back to the place where he had tethered his horse. He put the parchment in one of his saddlebags and rode off toward Jaffa.

Gerard avoided the main road to the seacoast, choosing instead a dry riverbed that lay about a half a league to the north. Gerard hoped that Saracen patrols would not be familiar with it. After riding for about an hour in the riverbed, Gerard's horse suddenly stumbled, throwing him over the front of the saddle. When he regained consciousness, he saw his horse grazing a few yards away. Thankfully uninjured by the fall, Gerard stood up slowly. He was bruised in several places but nothing seemed to be broken. When he walked over to his horse, Gerard saw that he was not alone. Saracen horsemen stood watching him from the edge of the riverbed. His first instinct was to draw his sword and fight, but quickly thought better of it—particularly when he saw a Saracen arrow aimed directly at his heart.

The commander of the Saracen patrol rode forward. He studied the red cross on Gerard's mantle. "Are you a Knight of the Temple?" the commander asked in broken French.

Gerard nodded.

The Saracen signaled one of his men to take Gerard's sword and dagger. "Mount your horse, Templar, and come with us."

Gerard did not disobey. When he had mounted, a Saracen tied Gerard's hands behind his back and took the reins of his horse. At a signal from their commander, the patrol rode off to the north with their prisoner.

The commander of the patrol knelt before the Sultan. "We captured a Templar riding toward Jaffa, Great One. He had this parchment scroll in his saddlebag."

Sultan Hassan—the Light of the World and King of Egypt and Syria—looked at the parchment and saw that it was written in Hebrew. "Captain, bring this Templar back in the morning. Feed him and do him no harm."

After Gerard was led away, Hassan stood for a few moments looking at the Hebrew lettering on the scroll. Why would a Christian Knight be in possession of such a document, he wondered.

Hassan rang a bell, summoning one of his servants. "Tell Samuel ben Eleazar that I wish to see him."

A few moments later ben Eleazar entered the Sultan's tent. Although a Jew, ben Eleazar had gradually risen to become the Sultan's most valued counselor and confidante. Some even said that the two had developed a strong bond of friendship.

Hassan handed the scroll to ben Eleazar. "This parchment was taken from a young Templar knight. It is written in Hebrew. Translate it for me, Samuel."

Ben Eleazar bowed to the Sultan. "Of course, Great One."

Ben Eleazar studied the scroll carefully with the exacting eyes of a scholar.

"It is an ancient Jewish census record—nothing more There are many like this in Palestine, Sultan."

"Why would a Templar be carrying such a thing, Samuel? There must be a reason."

Ben Eleazar shrugged. "I do not know. Perhaps it is written in code. Let me look at it again."

After a few minutes, ben Eleazar put the document down and smiled. "Now I understand. There is no code here, Master. It is a census record from the Jewish year 3791. The writing is actually quite straightforward—too straightforward for some I imagine."

"What do you mean, Samuel?"

Ben Eleazar pointed to several lines of text near the bottom of the piece of parchment. "The document says that a man called Yeshua of Nazareth and a woman named Mary of Magdala were married during the Jewish year 3791 and gave birth to a boy and a girl. The boy, named David, was born in 3792. Tamar, the girl, was born the next year."

Hassan stared impatiently at ben Eleazar. "But you still have not answered my question. Why would this Templar be carrying this piece of parchment?"

"Great One, Christians believe that their Messiah, this Jesus, or Yeshua, as he is called in the manuscript, remained celibate all his life. If this census record is accurate, it could fracture Christendom, setting brother against brother."

"Fracture Christendom! What do you mean?"

"If Jesus had children, some would question the authority of the pope and look for descendants of Jesus' children to lead Christianity."

Hassan was silent for a moment. "Samuel, where do you think this Templar was taking the parchment? He was riding toward Jaffa."

"Most likely to Cyprus. The grand master of the Templars is reportedly there gathering an army to help defend Jerusalem."

"Given what is written here, Samuel, I think I should send this Templar on his way. If the manuscript causes a rift in Christendom, Muslim lives may be saved."

Ben Eleazar looked at the Sultan. "And Christian lives lost."

"Who lives or dies is for Allah to decide, not me. He is the one who balances the scales of life. If it is Allah's will that this Templar reach Europe with the parchment, it will happen regardless of what I do. If it is Allah's will that the parchment be destroyed, it will be destroyed. Samuel, have the Templar brought here."

Samuel bowed and left the tent. Several minutes later, Gerard de Montelambert was led before Hassan. As he entered the tent, Gerard was pushed to his knees before the Sultan. Defiantly, Gerard struggled to stand up. "I kneel only before God and his vicar on Earth, the Bishop of Rome."

The Sultan smiled at Gerard. "I could have your head cut off in an instant for such insolence. But I applaud your courage, my young Templar—it is uncommon among Christians. Our religion teaches that even the courage of an unbeliever must be rewarded. I give you your freedom. Let it be a testament to the goodness of Allah and the generosity of Sultan Hassan."

Hassan spoke to one of his soldiers. "Give the Templar a fast horse and put him back on the road to Jaffa."

As Gerard was led out of the tent, Hassan turned to Samuel. "Stay for a moment, my friend."

"Yes, Excellency."

Hassan sat at a table and poured a glass of water. "I do not understand these Christians. Their Jesus must be an evil and a vengeful God."

Samuel ben Eleazar shook his head. "No. The Christian Scriptures say Jesus is a God of love, not of vengeance."

"If that is what their Scriptures say, then their Scriptures must lie." Hassan pounded his hand on the table spilling the glass of water. "Look at what the Christians do in the name of their God. When they captured Jerusalem, they rampaged through the city, killing everyone—Muslim, Jew, even their fellow Christians. No one was spared."

"It is true, Excellency. When the Christians breached the walls, every Jew fled to the main synagogue."

"What happened?"

The Jew struggled with his emotions. "The Christians set fire to the building. Anyone who was not burned to death was butchered as they tried to escape."

"Muslims were treated no better, Samuel. The Christians promised refuge in Al-Aqsa Mosque. Once the faithful had crowded into the mosque, the Christians broke in and slaughtered every one of them. Then they proceeded to cut open their bellies."

"Why?"

"There was a rumor that Muslims had swallowed gold coins to hide them from the Christians."

"Hassan, in battle, men do terrible things."

"Who knows that better than I, Samuel?"

Ben Eleazar was concerned that he had offended his friend. "Great One, I meant no offense."

"I am not offended. When you lead men into battle, you kill because you must. But you kill soldiers. In Jerusalem the Christians killed defenseless women and children. For them it was a holy war—a jihad against the enemies of their God."

"You speak truly, Hassan. When the butchery and mutilation had ended in Jerusalem, their priests gave thanks to their Lord for their victory. They even quoted from the Torah: 'This is the day the Lord has made. Rejoice and be glad.'"

"Are these Christians human or are they wild beasts without compassion for others?"

"Hassan, your armies are only a day's march from Jerusalem."

"My soldiers will not repeat what the Christians did there, if that is what you are suggesting. Christian, Jew, or Muslim—we are all people of the book. If they surrender, I will not lift my sword against them."

Gerard reached Jaffa safely and took passage on an English ship, the *Brigantine,* which was scheduled to stop in Cyprus. Fortunately for Gerard, the captain of the ship, a heavyset Yorkshire man, was also a confrater of the Order of the Temple. He had made a vow to assist the work of the order and provided Gerard with ample food and money for the journey.

A severe winter storm in the Mediterranean, however, forced the *Brigantine* to take shelter in the port of Tripoli. While there, word came that Jerusalem had fallen to the Saracens. As people heard the news, panic spread throughout Tripoli. Wealthy merchants paced up and down the harbor front, begging for passage to Cyprus or Italy for themselves and their families. As the days passed, the merchants became more insistent; what had begun as entreaties gradually became threats. The captain of the *Brigantine* worried that a group of desperate merchants might commandeer the ship for their own purposes. Being a prudent man, the captain caught the high tide and sailed out of the Tripoli harbor during the night. He later explained to Gerard, "I'd rather face a Mediterranean storm than a pack of armed and desperate merchants."

When the *Brigantine* arrived in Cyprus, Gerard wasted no time before seeking an audience with Jacques de Molay.

Chapter XIV

THE PARCHMENT

THE GRAND MASTER brightened as the young Montelambert entered the room. "Gerard! I've thought of you many times during these last months. Hassan surrounded Jerusalem before I could get back to the city."

"When I returned to Jerusalem, Grand Master, I learned what had happened."

"These are dark days. The loss of Jerusalem has been a terrible blow for Christendom. The seneschal and over sixty members of our order were killed during the siege. Many were friends." The grand master fought back his tears.

"And the women and children—did Hassan slaughter them?"

"They were spared. But enough talk of Jerusalem! What did you find in the cave?"

"More than I expected."

"'More than you expected!' What do you mean?"

Gerard laid the parchment scroll in front of de Molay. "Grand Master, I discovered this Hebrew census record buried in the cave. I have translated it into French."

"Let me see it." Gerard handed de Molay the translation. After he finished reading it, de Molay threw the document on the table in front of him. "Gerard, this is a crude joke."

"I wish it were."

"Then your translation must be wrong."

"No, Grand Master. I compared my translation with the Hebrew text several times. There is no mistake."

"Then this parchment is a blasphemy against God and his holy Church. The rule given to us by St. Bernard counsels 'if any brother does not take the vow of chastity he cannot come to eternal rest nor see God.' If this is true, how is it possible that Jesus...?"

"Grand Master, I cannot answer your question."

Gerard was suddenly drawn back to the night of his initiation. He remembered the litany spoken in the chapel. "I am not who I appear to be. When you come, then will you understand who I am." Could these words be a clue to understanding the parchment?

"Listen to me carefully, Gerard. As a Templar, you vowed obedience to me as grand master of the order. Under pain of damnation, never divulge the contents of this document to anyone."

"Yes, Grand Master."

"With Jerusalem lost, this parchment could lead to chaos in the Church. It could convince Christians that we were fighting in Palestine for a false God—that all the Church has taught us about Jesus is wrong."

"I understand."

"Many months ago, you told me about the symbolism of the Cross, how it has two bars. I have thought often about what you said. Today we must attend to the horizontal bar in order to protect God's holy Church from division and scandal. Leave the parchment with me."

"As you wish, Grand Master."

Gerard handed the parchment to de Molay, bowed, and left the room.

The grand master bent over and looked carefully at the census record. If Gerard's translation is accurate, this piece of parchment puts into question thirteen hundred years of belief about the man Jesus was. The parchment also questions the legitimacy of the apostolic succession of the papacy—that Jesus left the Church to be governed by the successors of the Apostle Peter. But if Jesus had children of his own, perhaps he would have wanted their descendants to govern the Church, not the elected bishops of Rome.

De Molay walked to a casement window and looked out to the sea. He knew that there was something else at stake here—the very survival of the Order of the Temple. The Italian city-states were arguing that the Templars should be disbanded, now that

Jerusalem and the Holy Land had been reconquered by the Saracens. Used strategically, this manuscript could protect the Order of the Temple from any such fate. As he stared again at the parchment, de Molay remembered the Latin motto of the order. *Non Nobis, Domine, Non Nobis Sed Tuo Nomini Da Gloriam*—"Lord, give the glory not to us, not to us, but to your name."

Jacques de Molay left Famagusta, Cyprus, on a Templar galley bound for France. As befitting his station, a large retinue accompanied him—Gerard de Montelambert included. When they reached Marseilles, the Templars boarded flat-bottomed barges for the trip up the Rhone to Avignon where Pope Clement had taken up residence. De Molay politely refused the pope's invitation to accept lodging in the Palais des Papes.

"We have a commanderie in Villeneuve just across the river from the Palais," the grand master wrote the pope. "The simple quarters of my order will be adequate for my needs."

The Templar commanderie lay on a bluff overlooking Villeneuve. The barges carrying de Molay's entourage arrived quietly at the docks of the town. The grand master insisted that there be no panoply to mark his arrival. Even the Bishop of Avignon was politely asked not to come to greet de Molay.

Gerard was assigned the job of transferring provisions from the Templar barges to horse carts for the trip up the hill to the commanderie. As Gerard bent down to lift a heavy chest onto one of the carts, a large hulk of a man stood over him, blocking out the sun. Gerard knew immediately who it was.

"Brother Michael!"

"By the bones of St. Peter, what are you doing here, Montelambert? And a Templar, no less."

The two men embraced.

"How long have you been in Villenueve, Brother Michael?"

"When the Crusaders abandoned Tortosa, the grand master ordered me here. I must admit I prefer Tortosa to Avignon."

"Why is that?" asked Gerard.

"In Palestine snakes crawl; here they walk."

Chapter XV

EXTORTION

THE LARGE OAKEN chair all but engulfed the small frame of Bertrand de Got, formerly Archbishop of Bordeaux and now the Vicar of Christ, Pope Clement V. To be chosen Bishop of Rome and Supreme Pontiff of the Roman Catholic Church was an honor bestowed on few men. Devout Catholics believed that the Holy Spirit inspired Clement's selection. Clement, however, knew better. He owed his election not to the Holy Spirit but to a man—King Philip IV of France. Wanting a French pope, Philip had bought the final votes needed to give the election to Clement. In return for his election, Philip had already forced Clement to move the papal household from Rome to Avignon. Clement knew there would be new demands to come.

A knock on the door made Clement look up from the letter he was reading. An elderly cardinal entered the room. "Ah, Pierre, thank you for coming so quickly." Cardinal Pierre de Saone was the camerlengo of the Church and Clement's most trusted adviser.

"De Saone, this letter just arrived from the Patriarch of Constantinople. It is dated June twenty-ninth."

"The feast of Saints Peter and Paul. What does the Patriarch want?"

The pope looked upset. "He threatens a schism unless the Western and Eastern Churches reach some accommodation on the status of the Bishop of Rome and the Patriarch of Constantinople."

"What 'accommodation' does the Patriarch want?" The cardinal asked the question sarcastically.

"He proposes that we both have equal status in the Church. Each would have a veto over the other in doctrinal and ecclesiastical matters. He concludes by saying that, just as Peter and Paul settled their differences amicably, the two of us must do the same for the good of Christianity."

"What the Patriarch proposes is out of the question, Your Holiness. You are the Vicar of Christ on earth. The Patriarch must accept the primacy of the Bishop of Rome."

"Of course I cannot accept the Patriarch's demands. But his threat of a schism is still ominous."

"I know it is, Holiness."

"These are desperate times, de Saone. The world seems to be coming apart. The infidels have reconquered Jerusalem, and Christ's tomb is again in shackles. The remaining crusaders in Palestine stream back to Europe defeated and demoralized. Here in France, Philip maneuvers to take more and more power from the Church. Already he has forced me to move my household here to Avignon. Who would have believed that one day the Bishop of Rome would sit captive in a French city! But I dare not oppose Philip. You saw what he did to my predecessor Pope Boniface. These papal vestments are no protection from Philip's anger."

"The Archangel Michael would strike Philip dead if he ever dared harm you, Clement."

"Let me tell you a story. Remember the recent deportation of the Jews from France."

"Of course. Phillip expelled them so he could confiscate their wealth."

"When he first told me of his plans for the Jews, I objected in the strongest terms. I threatened to place France under an interdict and forbid the distribution of the sacraments. I told him the interdict would remain in place until he relented and allowed the Jews to return to France."

"And what did he say to that?"

"Here is what he said: 'Boniface placed France under an interdict and look what happened to him. If you follow his lead, Clement, there will soon be another Frenchman on the Throne of Saint Peter.' What do I do, de Saone? I am not as brave as Boniface. I fear Philip."

"You are right to fear him. Philip stops at nothing to get his way. Yield to his political ambitions. Flatter him — call him the new Charlemagne. But you must not let Philip gain control in matters of religion. You are the Vicar of Christ and the conduit of his graces, not King Philip."

"It sounds so easy when you say it, Pierre." Clement poured himself a glass of water. "Philip is not the only problem that must be dealt with. Jacques de Molay has come from Cyprus to see me. He wishes to discuss the future of the Order of the Temple now that Jerusalem has fallen to the Saracens. But I fear that the grand master comes with something else on his mind. I do not trust him."

"You are right to be cautious, Holiness. What is good for the order is not always good for the Church."

"I trust your judgment in these matters, Pierre. Stay to hear what he says."

A servant knocked on the door to the pope's chamber. "Your Holiness, the grand master of the Templars waits outside,"

"Show him in."

Clement rose from his chair to greet his famous guest. De Molay genuflected before the pope and kissed his ring. "Your Holiness, it is good of you to receive me so soon after my arrival in Avignon."

Clement opened his arms expansively. "The grand master of the Temple is a welcome guest in our palace. I only wish I could welcome you more appropriately. Philip forces me to live in this crowded pigsty of a city. The streets are so dangerous that members of the curia have built skyways from their houses to the Palais des Papes."

De Molay smiled. "I have seen them throughout the city."

"On top of everything else, this dingy palace that Philip has provided me is too small for my household. But, Grand Master, I am sure you did not come all the way from Cyprus to listen to my complaints. You know, of course, Cardinal de Saone. I have asked His Eminence to join our discussion."

"I know the camerlengo's reputation for wisdom and unswerving devotion to the Church. He has always been a loyal friend of our order."

De Saone quickly grew impatient with the customary rounds of diplomatic niceties. "Your order has also contributed much to the work of the Church, Grand Master. But now tell us why you have come. Although the spring sun is warm in Avignon, I do not think it was the weather that brought you here."

"You are right, Your Eminence. I am here for a reason." De Molay turned and addressed Pope Clement directly. "As you are aware, Holiness, I have asked to speak to you about a matter of the gravest concern to my order and to Christendom. The holy places are again in Saracen hands. The crusading armies have returned to Europe. Two hundred years ago, your blessed predecessor Pope Urban rallied all of Europe to the banner of the Cross. For a time, the Tomb of Christ was in Christian hands. I beg you, Clement, follow the example of Pope Urban. Preach a new Crusade. Western Christendom must retake what it has lost."

"Grand Master, I am told you are someone who is both realistic and skilled in the art of diplomacy. You know as well as I that there can be no Crusade at this time. There have been six already. The kings of France and England are preoccupied with matters here in Europe. They have neither the money nor the inclination for new adventures in the Holy Land."

"But, Your Holiness, you could bend them to your will. Threaten them with an interdict."

"For all your reputation as a shrewd diplomat, de Molay, I am surprised at your naïveté. There will be no Crusade. I do not have the power to convince any of the kings of Europe to join in such an effort."

"You are the Vicar of Christ, Your Holiness. I must insist that you reconsider your decision."

"'Insist!'" Clement bristled when he repeated the word. "Do not forget to whom you are speaking, Grand Master."

"Your Holiness, I wish to show you something that may change your mind."

De Molay unrolled an ancient parchment scroll and laid it on a table. "This parchment was discovered several months ago in Palestine by a young Templar. It is written in Hebrew. I understand

Your Holiness is fluent in Hebrew so you might wish to read it for yourself."

The pope sat down at the table where de Molay had unrolled the manuscript. "I will not indulge you much longer, Grand Master."

After studying the manuscript for several minutes, the pope suddenly stopped. His face grew pale and his body trembled. Clement handed the parchment to Cardinal de Saone. "This writing, de Molay, is the product of the Devil. It is rank heresy. If you or any of your Templars believe in such things, then you should be excommunicated from the Church."

"Your Holiness, what I believe — for the moment at least — is irrelevant. What is relevant, however, is the parchment. As of this moment, just four people know the contents of this document — three of whom are presently in this room. And so it will remain — on one condition."

"And what is that, de Molay?"

De Molay looked squarely at Pope Clement. "That you call for a new Crusade to free the Holy Places."

The pope was shocked at de Molay's challenge. "And if I refuse?"

"The contents of the parchment will be revealed. You can imagine the impact it will have on the papacy, Your Holiness. If there is a bloodline of Christ Our Savior, many devout Christians will believe that his descendants, and not Peter's successors, should lead the Church."

"Who would believe you, de Molay?" Clement looked contemptuously at the grand master. "We all know that many in your order are capable of forging this Hebrew document. That is what the people will believe. As for this claim that issue was born to Jesus and the Magdalene, it is simply preposterous. In the Gospel of Matthew, Jesus says that He chose to be celibate. The faithful will not believe that, despite His words, Jesus had relations with a woman. He was God."

"But he was also fully human, Holiness."

The pope became visibly agitated at the grand master's words. "Don't engage me in theological debate, Grand Master."

"Your Holiness, that was not my intent. But there is more to this than may meet the eye. There are political overtones to this parchment."

"Political overtones?"

"You know that as well as I, Holiness. For years there have been rumors in France that there was a bloodline of Christ, and that it ran through the Merovingian dynasty of French kings. Your sponsor, King Philip, is a Capetian."

"The Capetians have ruled France for over three hundred years, de Molay. Their throne is secure."

"Perhaps not as secure as you may think, Your Holiness. Rumors about a bloodline of Christ resurfaced during the recent Crusades against the Cathars. Some even believe that the Capetian's brutal suppression of the Cathars was aimed at destroying the bloodline."

"These rumors are no threat, de Molay."

"I respectfully disagree, Holiness. In the right hands, this parchment will refuel these rumors and give them more credibility. There could be efforts to depose the Capetian dynasty in favor of the Merovingians. Imagine what your King Philip will think if he learns that you had the chance to destroy the manuscript but did not!"

Cardinal de Saone angrily interrupted. "This is extortion, de Molay!"

"Call it what you will, Eminence. I do what I must do for my order."

De Molay turned again to Clement. "Your Holiness, I ask you for a second time — will you agree to preach a new Crusade to recapture the Holy Places?"

"De Molay, Templars take a vow to obey me in all things. I call on that vow. Do not reveal the contents of this parchment. Many will die, brother will fight against brother."

"I must act for the good of the Templars, Holiness."

"If you do not honor your vow of obedience, damnation awaits your immortal soul, de Molay."

The grand master stood firm. "Holiness, I require your answer."

Clement sat silent for a moment. "I need more time to consider what you have said."

"Three days is all the time I can give, Your Holiness. I will return then for your answer."

The grand master bowed stiffly to the pope and Cardinal de Saone and walked out of the room. As he left, de Molay did not kiss Clement's ring.

When the grand master returned to his quarters, he scribbled several lines on a piece of parchment and then summoned Gerard de Montelambert.

"Gerard, I have an important mission for you."

"Does it involve the parchment, Grand Master?"

"Yes. I have just come from an audience with Pope Clement. I asked him to preach a new crusade to retake Jerusalem. I threatened to reveal the contents of the manuscript if he refused."

"What did he say?"

De Molay looked upset. "He stalled for time. I do not trust him. Either the pope or his sponsor King Philip may try to have me arrested and the parchment destroyed. Until their intentions become clear, take the parchment out of Avignon."

"Yes, Grand Master. If Clement or Philip tries to harm you or members of our order, I will give the parchment to their enemies."

De Molay shook his head. "No. I will not act to harm the Church."

"Not even to save the Templars?"

"Not even to save the Templars. Remember your story about the two bars on the Cross. In the end, a Christian must follow the vertical bar."

"But, Grand Master...!"

"Enough, Gerard. Speak no more of this! Take the parchment and leave Avignon tonight. I fear we have little time."

"I will do as you say, Grand Master."

Jacques de Molay walked to a window and looked across the Rhône to the narrow streets of Avignon. In the withdrawing light of the day, river glowed a bright orange. "What of your faith,

Gerard? Would it matter if Jesus and the Magdalene lived as man and wife?"

"Palestine taught me that the real Jerusalem was different from the Jerusalem I had imagined as a child. Perhaps the real Jesus is different from the Jesus the priests have taught us."

"'I am not who I appear to be.'"

Gerard looked at de Molay. "Grand Master, you spoke those words at the initiation ceremony."

"Yes, I know. Go now, Gerard. Take these words I have written you. God has chosen you to protect this parchment for a future age."

As Gerard was about to leave, Jacques de Molay put his hand on the young Templar's shoulder. "You have been a courageous and loyal Templar, Gerard de Montelambert. I hope we meet again."

They never did.

Chapter XVI

HERESY AND CAPTURE

After de Molay had left, Pope Clement fell back into his chair as if a great weight had collapsed on him. "De Saone, this manuscript must be a forgery. There could be no truth to it."

"Sometimes what is important, Holiness, is not truth, but what people perceive to be the truth. We both know that if the parchment is revealed, there will be great scandal among the faithful. Many will question the divinity of Jesus. Some will abandon the sacraments altogether. No matter what the cost, the parchment must be destroyed."

"But how can I do that? I have no army to take it away from the Templars."

"You must speak with Philip. What alternative do you have? To save the Templars, de Molay would destroy the Church."

King Philip was visibly annoyed as he entered Pope Clement's apartment in the Palais des Papes. The pope extended his hand to the king but Philip angrily brushed it aside.

Philip IV was a tall and muscular man with blond curly hair and a fair complexion. His good looks and regal bearing had earned him the sobriquet Philip the Fair. Yet his princely demeanor was marred by one feature—his eyes. They were the hard metallic color of steel. They displayed no warmth, only the cold and pitiless inhumanity of a predator. Philip's father, King Philip III, once cautioned his chief minister: 'If you live to serve my son Philip, be on your guard. He is as rapacious as the wolf and as wily as the serpent. Worse still he trusts no one, not even his father.'"

"Clement, what is this urgent matter about the Templars and de Molay? Your courier interrupted a most pleasant ride in the countryside with Mademoiselle Heurbon."

"De Molay has a manuscript that purports to show the existence of a bloodline of Jesus Christ."

"Clement, are you mad? Is this why you called me here?"

"De Molay must be taken seriously. Unless I agree to preach a new Crusade, he threatens to reveal the contents of the document."

"So what! No one will believe him. Those who credit such things are excommunicated from the Church."

"I told de Molay that. No scriptural text, no Father of the Church, nothing in the entire Christian canon mentions such a thing. But. . . ."

"But what?"

"You know, Philip, there have been legends about the Magdalene's coming to France."

"Yes, I have heard them all. My nurse was very devout. Her favorite was the tale of the three Marys—how they were put to sea in a boat without oar or sail."

"Some say there were others in the boat—the Egyptian slave Sarah and the two children, David and Tamar."

"Yes, and some say Joseph of Arimathea as well, or was it Nicodemus? Maybe in the end, Pontius Pilate came along for the ride." Philip snickered. "Legends about these two children are just that—legends."

"Do not dismiss them so quickly, Philip. Look at this." Clement handed the king a round piece of bronze.

"What is it?"

"A medal struck in the town of Saintes Maries-de-la-Mer not far from here. Look carefully at the picture and the inscription."

"It says 'St. David and Ste. Tamar, *Liberi Christi.*'"

"Yes, 'the children of Christ.' People here in Provence believe in a divine bloodline."

Philip laughed. "What do I care about the beliefs of fishermen in Saintes Maries-de-la-Mer!"

"The Templars are admired for their honesty and courage. They also have a network of lay *confratres* all over France, some even in your own household."

"What is your point, Clement?"

"If the Templars say the contents of the parchment are true, many will believe them."

"This is your problem, not mine." Philip got up to leave.

"Not so. The legend of these children threatens not only the papacy; it threatens your throne as well."

Philip stopped at the door of the pope's chamber.

"What the fishermen in Provence believe does not threaten the throne of France."

"But it does. You are a Capetian. Your ancestors have ruled France for over three hundred years. But the Merovingians ruled these lands long before your family."

Philip was becoming visibly angry. "Do not lecture me on the history of the French monarchy!"

"Majesty, I do so to make a point. The Merovingians trace their lineage far back in history—to the time when the Magdalene came to France with these two children. There are legends. . . ."

"Ah, more legends."

"Yes, more legends! For a king, legends can be more dangerous than enemy armies."

"I grow impatient with all this."

"Legends say that the children of Jesus married into Merovingian families. Many believe that, because they are of the holy bloodline, the Merovingians are therefore the rightful kings of France."

"Clement, Jacques de Molay is a clever man. Now that Palestine is gone, his order is hemorrhaging. To stop the hemorrhaging, he needs you to preach a Crusade. He hangs the census record over your head like the sword of Damocles."

"And over yours!"

"No one threatens the king of France with impunity. How many Templars know about this parchment?"

"Only two. De Molay and the Templar who discovered it."

"Good. If we are to succeed, we will have to act quickly. De Molay and this other Templar must be arrested. We know that de Molay brought the parchment here to Avignon. I am sure the Templar who found it is here with him. When does de Molay expect an answer about a new Crusade?"

"In three days."

"There is time then. Summon de Molay to your apartment tomorrow morning. Have him and his entourage arrested. I am sure we will find this young Templar among them. A little persuasion from the inquisitors should uncover the parchment."

"But you forget one thing. There are many hundreds of Templars here in France. Do you think they will all sit idly by and watch their grand master and a fellow Templar arrested and tortured, even if the command comes from the pope himself?"

"You are right. We must strike more boldly."

"More boldly?"

"Yes, all the Templars in France must be imprisoned. We cannot flinch from our purpose. As you have said yourself, at stake here is the Throne of Peter and the throne of France."

"What charges will you bring against the Templars?"

"Heresy, of course. Accuse de Molay and the others of committing sacrilegious practices."

"What sacrilegious practices?"

"Accuse them of spitting on the Cross and trampling on the consecrated bread and wine. Some say they worship an idol—add that to your list. More charges can be brought later."

"This goes too far, Majesty, much too far. No one will believe these lies about the Templars."

"You are wrong, Clement. If the Templars are respected in some quarters, they are envied and resented in others. Envy and resentment are powerful weapons. Christians, even devout Christians, will believe whatever we say about the order."

Philip turned to leave. "Before I go, there is one thing more. What will be done with the Templars' properties once they are arrested?"

"I will appoint custodians to administer them."

Philip shook his head. "No, Clement. All Templar properties must be confiscated and turned over to the king of France."

The pope blanched. "Impossible! How can I justify such a thing?"

"Many call France the eldest daughter of the Church. Say it is a reward for her long and steadfast support of the papacy."

"Philip, this will effectively destroy the Templars!"

"So be it. But why should we kill the bees and not enjoy the honey?"

A short while after the king had left, Cardinal de Saone entered the pope's library. "Your Holiness sent for me."

"Yes, Pierre. To find the parchment, Philip would have me arrest de Molay and every Templar in France on charges of heresy."

"Every Templar in France?"

"Yes, Philip cares little about protecting the Church. He uses the threat of the parchment to confiscate Templar property."

"What do you mean?"

"Once the Templars are arrested, Philip would have me transfer their property to him."

"Confiscating the Templars' wealth is his price for destroying the parchment?"

"Yes."

De Saone delivered his judgment without any hesitation. "Holiness, the Templars have done much for Christendom. But that was in the past. Now they must be sacrificed for the good of the Church."

"This is too high a price, Pierre."

"Clement, a doctor must often amputate a limb to save the body."

"But the limb you would have me amputate is the Order of the Temple, the right arm of the Church."

"Holiness, right or left makes little difference in such a serious situation."

"So you would have me do what Philip asks?"

"You have no choice. A pope's responsibility is to the Church as a whole, not to any one part of it. If de Molay seeks to harm the whole of the Church, then you must act against him."

"But, except for de Molay, the Templars have done nothing to harm the Church."

"If a man threatens to attack you, Holiness, must you wait for the attack before you strike?"

"No."

The morning dawned dark and overcast in Avignon. Cold mistral winds blew down the Rhône Valley with a ferocity not felt in months. Despite the weather, Jacques de Molay and senior members of the order arrived promptly at the Palais des Papes just after eight o'clock in the morning. Pope Clement had summoned de Molay to a meeting at 8:15. A contingent of French soldiers suddenly confronted the grand master and his entourage.

"Captain, stand aside. You block the way of the grand master of the Order of the Temple. Out of the way!"

"Grand Master, my orders are to arrest you and your men on charges of heresy."

"Heresy! The grand master of the Temple! This is laughable. Out of the way. Pope Clement expects us in a few minutes."

"I am not here to debate, Grand Master. My orders are to arrest you and your retinue. If you resist, I will have to use force."

"The Templar oath requires us to fight against the Saracen, not fellow Christians. We will not unsheathe our swords. But tell Pope Clement one thing; what he seeks will not be found."

At first light, a contingent of French cavalry sought entrance to the Templar commanderie in Villeneuve. Roused from a deep sleep, the old castellan unlatched the front gate to the courtyard. Although it was earlier than usual, the arrival of the French military patrol did not arouse the gatekeeper's suspicions. French patrols often came to the commanderie to buy food and drink.

"Who's in charge here?" The French Captain spoke brusquely to the old man.

"Brother Michael. If you wish to see him, you must wait. He is in chapel for matins."

"Good, this will make our task easier."

"What task?"

"Out of the way, old man!" The French officer drew his sword.

"You cannot enter the chapel with weapons drawn, Captain. It would be a sacrilege.

"I said out of the way!" The Captain spurred his horse past the gatekeeper, knocking him to the ground.

At a signal from the Captain, the French soldiers dismounted and entered the chapel. The Templars knelt around the altar reciting the Holy Office.

The Captain spoke in a loud voice that echoed throughout the chapel. "By order of King Philip, you are all under arrest."

Astonished at what he heard, Brother Michael slowly stood up from his *pre-dieu* and walked menacingly down the center aisle of the chapel to where the French captain stood.

"No French soldier can arrest a Templar. We are under the direct jurisdiction of the pope. Philip has no authority here." Contemptuously, Brother Michael made a dismissive gesture and turned his back on the French officer. Infuriated, the captain drove his sword into Brother Michael's back. The Templar staggered forward from the force of the blow. Blood spurted from his nose and mouth. Then, like a wounded bear charging the hunter, Brother Michael lunged for the captain, catching him around the neck. Lifting the captain off the ground, he hurled his body across the chapel. The captain hit the wall with a thud and fell to the ground unconscious.

Brother Michael's courage emboldened the others. A young Templar grabbed a gold cross from the altar and charged the startled French soldiers, shouting "For God and Beauseant." When the others heard their battle cry, the Templars to a man jumped up and ran toward the French soldiers—some bare handed, others brandishing brass candlesticks taken from the altar.

Fifteen Templar knights died fighting at the commanderie in Villeneuve; the rest were taken back in chains to Avignon. On that day, many hundreds more were arrested throughout France.

The spikes on the wheel dug deeply into his flesh. De Molay flinched in pain but did not cry out.

The inquisitor bent over him. "Where is the manuscript? Tell me and you will be given the Holy Sacraments of Penance and the Eucharist."

De Molay spat at the inquisitor and said nothing.

"Jailer, turn the wheel more."

De Molay writhed in pain.

"Jailer, more."

De Molay spat a second time at the inquisitor. This time his spittle was red with blood.

"The manuscript is where you will never find it. Tell that to the whores Clement and de Saone and their madame Philip."

"Brave words for someone in your predicament, Templar scum."

The wheel was turned again, this time at an excruciatingly slow pace.

"De Molay, one of your Templars has testified that he saw you urinate on the Cross. Is that true?"

De Molay glared at the inquisitor. "A man will say anything under torture."

"I am told that you and the members of your order mocked the sufferings of Our Lord Jesus Christ. Maybe if you suffered like him you would repent of your blasphemy and tell us what we want to know."

The inquisitor motioned to one of the jailers. "Bring some spikes and make a crown of thorns."

The inquisitor turned and looked at his prisoner. "While you are being crowned, de Molay, I will give you something to think about. If you will not tell us where the parchment is to save yourself, perhaps you will tell us to save the members of your order. Templars have been arrested all over France."

"Rot in Hell, priest."

The inquisitor smiled at de Molay. "You may be sure there will be more Templar arrests. How they are treated depends on you."

De Molay struggled to break free from his bonds but they held.

"Jailer, you know what to do. Push the spikes in deep." The inquisitor turned and left the room.

CHAPTER XVII

A JOURNEY TO ROME

"Your Holiness, we have tortured de Molay for three days." The inquisitor squirmed as he addressed the pope and the king of France. "He will not tell us anything. He insists that the manuscript is in a place where you will never find it. De Molay is a brave man; he will not succumb to our torture."

King Philip rose from his seat in anger. "My good inquisitor, if you cannot break the man, then you must kill him. There is really no alternative. Pope Clement and I have a vested interest in de Molay's guilt. If you need a reason to kill the grand master, I have told you before; condemn him as a heretic."

The pope signaled the inquisitor to leave the room. When the door closed behind him, Clement looked incredulously at Philip.

"Your Majesty, you cannot be serious—kill de Molay as a heretic?"

"Yes, I am deadly serious."

"Not for one moment do I think de Molay is a heretic, and I do not think you do either."

"De Molay is using this manuscript against both of us."

"He is using the manuscript to save his order, not to spread heresy. He is acting as any grand master would."

"Bertrand de Got, remember your Bible." Philip was wont to use the pope's baptismal name when he was about to lecture him on some matter. "Jesus of Nazareth was put to death as a heretic."

"Yes, the Jewish priests accused him of blasphemy."

"But Pilate's reason for crucifying him was quite different. Jesus had caused the Romans a political problem by claiming to be 'king of the Jews.'"

"What are you saying, Philip?"

"The parallel to de Molay should be obvious. We will accuse him of heresy but kill him because he threatens the papacy and the throne of France. A charge of heresy is simpler than trying to explain such complex issues."

"I will not join you in this, Majesty."

Philip smiled coldly at the pope. "You forget yourself, Bertrand de Got." Philip's tone of voice became coldly matter of fact. "You sit on the Throne of Saint Peter because of me. Your predecessor Boniface no longer sits on the Throne of Peter—also because of me. I will not tolerate opposition on how we deal with de Molay. He poses a threat and the threat must be ended. If you stand in my way, you will be removed from your throne."

The king left the room. Pope Clement realized that he was powerless to save de Molay's life. Even worse, he realized he was afraid to try.

When Gerard left Avignon, he rode north to the village of Divanche. He found lodging in a barn owned by a confrater of the order. On his third night there, news came that Clement had ordered the Templars arrested. Rumors also spread that the grand master had been turned over to the inquisitors.

Gerard knew that he must leave the area immediately. Philip's soldiers would soon be scouring the countryside looking for the parchment. He took out the letter de Molay had given him and read it. "Gerard, the Hebrew manuscript is in your safe keeping. Hide it well. Someday the world may come to learn whether there is a divine bloodline."

As he was putting the letter back into his saddlebag, word came that the confrater's only son, a Templar initiate, had been killed in the fighting at the commaraderie in Villaneuve. Disconsolate, the confrater fell on the ground and sobbed.

Pitying the man, Gerard helped him to his feet. "God will punish Clement. He usurps the Throne of Peter. I have proof."

The confrater grasped Gerard's arm. "What proof is there? Let me see it."

"I cannot show it to you. I have given my vow to the grand master of the order not to reveal it to anyone."

"But if it would avenge my son's death. . . ." The confrater struggled with Gerard as the Templar tried to mount his horse.

"Stop, old man."

Gerard's horse reared up and his hoof struck the man in the head. The confrater fell against a rock and lay unconscious on the ground, blood pouring from the back of his head. Several farmhands came running as Gerard mounted his horse and rode quickly away.

Gerard de Montelambert took many months to travel from Avignon to Rome. With the arrests of his fellow Templars in France, he proceeded cautiously. He shaved off his Templar beard and substituted a plain cloak for his white Templar mantle. To avoid detection, Gerard stayed off the main routes to the French-Italian border. Late snows and severe spring flooding in northern Italy further delayed his progress. When he finally arrived in Rome, Gerard took lodging at an inn near the old papal library.

Although the papal household had been moved to Avignon, most of the Church's records had been left behind in Rome. Gerard knew that the founder of the Order of the Temple, Hugh des Payens, had stored the major portion of early Templar documents in the papal library. Gerard remembered the lesson he had learned from his Uncle Edouard. "If a man wishes to hide, he should not hide in the forest; people will look for him there. He should hide instead in the open, preferably in the town square next to the parish church. People forget to look in the most obvious places." Gerard was about to put Edouard's lesson to the test for a second time. He entered the library and asked an old librarian where the records of the Knights Templar were kept.

"No one has asked to see those records in many months—not since the Templars were suppressed by the pope. People are afraid that they will be accused of heresy by just looking at them. Why do you want to see them?"

"I look for a record of my birth. All my mother would tell me was that I was born on a Templar commanderie in Provence."

"I hope your mother did not take up with a Templar. There were many such relationships. Good luck in your search."

Gerard was escorted to a small room far in the rear of the library. After the librarian had left, Gerard took out the parchment from a shoulder bag and looked at it one last time. What would the future hold for it, he wondered. Making the sign of the Cross, he opened an old oaken chest that was inscribed with the Templar motto—*Non Nobis, Domine, Non Nobis Sed Tuo Nomini Da Gloriam.* The chest was piled high with accountings from several Templar commanderies in Aquitaine. Gerard put the parchment in the middle of the pile. Edouard would be proud of him. He had hidden it in a particularly obvious place—among Templar documents in a chest inscribed with the Templar motto in the main library of the Catholic Church. Gerard rang a small bell to summon back the librarian.

"Thank you for your help. I am finished."

"Did you find the date of your birth?"

"No."

"These Templars were strange ones—rich and powerful. I don't think they deserved their fate, however. What do you think?"

"All of this is too much for a simple man like me."

As Gerard left the papal library, he thought again of the motto of his order inscribed on the wooden chest: *Non Nobis, Domine, Non Nobis Sed Tuo Nomini Da Gloriam.*

Gerard de Montelambert left Rome that day and vanished into the Italian countryside.

"An amazing tale, Jean!"

Calvaux smiled. "There's actually a sequel that I haven't told you."

"Tell me, please. It's fascinating."

"They say that ten years after Gerard disappeared, there was an outbreak of plague in Cours-des-Trois. Gerard's father had died many years before but his mother still lived in the manor house. Although she was old and feeble, the Marquise walked through the town every day bringing food and blankets to those who were dying. It was not long, however, before the Lord saw fit to bring her to himself. On the Wednesday before Pentecost, the Marquise contracted the disease. The red boils soon covered her body. The night before she died, the parish priest was walking through the square, when he noticed something strange. The cross that had stood in the square from the day Gerard had left on crusade was gone. The curé could see a faint glimmer of light coming from inside the church. When he opened the door of the church, he saw that the cross had been put back on the altar. Out of the corner of his eye, the curé saw the shadow of a man leave the church by the side door.

The next morning, the curé ran to the manor house. He went into the room where the Marquise lay dying. "My Lady, there has been a miracle. The cross has been returned to its place on the altar."

The Marquise smiled. "Gerard, my son, has come home." These were her last words."

The two cardinals sat in silence. Although he could see that Barbo had been deeply engrossed in the Montelambert legend, Calvaux did not understand why. Finally Barbo spoke.

"So this parchment exists somewhere?"

Calvaux shrugged his shoulders. "It may or may not. It's a legend."

"But if it did exist and were proven accurate, think of the impact it would have on millions of the faithful who were raised to believe Jesus never had relations with a woman."

"I've had many years to consider this possibility. My faith in Jesus depends on his Resurrection, not on whether he was married or single."

Barbo's cell phone rang.

"Excuse me Jean. I must take this call. It's from the camerlengo's office. But I'd like to talk to you more about the parchment Gerard discovered."

"That he allegedly discovered, Francesco. If the parchment exists, one thing is certain—no one has seen it for almost eight hundred years."

Chapter XVIII

ABDICATION

THE OLD MAN was preoccupied as the taxicab stopped in front of number 35 Via Mascherino. Somehow he sensed that this morning's invitation was not purely social. He paid the driver and slowly maneuvered himself out of the taxicab. As he closed the door, the man realized that he had left his purse in the backseat of the cab.

The driver saw what had happened and jumped out of the taxi to help. "Let me get it for you, Eminence."

The old cardinal smiled at the driver. "Thank you. I'm usually less forgetful."

Agostino Cardinal Marini rang the doorbell to the secretary of state's apartment. A young priest came down to the lobby and escorted him upstairs.

Cardinal Barbo greeted his guest warmly. "It's good to see you, Agostino. Please sit. I thought you might like some breakfast. My cook has prepared scrambled eggs and cereal. The orange marmalade is from England—try it on the toast."

Cardinal Marini was kind and affable with a disarming smile. A simple man from Genoa, Marini eschewed wearing cardinatial dress. It was rumored that, when Pope Benedict appointed him to the Sacred College, Marini told the Holy Father that, unless he was specifically ordered to do so, he would not walk about the Vatican looking like some Prussian field marshal. Because of his unpretentiousness, Pope Benedict chose Marini to be the camerlengo of the Church—the prelate given the responsibility of administering the Holy See during the *Sede Vacante,* the period during which the papal throne is vacant.

Marini poured himself a second cup of espresso. "Thank you, Francesco. As enjoyable as breakfast with an old friend is, I sense this morning's invitation is not purely social."

Barbo hesitated. "It is not."

Cardinal Marini looked ominously at Barbo. "Call it a premonition but is there a problem with the pontiff's health?"

"Yes, Agostino. The Holy Father has Alzheimer's disease. The symptoms have progressed far enough that he is no longer able to manage papal affairs. He wishes to abdicate for the good of the Church."

Marini's cup clattered to his saucer. "Pope Benedict! Abdicate! You can't be serious."

"I'm very serious." Barbo removed a medical file from a desk drawer. "Read it if you want, Agostino. The doctors agree that the Holy Father is no longer competent to administer the Church. He still has lucid moments but they are becoming less and less frequent."

"There must be drugs. . . ." Marini groped for words.

"There are, but the pope's condition doesn't respond to them."

Marini slowly regained his composure. "There have been rumors about Benedict's health but no mention of abdication."

"It is the Holy Father's decision. No one else can make it." Barbo paused and looked at his old friend and colleague. "Once the pope resigns, Agostino, the Church will become your responsibility. The intrigue over Benedict's successor will start at once. Diefenbacher will be out rallying his supporters."

Marini's eyes grew somber at the sound of Diefenbacher's name. "Yes, I know about his ambitions. He has wide support among our European and North American colleagues. The Africans may also support him because of his record on civil rights."

Barbo nodded. "He's been a strong opponent of apartheid."

Marini glowered. "Diefenbacher should remain Archbishop of Durban. He will not get my vote."

"Why are you so opposed to him, Agostino?"

"He's a whitened sepulcher. He would destroy the papacy with his ideas. The notion of giving doctrinal autonomy to local bishops is absurd." Marini's face darkened. "But enough about Diefenbacher! How can I help you, Francesco? Pope Benedict has been like a father to you. It must be difficult."

"Yes. I must help him through this without a loss of dignity. He was always a dynamic and vigorous man." Barbo handed Marini a picture of Pope Benedict hiking in the mountains, followed by three Vatican aides visibly straining to keep up. "This is the way he should be remembered, not as a confused and drooling old man."

"Francesco, my office draws up the formal papers when a pope dies. I will adapt them to fit an abdication. Is the Holy Father aware enough to sign them?"

Barbo nodded. "Doctor Hendricks thinks so but to be on the safe side he suggests the signing be kept private. The cameras and crowds of reporters would most likely confuse the Holy Father. You will have to make the formal announcement, Agostino."

Marini thought for a moment. "The Sacred College will have to be notified before the public announcement. When will the Holy Father sign the documents?"

"Can you have them prepared by Holy Thursday morning?"

"Of course, but we should delay the abdication until after Holy Week. It will overshadow the Easter liturgy."

"What alternative do we have, Agostino? If the Holy Father cannot carry the cross through the Coliseum on Good Friday—or worse, fails to appear for Mass in St. Peter's on Easter."

"You're right. The documents will be ready late Wednesday. When on Thursday will they be signed?"

"At 8:30 in the morning."

"I will call a meeting of the Sacred College at 10:30, after Holy Thursday Mass."

"Call the meeting in the Holy Father's name. If you call it as camerlengo, rumors about the pope's health will start to fly. We don't want that."

"Francesco, calling the Sacred College together on such short notice during Holy Week will start the rumors flying in any case. It's unavoidable."

"Not necessarily." Barbo replied. "Our Middle East nuncios are in Rome for consultations over the crisis in the Church of the Holy Sepulchre. No one will be suspicious if the pope calls a meeting. It will look like it has something to do with the Middle East."

As the full significance of what was happening dawned on Marini, his face tensed. "After the meeting of the Sacred College, I will make the formal announcement on Vatican Radio."

As Marini was about to leave, he turned to Barbo. "Francesco, I have worked here in the Vatican for just over fifty years. For me, the Vatican is not only the home of the Church; it is my own home. In a very real sense, the pope is not only my priest and bishop; he is also my employer and landlord."

"The pope as landlord!" Barbo smiled. "I've never thought of it like that before."

Marino pointed in the direction of St. Peter's. "Pope Bendict knows the name of every Swiss Guard, every secretary and postal worker on the Vatican staff. I once caught him debating with a gardener over how best to prune rose bushes."

"Benedict cares deeply for people, Agostino." Barbo held back for a moment. "He used to tell me, 'God is in all of us. Whether I talk to a king or to a grocer, I am talking to God. That is the meaning of Mystical Body.'"

"Yes, a person's humanity is what makes one godlike. I will cast my vote in the conclave for the person who will make the best landlord. He will also make the best pope."

A red leather binder lay open on the gilded table in the pope's bedroom. Cardinal Marini scanned the documents one last time. "Francesco, I think we should begin."

Barbo nodded. Sister Consuela helped Benedict to the table and sat him comfortably in his chair. The pope was dressed in his white cassock and zucchetto. Sister Consuela had draped over his shoulders the wool pallium, symbolizing his universal authority in the Catholic Church.

Cardinal Marini touched the pontiff on the shoulder. "Your Holiness, these documents in front of you state that by your own volition, you are abdicating the Throne of Saint Peter—that henceforth you will no longer be the Vicar of Jesus Christ, the Supreme Pontiff of the Roman Catholic Church, the Primate of Italy, or the Bishop of Rome. Do you understand the step you are about to take?"

Benedict smiled at the camerlengo. "You forgot my most important title, Agostino—Servant of the Servants of God."

The pontiff picked up a gold pen that Cardinal Marini had lain next to the red leather binder. Sister Consuela looked away. This was the moment she had dreaded.

"Consuela, please don't be upset. This must be done for the good of the Church." Sister Consuela sobbed aloud. The Holy Father had never called her simply "Consuela" in all the years she had worked for him.

The pope slowly traced his name at the bottom of the abdication document. "I do this of my own free will and volition."

Cardinal Barbo witnessed Benedict's signature as required by canon law.

Benedict struggled out of his chair and kneeled before Barbo. "Francesco, I ask for your blessing."

Struggling to hold back his tears, the secretary of state blessed his old friend.

"Thank you, Francesco. I'm tired. Sister, sit me up in bed so I can read my breviary."

As cardinals Marini and Barbo prepared to leave the room, the pope fumbled for something in the pocket of his cassock.

"Sister Consuela, give this to Cardinal Marini."

It was the Ring of the Fisherman.

At 10:30 in the morning, approximately forty members of the Sacred College of Cardinals gathered in the conference room of the

Apostolic Palace. As Barbo had expected, the reason for the meeting was assumed to be the Middle East. Several cardinals had even phoned the secretary of state the night before to ask whether there had been new incidents in the area. Even the Italian media gave the meeting only cursory attention. Rome's morning newspaper, *Il Messaggero,* for example, made no mention of the meeting but did run a small story on how Archbishop Finnergan's conduct had compromised the Vatican's perceived neutrality.

A murmur passed through the assembly when cardinals Marini and Barbo entered the room. The pope was not with them. Since his election, Benedict had made it a point to attend all meetings of the Sacred College. If anything, however, it was Cardinal Marini's appearance that unnerved many in the room. Despite his customary aversion to ecclesiastical dress, the camerlengo wore his scarlet zucchetto and sash.

Marini walked slowly to the podium and leaned on it as if to steady himself. "I have sad news, my Brothers in Christ. At 8:30 this morning, the Holy Father signed formal documents of abdication. An announcement of his abdication will be made over Vatican Radio at noon.

The room sat in stunned silence. His face ashen, Cardinal Vaggio, the Archbishop of Florence, finally struggled to his feet. "Marini, what happened to the Holy Father? Why did he do this?"

Barbo stepped to the podium. "I should answer that, Agostino. The pope has developed Alzheimer's disease. He began to show the first signs a year ago. Doctor Roger Hendricks from the Mayo Clinic, a pioneer in Alzheimer's research, came to Rome to treat the Holy Father. Unfortunately His Holiness did not respond to medication. Inexplicably the pope's condition has worsened dramatically in the past few weeks. Doctor Hendricks and the other specialists he consulted believe His Holiness is no longer competent to govern the Church. The Holy Father himself made the decision to abdicate."

"Francesco, there must be new treatments." Cardinal Viaggio's voice still echoed with disbelief.

"There are but the pope does not respond to them. I have asked Doctor Hendricks to address this meeting at noon. He will answer any medical questions you may have with respect to the Holy Father's condition."

"How can a pope abdicate?" Cardinal Cornelius Reysin, Archbishop of Houston, Texas, jumped angrily to his feet. "This is absurd! An abdication cannot divest the pope of his spiritual authority. There is no term of office for a pope. He can neither be voted out of office nor resign from office. Benedict's abdication is invalid as a matter of ecclesiastical law. In my view, Benedict is still the Holy Father."

Although Barbo was reluctant to be drawn into a prolonged debate with a cardinal best known for his harmonica playing, his temper, and his long-windedness, he felt he had to respond.

"A pope does have a term, Cardinal Reysin. The term, however, is indeterminate—it lasts only as long as the pope can function in the office. Pope Benedict realized that he could no longer perform his responsibilities. He made the courageous decision to abdicate."

Cardinal Calvaux asked to be recognized. "Cardinal Reysin, the secretary of state is correct in his reading of canon law. There have been papal abdications in the past. This is not the time to challenge Pope Benedict's decision. Instead we must rally in support of the camerlengo."

Reysin glared at Calvaux. "Your fancy French theologians are wrong, Calvaux. I do not accept the legitimacy of what has been done." Reysin angrily left the room.

Cardinal Agostino took the podium.

"His Eminence Cardinal Reysin can express his views as forcefully as he wishes. He may be able to walk out of this meeting, but I do not have that freedom. The Church must endure. There are no procedures to guide us when a pope abdicates. Unless Your Eminences object, I plan to follow the procedures applied when a pope dies—with whatever modifications may be required.

Cardinal Muñoz, the Archbishop of Quito, Ecuador, slowly lifted his heavy frame from his chair. As a prominent member of the conservative wing of the Sacred College, Muñoz was a respected and powerful figure in the Church. Barbo knew that, if Muñoz were to attack the legality of the abdication, it would create a serious fissure in the Church.

"I think I speak for all of us, Agostino. Do what you must. We sail on uncharted waters." There was a murmur of assent from the cardinals in the room.

"Thank you, Cardinal Muñoz."

Marini looked at his watch. "Before I leave to make the announcement on Vatican Radio, there is one matter of business that must be attended to. When there is a *Sede Vacante,* the rules require all cardinals in Rome to meet in General Congregation on a daily basis. The first session of the General Congregation has been scheduled at nine o'clock tomorrow morning in the Apostolic Palace. I need not remind Your Eminences of how important these meetings are. They are an integral part of the process of electing a pope."

Everyone in the room knew what Marini meant. The meetings provided an opportunity for the cardinals to begin assessing the strengths and weaknesses of potential candidates to succeed Pope Benedict. Vatican experts often quipped that, during the meetings of the General Congregation, more work was done around the coffee bar than inside the meeting room.

Cardinal Muñoz asked the question on everyone's mind. "When will the conclave begin, My Lord Camerlengo?"

"Given the extraordinary circumstances of Benedict's abdication, I have decided to convene the conclave in twenty days—the maximum time permitted by canon law."

Cardinals Marini and Barbo arrived unannounced at the offices of the Vatican Radio at 11:45 A.M. The visit of the two cardinals produced a flurry of activity. Espresso and dolci materialized from nowhere. The director of the radio station, a young Canadian Jesuit named John Peters, sprinted out of his office to greet his distinguished guests.

"Your Eminences, if I had known you were coming."

"Father Peters, we must speak to you about a matter of great importance."

"Of course, come with me." Peters escorted the two prelates down the hallway to his office and closed the door.

Cardinal Marini spoke first. "Pope Benedict abdicated at eight-thirty this morning. Vatican Radio's scheduled broadcasting will have to be interrupted. I will make the formal announcement."

For a moment, Father Peters stood stock still, as if he did not understand what Cardinal Marini had just told him. Then his training as a reporter clicked in. "The 'Angelus' is broadcast at noon. After that, there's fifteen minutes of international news. We will cut into the broadcast before we start the news. Cardinal Marini, do you wish the announcement televised?"

Marini looked at Barbo. Shaking his head Barbo answered the question. "No. Pope Benedict would not want that."

Cardinal Marini sat in front of the microphone waiting for the signal to begin speaking.

At the conclusion of the "Angelus," Father Peters interrupted the radio broadcast. "Cardinal Agostino Marini—the camerlengo of the Church—has an important announcement regarding the Holy Father, Pope Benedict."

"At eight-thirty this morning, His Holiness Pope Benedict XVI abdicated his position as Supreme Pontiff of the Holy Roman Catholic Church. His abdication was the result of advanced Alzheimer's disease. Pope Benedict made the decision to abdicate after his doctors informed him that they could not slow his deteriorating condition. Pope Benedict's eighteen-year pontificate was a blessing not only to his Church but also to the world as a whole. As camerlengo, I have the responsibility of overseeing the affairs of the Church during this interregnum period and for organizing the conclave to choose his successor. Tomorrow morning that process will begin. May God bless Pope Benedict and the Catholic Church."

When the announcement was made, those in the broadcast studio seemed unable to move. A young woman slowly began to cry. Fighting back her tears, she spoke to Cardinal Agostino.

"Could you lead us in prayer, Your Eminence? The Holy Father spoke to me once. He was walking up the center aisle in St. Peter's. When he recognized that I worked in the Vatican, he stopped and asked after my family. He is a kind and holy man." Marini took the woman's hand and recited the Lord's Prayer.

The buttons on Father Alessandri's phone were flashing wildly as Barbo entered his office.

"Eminence, it's been this way since noon, when Marini made the announcement. Even the White House called."

Barbo's cell phone rang. It was the Italian Prime Minister calling from Turin.

"Francesco, I apologize for calling you on your private number but all lines into the secretariat are tied up. My secretary has tried to get through for two hours and all she gets is a busy signal." Barbo could hear the Italian Prime Minister was struggling with his emotions.

"All our embassies are calling for instructions."

"I had no idea this was happening to the Holy Father. How can I help him?"

"The pope needs a few days of bed rest. Tonight he will be taken to Castel Gondolfo."

The prime minister saw a way to help. "I will send an ambulance to take him."

"Thank you for your generosity, but I think the Holy Father would be more comfortable in a Vatican car, Mr. Prime Minister."

"Let me at least send a police escort."

"That would be helpful." Barbo knew that it would be impolitic to refuse all assistance from the Italian government.

"And what of the conclave, Cardinal Barbo? I have heard your name mentioned as a possible successor to Pope Benedict."

"Vatican watchers always make the secretary of state a candidate—Rampolla, Gasparri, Pacelli. It happens by dint of office, whether the person is qualified or not."

The prime minister laughed. "But Pacelli became Pius XII."

"Pacelli was a man blessed with innumerable talents. Rest assured, Mr. Prime Minister, the Holy Spirit will not land on me."

A black Mercedes waited at the rear entrance to the Apostolic Palace. Two unmarked police cars stood idling nearby. When Pope Benedict emerged from the doorway, a police lieutenant knelt and kissed the Holy Father on the hands.

"The Ring of the Fisherman is gone, Lieutenant."

"Holy Father, in my eyes, you will always be God's Vicar here on earth."

Cardinal Barbo walked around the car to where the officer stood. "Lieutenant, please—Pope Benedict is tired."

"I'm sorry. The Holy Father has been my bishop for so long."

"I understand, but it's getting late. We've got to go."

Barbo motioned the driver and Sister Consuela to get into the front seats of the Mercedes. He sat next to Benedict in the back. Barbo pushed open the sliding glass panel separating the front and back seats of the car.

"It's time to start, Marco."

"Yes, Your Eminence."

One of the police cars led the way out through the Vatican gate. The second police car followed behind the Mercedes. As the cars crossed the Tiber and headed north out of the city, Cardinal Barbo heard the sound of a helicopter. He smiled to himself. The prime minister must be making sure Pope Benedict leaves Rome safely.

As the pope's car reached the turnoff for the autostrada, Barbo looked at his watch. It was already 9:00 P.M.

"Marco, take the autostrada. At this time of night we should reach Castel Gondolfo in less than two hours."

As Barbo sat back in his seat, he heard a soft voice next to him.

"Yes, Francesco, at this time, the autostrada is best."

"Your Holiness, I didn't know you were awake."

"Although it was for the good of the Church, my abdication creates problems for my successor."

"What problems, Your Holiness?"

"You saw the police officer in Rome. In his eyes, I will always be the Vicar of Christ."

"Don't worry about this."

"But I do. Wherever I go to live, there will be tourists and curiosity seekers who'll want my blessing or want to receive the Eucharist from my hands. I won't let that happen."

"The curiosity will be over in a few months."

The pope leaned his head back on his seat and closed his eyes. Barbo could see that the conversation had tired him.

"Francesco, I know where I want to live out the rest of my life."

"Where, Holy Father?"

The pope closed his eyes.

"Not yet, Francesco."

Chapter XIX

THE GENERAL CONGREGATION

Bishop Pellent skimmed through the diary and marked several entries with bookmarks. He rang for his secretary.

"Send this to Cardinal Barbo in Rome by air courier."

"Your Eminences, please be seated." The camerlengo rapped his gavel on the podium. "We have much to do." Cardinal Reysin sat glumly in the back of the conference room, his anger cooled but not eliminated by a night's sleep.

The camerlengo took Pope Benedict's ring, the symbol of papal authority, and scratched it with a sharp metal tool. He did the same with Benedict's lead seal. When both the ring and the seal had been defaced, he threw them into a brazier of hot coals. The camerlengo would usually perform this ritual defacement with only a select number of cardinals in attendance. Given the circumstances, however, Marini decided to carry out the ritual in full view of the General Congregation. The camerlengo hoped the defacement would bring closure to the cardinals who were still stunned by Benedict's abdication.

Two ceremonial matters still remained to be done. The camerlengo formally requested Cardinal Bargarian, the Dean of the Sacred College, to send copies of the abdication documents to the members of the diplomatic corps accredited to the Holy See and to all heads of state. Marini then asked Cardinal Desion, as prefect for bishops, to notify the other members of the Sacred College in dioceses throughout the world to come to the Vatican for the upcoming conclave.

Once these ceremonial matters had been concluded, Cardinal Marini called for a discussion of the first issue on the agenda—the use of technology in the conclave. Cardinal Reysin was the first to be recognized on the issue.

"Many in this room head archdioceses. During the conclave, matters may arise that our auxiliary bishops cannot handle. If there's an emergency, there should be a way for them to contact us. A cell phone or a laptop is the most efficient method of communication. I ask that the restriction on bringing them into the conclave be lifted."

Barbo knew what was driving Cardinal Reysin's request. It was not solicitude for his auxiliary bishops but fear for himself. In recent weeks, rumors had circulated that Reysin might be indicted for destroying documents in several ongoing criminal investigations dealing with clerical pedophilia. There were also rumors that large financial settlements might force his archdiocese of Houston to consider filing for bankruptcy. A cell phone or a laptop would allow Reysin to monitor developments.

When Cardinal Reysin sat down, the Primate of Mexico, Cardinal Miguel Chavez, rose from his seat. Although a member of Opus Dei and an archconservative politically and theologically, the congenial Chavez was a popular and influential figure in the Church hierarchy. He had been educated in Rome and had filled several curial posts before being chosen Archbishop of Mexico City and Primate of Mexico.

"His Eminence Cardinal Reysin was not present at the last conclave. If he had been, he might be less enthusiastic about technology. When that conclave was over, the Swiss Guards found listening devices hidden in almost every room and chapel in the conclave area. They even discovered a small device in one of the candlesticks in the Sistine Chapel. Luckily, it had malfunctioned. It seems the Russians wanted detailed information about each step of the process. The camerlengo has assured me that Vatican security will sweep the conclave rooms twice a day. But this will only uncover listening devices hidden inside the conclave. If we bring computers or cell phones into the conclave and send messages to our offices or staff, they can be listened to by monitors set up outside the conclave. The Swiss Guards cannot discover them so easily."

When Chavez had finished, Cardinal Vaggio, the Archbishop of Florence, asked to be recognized. "Cardinal Reysin comes from a rich and powerful country. I can understand his fascination with technology. Who would deny its usefulness? But there are limits. We turn off our cell phones during dinner with our family and friends. Why? Because dinner is a time to reflect and listen to others. It is the same with a conclave. It is a time to put aside the distractions of daily life and listen to one another and to the Holy Spirit. An old nun from Sicily once told me 'Eminence, the Holy Spirit doesn't fly in a thunderstorm.' What a wise woman! Given this, no elector except Cardinal Lawrence, the Major Penitentiary of the Church, should be permitted to communicate with anyone outside the conclave. We make an exception for the Major Penitentiary because he oversees papal dispensations. God's mercy cannot be interrupted even for a conclave. Who else among us could claim such a privilege?"

"I agree with Vaggio," Cardinal Muñoz spoke from his seat. "Let me remind my brothers that the Latin roots of the word *conclave* are *'cum'* and *'clavus.'* Together, the words mean 'with a key.' We are locked into the area of the conclave so that we are cut off from the noise of the outside world."

Cardinal Reysin bridled with anger. The crusty old archbishop had once grumbled that he knew only five words of Latin and was proud of it. He could not help but think that Muñoz was patronizing him by explaining the Latin derivation of the word conclave.

Muñoz continued. "But, Cardinal Reysin, I have more fundamental objections than Latin roots for prohibiting cell phones and laptops in the conclave. They are a near occasion of sin. The less noble-minded among us might begin using email to campaign for support. More troublesome still would be the temptation to use a cell phone to leak the name of the new pope before the formal announcement in St. Peter's Square. The best defense against temptation is to remove its source."

A hush fell over the room as Cardinal Diefenbacher rose to speak. Cardinal Cabrillo from Manila unobtrusively turned up the volume on his hearing aid.

"These are extraordinary times, my brothers. Pope Benedict's abdication has left a great void in the Church. He was truly a man chosen by the Holy Spirit. Today we begin the search for his successor. As at the time of the Reformation, our Church faces grave problems—problems that, without exaggeration, threaten its very survival as an institution. Many Catholics challenge the teaching authority of Rome. Others say that the structure of the Church has become fossilized and that national episcopal conferences and local bishops must have more say. The celibacy of the priesthood and the place of women in the Church are divisive issues in some areas of the world. When I began my remarks, I addressed this assembly with the words 'My brothers'—someday a future cardinal will stand here where I do and open with 'My Brothers and Sisters.' This is not an opinion; it is a fact.

"The Sacred College has the responsibility to save the Church. Two thousand years ago, the Romans mastered the art of knowing when to be rigid and when to be flexible. With that skill they built the greatest empire then known to man. So as not to forget the need for balance, the Romans put a statue of the god Janus in their holiest Temple. Janus has two faces—one looks to the rising sun of challenge and opportunity, and the other is turned to the evening sun of tradition and experience.

"Cardinal Reysin's laptop is not the real issue here. What is at issue here is medievalism versus modernity. When we sit in the Sistine Chapel to ballot for Benedict's successor, look up to Michelangelo's magnificent frescoes. Unless they had been restored with the best of modern science, they would have long since fallen into decay. We must embrace tradition but be willing to change it when necessary. If not, the Church will become an institution frozen in time. Even if one of us deliberately emailed the name of the new pope to the Associated Press before Cardinal Marini announced it in St. Peter's Square, would that be so terrible? Would it dim the excitement of seeing the new pope impart his first blessing? No! Would it dim the feeling of pride and unity that will sweep through the square when the new pope appears? No! We hold too tightly to medievalism."

The vote in the General Congregation was close, but a three-vote majority banned all forms of electronic and computer communication equipment from the conclave.

As the cardinals left the General Congregation, Barbo walked over to where Reysin was seated, still angry over being outvoted by his colleagues.

Barbo sat down next to him. "Cardinal Vaggio was sending you a message."

"What message?" Reysin was not in the mood for conversation, even with the secretary of state.

"Talk to the Major Penitentiary. Cardinal Lawrence's job is to allow exceptions to rules."

"Why didn't Vaggio come out and say it?"

"That's not the way here in Rome. Footnotes and cross-references are more important than text. You Americans are more direct."

Reysin look relieved. "Thank you, Francesco. I will speak with Cardinal Lawrence."

Father Alessandri handed a package to Barbo. "Your Eminence, this just arrived from Avignon. Bishop Pellent sent it by air courier."

"Hold my calls unless it is from Sister Consuela."

When Barbo opened the package, he saw it contained an ancient diary. A one-line note from Pellent accompanied the book. "Your Eminence, I think you will find this a disturbing tale."

Barbo opened the diary to its first page.

Chapter XX

THE DEATH OF A POPE

On this nineteenth day of March in the year of Our Lord 1314, I, Ricard de Treden, Abbot of the Cistercian Monastery of Valmagne, have decided to reduce my private thoughts to writing. I must begin with the events of yesterday in Paris.

"Jacques de Molay, Grand Master of the Order of the Temple, I condemn you to death as a heretic and as a blasphemer. In the name of Jesus Christ and His Holy Church, repent of your sins. If you do, I can save you from the stake."

De Molay spat at his executioner. "You will never find what you seek."

"It is finished then. May God have mercy on your soul."

Cardinal Pierre de Saone, camerlengo of the Church, stood on the small Ile des Javaux in the middle of the River Seine. Thousands of Parisians milled sullenly along both banks of the river to witness the death of the grand master. De Saone signaled an inquisitor to light the pyre. The flames and smoke quickly engulfed de Molay's body. Then for a moment the wind blew the smoke away. The grand master, his skin blistered and scorched by the heat, glared defiantly at the cardinal.

"I curse you, de Saone—and with you King Philip and Pope Clement. Before the year is out, God's holy angels will bring you three before His Judgment seat to answer for what you have done to the Church and to the Knights of the Temple."

The cardinal nervously lifted his pectoral cross as if to shield himself against de Molay's words and the angry stares of the crowds. The smoke blew back over de Molay's face. The sound of the fire drowned out his words. Then out of the smoke came one final terrible cry of pain. "De Saone, remember we will meet again before the year is out!"

As the ashes of the grand master were being gathered for burial, the crowds that had remained silent during the execution now became unruly. Bystanders hurled rocks and clumps of manure at Cardinal de Saone. French soldiers had to hurry the cardinal into Notre Dame Cathedral to avoid injury.

On the night of April 20, 1314, the people of Avignon stood vigil for the pope. There were rumors that Clement was near death and would not last until morning. As the night wore on, women left marzipan candies in front of the Palais where the pope lay dying. According to ancient folklore, the marzipan candies, *gateaux de Saint-Pierre,* would bribe St. Peter to open the gates of heaven.

A cold wind blew down from the north, forcing the boats along the Rhône to be doubly secured. Near St. Bénézet Bridge, a large crowd of merchants and tradesmen huddled around fires to keep warm. An old woman, bent from years of carrying water kettles on her back, moved slowly through the crowd selling hot tea. "We should all light candles. They will help guide the angels to find Clement's soul and bring it to heaven."

An old blacksmith, his hands bruised by years of heavy work, angrily pointed a bony finger at the woman. "I will light no candle for Clement. The pope allowed the Templars to be tortured and killed as heretics. For thirty years I worked for the order at their commanderie across St. Benezet Bridge in Villenueve. They were not heretics but good and god-fearing men."

"And don't forget, my friends, the Templars were good for business." The speaker was a heavy-set merchant who lived in the center of Avignon near the Palais. Well dressed in a fur-trimmed jacket and velvet hat, he exuded the brash swagger of the recently established mercantile guilds in Avignon. "Some days as I walked along the harbor, I used to count the boats flying a Templar standard. I could easily count six or seven."

"Son of Satan." The old woman hissed at the merchant. "Clement is the pope, our Holy Father—the successor of St. Peter. The Templars were heretics and the world is well rid of them."

Smirking with contempt, the merchant pulled out a scented handkerchief and waived it theatrically in front of his face. "Toll your beads, old crone. You will not pollute the air of Avignon much longer."

A tanner broke into the conversation. "You are wrong, merchant. The pope, not the Templars, brought prosperity to Avignon. Since Clement came, our docks are filled with goods from all over Europe—wool from Flanders, leather from Florence, spices from Damascus. Yesterday I even found a small piece of lapis from Persia for my wife. It was not always this way. I will light a candle for Pope Clement."

"I was a confrater of the Order of the Temple." A tall gaunt man pushed his way to the center of the crowd. "I took a vow to help the Templars in whatever way I could. God has given me the ability to paint. Every month I donated part of my income to the order. The Templars fought to defend the Church. Their reward is to be tortured as heretics. I hope Jesus casts Clement into hellfire for what he did to them."

A student from the university tried to turn the conversation away from the Templars. "It is rumored that King Philip bought enough cardinals' votes to make Clement pope."

"There is no truth to such a rumor!" the local curé angrily interrupted the student.

The mention of money and bribery lured the merchant back into the conversation. "Your parish must lie deep in the forest, priest. Not only did Philip buy votes in the last election; he is prepared to do so again. Of that I am sure."

The curé ignored the merchant's taunt. "De Molay is dead only a month and he already comes for Clement's soul. Maybe the Templar is in the Palais already."

The student looked puzzled. "If the pope is dead, why have the bells not tolled?"

"The cardinals await the arrival of King Philip. Nothing will happen until then." The merchant's response had a gleeful tone to it.

"People say that many cardinals are angered by what Clement and Philip did to the Templars. The Italians want the papacy returned to Rome."

"To Rome?" The merchant roared with laughter. "Philip would disembowel every cardinal before he would allow that. Philip wants the papacy to remain here in Avignon. No one in Europe would dare stand up against him."

The tanner looked thoughtful. "I hope you are right, merchant. If the new pope decides to return to Rome, where will that leave us?"

The old woman spat on the ground. "Business and money. That is all you people think of. What about God and his Church?"

A passerby overheard what she said. "This woman is right. Christians must pray that God will guide the Church through these days."

"But only until the next French pope is elected. Then King Philip will again guide the Church." The merchant laughed as he walked away from the crowd toward the city square.

The old woman picked up a rotted apple core and threw it after him. "I hope you burn in hell."

When it became clear that Pope Clement was near death, the members of the Sacred College began a vigil. Two cardinals remained in his bedchamber at all times. As the hours passed, Clement became more and more agitated. At about eleven o'clock that evening, he began to cough up dark blood. When the pope's physician saw the color of the discharge, he motioned to Cardinals Paolo Nitolli, the Archbishop of Padua, and François Taserant, the Archbishop of Lyons, to meet him outside the pope's chamber.

"My Lords, the pope will not last the night."

Taserant looked at Nitolli. "We must tell the camerlengo."

The two men hurried to Cardinal de Saone's quarters in the Palais. As camerlengo, de Saone would perform the sacred rituals that the Church requires when the Vicar of Christ dies.

Nitolli knocked on the heavy oak door to Cardinal de Saone's apartment. Père Beneton, the camerlengo's secretary, opened a small hatch to see who the visitor was.

"It is Cardinals Nitolli and Taserant. We must see the camerlengo at once."

Beneton opened the door and bowed to the cardinals. "The camerlengo is in his chapel. He asked not to be disturbed."

"Tell the camerlengo the time has come."

In a few moments, Cardinal de Saone walked slowly across the room to greet his fellow cardinals. "Is Clement near death?"

"Yes, de Saone, Cardinal Nitolli and I just came from his bedchamber. You must hear his confession and anoint him with chrism."

"Give me a moment." De Saone retreated into his chapel and returned with a gold container of holy oils.

As the three prelates walked to the door of de Saone's apartment, Cardinal Taserant stopped for a moment and spoke to the camerlengo. "Be prepared for one thing, de Saone. Clement is having hallucinations. One minute he sees de Molay's ghost, the next minute he starts shouting that de Molay's death was all your doing. Then his mood changes and he begs you to come and absolve him of his sins. Through all of this he keeps asking about a Templar manuscript. It has something to do with Jesus and the Magdalene. I do not understand him."

"Taserant, de Molay cursed Clement for suppressing the Templars. He called him to God's judgment seat before the year was out."

"You heard the curse, de Saone?"

"Yes, Taserant, I was there when de Molay made it. At first I was afraid to tell Clement what had happened but I could not lie to the Vicar of Christ."

"What did Clement do when you told him?" Taserant's curiosity was palpable.

"At first, nothing. He just stared vacantly at me. Then his body began to tremble as if he had been struck with the palsy. He grabbed my arm and begged forgiveness for what he had done to de Molay and the Templars. Nightmares have haunted him since that day."

Nittoli interrupted. "Is it true that de Molay cursed both Philip and Clement?"

"Yes, Nitolli, and the camerlengo of the Church as well."

"You, too?"

"Yes."

Nittoli stopped for a moment before he continued speaking. "Many in the Sacred College are angry that Clement agreed to suppress the Templars. He succumbed to King Philip's power. The king of France holds the papacy captive here in Avignon."

Taserant's eyes flashed angrily. "Where does this lead us, Nitolli?"

"Do not patronize me, Taserant. Several of your French colleagues have already met and pledged you their votes in the next conclave. You even sent emissaries to speak with King Philip about your papal ambitions."

Taserant smiled at the Italian cardinal. "Philip will insist on a French pope."

"Taserant is right, Nittoli. Philip will want another Clement."

Contemptuously turning his back on Cardinal Taserant, Nittoli addressed de Saone. "Some of us in the Sacred College may try to hold a separate conclave in Rome." The Archbishop of Padua knew that the camerlengo, although a Frenchman, was no friend of Philip. De Saone could be a key ally if any attempt were made to move the next papal election to Rome.

"Nitolli, think hard before doing that." De Saone's words were blunt. "Philip is the most powerful monarch in Europe."

"But we have enough votes to block Philip and with your help. . . ."

"I am no friend of the king, Nittoli. But I will not support your schemes. As I have grown older, I have become less courageous."

"A prudent answer, My Lord Camerlengo." Cardinal Taserant opened the door to Clement's chamber and went inside.

Nittoli held the camerlengo back. "De Saone, reconsider. We have enough votes to. . . ."

The camerlengo smiled and handed Nittoli a gold sovereign. "You have enough votes until your Italian colleagues feel the weight of Philip's purse."

De Saone followed Cardinal Taserant into Clement's bedchamber.

Pope Clement was pointing his finger to the entrance of his bedchamber. "He will be here soon. Bolt the door. I must hide." Squirming, Clement sought to break free of his restraints. He grew increasingly agitated as two servants tried to keep him in bed. "Please help me. The Templar comes for my soul."

The pope's physician put cold compresses under Clement's arms to bring down his fever. When he felt the cold, Clement angrily pulled the compresses off and struggled again to get out of bed. He thrashed about, kicking his physician in the mouth.

When he saw the camerlengo enter the room, the pope cringed with fear. "You did this, de Saone. You wanted the parchment." De Saone could see the look of terror in the pope's eyes.

"Clement, I came to absolve you of your sins."

"Absolve me of my sins? Yes, of course. I must have absolution before I face God. I have seen Jesus pointing me. . . ."

"Pointing you where?"

"To the fires—Jesus was pointing me to the fires of hell."

"Why, Your Holiness?"

"For the slaughter of the Templars, de Saone. They were good men."

"Holiness, you must rest. These are only wild dreams. No matter how you have sinned, God will forgive you."

"No, He will not forgive me. There has been too much blood—too many have died. But, de Saone, you were there—you know what happened. What could we do?"

The pope began to whimper like a child. "De Saone, please my sins—you must forgive my sins." Clement's voice was hollow and distant.

The pope started to cough uncontrollably. A physician rushed to apply leeches to Clement's right arm.

"Your Holiness, you must let me. . . ."

"Out of here, physician! Christ shed His blood on the cross — mine is fed to leeches."

The physician tried to calm Clement. "Your Holiness, the treatment. . . ."

"Go, I say or you will meet the devil before I do."

Clement grasped de Saone's arm and pulled himself up to a sitting position. He kept looking at the door across the room. "De Molay, Jacques de Molay, where are you? Will you not come to claim your victory?"

The pope coughed violently. Blood stained his bed sheets. As he gasped for breath, Clement pointed again to the door. "They are here. De Molay and his Templars are here. Do you see them, de Saone? There by the door! De Molay taunts me with the parchment."

Wild-eyed, the pope tried frantically to get out of his bed. "He comes for me! The Templar comes for me. We must take the parchment away from him. We must save the Church. Help me!"

"Holiness, you must get some rest."

"The way is dark."

Clement reached for a cross that lay on a table next to his bed. He touched it and slumped back on his pillows. The cardinal could see that the pope was dead. De Saone gently loosened Clement's grip on his arm. The camerlengo raised his right hand and made the sign of the cross over Clement's body. The pope had not confessed his sins to the camerlengo.

Barbo looked up from the diary. The abbot's entry linked Pope Clement's death to the persecution of the Templars — something that Barbo had always suspected but could never prove. The cardinal poured a glass of water and telephoned Castel Gondolfo to speak with Sister Consuela. Barbo knew how difficult these days must be for Pope Benedict. After checking on his friend's condition, he picked up the abbot's diary and continued reading.

Cardinal de Saone knew what must be done. As camerlengo, it was his responsibility to confirm the death of the pope. The rituals that must be followed were ancient. After Clement's body had been washed and wrapped in a white shroud, de Saone took a small silver mallet out of a velvet pouch. He walked to Clement's bedside, and as those in the room watched, the cardinal tapped Clement's forehead.

"Bertrand de Got, arise."

When an individual is elevated to the papacy, tradition requires that he choose a new name that will mark his Pontificate. When Bertrand de Got, Archbishop of Bordeaux, was chosen pope, he took the name Clement. Papal ritual required that the camerlengo now address the pope by his family name and not by his papal name. In God's eyes, it was Bertrand who had died, not Clement. The papacy lives forever and the gates of hell will not prevail against it.

De Saone tapped Clement's forehead a second time. "Arise, Bertrand."

He stood for a moment and then tapped Clement's forehead for the third and last time. "Bertrand de Got, arise from your bed."

When there was no response, the camerlengo intoned the ritual words: *"Bertrandus mortuus est."* Once the camerlengo had spoken these words, the Church officially came to a halt. Until a new pope was elected, the Church was without a successor to Peter.

One more task still awaited the camerlengo. De Saone removed the papal ring from Clement's finger and placed it and the pope's seal in a brazier of hot coals. As several members of the Sacred College watched, the heat from the coals gradually melted the ring and seal into a liquid paste. With the symbols of papal authority destroyed, the sacred rituals were concluded.

The camerlengo walked to the chapel next to the pope's bedchamber and pulled a bell rope to begin tolling the death knell for Clement. The mournful cadence grew louder as more and more bells joined in the tolling. The sound reverberated through the streets of Avignon, then across the Rhone until it became lost in the hills beyond Villenueve.

The merchant, warm in his house near the Palais des Papes, was awakened by the bells of the cathedral. Annoyed, he rolled over and went back to sleep.

When they heard the bells begin to toll, those still gathered near St. Bénézet Bridge grew silent. The old woman dropped to her knees and made the sign of the cross.

Kicking a stone along the street, the blacksmith walked away, smiling. "The Templars have been avenged. Clement has come before the judgment seat of God. King Philip and Cardinal de Saone will be next."

As the camerlengo walked back to his apartment, he was frightened. A strong wind blew along the cloisters causing his cape to billow behind him like the sail of a ship. It was as if the wind and the sail were pushing him back into the past—to that morning on the Ile des Javaux in Paris when de Molay was burned at the stake. How could he ever forget the horror of that day—de Molay's defiance as the flames engulfed him, the smell of burning flesh, the cries of agony. But it was de Molay's curse that most terrified de Saone. As de Molay had predicted, Clement had come before God's judgment seat within the year. Would de Molay soon come for de Saone as well?

The camerlengo heard footsteps behind him. He looked over his shoulder but no one was there. The footsteps came again—this time they sounded closer. The cardinal became frightened. "Is it you, de Molay? Show yourself." As if in response, the wind blew stronger. De Saone was sure that he could hear de Molay whisper to him. "I am coming soon for your soul." Haunted by the sounds of the wind, the old cardinal hurried faster down the corridor.

The sound of hooves awakened the mayor of Auclaire. It was unusual to hear horses so late at night. Lighting an oil lamp, he hastily threw a mantle over his shoulders and ran out to the street. The mayor could see a large contingent of horsemen—perhaps forty in number—riding into the town at a gallop. A carriage pulled by four white horses followed them. The mayor could make out a gold fleur-de-lis painted on the carriage door. With such an escort, the mayor knew that someone either very important or very wealthy must be in the carriage. Perhaps it could be the new governor of the province. As he hurried toward the carriage, one of the horsemen dismounted and blocked his way.

"No farther, old man."

"I am the mayor of Auclaire. I come to greet our visitor."

"I do not care if you are St. Michael himself. Stay back."

Suddenly the carriage door opened and a man stepped out.

"On your knees, old man. You are in the presence of the king of France."

The soldier pushed the mayor of Auclaire to the ground. Philip looked contemptuously at the figure cowering in front of him. "Is this peasant the messenger from Avignon? He reeks with garlic."

"No, Sire. He says he is the mayor of the village."

"The mayor? My subjects deserve better than this. Throw him into the Rhône for a cleaning."

Just then a lone horseman rode into Auclaire from the direction of Avignon. The rider jumped from his horse and knelt before the king.

Philip pulled the messenger to his feet. "Is he dead? Tell me, is Clement dead?"

"Yes, Your Majesty. The bells announce that Christ has come for the pope's soul."

"'That Christ has come for the pope's soul?'" Philip laughed. "If anyone came for his soul, it would have been the devil—or maybe Jacques de Molay. He threatened Clement and me that we would soon stand before the judgment seat of God." Philip smiled. "I put Clement on the papal throne because he possessed the qualities I most admire in a pope—weakness and indecision. Clement has not disappointed me on either score."

Philip turned to the messenger. "Ride back to the city—have the Papal Palace surrounded. No one is to enter or leave—especially my lord cardinals."

"And the roads in and out of Avignon, do you wish them guarded as well, Majesty?"

"Yes, and the river, too. Some cardinals may try to escape by boat to Rome."

"No one will leave, Sire."

"Bring the camerlengo, Cardinal de Saone, here so we may organize a conclave to elect another French pope."

As the messenger rode back toward Avignon, Philip beckoned to the captain of his escort. "Is there lodging nearby? I will stay out of Avignon until Clement's successor is chosen. Appearances must be preserved."

"There is a Templar commanderie half a league from Auclaire, Majesty. Several Templars are imprisoned there."

"Templars! They will provide interesting company while I wait for the next French pope to be elected."

King Philip walked down the wet stairwell to the dungeon under the commanderie. Seven Templars were shackled to the wall of the damp cell. When they saw the king, one prisoner spat on the ground. "Why does the devil come to see us?"

"Speak more politely to the king of France, Templar heretic. I assume your accommodations are satisfactory. The seal of your order shows two Templars sharing a horse. I have allowed you to be even thriftier—seven of you share one cell."

"You will die for what you have done to us and to our grand master, Jacques de Molay."

Philip laughed and turned to leave. "I am late for dinner."

As Philip started back up the dungeon stairs, he spoke to the jailer. "Share the leftovers with these heretics. The king of France is a generous sovereign, but a sovereign who still punishes the sinner. Give them no wine to wash down their food. If they are thirsty, let them drink from the latrine."

At noon, the Mass of the Dead was offered for Pope Clement. As the papal choir intoned the *Dies Irae,* a long procession of cardinals and bishops wended its way from the Papal Palace to Avignon's

Cathedral des Doms, fifty yards away. A lone priest followed the prelates, carrying the papal tiara on a red velvet cushion. The tiara was made of three jeweled circlets, each symbolizing one of the pope's powers: to rule over the people; to judge their sins; and to teach the word of God. Behind the priest, members of the nobility pulled a caisson draped in black cloth on which the body of the pope lay. At the rear of the procession walked the three prelates who would concelebrate the pope's funeral Mass. By tradition they were the camerlengo, the dean of the college of cardinals and the youngest member of the Sacred College, in this case, the Cardinal Archbishop of Genoa.

One mourner, however, was conspicuously absent from the procession. King Philip had sent word that he would not attend Clement's funeral Mass.

At the entrance to the cathedral, the procession paused as the pope's body was lifted off the caisson and placed on a catafalque. Thurible in hand, de Saone circled the coffin three times, each time incensing Clement's remains.

De Saone thought back five years, to the first time Clement had entered the Avignon Cathedral. King Philip had invited Clement to live in Avignon for the pope's own safety. Rome, Philip insisted, was no place for the head of Christendom.

"When the weather in Rome is cool, there are riots; when the weather is hot there is plague. The Rhône flows more calmly than the Tiber."

Clement knew, however, that Philip's concern about his health and well being was an act. The king's real motives were less noble. Clement's predecessor, Pope Boniface VIII, had excommunicated Philip for taxing Church properties. Philip swore he would never allow a pope to challenge him again. The easiest solution was to hobble the pope's power by forcing him to live under the watchful eye of the king. Clement knew that it would be unwise to refuse King Philip's invitation. On March 23, 1309, followed by King Philip, Clement had ridden through Avignon's San Roch Gate to the thunderous cheers of the faithful. As the papal entourage moved through the crowds, the devout, and even some of the not so devout, covered the streets with rugs. Others tossed sprigs of lavender and flower petals from tenement windows in a blinding rain of color. Men ran next to the pope's horse, holding up children for him to bless. At the Avignon Cathedral, hundreds of prelates and nobility waited outside to greet him. As Clement dismounted, the bishop of Avignon knelt before him and kissed his ring. Then as the choir thundered the *Tu es Petrus,* the pope and the king of France walked into the cathedral for a pontifical Mass celebrated by Clement.

Now, of course, things were very different. There were no cheering crowds, no showers of lavender, no trumpets, and most significantly, no King Philip. As de Saone watched the faces of his fellow cardinals, he could see that their minds were not on Clement but on the upcoming conclave. De Saone had already received a foretaste of what was to come. Earlier that morning, two French cardinals had secretly come to his quarters in the hope of persuading him to allow Cardinal Taserant to preach Clement's eulogy. The camerlengo indignantly refused. "I was blessed to have Pope Clement as my friend. His funeral Mass will not be used to promote Cardinal Taserant's papal ambitions." As the French cardinals stormed out of his apartment, de Saone recalled that it was Clement who had elevated Cardinal Taserant to the Sacred College and appointed him Archbishop of Lyons, the wealthiest diocese in France. But now, there was no gratitude, only Taserant's naked ambition to be Clement's successor.

The signal was given for the procession to enter the cathedral. When the cardinal camerlengo walked into the immense twilight of the nave, he thought he saw a helmeted figure standing on the high altar. He hesitated for a moment, letting his eyes adjust to the darkness. When he looked again, whatever he had seen was gone. As he started down the center aisle, he passed a painting of the triumphant Jesus appearing to the Magdalene. Then the camerlengo saw it again—a wraith-like figure was beckoning him toward the altar. De Saone thought he saw a scroll of parchment in the figure's hand. The cardinal began to lose his composure and paused. The figure dissolved in the smoke from the incense.

At the altar, de Saone began the Mass. The cardinal always found comfort in the sheer predictability of the ceremony. The words of the liturgy never changed, even for a funeral of the Vicar of Christ. He recited the offertory prayers and prepared the bread and wine for consecration. De Saone prayed the Sanctus and genuflected before the altar. Taking the bread in his hand, he bent over the altar to recite the words of consecration. Suddenly, de Saone sensed the mysterious helmeted figure standing beside him on the altar. As de Saone lifted the consecrated host for veneration, he felt the phantom pulling his arms down. Trembling, he laid the host back on the altar. De Saone bent low over the wine. *"Hic est Calix sanguinis mei"*—he could barely speak the Latin words of consecration. As he lifted the cup of Christ's blood high above his head, it felt like a stone of immense weight. The cardinal lost all sensation in his arms. The chalice fell on the altar, spilling red wine over the white altar cloth. As he looked down at the altar, de Saone shrank back in terror. In the pool of wine, he saw the face of Jacques de Molay. The Templar smiled at de Saone and held out the parchment scroll as if taunting him to take it.

Père Beneton ran to the camerlengo's side when he saw the chalice hit the altar. Wild-eyed, the old man stood alone. Then, as if he were looking into the abyss itself, de Saone let out a loud, animal cry: "God protect me from the Templar." He struggled to pick up the chalice a second time but collapsed on the marble floor of the altar. Beneton carried the camerlengo to a chair on the right side of the sanctuary. When he regained consciousness, de Saone's face was ashen and his breathing labored. Père Beneton knew the cardinal would not be able to finish saying the mass. Steadying the old man, the priest led the cardinal into the sacristy and helped him remove his black vestments. As de Saone looked back to the altar, he saw Cardinal Taserant had replaced him as the principal celebrant.

When Mass was over, the sacristan burned de Saone's black vestments and the white altar cloth. Both had been stained with the Blood of the Savior.

An hour later, de Saone was still trembling as he entered his apartment. Beneton poured water into a metal basin and wiped the cardinal's face.

"Beneton—my nephew Etienne—bring him here as quickly as you can."

"It will be difficult, Emenence."

"Difficult! Why?"

"The Papal Palace has been sealed off. King Philip's soldiers are everywhere."

"Clement's body is hardly cold and already the struggle over succession begins."

De Saone scribbled a message on a piece of parchment. "Take this, Beneton. Tomorrow the College of Cardinals will inter Clement's remains under the altar of the cathedral. I need my black cope and stole from my palace in Villenueve to participate in the burial liturgy. No one will stop the camerlengo's secretary on such a mission."

"Yes, Eminence."

"One thing more, Beneton. My nephew must disguise himself when he comes here. If King Philip knew that Etienne was visiting me today, there would be some inconvenient questions."

"Finding Etienne's whereabouts may be harder than bringing him here, Eminence."

Chapter XXI

A Trip to Avignon

"HALT!" FRENCH SOLDIERS blocked the road. "Go back. No one may leave the palace."

Père Beneton took de Saone's letter from under his cloak. "Stand aside. My orders are under seal of the camerlengo."

A soldier read the letter and handed it back to Beneton. "No one can leave—not even the camerlengo himself."

"It is the pope who is dead, not some poor beggar in the street. It would be sacrilegious to deny him the rites of the dead."

The soldiers spoke among themselves. Finally, the ranking soldier turned and looked uneasily at Beneton. "Go ahead. We do not want the pope's soul on our consciences."

Père Beneton continued down the hill. When he reached the town center, the marketplace was bustling with people. The pace of commerce stops for no one, Beneton thought, not even for Christ's Vicar on earth.

Beneton decided to go first to L'Auberge Carrée to look for Etienne. The priest had often seen the camerlengo's nephew leaving the bordello at odd times during the day. Knowing Etienne as he did, Beneton was certain that Clement's death would not keep him from the pleasures of a woman's bed.

"Below!" Beneton heard the cry just in time. The contents of a slop-pot splashed on the ground, barely missing him. A toothless old woman looked down from a tenement window smiling.

"You dried-up hag. You did that deliberately."

"Come up and visit me, priest." The woman pulled up her dress. "I can still teach you a thing or two."

As he was staring at the woman, a French patrol came galloping down the street, scattering pedestrians in every direction. Beneton jumped into a doorway, barely escaping injury. A merchant shared the space.

"Cesspools—that is what these streets have become. The worst plagues are the rats."

The clock in the bell tower began to toll noon. The merchant took a piece of hard bread out of his pocket and threw it in the street. "Watch! It will be gone before the bell tower sounds the twelfth stroke."

The bread had hardly hit the ground when rats darted out from gutters and clumps of sewage that had been thrown in the street. As Beneton watched in disbelief, the piece of bread was devoured in an instant. Then as if nothing had happened, the sidewalk was empty again.

The merchant walked away shaking his head in disgust. "I thought purgatory came after death, not before."

When Beneton went through the door of L'Auberge Carrée, Madame Therese greeted him warmly.

"Ah, Père Beneton, we have not seen you here for weeks. Marie still asks after you."

Tall and buxom with pockmarks on her skin caused by several bouts of venereal disease, Madame Therese presented a commanding figure, leaving little doubt that she was the proprietor of L'Auberge Carrée.

"Therese, I am looking for someone—Etienne de Saone."

"He is not here. Come back tonight."

"His uncle wishes to see him."

Madame Therese shrugged her shoulders. "Wait a minute. . . ."

Several minutes later an angry Etienne de Saone stormed down the corridor of the bordello, tucking a linen shirt into his pants. "Damn it, Beneton. . . ."

"The pope is dead. Your uncle needs you immediately."

Although Etienne seldom tolerated interruptions in his pleasures, he sensed that the matter was serious. In any case, he could always return. As the two men left the bordello, Madame Therese walked over to where a merchant sat drinking absinthe.

"One of the men who just left was Etienne de Saone, the nephew of the camerlengo. His uncle wants to see him immediately. It has something to do with the pope's death."

The merchant handed the woman a gold coin. "Thank you, Therese." Finishing his absinthe, the merchant arose and left the bordello, heading for the post of the commander of the king's guard.

As Père Beneton and Etienne walked quickly toward the Papal Palace, they slipped into a quiet alley. "Throw this monk's cassock over your uniform, Etienne. You must not be recognized. Too many questions will be asked."

When they reached Cardinal de Saone's quarters, Etienne could see that his uncle was upset. The cardinal's hands trembled as he paced up and down in his study.

"Etienne, I have a mission for you. Go to the Cistercian abbey of Valmagne and bring Abbot Ricard here as quickly as possible. He is my confessor."

"Now, Uncle?"

"Yes, Etienne. Go down to the harbor and find a barge stopping at the village of Dupais. The abbey is a four-hour walk from there. God willing, you can be at the abbey by noon tomorrow."

"As you wish, Uncle."

"Take this gold pectoral cross. It was a gift from the abbot. If you are refused entry to Valmagne, have this taken to Ricard. He will see you."

There was a loud knock on the door of the camerlengo's apartment. De Saone and Beneton looked apprehensively at each other. The cardinal pointed to a door at the far end of the room. "Etienne, hurry—hide in my chapel. You cannot be seen here."

As Etienne entered the chapel, the camerlengo motioned Beneton to open the door. Two armed soldiers stood outside.

"King Philip wishes the camerlengo to attend him. He has sent a carriage."

"I will inform His Eminence."

The cardinal overheard what the soldiers had said. "One dares not keep the king waiting. Beneton, bring me my cloak."

When the cardinal had left, Etienne came out of the chapel.

"Be careful, Etienne, French soldiers are everywhere."

"They will not stop me."

"It will be cold on the river tonight. Take this." Père Beneton handed Etienne a goatskin bag.

"Good wine will help."

As Cardinal de Saone alighted from his carriage, King Philip stood waiting in the courtyard of the Templar commanderie to greet him. "I hope your trip from Avignon was comfortable."

"As comfortable as could be expected, Majesty. Your soldiers did not tell me the purpose of this meeting."

"Come have some wine."

The old cardinal followed Philip into the hall of the castle.

"With Clement dead, you administer the Church."

"Yes, Your Majesty."

"And you are responsible for convening the next papal conclave."

"This is common knowledge, Sire."

"Then let me make my wishes clear. The conclave will be held in Avignon, and the new pontiff will be French."

"The Italians may vote to return the conclave to Rome."

"Remind their Eminences of the Templars' fate. No one leaves Avignon until a French pope is elected."

"You cannot select the next Vicar of Christ, Philip. That choice belongs to the Holy Spirit."

"Don't talk to me of fairytales, de Saone."

"The will of God is not a fairytale."

"Tell your fellow cardinals that I have caged the Holy Spirit. He acts through me."

As the king turned to leave the room, he stopped. An uneasy look crossed his face.

"Do you believe in de Molay's curse, de Saone? The people say he came for Clement's soul."

"He said that he would come for our souls as well—yours and mine."

"Certainly, you do not believe in such things."

"I believe in the resurrection of the body, Your Majesty. Such things can happen."

"De Molay's curse is merely another fairytale, de Saone."

Etienne walked along the busy quais of Avignon. At a wharf just north of St. Bénézet Bridge, several stacks of Toledo armor lay on the deck of a barge. One sword in particular caught Etienne's attention. Walking over to the barge, he picked up the weapon to feel its weight. Never had he felt such perfect balance. He ran his hand over the finely worked blade. The engraving depicted the legendary knight Roland. Ambushed by a Saracen army in the Pyrenees, Roland lifts his horn to recall Charlemagne and his men to help drive off the Muslim attack. Absorbed by the beauty of the sword, Etienne did not see a man approaching from the rear.

"It would take the treasuries of fifty abbeys to buy that sword, monk. Put it down or by the Blood of our Savior, you will see the devil before nightfall." Still wearing the cassock of a monk, Etienne spun around and saw the captain of the barge standing directly behind him. From his girth, Etienne could see that the captain was a man who enjoyed his wine and venison. Despite his menacing tone, however, there was something about the man that Etienne instinctively liked.

"I intended no harm. The sun reflected off the blade like. . . ."

"Move on, priest. We sail up river tonight."

"Do you stop in Dupais?"

"Dupais? Now there's a destination for you. The rats are plentiful there. When we stop there tomorrow, the dock may be gone—the rats eat quickly."

"Is there room for one more passenger?"

"There's always room for someone who pays his carriage. But prayers are no substitute for money."

"What is the cost to Dupais?"

"Ten copper coins."

"Five."

"Your mother must have never taught you to count. Eight it will be and not one coin less."

"Six and half my wine."

"Let me taste it."

Etienne gave the captain Père Beneton's goatskin of wine.

"Where did you get this, monk? If priests drink this well, I might even return to the church. Six it is and half the wine."

At eight o'clock in the evening, the barge left Avignon, and the captain steered the boat out through some sandbars close to the shore. When it was safely in the main channel of the river, the captain fastened two torches to the front of the barge to avoid nighttime collisions. "That should prevent us from getting rammed. Now for some of your wine."

At four o'clock in the morning, the barge docked at the village of Dupais. Before he stepped off the barge, the captain tested the strength of the dock.

"The rats must be eating more slowly. The planks have survived another night."

"When do you return to Dupais?"

"Late tomorrow afternoon."

"Do you have space for two passengers?"

"Yes, but it will cost twelve copper coins and more good wine."

Etienne followed the forest path west from Dupais. When the sun began to rise, he stopped to eat some blackberries that grew along the path. Two young fawns darted out of the woods and stood blinking in the light. Etienne moved slowly toward them holding out some of the berries. The fauns looked at him as if puzzled by his offer of food. Etienne heard a sound behind him. Turning, he saw a large stag walk out onto the forest path. The stag pawed the ground and shook his antlers menacingly. Etienne backed away. An owl had observed the confrontation and hooted a comment on the wisdom of Etienne's strategic retreat.

Continuing along the path, Etienne heard the sound of far-off bells. The path wound steeply upward until the land fell off abruptly, exposing a large valley. In the center of the valley stood the Abbey of Valmagne. The early morning light made the travertine walls of the monastery glow with the softness of gold. Everywhere he looked, Etienne saw meticulously tended fields, bounded by stands of orange and lemon trees. Far off in the distance was the abbey's vineyard. The vines, neatly spaced in rows, reminded him of the stripes on a tiger's back.

The monks were already at work in the fields, harvesting a crop of barley. Etienne laughed at a flock of crows, hungry for scraps and cawing impatiently as they waited for the monks to leave the field. Off in the distance a rather portly monk chased a duck that had escaped from its coop.

When he reached the gate to the abbey, Etienne knocked loudly on the wooden door. There was no answer. He knocked again. Finally an old servant opened a small slide in the door. "It's too early for visitors. Come back later."

"I have come to see Abbot Ricard."

"If it is the abbot you wish to see, then come back tomorrow. He will be busy the whole of today."

"Cardinal de Saone sent me." Etienne showed the gold pectoral cross to the gatekeeper.

Unlatching the metal bolt from within, the old man opened the door. "I recognize the cross. Come with me. The abbot has been in the chapter room for two days trying to resolve a dispute between the Bishop of Autun and the villagers of Lemeux."

"What is the dispute?"

"Another problem inherited from the Templars. When King Philip confiscated the Templar lands and their wealth, he gave the vineyards on both sides of the Durand River to the Count of Provence. The count gave the vineyards north of the river to the Bishop of Autun and those south of the river to the town of Lemeux. It did not take long before the bishop and the town began feuding over how much water each party could take from the river. Tempers ran high. The Count of Provence asked the abbot to settle the dispute."

"Murderer!"

"You dare call a bishop of the Church a murderer?" The Bishop of Autun hoisted himself from his seat and glared at his accuser.

An old man stood pointing a bony finger at the corpulent bishop wrapped in yards of purple cloth. "That and more. You are a liar and a fornicator as well."

"Old man, for those sinful words, you will be denied the sacraments. No absolution, no communion, no. . . ."

Abbot Ricard stepped between the bishop and the old man. "Lord Bishop, people say many things in the heat of passion. Please take your seat."

Etienne looked carefully at Abbot Ricard. He was a tall handsome man with a wide and pleasant face. The abbot had been born into a wealthy mercantile family in the Auvergne in south-central France. It is said that the people of the Auvergne believe that their beloved mountains, their Catholic faith, and their families are somehow mystically bound together, each a part of the other two. Ricard's own parents held tenaciously to this belief.

Ricard had shown exceptional intelligence as a child. He was sent to study law at the University of Lyons. While at university, his parents betrothed him to Genevieve de Fereine, the youngest daughter of the mayor of the neighboring village of Cresson. After three years of marriage, the couple conceived a child. While in the fifth month of her pregnancy, Genevieve went to Cresson to visit her father. On the way home, her carriage was ambushed by a band of highwaymen. When the driver tried to escape, the carriage plunged down the side of a cliff, killing Genevieve and the baby. Inconsolable, Ricard entered the monastery at Valmagne. Five years later, his fellow monks elected him abbot.

Now Abbot Ricard stood up from his chair and bowed to the Count of Provence who sat archly at the front of the chapter room. Ricard stood for a moment until there was absolute silence in the room.

"This dispute is not about water, my friends. It is about money to feed wives and children."

At the mention of children, the bishop of Autun squirmed in his seat. Despite his promise of celibacy, he had fathered three children.

The abbot continued. "God created the mountains and the valleys. He created the rivers to bring water from the mountains to the valleys below. I cannot improve on that. But people created money and can distribute it as they please."

"What do you mean, Abbot?"

"My Lord Bishop, when a priest begins to say Mass, he kisses the altar stone. Why?"

"Because it contains holy relics."

"Precisely. My Lord Count, you have many relics in your treasury, including the bones of St. James, the brother of Jesus."

"What do the bones of St. James have to do with this water dispute?"

"Relics should be venerated by the faithful, My Lord, not kept in a dark vault. If you loan the bishop the relics of St. James, he could place them in his cathedral. Many pilgrims would come to pray before them."

"Ah, now I am beginning to see your point." The count smiled at Ricard. "The monies from the pilgrim trade will make the bishop rich in exchange for pulling up his vines!"

The abbot looked hard at the count. "Your Grace, the relics of St. James are the key to solving this dispute."

"I will agree to your plan if the others do."

The villagers from Lemeux howled with joy. "His Amplitude gets the relics, we get the water."

The bishop of Autun heaved his body out of his chair. "I will not accept this! Autun has always produced wine. It will continue to do so as long as I am bishop."

The villagers continued their chant. "His Amplitude gets the relics, we get the water."

Furious at their slur, the bishop's face turned cardinal red, and he hurled his chair at the jeering villagers. It fell short and broke into pieces.

"Lord Bishop, please hear me through on this. This solution will make you a wealthy man."

"How is that?"

"The pilgrims who come to your cathedral will need wine to drink. For every liter of Lemeux wine sold in Autun, Your Excellency would receive a ten percent commission."

"Ten percent is not enough. These thieves should pay me more."

"Think like a merchant, Your Excellency. You can increase your profits by as much as fivefold."

"How is that?"

"Call the wine 'The Blood of St. James' and sell it in the Cathedral of Autun. Pilgrims will confuse their devotion to the saint with their love of wine. Word of a holy wine will spread throughout France."

The bishop of Autun warmed to the idea. "With the increased profits, we can build inns for the pilgrims, places for them to eat, places to wash...."

A villager stood up and gleefully shouted: "Perhaps even a new bordello or two for His Amplitude!"

The bishop glared at the villager but quickly turned to Abbot Ricard and smiled. "I agree with your proposal."

The abbot bowed to the Count of Provence. "My Liege, the bones of St. James have settled this matter."

When the parties had left, the abbot asked that Etienne be brought to his room. "I understand you have come from the camerlengo."

"Yes, Your Grace. I am Etienne de Soane."

"Ah! The cardinal's nephew."

"Your Grace should be congratulated. The dispute seems to have been settled to everyone's satisfaction."

"To everyone's satisfaction but mine."

The abbot's answer startled Etienne. "I do not understand."

"This was Templar land taken in blood. Instead of rejoicing in what they received, the bishop and the townspeople covet more. They act like maggots feeding on the dead flesh of the Templars." Ricard paused. "For the last weeks, my diary is full of entries about vines, rivers, and soil composition. Someday I am sure I will look back on this and laugh, but not now—but enough of this. Word has come that Pope Clement is dead. Is this true?"

"Yes."

The abbot made the sign of the cross. "May his soul rest in peace. It will be difficult for the Church until a new pope is chosen."

"King Philip will have much to say about that."

"Yes, too much I am afraid. But tell me, why did the camerlengo send you to Valmagne?"

"I must bring you to Avignon as soon as possible. You are his confessor."

"I will come immediately."

"A barge leaves Dupais for Avignon tomorrow afternoon."

"Good. I will ask Father Matteo for some peasant shirts and hose. Eyebrows would be raised if the camerlengo's nephew and the Abbot of Valmagne were seen traveling together to Avignon at a time like this."

The following morning, a young postulant from the abbey drove an oxcart along the forest path to Dupais. Disguised as farm hands, the abbot and Etienne sat in the rear of the cart. The morning air was thick with pollen and Etienne dozed off to sleep. The abbot read his breviary, occasionally looking up at the sky. A large hawk followed the cart. The abbot shook Etienne to wake him.

"Is that Philip's spy?"

Etienne smiled. "I would like to think instead that it is the Holy Ghost watching over us."

When they reached the outskirts of Dupais, the abbot and Etienne got out of the cart. There would be less suspicion if they walked into the village. The postulant kissed the abbot's hand and drove the cart back to the monastery.

Late in the afternoon, the barge docked at the village. The captain of the barge greeted Etienne with a skeptical look.

"I see you have changed professions overnight—from monk to farmhand. I hope you still have a good vintage to pay for your return passage?"

"Yes, from the abbot of Valmagne's own stock."

The captain smiled in anticipation. "Good, we will drink well tonight."

The shadows along the river were already lengthening as the barge left Dupais. Etienne and the abbot found a comfortable spot on the deck for the overnight journey. After the captain steered the barge into the center channel, he joined the others to claim his share of the abbot's wine. After several cups, Etienne and Ricard were lulled to sleep by the comforting rhythm of the oars.

At about two in the morning, Etienne heard a voice from the water hail the captain. "We wish to board."

Etienne knew it had to be a French skiff patrolling the river. He pulled out his dagger.

The captain called back. "You are welcome to search the barge. We carry Flemish wool to Avignon."

Etienne woke the abbot. "French soldiers are coming aboard. Take this dagger and use it if you have to."

Ricard shook his head vehemently. "I am a priest. I will not use it."

"Take the knife, Your Grace. Worry about your religious scruples later."

Etienne turned to the captain. "When the soldiers board, I will offer them some wine. If they ask, I am your cousin. I go to Avignon for the women."

"And your friend?" asked the captain.

"Tell them I am a mute. You took pity on me and gave me passage to Avignon."

Three French soldiers stepped onto the barge. They looked quickly around the deck and then returned to the captain.

"We are looking for a French knight, Etienne de Saone. He is wanted for questioning. Who is this man?" The leader of the boarding party pointed at Etienne.

"My cousin. He goes to spend the night in a brothel as usual. I am amazed he has not caught the pox."

"And this one?" the French officer pointed to Ricard. "He looks a little too well bred to be a farmer."

"He does not speak. The people in Dupais say he has not uttered a word since his wife died ten years ago."

The officer in charge laughed. "A few more like him and the streets of Avignon will be less noisy."

Etienne appeared with a jug of wine.

"Ah, look at what my cousin has brought us. In honor of King Philip, share some refreshment with us. It is cold on the river tonight."

Etienne poured wine into earthenware cups and handed them to the soldiers.

The leader of the French patrol savored the taste of the wine. "You are right. It is cold on the river tonight. Wine warms the blood and fortifies the soul."

After several cups, the soldiers left the barge and returned to their skiff.

As dawn began to break, Abbot Ricard awoke and prayed silently. The sun edged over the horizon, and the towers of Avignon appeared in the far distance.

"The center of Christendom!" Abbot Ricard murmured sarcastically. "But not the city chosen by St. Peter and not the city that has seen 1300 years of popes."

Etienne worried about the forthrightness of his companion. "My Lord, you must keep such thoughts to yourself. French soldiers patrol everywhere in Avignon."

"Do not worry, my friend. An abbot spends most of his day in silence. I know how to be careful."

Etienne looked down river. "The barge will reach Avignon by noon. Before we go to the Palais des Papes, we must stop at an inn."

"No, Etienne, we can eat later. Your uncle is waiting for us."

"It is a dangerous time in Avignon, Your Grace. We go to the inn not to eat but to listen."

The abbot put a hand on de Saone's shoulder. "But the French soldiers are looking for you."

Etienne drew his sword. "I will be careful. After all, I am a French soldier myself. I know their habits."

When they reached Avignon, the captain of the barge walked over to Etienne and gave him a farewell thump on the back.

"Goodbye, Etienne de Saone. Your disguise did not fool me. But for your sake, I hope it fools Philip's soldiers."

Etienne and Ricard stopped at a small tavern near the road up to the Palais des Papes. They learned that Philip had effectively sealed off Avignon and vowed to keep it that way until the cardinals elected a new French pope. They also learned that Philip had decided to remain on the outskirts of Avignon until the election had taken place. He was leaving nothing to chance.

When Etienne and the abbot left the inn, a French soldier followed them into the street. The soldier stared hard at Etienne with a puzzled look.

"Etienne de Saone?" the soldier asked.

"You are mistaken, soldier. I am a farmer from Dupais."

The soldier continued to follow the two men.

"You do not have the demeanor of one who tills the soil. You are Etienne de Saone—I am sure of it. Come with me peaceably; you are wanted for questioning."

"Leave me alone, soldier. I am not this Etienne de Saone."

The soldier drew a knife and held it to Etienne's throat. "I said 'Come with me!'"

The soldier suddenly gasped for breath. A dagger protruded from his belly. At first, Etienne thought it was the soldier's own weapon until he saw blood on Ricard's hands.

Etienne was incredulous. "Abbot, you killed that soldier with the knife I gave you on the barge!"

"He threatened your life. I stabbed him to save you, not to kill the soldier. It is permitted for a monk to act in such a way."

Etienne dragged the soldier's body into the alleyway and concealed it behind several empty wine barrels. "It will look like a random killing. Dozens occur in Avignon every month. We must go quickly."

"Wait!" The abbot knelt on the ground and drew the sign of the cross on the soldier's forehead.

"Requiescat in pace." Whispering the age-old farewell to the dead, the abbot pulled a discarded gunnysack over the soldier's face.

A cold mistral wind blew through Avignon as Ricard and Etienne climbed the hill to the Palais des Papes. When they reached the gate to the palace, French soldiers stopped them.

"What business do you have in the Palace?" The soldier's voice was brusque.

Ricard answered. "Cardinal de Saone ordered us to bring his gold pectoral cross."

"Let me see it," one of the soldiers demanded.

Ricard took the gold cross from under his cloak and handed it to the soldier. The soldier weighed the cross in his hand. "The cardinal must trust the two of you very much if he allows you to carry something as valuable as this. Pass on."

Ricard and Etienne found Cardinal de Saone's apartment, and when they were certain that they had not been followed, Ricard knocked softly on the door. Père Beneton opened it slowly as if he feared what might be on the other side. "Ah, thank God it is you, Abbot Ricard. A hundred times, his Eminence has asked when you are coming. He has not slept in two nights."

Père Beneton led Ricard and Etienne to the cardinal's study.

Although he was wrapped in a fur-lined robe, the camerlengo was shivering. The fingers that grasped the edge of the heavy robe appeared gray in the afternoon light.

"Ricard, thank God you are here. You must hear my sins before it is too late."

"Of course, Your Eminence. Etienne, please leave us alone for a while."

When they were alone, the Abbot knelt and kissed the cardinal's ring. The camerlengo's hand felt cold and clammy.

"Your Eminence, are you ill?"

Cardinal de Saone looked at Ricard. "Yes, in my heart."

"What do you mean?"

"The nightmares ... the Templar taunted Clement with the parchment. He was at Clement's bedside, to take his soul."

The camerlengo grabbed Abbot Ricard's arm and pulled him close, as though he feared someone would overhear. "De Molay cursed me, too. He said he would come for my soul within the year. At night, I have heard him breathing in my room, waiting for the time."

"What does de Molay have to do with all of this? And what is this 'parchment' he has? I do not understand."

"The parchment is blasphemous. It says that Jesus and the Magdalene were husband and wife and bore two children. The Templars hid it from us." As he spoke, de Saone grew increasingly agitated. His body trembled.

"Ricard, terrible things have happened these last months. I thought it was for the good of the Church. But God is angry. He will not forgive the torture and the killing of innocent men."

"Your Eminence, this is not true." The abbot spoke in a reassuring voice. "God did not forbid all killing. It is his law that one can kill in self-defense."

"Ricard, please grant me forgiveness for my sins. These cardinal's robes will not shield me from God's vengeance."

"God forgives the sodomite and the blasphemer. He will forgive you too as long as you sincerely repent."

"But so many innocent Templars have died."

"Forgiveness requires that we experience the full sinfulness of our acts. If we do that, God will forgive us."

"But will God's forgiveness protect me from de Molay's curse?"

Ricard paused for a moment. "To do that, you must forgive yourself also. Only then will de Molay's curse be gone."

"But there has been so much blood."

Barbo put down the diary. He wondered about de Saone; was he a large or thin man, tall or short? A small piece of parchment fell from the book. Barbo could see that it appeared to be written by Abbot Ricard.

"Two days ago the body of Cardinal de Saone was found floating in the Rhône River near Saint-Bénézet Bridge. I fear that he died from remorse for what he had done to the Templars. And this morning there is news that King Philip has been killed in a hunting accident. The people say that Jacques de Molay has finally been avenged."

Barbo stood up from his desk and walked to the window. It was one of those magical late afternoons in Rome, when the mere use of one's eyes brings serenity and peace. In the distance, Barbo could see Trinita dei Monti standing regally above the Spanish Steps. Off to the east was the elaborate monument to Vittorio Emmanuele II, dubbed the wedding cake because of its decoration and brilliant white color. When he was a young seminarian, Barbo remembered taking his family to experience the grand scale of the memorial. For weeks his mother could speak of nothing else. Immediately below him was the magnificence of St. Peter's. Bernini's columns encircled the square like a mother's arms embracing the crowds of the faithful who walked within them. Standing guard over the square like a benevolent sentry was the massive stone facade of the basilica.

Almost by happenstance, Barbo saw the large statue of the Risen Christ behind the Jesuit Mother House on the Borgo Santo Spirito. In five days it would be Easter Sunday. As a child, Barbo had always looked forward to Easter more than any other day in the year. Easter meant big family dinners and colorful new clothes—and *uova di Pasqua,* the traditional chocolate eggs his mother made. After dinner, the family would go out into the street and light Roman candles and sparklers. As he grew older, the cardinal continued to indulge his "secular pleasure" at Easter time. Every Holy Saturday night, he would join the tens of thousands of Romans and watch the *fuochi d'artificio* display over Castel Sant'Angelo.

To a priest, however, Easter was much more than new clothes and family dinners. It was the day when Jesus triumphed over death—the central belief of all Christianity. The Easter gospels had always puzzled Barbo. Three of the evangelists report that, after he rose from the dead, Jesus appeared first to the Magdalene and then to Peter, John, and the other Apostles. And now the discovery of this Hebrew manuscript. If Jesus and the Magdalene were man and wife, it would explain why he appeared first to her.

The exhaust backfire of a tourist bus ricocheted through St. Peter's Square like a gunshot, scattering flocks of pigeons in all directions. The loud noise startled Barbo. He heard the phone ring in his office. He hoped it was something Alessandri could handle.

Alessandri picked up the phone.

"Excuse me, Your Eminence. There's a Pietro Visconti on the line. He insists on talking to you."

Barbo had avoided telephoning Visconti since the night of their meeting in Trastevere. Like a small child, he had hoped that the ghost in the closet would simply go away. But now he knew what he had to do: Above all else, he had to protect the Church. Barbo knew the Church is not a club for smug American and European Catholics who attend services on Christmas and Easter. For them, women priests, priestly celibacy, and the power of local bishops are hot-button issues. More and more, however, the power in the Church is shifting to the poor and the working classes in Africa, Latin America, and Asia. The Catholics there believe in relics and miracles and do not care about the ordination of women so long as the Blessed Virgin remains a part of their lives. The knowledge that Jesus had sexual relations with the Magdalene would shatter their faith in the Church. There is a natural momentum to such things. If people begin to question their belief in Jesus' celibacy, they might also begin to question their belief in the Virgin Birth and, ultimately, in the Resurrection itself. Although he had suffered guilt and remorse, de Saone had made the same decision that now Barbo would have to make—to suppress the parchment and protect the Church.

The secretary of state took the phone from Alessandri. "Pietro?"

"Ah, Eminenza, thank you for taking my call. Have you had time to consider what we talked about in Trastevere?"

"Yes, Visconti. I will accept your offer. There are issues that will have to be worked out—particularly access to accounts." The secretary of state tried not to be too specific; he did not trust telephones when discussing such sensitive matters.

Barbo could hear the satisfaction in Visconti's voice. "Even when friends agree, there are always the details of implementation." Visconti paused for a moment. "Eminenza, I'm glad you accepted. I didn't want to help Diefenbacher's papal ambitions. Our friends in South Africa say he is not a man to be trusted."

"There is one condition, Visconti."

"What is that?"

"The parchment must be authenticated by someone from the Vatican Library."

"As you wish. The parchment has already been subjected to carbon dating and pollen tests that confirm its authenticity. But you need not accept my word on that. Send your expert tomorrow morning at eight o'clock."

"Where?"

"The manuscript will be in Professor Baldini's office at the University of Rome. He will arrange for the tests."

Chapter XXII

TRUST IN THE LORD

Martin Fellows, Curator of Hebrew Manuscripts at the Vatican Library, walked into Cardinal Barbo's outer office.

Alessandri looked at the list of Barbo's scheduled appointments.

"Martin, there is no room in his schedule for today. How about tomorrow?"

"His Eminence left a voice-mail message. He wanted to see me as soon as possible."

"Let me speak to him." Alessandri buzzed the cardinal's inner office. "Martin Fellows is here to see you, Your Eminence. He's not on your calendar."

Barbo sounded impatient. "Show him in, Alessandri."

Fellows was something of an anomaly on the Vatican Library staff. He was a renowned authority on Hebrew manuscripts, but he was not a Catholic. In fact, as a born-again Christian and an avowed Freemason, he had pronouncedly anti-Catholic views on many subjects. What redeemed Fellows in most people's eyes, however, was his close friendship with Cardinal Barbo. Given Barbo's interest in the Knights Templar, the two men—cardinal and Freemason—spent many nights discussing medieval history and poring over ancient texts from the Vatican Library collections. It was a relationship that both men valued.

Barbo motioned Fellows to take a seat. "Martin, I need your expertise. It's a matter of some urgency."

"Of course, Francesco." Few nonclerics dared address the secretary of state by his first name.

"Two American professors claim they have found a first-century Hebrew manuscript containing census records."

Fellows laughed. "You can find these census lists in almost any manuscript library in the world."

Barbo stood up. "But this one's different."

"How?"

Cardinal Barbo hesitated for a moment. "Because it lists Jesus and the Magdalene as man and wife."

"Sounds like a forgery to me. Let me look at it. If I have to, I'll do a carbon dating."

"Do you know Professor Baldini?"

"At the University of Rome? Yes, of course."

"The manuscript will be at Baldini's office tomorrow morning at eight o'clock."

"Okay—if I have to carbon date it, I should have preliminary readings by about nine o'clock at night. Final results will take much longer."

After Fellows left, Barbo quickly finished reading some diplomatic cables and buzzed Alessandri on the intercom.

"Enrico, have a Vatican limousine meet me downstairs in fifteen minutes. I am due at the Pontifical University for a reception of the Latin-American cardinals."

The Pontifical University of St. Thomas is located in the heart of Rome at the bottom of Via Nazionale. Nicknamed the "Angelicum," the university is normally a half-hour ride from the Vatican. But not this evening. A snarled traffic jam near Ponte Sant'Angelo caused Cardinal Barbo to be twenty minutes late for the reception. As he walked into the room, he was surprised to see Cardinal Calvaux at the far end of the room. At least Barbo would not be the only guest from outside Latin America.

"Your Eminence, thank you for joining us." Cardinal Alejandro Obregon, the Archbishop of Lima, Peru, hurried over to greet his distinguished guest. "It's not often that we in Latin America have a chance to meet privately with the Vatican secretary of state."

"Thank you for inviting me, Alejandro."

Obregon took Barbo's hand and kissed his ring. The tradition of one cardinal reverencing the ring of another was sharply criticized by those in the liberal wing of the Sacred College. Diefenbacher had given several speeches in which he called the tradition a medieval practice of self-glorification. Therefore, Obregon's public gesture of reverencing Barbo's ring caught everyone by surprise. The Peruvian cardinal was sending a message to his colleagues. It was unclear, however, whether the message was one of respect for Barbo or contempt for Diefenbacher.

"Francesco, come join the discussion. Cardinal Ramera had just begun talking to us about the poor in his diocese. Continue, Ramera!"

"One night, about a month ago, I walked through the streets of Recife. I saw a young boy no more than ten years of age lying in the streets. He was dying from AIDS. I drove the flies away and kissed him. He died in my arms. Madonnas and wooden santos are not what he needed. He needed to be given a chance to live a fully human life. A chance to have a wife and family—a chance to have friends and to laugh and sing."

Cardinal Chavez, the Primate of Mexico, angrily interrupted Ramera.

"Your Eminence, Jesus said that the poor would always be with us. The Church cannot correct disparities between rich and poor. All we can do is provide the poor with the hope of an afterlife."

Cardinal Viateste, the Archbishop of Managua, Nicaragua stood when Chavez had finished speaking.

"The Church is all that the poor have. We cannot desert them. If we need to confront the social order to help them out of poverty, then we must do so."

Cardinal Obregon made a sign of mock horror. "I don't know how to load a gun, Viateste. Short of that, all of us in this room do try to help the poor. Every Sunday in Lima, my staff gives away tons of food and medicine."

Viateste challenged Obregon. "But the poor come back the next week. In reality, there is no change."

Chavez was adamant. "In my country, the poor worship Juan Diego and the Madonna of Guadalupe. When I see their faith and devotion, I cry. They believe so devoutly in their God—it gives them hope."

"I wonder, Chavez, whether Juan Diego and the Virgin would satisfy you if you had no bread for your children." Viateste stared angrily at Chavez. The room suddenly grew quiet.

Obregon broke the tension by changing the subject. "Gentlemen, in a few days the conclave will open. We must choose Pope Benedict's successor. The fundamental question seems to be, do we look for another pastor like Benedict or an administrator?"

"That is not the right question, Alejandro." Cardinal Ignacio Muñoz of Ecuador spoke from his seat.

"Well, how would you phrase it, Ignacio?"

Muñoz declared loudly. "Do we choose a pope who will decentralize power or one who will keep it in Rome?"

"And how would you answer the question, Ignacio?" Cardinal Barbo smiled at his old friend from curial days.

"Our distinguished guest puts me on the spot. Well, I will answer his question. In Chavez's country, there are Mexican bishops who preach that the story of Guadalupe is merely a myth—that the Virgin never appeared to Juan Diego. Can you imagine a churchman in Mexico calling the central symbol of Mexican Catholicism a myth! But these bishops do it and get away with it. Benedict would not silence them."

"It's worse than that, Ignacio." Chavez's face was flushed with anger. "Bishops throughout Latin America openly flaunt Rome on theological matters. Some even intimate that the Eucharist contains the body and blood of Christ only in symbolic form. Bishops like these must be excommunicated if we are to maintain one universal church with one set of beliefs."

"But, Your Eminence, whether the Virgin appeared to Juan Diego or not is hardly a question of theology or dogma. It's a question of belief." All eyes turned toward Cardinal Calvaux who stood near the back stairs of the conference room. "We must always uphold the truth. Obviously, a powerful force touched Juan Diego. It changed his life and the life of the Mexican people. In all this debate about whether the Virgin appeared to Juan Diego, we should not lose sight of the fundamental truth. God touched the Mexican people deeply through the story of Juan Diego and the Virgin."

"But would you vote for a centralist or a decentralist, Jean?"

Calvaux spoke from his heart. "I will look for a pastor. The Holy Father is the spiritual leader of a billion Catholics. Whoever is chosen as Benedict's successor should have the ability to project his care and love to all of the faithful."

Cardinals Ramera and Viateste nodded in agreement.

"I cannot agree with Cardinal Calvaux, even though we are distant cousins." Obregon was no longer the gracious host. "The Holy Father has been an inspiration for me and for Catholics everywhere. But he seemed afraid to uphold the Magisterium of Rome. He was too tentative when it came to clamping down on rogue bishops. We need a pope who will reassert the central authority of Rome. Wouldn't you agree, Francesco?"

Barbo smiled. "I will not be drawn into the debate, Alejandro. But I do know that many who were in the conclave that elected Pope Benedict told me they could feel the presence of the Holy Spirit in the Sistine Chapel."

Chavez nodded. "Francesco is right. I was there. There was a feeling of incandescence in the room—as if the air in the chapel was about to ignite."

Barbo looked at Obregon. "We must keep our hearts and minds open. The choice of pope is not ours. The Holy Spirit will guide us to the right man."

Cardinal Obregon could not resist a chuckle. "I see the Cardinal Secretary of State will not be pinned down."

Cardinal Chavez looked at his watch. "It's after ten o'clock, gentlemen. Tomorrow morning we have Mass and then we meet in General Congregation. I for one need to be rested if the Holy Spirit is to guide me."

As the cardinals bade their farewells to their host Cardinal Obregon, Barbo walked over to Calvaux.

"Jean, I didn't know you would be here."

"Nor did I until earlier this evening. The Montelamberts might be better described as a dynasty than a family. Obregon is a distant relation. He called and invited me to the reception."

"You spoke eloquently tonight. I was impressed with your candor."

"Thank you. I believe strongly that the next pope should be a pastor. What about you, Francesco? You were close to Benedict."

Barbo smiled. "Jean, I'm a member of the Curia—I've had no pastoral experience."

"I said we should choose a pastor, not necessarily someone with pastoral experience. They're not the same. The qualities of a good pastor can be found even among the members of the Curia."

Cardinal Barbo could not hold back a laugh. "'Even among the members of the Curia!' Jean, by this time you must have some inkling of how the Curia works. A bureaucratic process determines orthodoxy. If I were to advance a position, it would be reviewed and compromised for weeks until what emerges would bear no resemblance to my initial position. In the Curia, you'll find your share of canon lawyers and theologians, but not too many pastors. Benedict tried to dismantle the bureaucracy but with little success."

"You said tonight that we must open our hearts to the Holy Spirit. We priests often forget that the advice we give others applies to us as well."

Barbo's limousine left the Angelicum and headed toward the Vatican. As the car approached the Tiber, Barbo saw flashing lights ahead. A police barricade blocked the street. Barbo got out of the car and walked inside the stanchions.

A police officer pushed Barbo back. "You must stay behind the barricades."

"What happened?" asked Barbo.

The policeman answered. "A woman is threatening to jump from a building. She's holding a baby."

"I'm a priest. Let me through."

"I guess it can't hurt." The policeman pushed the barricade aside.

Barbo ran toward the building. When the cardinal reached the entrance way, he was stopped. Barbo recognized a familiar voice. "Detective Cameri, let me try to save the woman."

"I apologize, Your Eminence. I didn't recognize you. But you cannot go inside the building when someone is threatening suicide. It's against policy."

"For God's sake, Cameri, let me try."

The detective looked up at the woman standing on the ledge of the building holding her baby. He shrugged his shoulders. "All right, go ahead. She's a prostitute. We think she was beaten by some junkies and then gang raped. They went after the baby too. It's not a pretty sight."

"Thank you, Detective."

"I'll go with you. Try to get her to give up the baby. It'll give her a reason to live."

Barbo climbed the stairs and walked out on the roof. He tried to sooth the woman. "I'm a priest. Are you a Catholic?"

"I was a long time ago." The woman began to cry.

"What is your name?"

"Maria."

Barbo moved closer to the woman. "God loves you, Maria. He loves your baby, too. What is her name?"

The woman hugged the baby. "I call her Eva. It was my mother's name."

"Where was Eva born? Here in Rome?"

"Yes, but there's no life for my baby here. Look what they have done to her!"

She lifted the baby for Barbo to see. The movement caused her to lose her balance. Barbo caught the baby as the woman fell from the ledge to the street below.

"I must anoint her." Barbo pushed the baby into Cameri's arms and ran down to the street.

A police car had broken the woman's fall. When Barbo reached the street, she was still breathing.

Barbo bent down and kissed the woman. "God will lead you into paradise, Maria."

Barbo blessed the woman and held her hand while she died. Cameri placed the baby in her dead mother's arms for a final farewell.

When the ambulance took the baby away, Cameri walked over to where Barbo was standing. "Tonight took guts, Your Eminence. You tried. Just remember one thing. Maria is just another casualty of your friend Visconti's clients."

Barbo stared for a moment at Cameri and then walked slowly back to his limousine. Cameri could see that the secretary of state was holding back tears.

Barbo showered when he returned to his apartment on Via Mascherino. The water washed away the blood but not the emotions he had experienced on the street tonight. For the prostitute Maria, he was not Francesco Cardinal Barbo, Vatican Secretary of State, but a simple priest helping another human being die. He hoped he had mattered in the woman's life.

"Open your heart to the Spirit." Calvaux was right. Barbo had spoken those words on innumerable occasions to innumerable people, but he had never opened his own heart.

Barbo's thoughts returned to Visconti. He could easily justify giving in to Visconti's demands—after all, he would be acting to protect the Church and the papacy, let alone the millions of poor and uneducated Catholics who would be scandalized by the contents of the parchment. If protecting the Church meant that Visconti's clients would profit, then so be it. The profit would be the unintended consequence of achieving the greater good. But tonight, perhaps for the first time in his life, Barbo had seen the faces of those unintended consequences—Maria and her baby.

"Open your heart to the Spirit. You might be surprised at what happens."

Barbo poured brandy into a snifter. Suppose he told Visconti there would be no deal—that he would not help those who contributed to the death of Maria and the rape of her baby. Suppose he told Visconti that he would not compromise the Church's integrity or his own for this piece of parchment?

The phone rang, and Barbo looked at his watch. It was almost two o'clock in the morning. The caller-ID panel showed the call originated in Castel Gondolfo. He picked up the receiver.

"Francesco?" The pope's voice was strong despite the lateness of the hour. "I could not find the telephone number for your apartment. I had to wake Sister Consuela to get it."

"Tell Sister Consuela that I was not the cause of her losing a night's sleep."

"I will, Francesco. I was kneeling by the side of my bed praying when I saw you kneeling next to me. You were troubled by something. We are old friends, Francesco. Can I help?"

Barbo yearned to ask his old friend about the Magdalene parchment and Visconti's blackmail but dared not. Doctor Hendricks had laid down strict rules that the Holy Father must be shielded from any talk of problems or difficulties. They would only deepen his sense of guilt over abdicating.

"Whatever it is, Francesco, have the courage to put your trust in God. He will help you."

Pope Benedict clicked off the phone.

Rarely in one's life—never for some—there are moments of moral clarity when a person sees exactly what must be done. For Barbo, that moment came when Benedict said: "Have the courage to put your trust in God." Calvaux's words, the sight of the dying prostitute, Benedict's phone call—they were all parts of the same message. Barbo knew what he had to do.

Fellows had said there would be a preliminary report on the carbon dating at about nine o'clock this evening. If, by some miracle, the parchment turned out to be a hoax, the force of circumstances would end the deal with Visconti. If the document proved to be genuine, however, he would tell Visconti there would be no deal. Barbo would put his trust in God.

As Barbo took his seat in the General Congregation, Cardinal Desion, the prefect of the Congregation for Bishops, sat next to him. The prefect's position perfectly suited Desion's personality. Anyone who sought an episcopal appointment had to pass his scrutiny. In many ways, Desion was a bellwether. Because of his dealings with the hierarchy, Desion knew the thinking of most Church leaders around the world. Even more significant, perhaps, many of the cardinals who would select Benedict's successor owed their episcopal appointments to Desion.

"Francesco, come join me for a cappuccino at the coffee bar. We have a few minutes before Marini starts the meeting."

Barbo and Desion found a table in the corner farthest from the door. Although Desion exuded Gallic charm, Barbo knew him to be a wily and tough adversary.

"Extraordinary—the pope abdicating like this. Who could have predicted such a thing?" Unconsciously, Desion put his hand to his face to conceal a childhood scar.

"Pope Benedict was a great leader, Desion. In our ranks, there are few like him."

"You are right, Barbo. The Church will miss his gentle but steady hand." Barbo knew that Desion's words were leading to a different subject.

"You know, Barbo, as prefect of the Congregation for Bishops, I met weekly with the Holy Father to review episcopal nominations. We spoke often about the future leadership of the Church. He told me once that he gave you a cardinal's hat not as a reward for your past accomplishments, but for what you would do in the future. Pope Benedict had a high regard for your talents, Barbo. "

"I was privileged to work closely with the pontiff. He had a firm grasp of even the most complex problems."

"The Holy Spirit will guide us to the next pope. But many think they hear him hovering over you, Barbo." Desion chuckled.

"I will not be chosen, Desion. There are many others."

"The papers mention you as a cardinal who has many of the qualities the Church needs on the Chair of Peter."

"Desion, I'm too old to be elected."

"You're seventy. After the long reign of John Paul II, some of our colleagues will regard your age as one of your most appealing qualities."

Barbo smiled. "In other words, Desion, my pontificate will be short."

"I'd rather say that your pontificate would not be too long."

"But longevity runs in my family. My father died when he was ninety-four."

Desion chuckled. "Keep that fact to yourself, My Lord Cardinal Barbo."

A bell rang.

"Cardinal Marini calls us to our task, Francesco."

The camerlengo rapped his gavel to bring the session of the General Congregation to order. "My brothers, we have much to do."

As he rapped the gavel a second time, a Vatican staff member hurried up to the podium and handed Marini a note. The camerlengo was dumbstruck at what he read. "His Eminence Cardinal Obregon has suffered a massive stroke. The doctors say he will not live out the day."

There was stunned silence in the room.

His face ashen, Cardinal Chavez rose from his seat. "Alejandro was my close friend for many years. I must go to his bedside." Tears rolled down the Mexican cardinal's cheeks as he tried to remain composed.

Cardinal Muñoz stood up and started to follow Chavez out of the room. Chavez shook his head. "No, Ignacio. Alejandro would want us to proceed as before. The Church must have a new Holy Father."

When the shock of Cardinal Obregon's stroke had worn off, Cardinal Marini opened his briefcase and took out a letter. "There is more bad news. Cardinal Tien has emailed me from Hong Kong.

His doctors are concerned that he may have been exposed to a new and virulant strain of Kowloon flu."

"Then he must not come," insisted Cardinal Vaggio from Florence. "Can you imagine a serious outbreak of flu in the conclave?"

Marini nodded in agreement. "I will inform Cardinal Tien. I'm sure he won't be surprised by the decision."

Marini bent over and rummaged through his briefcase. He took out an envelope sealed with red wax. "Yesterday the papal chamberlain found this among Benedict's papers. It is labeled 'cardinal nomination *in pectore.*'" There was a murmur in the room. Barbo stood to be recognized. "Pope Benedict did tell me at the last Consistory that he was nominating one cardinal *in pectore.* The pontiff was convinced that public nomination of the individual should be deferred to a later date. Cardinal Krause, you are the most knowledgeable canon lawyer among us. What should we do?"

"If a nominating pope dies without revealing the name of the 'in pectore' appointment, the nomination is void. *Mutatis mutandis,* the same rule should apply when a pope abdicates. The *in pectore* nomination should lapse. We should burn the document."

"Why don't we just ask Benedict who it is and give him his hat?" Cardinal Reysin shouted out his remarks as he walked down the center aisle of the meeting room.

"It's a question of canon law, Cardinal Reysin. Even if Benedict announced the name today, the appointment would be void."

"Krause, I thought you said that the rule specifically applied only to a papal death, not to a papal abdication."

"Yes, but a rule of canon law must also be applied *'in consimili casu'*—for these purposes, an abdication is similar to a death."

Reysin muttered for all to hear, "Between canon lawyers and the Curia, it's amazing that the Catholic Church has managed to survive and surge into the eighteenth century."

As the cardinals left the meeting room at the end of the afternoon session, Cardinal Desion walked out beside Barbo. "I would say it's been a good day for Diefenbacher. Obregon won't be around to speak against him. And Tien! He would never have voted for

Diefenbacher if he were the last candidate on earth. As for Reysin—his little exchange with Krause probably pushed the American farther into Diefenbacher's camp."

Professor Baldini handed the wet sheet to Fellows. "Martin, the preliminary carbon dating results confirm my earlier test. The parchment is first century—it's not a forgery."

Fellows's face was impassive as he looked at the results of the test. After a few moments, Fellows excused himself and left Baldini's office. "I must call Cardinal Barbo with this information."

Barbo walked back to his apartment on Via Mascherino. As he passed the Church of San Dominico, he stepped inside and knelt in a back pew. When he had first been appointed secretary of state, Barbo often stopped at the church to say Mass on his way to the Apostolic Palace. But it must have been two years since he had done so.

Barbo saw an old woman patiently cleaning the votive candleholders throughout the church. Picking up each holder, she would scrape off the congealed wax and insert a new candle. Barbo could see that for the woman arranging each new votive candle was a prayer.

"Signora, I would like to say Mass at one of the side chapels. Could you open the sacristy so I can vest?"

The woman was about to refuse Barbo's request when she noticed his skullcap and the scarlet piping on his black cassock. "Of course, Your Eminence." The woman hurried to unlock the sacristy. She had never spoken to a cardinal before. Her children would be impressed.

"Serve the Mass for me, Signora."

"The pastor does not permit women to do such a thing, Your Eminence."

"It will be our secret then."

"I do not know the words."

"They are not hard. I will help you."

At approximately 9:15, the phone rang in Barbo's apartment. Nervously, he picked up the receiver. "Well, Martin, what are the results?"

"The carbon dating shows the parchment to be first century—it was probably made sometime around 30 A.D. I'm sorry."

"Are you absolutely certain?"

"Not absolutely certain. I would have preferred doing the test in a more up-to-date lab, but even if we did, I doubt there would be a material change of results."

"There must be other tests."

"One of Baldini's colleagues tested the parchment for pollen. There were spores on the manuscript that are characteristic of Palestine."

"Could the translation be wrong?"

"Anything's possible, Your Eminence, but I wouldn't hold out too much hope. I'll go over the whole document again myself to be absolutely sure, but from a quick read it does seem to say that Jesus and the Magdalene were married according to Jewish law in their year 3791. It also mentions the birth of two children."

Barbo put down the phone. Trust in God does not bring immediate results. He looked in his Rolodex and dialed Visconti's home number.

"Ah, Eminenza, I'm sad to say the results of your carbon dating test coincide with Baldini's. They both show the manuscript to be genuine. You probably had hoped for a different result."

"Yes, but it doesn't really matter, Visconti. I've decided not to accept the demands of your clients."

There was a long pause on the other end of the phone. "As you wish Cardinal Barbo. Diefenbacher will pay us handsomely for the manuscript. Think of the impact it will have in the conclave. It could very easily make him pope."

"Thank you for the warning, Visconti. By the way, commend your clients in Sicily. Theirs was one of the more innovative attempts at blackmail."

"I admire your courage, Eminenza, but I question your judgment. I hope we do business again. Religion and business are separate sides of life. One should not interfere with the other."

Chapter XXIII

THE PRELATE FROM DURBAN

SEVERAL BUSES PULLED up in front of the Arch of Titus, disgorging scores of Japanese tourists intent on photographing whatever there was to see in the Roman Forum. Sitting on a bench in the shade of the arch, Cardinal Hans Diefenbacher looked on in amusement as tour guides with their pennants and handheld microphones divided their customers into manageable groups. With his graying hair and round face, Diefenbacher was the epitome of ordinariness.

An elegant-looking man climbed out of a taxicab on Via Imperiale and walked toward the seated cardinal. "It is good to see you again, Your Eminence."

Diefenbacher stood and shook Pietro Visconti's hand. "Your telephone call intrigued me. What was it you wanted to show me?"

Visconti raised his hands in mock self-defense. "Eminence, first a bottle of wine and perhaps some risotto ai funghi.... There's a wonderful trattoria across Via Imperiale near the Church of San Pietro in Vincoli."

Diefenbacher shook his head. "I appreciate your offer, but I do not drink alcohol. The conclave begins in a few days and there's much to do."

"As you wish, Your Eminence." Visconti opened his attaché case and laid a photocopy of a manuscript on a large stone.

"What's this?" Diefenbacher asked.

"Read the Hebrew yourself, Eminence—particularly the place I've marked."

Diefenbacher looked at the lines Visconti had circled. When he had finished reading, the cardinal smiled and handed the copy of the manuscript back to Visconti. "Did you really think I would be fooled by this?"

"Then you might want to look at these, Your Eminence?" Visconti took a manila envelope out of his attaché case and handed it to Diefenbacher. "Inside the envelope are the results of carbon and pollen tests conducted by a Professor Baldini from the University of Rome. They show that the parchment originated in first-century Palestine."

Diefenbacher took the copy of the manuscript back from Visconti and read it a second time. Diefenbacher stared at Visconti. "Where did you get this?"

"Two American professors took the manuscript from the Vatican Library and offered to sell it to one of my clients. My client thought it prudent to take the parchment away from them. Unfortunately in the process one American was killed and the other is in critical condition in Gemelli Hospital."

"How much do you want for this?" Diefenbacher's voice was matter of fact, as though he were pricing a cassock.

"Ten million euros in cash."

Diefenbacher stood up angrily. "That's preposterous."

Visconti made his point directly. "I would have thought the papacy would be worth much more."

For a second, Diefenbacher seemed to waiver. "I need time to think," was all he said.

"The offer expires today. Why do you need time to think? You've always wanted the papacy. Here's your chance to have it."

"You forget one thing, Visconti. Suppose this professor in Gemelli Hospital recovers and accuses me of possessing stolen property?"

Visconti looked at Diefenbacher. "She would have very compelling reasons not to do something so foolish. Also, my clients can make sure that such an event will never happen."

Diefenbacher picked up the parchment and read it a third time. "It will take me several days to raise such a large sum of money."

Visconti spoke in an understanding tone. "The particulars of payment are always subject to negotiation."

"Signor Visconti, under the circumstances, I will accept your offer for some risotto. We must discuss specifics."

Leaving the Forum, the two men crossed Via Imperiale and walked toward San Pietro in Vincoli.

As the days counted down to the opening of the conclave, Cardinal Barbo spent the better part of his time in meetings of the General Congregation. Although curial appointments were terminated upon the death or abdication of a pope, Barbo continued to act as the de facto secretary of state. Dispatches had to be answered, ongoing foreign policy matters had to be managed, and a relief fund for victims of the Israeli assault on the Church of the Holy Sepulchre had to be set up. Barbo asked Cardinal Calvaux to monitor issues relating to Pope Benedict's peace initiative. Phone calls were coming in from those who had pledged to assist in the effort, wondering whether the Vatican would scrap the initiative now that Pope Benedict had abdicated.

Along with Cardinals Chavez and Diefenbacher, Barbo was frequently mentioned in the media as "papabile." Rome's *Il Messaggero* emphasized Barbo's detailed knowledge of the Vatican bureaucracy. The secretary of state knew intimately each and every member of the Curia. He was also an Italian and, as the newspaper pointed out boastfully, the country most heavily represented in the College of Cardinals was still Italy. The weekly magazine *Panorama* noted Barbo's linguistic and diplomatic skills and called him an "effective consensus builder." The only negatives mentioned were his lack of pastoral experience and his age. At seventy, some might regard Barbo as a little too old for the job. But as one Vatican pundit wrote, older men than Barbo have been elected to the papacy—John XXIII for one.

During the final sessions of the General Congregation, Barbo carefully watched Diefenbacher for the smallest hint of what he was thinking. By now, Barbo had to assume that Visconti had offered to sell Diefenbacher the parchment. Barbo knew that the South African was shrewd and calculating. Two things would worry him: the manuscript's authenticity and its provenance. The carbon dating and pollen tests should convince Diefenbacher that the parchment was authentic. The provenance of the manuscript, however, was a different matter. A cardinal with papal aspirations would not wish to be caught in possession of a stolen manuscript, no matter what it said.

Barbo suspected that Visconti would not divulge Barbo's involvement in the matter. Mentioning Barbo would only scare Diefenbacher off. But Visconti would likely tell Diefenbacher about Bielgard and Michellini. From Diefenbacher's perspective, with Bielgard dead, only two people knew the parchment was stolen—Visconti and Michellini. Diefenbacher knew that Visconti would not incriminate his client. Therefore the person who posed the greatest threat to Diefenbacher's papal ambitions was Jane Michellini. Was Diefenbacher capable of murder if it would assure him the papacy? Barbo feared that the answer was yes.

Barbo dialed Detective Cameri's office.

"Cardinal Barbo! I hope you're not calling about last night. The doctors were unable to save the baby."

After a moment's hesitation, Barbo responded, "Maybe I can save another life instead."

The detective was puzzled. "What do you mean?"

"The American professor in Gemelli Hospital, Jane Michellini."

"Yes, what about her?" asked Cameri.

"Her life is in danger."

"What evidence do you have?" Cameri quickly became the trained professional.

"None."

"Is Visconti involved in this?" Cameri asked bluntly.

"Yes," Barbo responded.

"I'll station someone outside Michellini's door." Cameri suspected that he had just been handed the break of a lifetime.

When he awoke the next morning, Barbo dialed the main number of Gemelli Hospital. The cardinal sat patiently as a recording ran through an interminable list of extensions. As if begrudging the release of the information, the recording finally yielded the schedule of visiting hours. Except for members of the immediate family, regular visiting hours began daily at ten in the morning.

Barbo dialed Cardinal Marini's number. "Agostino, we begin the conclave in two days. I'm coming around to your point of view. Whoever makes the best landlord for St. Peters will also make the best steward for the faithful."

Marini chuckled. "There could be worse ways of choosing a pope. By the way, Francesco, I spent a good part of last night assigning each cardinal elector a room in the Domus. I put Diefenbacher on a corridor with his liberal supporters. He can preach to the choir."

Barbo laughed. "Pope Benedict believed that he owed his election to Cardinal Misteau, the camerlengo at the time. Misteau lodged Benedict between two highly influential members of the Sacred College. 'Grand electors' was what he called them."

"Well, Francesco, I gave you a room on a corridor with Reysin and two other Americans."

"Why?"

"Because they're rumored to be Diefenbacher supporters! Maybe you can change their minds."

"In all your electoral manipulations, My Lord Camerlengo, leave some room for the Holy Spirit."

Marini spoke playfully. "He needs no allocation of space from me."

Barbo decided to take an early morning walk before visiting Professor Michellini in Gemelli Hospital. If he moved quickly enough, he could walk to the Trevi Fountain and still arrive at the hospital by ten o'clock.

The Trevi Fountain always intrigued Barbo—not for the romance associated with it, but for the purity of its waters. Legend has it that the spring water cascading through the Trevi is the sweetest in all of Rome. Before reaching the fountain, the water flows through much of the city, bringing life and beauty with it. To the cardinal, the waters of the great fountain were a symbol of God's grace flowing freely through the world—available to all who needed it.

As Barbo sat on the steps of the fountain, the first tourist bus arrived. In a matter of seconds, a crowd of men and women were throwing coins in the water to assure their return to Rome. Barbo glanced at his watch. It was already 9:30, and the ride to Gemelli would take close to half an hour. He walked over to a taxi stand in front of the Church of Saints Vincenzo and Anastasio.

As the taxi threaded its way through the narrow streets around the Trevi, a profound sense of peace came over Barbo. He had felt it years ago as a young priest in the hospitals of Lourdes. He could remember the tears of joy in the eyes of the sick as he blessed them and absolved them of their sins. He had felt it again two nights ago when he knelt beside the dying prostitute Maria. She and the others were his reason for becoming a priest, not the endless piles of communiqués that awaited him every day in his office. Over the years, he had allowed the communiqués and the telexes to dominate his life—to become his life.

When the taxi pulled up to the hospital, Barbo hurried up the entrance steps and stopped at the information desk. He asked the receptionist for Professor Michellini's room number.

"Are you a relative?"

"No, a friend."

"Professor Michellini died this morning at 7:32 A.M. We are contacting her family."

Barbo was stunned. "How did it happen?"

"For that, you must talk to someone on staff. I'll page Doctor Tolato."

In five minutes, a young intern arrived at the information desk. "Dr. Tolato is performing surgery at the moment. He asked me to meet with you. I understand you are a friend of Professor Michellini?"

"Yes, how did she die?"

"Dr. Tolato had just finished aspirating her right lung. She seemed fine until she started to cough up blood. We rushed her to the emergency room, but it was too late. I'm being frank. We just don't know what happened."

Cardinal Barbo asked for an envelope. "Do me a favor, Doctor. If Professor Michellini has any remaining hospital charges, take them out of this." Cardinal Barbo took off his ring and put it in the envelope. "If there's anything else that I can do, please contact me." Barbo handed the intern a business card.

"Certainly."

When the intern read the name on the card, he was at a loss. "Your Eminence, I'm sorry—perhaps some coffee—the director of the hospital will insist on greeting you."

"I'm sorry, but I must return to the Vatican. The conclave begins tomorrow."

The intern looked at a patient list. "Your Eminence, are you aware that Cardinal Galliardin was admitted to the hospital last night?"

"Pierre Galliardin?"

"Yes, his secretary brought the cardinal to the emergency room. He's resting in a private room. The cancer has spread."

Barbo was visibly upset. "Take me to his room. He is an old friend."

The intern escorted Barbo to a floor reserved for cancer patients. "Cardinal Galliardin is in the last room on the right." The intern hurried off to tell the hospital director that a leading candidate for pope was in his hospital.

Barbo tapped lightly on the door and pushed it open. Galliardin sat propped up in bed reading a magazine.

"Pierre, no one told me you were here." Barbo was shocked at how pale and gaunt Galliardin looked. His cheeks were as white as the sheets on his bed.

"Francesco, I have grown old. Unfortunately, my cancer has grown as well. Now there are lesions in the liver. But enough talk about my health. Tell me about the General Congregation. Does Diefenbacher have a chance? I hope not."

"There are many who support him."

"Fools, all of them!" Galliardin hurled his magazine to the floor. "Are they blind to the harm he will cause the Church? I'm eighty-eight, but they won't let wise old owls like me be heard in the conclave." Barbo could see that Galliardin was becoming agitated.

"We have been friends for a long time, Francesco. You have grown in the job of secretary of state. I've watched from the sidelines. You have the natural instincts of a diplomat."

Barbo laid a hand on Galliardin's shoulder. "I had a good mentor. You taught me the importance of nuance and subtlety—how an arched eyebrow can speak volumes."

"I understand there's much talk of your becoming our next Holy Father. Some see it as a choice among Diefenbacher, Chavez, and you. They say Diefenbacher will come close but fall short of the necessary eighty-three votes. Chavez will not be able to get that many either. Both sides will turn to you as a compromise choice."

Barbo laughed. "What's the saying? 'He who enters the conclave pope comes out cardinal.'"

Galliardin got out of bed carefully and walked slowly to a chair. "Before I was admitted here last night, I received a call from an old friend, Aldo Cacaglio."

"The mayor of Palermo?" Barbo had met Cacaglio at a dinner party at Pietro Visconti's home.

"Yes. He wanted to know what would happen in the conclave."

Barbo gave Galliardin a good-natured look. "Cacaglio chose the right person to call."

"Thank you, Francesco. But there was more to what he said."

"More?" Barbo bent down to pick up the magazine Galliardin had thrown on the floor. Barbo saw that the front page story was an interview with Cardinal Calvaux.

"Cacaglio was quite circumspect, but he was clearly using me to pass a message to you. He knows that we are friends."

"What was the message?"

Galliardin hesitated before continuing. "The Mafia could help you become the next pope. There are at least five cardinals who will do their bidding."

Barbo smiled at his old friend. "There's always talk of this or that bishop being connected to organized crime, but to say that there are five electors who would vote for the candidate selected by the Mafia—I refuse to accept that."

Galliardin poured himself a glass of water. "I'm amazed that there aren't more of them. It's costly to run a diocese."

"And the price for Mafia support?"

"Cacaglio didn't say. I'm not sure he even knows. All he said was that Barbo would know what the price is."

"Was there anything else in Cacaglio's message?"

"Yes. If you wish the support of the five cardinals, submit a blank ballot on the first vote of the conclave. When the tally comes up one short, they'll know you've agreed to what the Mafia wants."

"As well as anyone, you know that I won't allow myself to owe the papacy to the Mafia. I've already told them that I will not do business with them."

Galliardin cleared his throat. "The Catholic Church is like an old tree, Francesco. It produces good fruit and bad fruit. What is so remarkable is that with all its imperfections and with all its faults, it perseveres."

"You're not suggesting that I do the bidding of the Mafia?"

"I suggest nothing, Francesco. All I say is this. Anyone who sits in the Chair of Peter has made compromises along the way. The Church has learned—wisely I think—not to shine too much light on the complexities of a papal election. A glimpse or two by candle-light is more than sufficient. We all talk of the will of the Holy Spirit, but in the end, it is compromise that elects a pope."

"But these are criminals—they...."

"Francesco," Cardinal Galliardin scowled at his friend. "Didn't Pius XI sign the Lateran Treaty with Mussolini? Didn't he also sign a concordat with Hitler?"

"Yes."

"They were distasteful compromises, but Pius agreed to them because he was a man who had both feet rooted here on earth. He was a realist, not a dreamer."

"There's a difference between what Pius did and this. Mussolini and Hitler were heads of state; they were not ordinary criminals like those in the Mafia."

"So where does this logic lead us? Nations perform criminal acts just like individuals do. We could write a criminal history of any country. You choose—Italy, France, the United States. There's little difference between making a compromise with Mussolini and making a compromise with the Mafia."

"You argue your case well, my old friend, but I'm not convinced by your realpolitik."

"Francesco, I don't know what the Mafia wants of you and I don't care to know. But I do know one thing. You understand diplomacy, and you are a courageous and compassionate man. I would rather see you on the Throne of Saint Peter than Chavez or Diefenbacher."

"Even if I owed my election to the Mafia?" Barbo asked.

"Yes, even if you owed your election to the Mafia."

A lonely church bell rang eleven o'clock. Barbo looked at his watch. "I must go, Pierre. The camerlengo wants me to attend this morning's session of the General Congregation to answer any last-minute questions about the situation in the Middle East. Once we are out of conclave, I will come back to see you."

As Barbo stood up to leave, Galliardin took his hand. "You told me once about an image that the Templars used in their meditations. They concentrated on the place on the Cross where the vertical and horizontal bars come together."

"Yes. For them, it was a symbol of the need to integrate the spiritual and the material. You have a good memory, Pierre."

"The image stayed with me. I have often thought of it in my own meditations. Francesco, all I ask you to do is think of the problems facing the Church—the scandals in America, relations with Islam, the rise of Christian fundamentalism in Third World countries. Then decide where you should center yourself on the Cross."

"You leave little room for the Holy Spirit."

"The Holy Spirit works through our heads and our hearts. Consider what I've said, Francesco."

Anticipation filled the streets of Rome as the cardinals met for the final session of the General Congregation. Cardinal Marini's agenda listed only a few last-minute items. Two cardinals, each with a pacemaker implant, asked that medical technicians be allowed to accompany them into the conclave. The requests were granted without debate. The only item that required discussion was an unusual request from Cardinal Stewart, the Archbishop of Melbourne, Australia. Stewart had undergone hip-replacement surgery. The cardinal's doctors would not let him fly until a month after the surgery. As a consequence, the earliest flight he could take would arrive at Leonardo da Vinci Airport late on the first day of the conclave. His request to enter the conclave late was granted, although several Latin American cardinals supporting Chavez voted against it. They assumed Stewart was a supporter of Diefenbacher.

As the cardinals left the final session of the General Congregation, several reporters tried to interview Cardinal Barbo but he smiled and continued walking. He did stop to speak with a troop of boy scouts from Milan. With their sleeping bags and knapsacks, they planned to sleep in the St. Peter's Square until the new pope was chosen. He blessed the group and jocularly prayed that the weather would not turn cold.

As Barbo walked into his office, Detective Cameri was sitting in the reception area.

He jumped to his feet when Barbo entered the room. "Your Eminence, I must have a word with you right now. Professor Michellini is dead."

"Yes, I know."

Barbo escorted Cameri into his office and closed the door behind them.

"You know more than you're telling me. Who is behind this homicide? Visconti?"

Barbo did not respond. He knew what the alternatives were. He could meet privately with Diefenbacher and threaten that, unless the South African withdrew his candidacy for pope, Barbo would rise in the conclave and accuse Diefenbacher of having bought stolen property from Visconti. An accusation like this coming from a respected cleric like Barbo would doom Diefenbacher's chances of being elected pope. Not only that, the accusation would publicly humiliate him in front of his colleagues in the Sacred College. Given the consequences, Diefenbacher would have no choice but to withdraw his candidacy. If Barbo did that and nothing more, however, Diefenbacher would escape punishment for his possible complicity in Michellini's death. When the scandal over priestly sex abuse surfaced in the United States, Barbo was outspoken in his criticism of the subsequent cover-up by members of the episcopacy. If he failed to divulge Diefenbacher's possible involvement in Michellini's death, how was he any different from those American bishops? Failing to accuse a prince of the Church of possible complicity in murder was morally indistinguishable from failing to accuse wayward priests of child abuse.

"You must make me one promise, Cameri?"

"What is that?"

"What I tell you must be kept in confidence until you have proof of what I say."

"You have my word."

"I believe one of my colleagues—Hans Cardinal Diefenbacher—was involved in Michellini's death."

"A prince of the Church?"

"Yes."

"Why would Cardinal Diefenbacher conspire to kill Michellini?"

"Look at this, Cameri. It's a copy of a manuscript that Professors Bielgard and Michellini found in the Vatican Library. They used it to blackmail the Church."

"What does it say?"

"It says that Jesus and the Magdalene were married and had two children. Bielgard and Michellini hired Visconti to blackmail the Church on their behalf."

"But it didn't turn out that way."

"No, it didn't. Once Visconti knew what the parchment said, he decided that he would use it against the Church in his own way. He had two of his men take the manuscript away from Bielgard and Michellini that night on Via di San Marco."

"How much did he want from the Church?"

"It wasn't money. Visconti wanted favors for his clients—the use of Vatican bank accounts to transfer money, Vatican pressure on the Italian government to remove troublesome prosecutors. When I refused, he said he would sell it to Diefenbacher."

"Why would Diefenbacher want it?"

"Votes in the conclave!"

"Ah, now I see. The parchment showing Jesus was married would allow him to attack priestly celibacy and the role of women in the Church."

"Yes, he would become an instant hero of the liberal wing of the Sacred College. The parchment might be enough to put him in the Chair of Peter."

"And the connection to Michellini?" Cameri thought for a moment. "Of course, she would be the only person who could realistically hurt Diefenbacher's chances. It would not help his papal aspirations if he were found to have bought stolen goods from the Mafia."

"No, it wouldn't."

"So you think Diefenbacher arranged her death?"

"'Arranged' may not be the precise word, but at some level, I'm sure Diefenbacher was involved in it."

"Why have you told me all of this, Your Eminence?"

"I don't want Michellini's death on my conscience."

"I cannot prosecute you as an accessory in the murder of either Bielgard or Michellini."

"Can't or won't?"

"Can't. The Italian Government grants diplomatic immunity to both the pope as head of the Vatican state, and the secretary of state as head of the Vatican government. Office has its privileges."

"I will not hide behind my office or a technicality."

"I doubt the prime minister will want the Italian government caught up in a diplomatic controversy with the Holy See—particularly when it involves the Vatican secretary of state. But such immunity does not extend to Diefenbacher."

The phone rang at Interpol's headquarters in Paris. "This is Detective Cameri from the Rome Police Department. Is Ira Panner there?"

In a moment, a man came on the line. "How can I help you, Giorgio? You never call just to say hello."

"Ira, I need a quick search done. In the last week, have there been any major bank transfers from Durban, South Africa, to any accounts in Rome?"

"How big is major?"

"More than a million dollars U.S."

"That should be easy enough. I'll call you back in a couple of hours."

Later that day, a police officer handed the phone to Cameri. "It's for you, Sir. I think it's from Interpol."

"Cameri, this is Ira. I have the information you wanted. During the past week, there's been no transfer of more than a million from any Durban account."

"Damn it. I was sure there would be."

"Wait, I'm not finished. There has been lots of traffic out of Durban, but in amounts under $500,000—$300,000 to an account in Turin, $420,000 to one in Palermo. As of yesterday, the transfers totaled more than $2 million. What drew my attention to them were the transferee bank accounts—they're all on Interpol's watch list—suspected of being controlled by the Mafia."

"Thanks, Ira. I owe you one."

Barbo was exhausted as he unlocked his apartment door. The death of Michellini, the visit to Galliardin's bedside, the meeting with Cameri had all left him emotionally drained. As he took off his cassock, he noticed the message light on his phone was flashing. He pressed the button. It was a message from Cameri.

"Your Eminence, there has been an interesting series of bank transfers from Durban to Italian accounts. By the way, Gemelli thinks Professor Michellini died from minute amounts of cyanide injected into her IV. We're looking into it."

As he listened to the message, Barbo noticed that his housekeeper had left a FedEx packet on his desk. The return address was Castel Gondolfo. When he opened the envelope, he found a one-page letter from Benedict written in his own hand.

Barbo's heart jumped a beat when he read it. He quickly rang his office. "Enrico, arrange for a car to Castel Gondolfo. I must leave immediately."

"You sound upset, Your Eminence. Is Pope Benedict alright?"

"Have the car at my apartment in ten minutes."

Chapter XXIV

EXTRA OMNES

THE OPENING DAY of the conclave dawned cold and blustery—an inauspicious beginning for so momentous an occasion. Days before, the news media had staked out places in St. Peter's Square to film the cardinals as they processed from the Apostolic Palace to the basilica to celebrate the Mass of the Holy Spirit. Curious bystanders watched as cardinals arrived in limousines from their lodgings throughout Rome. Vatican staff removed suitcases and garment bags from the car trunks and carried them into the Domus Sanctae Marthae, the Vatican hotel that would be used for the first time.

At precisely 9:00 A.M., the door of the Apostolic Palace opened and a contingent of Swiss Guards paraded into the square. A large crowd of onlookers cheered as Cardinal Marini, the camerlengo, appeared in the doorway. The rest of the Sacred College followed behind him in order of ecclesiastical rank—cardinal bishops ahead of cardinal priests, and cardinal priests ahead of cardinal deacons. Loud applause erupted when Cardinal Chavez, the most senior cardinal priest, walked out into the square. Smiling, he waved to the crowds and blessed a group of Mexican tourists who held up a picture of Our Lady of Guadalupe.

The loudest applause, however, met the Archbishop of Tokyo, Misho Cardinal Yapok. Yapok had suffered a stroke several months before and had to be taken into the basilica in a wheelchair. Drums began to sound when the six-foot-five Archbishop of Kinshasa, Uganda, Aloysius Cardinal Muramba, processed across the square. As if embodying the confidence of the African continent, Muramba wore his tribal dashiki over his cardinal's robes.

The only disturbance occurred when Cardinal Diefenbacher appeared in the square. A woman pulled out a placard from under her raincoat. "The Archbishop of Durban is the Anti-Christ." Luckily for an embarrassed Diefenbacher, the message was written in Afrikaans, understood by few of those watching the procession. Swiss Guards wasted no time in escorting the woman out of St. Peter's Square. As he processed across the square, Cardinal Barbo looked tired and preoccupied. He barely responded to the applause of his staff, watching the procession from their office windows.

As the cardinal electors entered the great basilica for Mass, no one would predict how long the conclave would last. Three names continued to be mentioned as successors to Pope Benedict: Cardinals Barbo, Chavez, and Diefenbacher—the "B, C, D candidates" as one newspaper humorously referred to them. The consensus among experienced Vatican watchers was that, in the end, Diefenbacher or Barbo would win. Diefenbacher either did or did not have the necessary votes, which would become apparent early in the balloting. If he did not have the votes of eighty-three electors, the cardinals would most likely turn to a centrist member of the Curia like Barbo rather than to an archconservative member of Opus Dei like Chavez. Rome's influential daily, *Il Messaggero,* however, disagreed. Chavez knew the members of the Curia from the days when he worked in Rome. His charm and sense of humor made him a popular figure among liberals and conservatives alike. In the end, many cardinals might choose to overlook his conservatism and vote for his humanity. The fact that he was seventy-nine years of age was also a positive factor. If Chavez turned out to be a mistake, his advanced age might at least limit the damage. Rome's odds makers seemed to agree with *Il Messaggero.* In the *Totopapa,* the daily betting pool on the papal election, the odds were three to two for Chavez, and five to one each for Diefenbacher and Barbo. No one seemed to care that betting on a papal election could result in excommunication from the Church.

The master of ceremonies stood in the center aisle of the basilica. As each cardinal elector approached, the master of ceremonies bowed and escorted him to his seat in front of the high altar. Following tradition, the Mass opening the conclave, the Missa Pro Eligendo Papa, was concelebrated by the oldest cardinal elector from each of the three cardinatial ranks—in this case, Cardinal Bishop Bernardo Filistrini from Albano, Italy, Cardinal

Priest Stephen Verebrand from Munich, and Cardinal Deacon Agostino Marini, the camerlengo.

As Cardinal Barbo was ushered to his seat by the master of ceremonies, he thought of last night's sudden trip to visit Pope Benedict at Castel Gondolfo. He hardly heard the camerlengo's homily on the significance of what was about to take place. The sound of communion bells jolted Barbo out of his reveries. He received the Eucharist from Cardinal Filistrini and returned to his pre-dieu. The three concelebrants intoned the closing words *Ite Missa Est*—"Go forth, the Mass is ended." Barbo rose from his seat and processed with the other electors to the rear of St Peter's, where a corridor connected the basilica to the Apostolic Palace, where the conclave would take place. Once the cardinal electors had entered the Apostolic Palace, the area would be cordoned off from the rest of the world.

There was a pause in the procession while the camerlengo consulted with the captain of the Swiss Guard about some remaining security issues before the cardinal electors entered the conclave.

Cardinal Muñoz walked over to where Barbo stood in the line. "You look tired, Francesco. Are you ill?"

"Thank you for your concern, Ignacio. I visited the Holy Father at Castel Gondolfo last night and returned later than I expected."

Muñoz shook his head. "Poor Benedict. I pray for him every day."

"So do I."

"This conclave will be very different from the one that elected Benedict. Eighteen years ago, there were sixty-one electors—today there are one hundred twenty-three—double Benedict's number. European cardinals, even if they voted as a bloc, could no longer muster the necessary two-thirds-plus-one majority. They'd still be five votes short."

"Yes, to receive the necessary eighty-three votes, a candidate will need wide geographical support."

"Let's be frank, Francesco." Muñoz pulled Barbo aside. "Chavez and Diefenbacher will both have strong backing in the early ballots. But some of Diefenbacher's votes are soft. He will have to win quickly—probably on the first or second ballot. If not, his support will quickly erode."

Barbo did not respond. If Diefenbacher had indeed bought the parchment from Visconti, Cardinal Muñoz's conventional wisdom would be sorely tested. Releasing the manuscript might cause a sudden groundswell of support for Diefenbacher. Many cardinals might see the South African as the best candidate to deal with the issues of priestly celibacy and the status of women in the Church that the parchment raised.

"Francesco, we Latin American cardinals will support Chavez, of course, but the loss of Obregon has been a terrible blow to Chavez. If he cannot attract the necessary votes, then we must look elsewhere. We will not support Diefenbacher. He's your typical Jesuit intellectual who thinks he's smarter than everyone else. Worse still, I don't think he knows how to cry. Many of my colleagues talk about you as our next Holy Father."

"Ignacio, you are being frank with me, so I'll be frank with you. Many of my views would not sit well with Opus Dei."

Muñoz smiled. "Opus Dei is not some diabolical force. It is a movement infused with Spanish mysticism—the mysticism of John of the Cross and Theresa of Avila. If we went through a list of issues, one by one, you might be surprised. We would probably see eye-to-eye on most of them."

"And on the others?"

"We would agree to disagree. Members of Opus Dei do not believe that just because you disagree with us you also disagree with God. I understand that this was the attitude of the Order of the Temple, but it's not ours."

"I didn't know you were an expert on the Templars, Ignacio."

"Your dissertation became required reading for many of us."

"Think of what I have said, Francesco." Muñoz returned to his place in the line.

Out of one corner of his eye, Barbo saw Martin Fellows in animated conversation with a Swiss Guard. Somehow Fellows had gained entrance to the basilica, and the Swiss Guard was insisting that he leave immediately.

Barbo hurried over to the door of the church. "Officer, it is all right. This man works in the Vatican Library. He can stay for a moment."

"Eminence, my orders are to allow no one into the church. You saw the woman with the placard earlier today."

"Please, Francesco, I must speak with you. I tried calling you on your cell phone but there was no answer."

"Cell phones are not allowed in the conclave. Why must you speak to me?"

"It's about the parchment."

"The parchment? You told me that it was authentic."

"It is, but. . . ."

"But what?"

"Please, Your Eminence, I have something to tell you."

"Officer, excuse us for a moment."

Barbo and Fellows walked over to the doors of the basilica. "The parchment's a forgery, Your Eminence—at least a forgery of sorts."

"What do you mean, Martin, 'a forgery of sorts?' You told me earlier today that carbon dating showed the manuscript to be from the time of Christ."

"It is from the time of Christ, Your Eminence, but that's not the point."

"Martin, stop the riddle right now. It either is or is not a forgery."

"Your Eminence, when I translated the document, I noticed one of the letters in the name Jesus looked different."

"Different?"

"Yes, different. I can't describe it better than that. Call it a hunch, an intuition, call it what you like. But I looked at the manuscript under ultraviolet light. I could see that the name Jesus had been superimposed over another name."

"What name was under 'Jesus'?"

"It was the name 'John'."

Barbo was puzzled. "Why would someone blot out 'John' and write 'Jesus' over it? It makes no sense."

"But it does."

"What do you mean? Why would a forger try to convince the world that Jesus was the father of these two children?"

"Perhaps we're looking at this from the wrong angle. Remember Herod Antipas beheaded John the Baptizer. If I recall my New Testament correctly, John was preaching against Herod, condemning his adulterous marriage to his brother's wife. At a deeper level, however, John was challenging Herod's legitimacy to rule."

"True, but. . . ."

"If Herod Antipas knew that John had two children, he most likely would have tried to arrest and kill them. Substituting Jesus as their father in the Jewish census records would help keep them safe. You know that early on Jesus was a disciple of John. Wouldn't he have agreed to help protect his mentor's family?"

"So it was John the Baptizer who married the Magdalene. After John was beheaded, she became a disciple of Jesus."

"Yes, that's what must have happened."

"God works in strange ways. I had long since given up hope, but now you've brought me the miracle I prayed for."

"There's one thing more, Eminence. Baldini doesn't know about my ultraviolet test of the manuscript. He was out of the room when I did it."

Barbo's eyes widened. "You mean Visconti doesn't know the manuscript is a forgery."

"That's right."

"Thank you, Martin. You have been a great help."

As the Swiss Guard led Fellows out of the basilica, Barbo saw the procession start up again. Putting one's trust in God may not bring instantaneous results, but they do come at the right time.

When the last cardinal elector had entered the conclave area, the Prefect of the Papal Household stood at the door to the Apostolic Palace and formally intoned the words *Extra Omnes*—"Outside, Everyone." With Cardinal Marini at his side, the prefect closed the heavy bronze door to the palace and locked it from the inside with a large key. No one could now enter or leave the conclave area until a new pope was elected.

The next day at ten o'clock in the morning, the cardinals entered the Sistine Chapel for their first ballot. Each elector was provided with a chair and a small table covered in green velvet. The Apostolic Constitution governing the election of a new pope required that, on each day of the conclave, the cardinals take a total of four votes, two in the morning session and two in the afternoon session, until a new pope is chosen. After each session, the ballots from the two votes are burned in a metal stove standing next to the door of the Sistine Chapel. When the balloting finally elects a pope, the camerlengo pours a vial of chemicals over the paper ballots before burning them. The chemicals send white smoke up through the flue in the ceiling. When the voting fails to elect a pope, however, the ballots are burned without additives, producing black smoke. When white smoke appears, the waiting crowd in St. Peter's Square begins to cheer and chant *"Viva il Papa!"*

In the Sistine Chapel, Barbo sat between Cardinal McDermott from New York and Cardinal Vaggio from Florence. Like the others, when Barbo took his seat, he placed his scarlet biretta on the right-hand corner of his desk. The cardinal's red hat was a symbol of his authority in the Church and of his right to be present in the conclave.

The first order of business was to select by lot three cardinals as *scrutatores*—those who would oversee the voting. The ritual to choose the scrutatores took only five minutes. When they had been chosen, Cardinal Chavez unexpectedly rose from his seat.

"My brothers in Christ, as I'm sure you know, my name has been mentioned as a possible successor to Pope Benedict. Some have questioned whether my membership in Opus Dei disqualifies me from assuming that office. There have been innuendos and whispers. I wish to discuss my membership in Opus Dei openly and candidly. Some critics say that Opus Dei is too secretive an organization, as if secrecy were something evil in and of itself. Opus Dei is no less transparent than the Curia here in the Vatican. Others say lay members of our order take the vow of celibacy and practice acts of strict piety such as fasting and self-flagellation. Since when does piety exclude a person from becoming the head of the Catholic Church! If anything, the future of Catholicism lies in reigniting the spiritual practices of the faithful. Catholics from Europe and the United States criticize us for being out of step on important Church issues such as priestly celibacy and women in ministry. How can we be out of step for believing what the Magisterium of the Church teaches?

"Before I sit down, let me ask each of my brothers a question. Would you exclude a member of the Jesuits or the Dominican Order from becoming pope?" Chavez glanced at Cardinal Diefenbacher who was sitting impassively at his table. "I suspect not. If you would not exclude them, then you should not exclude a member of Opus Dei. Our Church has canonized the founders of the Jesuit and the Dominican Orders and has canonized the founder of Opus Dei, Father Escriva, as well. In God's house there are many mansions—many ways to follow the word of the Lord."

There was silence in the chapel after Chavez resumed his seat.

The Archbishop of Recife, Cardinal Ramera, raised his hand to speak. "Chavez speaks of Opus Dei. In my country, its members are rich and powerful. I do not speak on their behalf but on behalf of the anonymous ones—the poor who beg in the streets, the children who sell their bodies for food, the sick who line up for days, hoping to see a doctor. They have been robbed of hope. All they have left is Jesus. But we who lead his Church turn away from them and support their oppressors. We offer them joy in heaven in return for pain in this life. I ask only two things from our next pope—compassion for the poor and the courage to condemn their oppressors.

When no other member of the Sacred College rose to speak, the camerlengo motioned the scrutatores to begin the first ballot. Each member of the Sacred College wrote the name of his choice on a white card, which he then folded in half. The cardinals, in order of ecclesiastical precedence, walked in a line to a large gold chalice that stood on a table in front of the altar of the Sistine Chapel. One by one, the cardinals placed their ballot in the bowl and returned to their seats. Barbo wrote on his ballot in bold letters the name Jean

Cardinal Calvaux. Printing Calvaux's name in oversized letters was therapeutic for Barbo. He remembered Cardinal Galliardin's words in Gemelli Hospital: If you want the support of the Mafia, submit a blank ballot on the first vote. This was Barbo's way of telling the five cardinals beholden to the Mafia that he would not accept their support. The oversized lettering was also a sign of how strongly he supported Calvaux.

Before tallying the names on the ballots, the scrutatores compared the number of votes submitted with the number of electors present in the Chapel. When the scrutatores announced that there was no discrepancy, Barbo glanced around the room to see if he could determine who the five cardinals were. No expressions or gestures revealed their identities.

The scrutatores proceeded to count the votes according to the rules set down in the Apostolic Constitution. The first of the scrutatores removed each ballot from the bowl and read the name written on it. He passed the ballot to the second scrutator who also read the name aloud. The third and last of the three followed the same procedure, calling out the name inscribed on the ballot. The first four votes were for Chavez, and then in rapid succession came five votes for Diefenbacher. The remaining votes seesawed back and forth between Chavez and Diefenbacher, with sporadic votes for Barbo, Calvaux, and Cardinal McDermott of New York.

The final tally was fifty-four votes for Diefenbacher, forty-five for Chavez, thirteen for McDermott, eight for Barbo, and three for Calvaux.

Since no candidate received the necessary two-thirds-plus-one majority, the scrutatores called for another ballot. Just before the second round of balloting was to begin, however, Diefenbacher rose from his seat.

"I commend Cardinal Chavez for his forthright defense of Opus Dei. His willingness to stand before you in this conclave and unburden his heart has given me the courage to do the same. Cardinal Ramera's eloquence put it best: The Vatican often supports the oppressors, not the oppressed. The Curia forbids priests to help the poor and the disadvantaged in their struggles to create a better life for themselves. And, despite the widespread disavowal of its position, Rome continues to remain intransigent on birth control.

"There is one problem that faces the Church, however, and it surpasses all of the others. In the business world, it would be called an employment crisis. Our churches are full, but our seminaries are empty. If we are to survive as a religion, we must increase vocations to the priesthood. When the existence of the Church was threatened during the Reformation, new orders of religious were formed to challenge those who were bent on destroying us. Today we must take equally bold measures to survive. What stands in our way is the Church's attitude toward sex. Somehow it is deemed unworthy of a priest. But the Church is wrong. God's most precious gift should not be denied those who have chosen to serve Him."

Several cardinals twisted in their seats.

Diefenbacher continued. "In my view, priestly celibacy must become voluntary, except for members of the episcopacy. The Church should also take immediate steps to reinstate those who have left the priesthood to marry and raise a family. If a former priest wishes to return to the Church, we should receive him back with open arms. Finally there is the issue of the status of women. God calls all to the priesthood regardless of sex. We are all members of His one Mystical Body."

Cardinal Muñoz pounded his hand on his desk. "Cardinal Diefenbacher, Jesus himself was celibate and those who carry out his ministry must remain celibate as well."

Barbo stared at Diefenbacher. The secretary of state sensed what was coming.

"Suppose Jesus was not celibate, Cardinal Muñoz? Would that make you rethink your position on celibacy?"

Muñoz smiled. "What do you think, Diefenbacher? Rome is the center of the Church because Peter and Paul were martyred here. If we learned that they were martyred somewhere else, I would vote to move the papacy there."

"And the Curia too, Muñoz?" A ripple of laughter greeted Cardinal Marini's moment of humor.

Diefenbacher paused for a moment. He opened the drawer of his desk and took out a parchment scroll. "Three days ago I came into possession of this document. It is an old Jewish census record. There is little doubt about its authenticity. Carbon dating confirms that it is from the first century A.D. Cardinal Muñoz, let me read a passage from the manuscript. 'In the year 3791, Yeshua from the town of Nazareth married Mary from the town of Magdala according to Jewish law. A child named David was born to them in the year 3792 and a second child, Tamar, in 3793.'"

As Diefenbacher lifted the piece of parchment for everyone to see, the conclave dissolved into uproar and name-calling. A red-faced Cardinal Muñoz struggled to his feet, all the while pointing his finger at Diefenbacher. "Have you no shame! Take this manuscript out of the Sistine Chapel. You have polluted this holy place."

An enraged Cardinal Muramba of Uganda, at a loss for what to do or say, knocked Diefenbacher's cardinal's biretta off his table. "If you believe what this document says, Diefenbacher, you do not deserve to vote in this conclave." Many applauded Muramba's action.

Despite the uproar, Diefenbacher calmly picked up his biretta and waited until the camerlengo restored order. He then walked slowly to where Cardinal Barbo was seated. "My Lord Cardinal Barbo, you can read Hebrew. Tell Cardinal Muñoz and the rest of this conclave whether my translation is accurate."

Barbo looked at the manuscript. "Cardinal Muñoz, I see nothing that would contradict Diefenbacher's translation." Barbo chose his words carefully.

Diefenbacher had the satisfied look of someone who has trapped his opponent. "Well then, Cardinal Muñoz, you must reconsider your position on priestly celibacy. In fact, all those who support celibacy should rethink their positions. Jesus was both God and man. To be fully human, Jesus could not remain celibate. Here is the proof."

The tension in the chapel was electric. Diefenbacher walked to the steps of the altar and stood beneath Michelangelo's *Last Judgment*. "Jesus has given us authority over his Church. But we have failed in our responsibility to him. Unless we elect a leader who is capable of adapting to new structures and new ideas, his Church will wither and die. Look above me at Michelangelo's fresco! Where will Jesus put us on Judgment Day—with the elect or with the damned?"

When Diefenbacher walked back to his seat, an angry Cardinal Chavez demanded to speak. "Perhaps Cardinal Diefenbacher has forgotten—we are in conclave. There are no experts here. We cannot authenticate this manuscript. I, for one, will not take Diefenbacher's word on a question of such importance. Like all Jesuits, he's a master of legerdemain."

Diefenbacher glared at the Mexican cardinal. "I will let that slur on my order pass without comment, Chavez. As for the manuscript, it has been carbon dated. An expert at the University of Rome has authenticated it. Here is his certificate."

Chavez exploded in anger. "I will not accept this certificate. My brothers, this is the work of the devil—not the Holy Spirit. Without further testing, we must not consider this. I will call the Swiss Guard to have this document removed from the Sistine Chapel."

Chavez pulled out a cell phone from under his robes. When he realized what he had done, Chavez quickly put the phone back in his pocket.

Cardinal Barbo rose from his desk. "Chavez, there have been more tests. Cardinal Diefenbacher is right—the manuscript is from first-century Palestine." The Mexican cardinal spun around to see who had spoken. "In addition to carbon dating, the parchment has been subjected to a pollen test. It shows definitively that the parchment was from first-century Palestine."

"How do you know about this manuscript, Barbo?" Chavez trained his eyes directly on the secretary of state.

Barbo stood calmly as he answered Chavez's question. "An agent of the Mafia offered to sell it to me for ten million euros. If I refused to buy it, the individual threatened to make the document public and harm the Church. I would be a liar if I denied that I was tempted to pay the blackmail. Just today, I discovered it was a forgery."

Diefenbacher turned pale. His hands began to shake uncontrollably. "It is not a forgery, Barbo. You yourself said it was authentic."

Barbo shook his head. "You didn't listen carefully, Diefenbacher. What I said was that I saw nothing to contradict your translation and that the manuscript was from first-century Palestine. All of this is true."

For a moment the South African prelate seemed relieved. "So then the parchment is authentic."

Barbo walked to Diefenbacher's desk and picked up the document. "It's an authentic first-century parchment from Palestine alright. But what it originally said has been altered."

Diefenbacher's face twisted with anger. "This is preposterous, Barbo! Are you saying that someone today found this first-century parchment and forged the name 'Jesus' on it?"

"Not precisely, Diefenbacher. The alteration was done in first-century Palestine. If you examine the manuscript under ultraviolet light, you will see that the word Jesus has been superimposed over the original name, John."

Chavez interrupted Barbo. "Why would such a thing be done?"

"Remember your New Testament, Ignacio." All eyes were riveted on the secretary of state. "Herod Antipas had just beheaded John the Baptizer—if he had known that John had children, he would have killed them as well. John's followers falsified the census records to protect his family. Jesus was a cousin and one of John's earliest disciples. He agreed to substitute his name. I asked the Swiss Guard to place an ultraviolet light in my desk." Barbo opened the drawer to his desk and removed a battery-driven light. "This ultraviolet light shows the forgery clearly. Anyone who wishes to see the proof may look for himself."

Chavez took the light from Barbo and shone it on the parchment. "Yes, I see the name John." Chavez handed the light to Cardinal Viaggio. "Chavez is right. The name John is under the name Jesus."

Barbo walked over and pointed at Diefenbacher. "This census record is a forgery, Hans. Not only that, but you bought this document with Church money from an agent of the Mafia."

Diefenbacher started to stand but fell back into his chair.

Barbo continued speaking. His booming voice filled the Sistine Chapel. "Your Eminence, when the conclave is over and the doors are reopened, Detective Cameri from the Rome police will wish to ask you some questions. I'm told there have been some suspicious money transfers from Church accounts in South Africa. Then there's the sudden death of an American professor in Gemelli Hospital. You'll have many questions to answer."

Later, when the second vote of the morning was called, the scrutatores counted the number of submitted ballots. The count came up one ballot short. The third of the scrutatores, the Archbishop of Bombay, Cardinal Padrosa, rose to make the announcement. "The last vote is declared null and void. The ballots will be discarded. I would ask Your Eminences to vote again."

When the ballots cast in the revote were counted, they matched the number of electors. After the scrutatores finished the tally, Cardinal Chavez had received sixty-one votes, Cardinal Barbo forty-one, Cardinal Calvaux eleven, and Cardinal McDermott nine. Diefenbacher received one vote. No one had obtained the necessary eighty-three-vote majority.

After this vote, Cardinal Marini gathered the used ballots from the two morning canvasses and put them in the stove. He lit a match and threw it on the paper ballots. When the camerlengo stood back from the flames, Cardinal Padrosa added the discarded ballots to the fire. "Agostino, you are the senior Cardinal Deacon, are you not?"

Marini nodded. "Yes, I am, Padrosa."

"The Senior Deacon must announce the name of the new pope from the balcony of St. Peter's. You should be an international celebrity by nightfall."

Marini smiled. "The choices have narrowed."

Not wishing to be overheard, Padrosa whispered. "It will be Chavez or Barbo."

"We'll see where the Holy Spirit takes us this afternoon, Padrosa. He can be full of surprises."

As expected, a cry of disappointment rose from the crowd in St. Peter's Square as black smoke was seen coming from the chimney.

The first two ballots, however, did not surprise the Vatican pundits. The consensus was that the factions supporting Cardinals Chavez and Diefenbacher had each held firm during the morning counts. If the Chavez and Diefenbacher supporters could not convince more electors to vote for their candidate, however, the Sacred College would soon have to turn to someone else and that someone else would most likely be Francesco Barbo. The odds makers in the *Totopapa* seemed to agree. When two ballots had not produced a pope, they increased the odds of Barbo's winning from five to one to three to one, replacing Chavez as the frontrunner.

The secretary of state returned to his room in the Domus Sanctae Marthae after the morning ballots. It was clear that Diefenbacher's bid for the papacy had failed. Cardinal Chavez had gained sixteen votes on the second morning ballot, but clearly he was not going to attract the necessary two-thirds plus one majority. Barbo knew that he would start picking up substantial numbers of votes as cardinal electors began to look for a compromise candidate. He might be elected as soon as the first or the second afternoon ballot. One last time, Barbo asked himself if he wanted to be the next Vicar of Christ? He heard the inner voice say again: "Have the courage to trust in God. He wants you elsewhere than in Rome." Barbo would read Pope Benedict's letter when the cardinal electors reconvened in the afternoon.

The news stations all filmed Cardinal Pierce's arrival from Melbourne at Rome's Leonardo da Vinci International Airport. A black limousine bearing Vatican license plates drove him to the Apostolic Palace, where he was immediately admitted to the conclave. He would participate in the afternoon ballots.

Chapter XXV

A New Pontiff

When the cardinal electors had taken their seats for the afternoon balloting, Cardinal Barbo rose to speak. "The Apostolic Constitution that governs this meeting allows for a letter from a deceased pope to be read in conclave. Although the circumstances are different, I asked the camerlengo whether a letter from Pope Benedict could be read to his College of Cardinals. Cardinal Marini has given me his permission."

Barbo unfolded a single sheet of white stationery. "My dear Brothers in Christ, the ways of God are mysterious. During my pontificate, I labored to bring peace to the Middle East. When I was diagnosed with Alzheimer's disease, I lost faith in the Lord. I despaired that he would let me continue my work to bring peace to the region. But I was wrong. He has answered my prayers in an unexpected way. My Alzheimer's disease has given me a new opportunity to work for peace in that sacred land. I wish to spend the rest of my days living in Jerusalem—in a new Center for Interreligious Studies. By living where Jesus died, I can be a witness to the love of God for the whole of humankind. God bless you all and God bless the new Holy Father."

Barbo's voice cracked with emotion as he slumped back in his seat.

"My God, he'll be shot by some fanatic." Cardinal Reysin exploded out of his chair. "This is the dumbest decision I've heard in a long time. Barbo, you're his friend. Convince Benedict that this is a crazy idea."

"The pope is stubborn when he makes up his mind to do something."

The Dean of the Sacred College, Cardinal Bargarian, rose to speak. "And what about his Alzheimer's? The progress of the disease must be monitored carefully. What Benedict asks is simply impossible. It should not be allowed."

"Cardinal Bargarian, I used the word *impossible* in front of Benedict. Do you know what he said? '*Impossible* is not a word in God's dictionary.' The pope will not be dissuaded from what he wishes to do."

Bargarian sat down. "Thank God the Israeli government will not let this happen. They don't want to be responsible for any harm that would come to him."

Barbo paused for a moment before he stood up from his chair and walked to the center of the Sistine Chapel. "I have decided to withdraw my name as a candidate for the papacy."

Stunned, the camerlengo, Cardinal Marini, fell back in his seat. He spoke but his words were barely audible. "Francesco, you must not do this. The Holy Spirit has begun to focus on you. With all due respect to my brother Cardinal Chavez, he will not be able to obtain the required eighty-three votes. You will be elected on the next ballot."

Barbo looked affectionately at Cardinal Marini. "Agostino, there are times when you must put aside ambition and even the wishes of the Church. At moments like this you must walk humbly in the presence of God. Benedict has been my closest friend for forty years. Now he begins a new journey. Over the years, the pope spoke to me of his wish to build a Center for Interreligious Studies in Jerusalem, a place where scholars from all faiths, Eastern and Western alike, could work toward a better understanding of God in all his many faces. I have decided to go with Benedict to Jerusalem and help him build the center."

Barbo stopped for a moment and tears welled up in his eyes. "I ask those who think me worthy to be the Supreme Pontiff of the Church to vote for My Lord Cardinal Calvaux, the Archbishop of Marseilles."

When the first afternoon ballot was counted, Cardinal Calvaux received eighty-six votes—three more than the necessary two-thirds-plus-one majority required for election.

At 3:30 that afternoon, a plume of smoke rose from the chimney that jutted from the roof of the Sistine Chapel. At first it was unclear whether the smoke was black or white.

"Sfumata Bianca!" "White smoke!" An old Italian woman began waving her arms as a sudden wave of excitement and anticipation rolled over St. Peter's Square. Tourists ran to get a place under the balcony of the basilica, where the new pope would make his first appearance. Word that the conclave had concluded spread swiftly through the streets of Rome. From all directions, Romans began to surge into St. Peter's Square. To those who lived in Rome, the pope was not just the Supreme Pontiff of the Holy Roman Catholic Church; he was also the Bishop of Rome, their bishop. They hurried to the square to receive the first blessing from the man chosen to be their spiritual leader.

After an hour, the doors of the central balcony overlooking the entrance to the basilica were finally opened and cardinals, dressed in scarlet robes, walked out into the bright sunlight. Reporters noticed that Cardinal Diefenbacher did not appear on the balcony. Word immediately spread through the press corps that Diefenbacher was the new pope. Commentators speculated over the papal name he would choose.

When the camerlengo, Cardinal Marini, appeared on the balcony, there was a roar of approval from the thousands packed into St. Peter's Square. Marini stood in the bright sunshine savoring every minute of the suspense. Almost playfully, he adjusted the microphone several times and spoke briefly to one of the cardinals who stood next to him. Finally Cardinal Marini motioned with his two hands for the crowd to be silent.

"Annuntio Vobis Gaudium Magnum. Habemus Papam." The camerlengo spoke the age-old Latin words that announced to the City of Rome and to the world that a new pope had been selected. The crowd again roared with approval.

"His name is ... the Most Reverend Lord Cardinal...." The camerlengo paused for a moment; it was the last time he could drag out the suspense. "... Jean Calvaux de Montelambert, Archbishop of Marseilles. He has chosen for himself the name of Paul and will be called Pope Paul VII."

As the camerlengo called out his name, the new pope dressed in a white cassock and zuchetto appeared on the balcony. Again the people roared. White and yellow Vatican flags appeared from nowhere and fluttered from windows throughout the square.

His eyes still squinting from the bright sunlight, Pope Gregory motioned for the vast crowd to be silent. He lifted his arm to impart his first papal benediction.*"Urbi et Orbi"*—to the City and the World. *"In Nomine Patris, et Filii et Spiritus Sancti"*—the Latin words of the blessing echoed across St. Peter's Square. When the blessing was over, the pope waved to the crowd and accepted their cheers. Finally, as the shouting subsided, Pope Gregory left the balcony to accompany the members of the Sacred College into the basilica to attend a Mass of Thanksgiving. Overhead the bells of the city thundered, greeting the new Bishop of Rome.

It was already early evening as the Cardinal Secretary of State walked back to his apartment. Although exhausted, Barbo felt satisfied with the events of the day. Barbo was humbled that the Holy Spirit had chosen him to play so important a role in selecting Pope Paul. As for himself, he could look forward to Jerusalem and the new challenges it would bring to his life.

When he entered his apartment on Via Mascherino, Cardinal Barbo saw on his caller ID that Pietro Visconti had telephoned. Curiosity drove Barbo to return the call.

"Visconti, this is Cardinal Barbo."

"Ah, Eminenza, I'm sorry you were not chosen, but there's so much excitement over the new pope. He's young and dynamic, much like John Kennedy when he was elected president of the United States."

"I'm sure the reason for your call was not to express your sympathies."

"No. It's to say goodbye. My clients think that my talents could be better utilized outside Italy, perhaps in Marseilles—particularly now. . . ."

"What do you mean 'particularly now?'"

"Nothing, Eminenza, I'm afraid I'm late. By the way, if you ever need to be in touch with my clients, please contact Signor Paolo Chiaramonte at his law office on Via Veneto."

As he hung up the phone, Barbo sensed that visconti had regretted his reference to Marseilles. Why was that, he wondered. He recalled what Galliardin had said. If Barbo wished the votes of those cardinals beholden to the Mafia, he should submit a blank ballot on the first tally. There had been a blank ballot cast, but it was on the second tally. At the time, Barbo thought nothing of it. Now he wasn't so sure. Perhaps there was a connection between the blank ballot and Calvaux's election. Could Visconti's trip to Marseilles have something to do with the new pope?

Barbo rang Cardinal Galliardin's room at Gemelli Hospital. A nurse answered the phone. "This is Cardinal Barbo. Could I speak with Pierre?"

"Cardinal Galliardin died at noon today."

Barbo uttered a gasp. "What happened?"

The nurse looked at the cardinal's medical chart. "It was complications from the cancer. The cardinal had been in great pain the past few days. He was taking large doses of morphine."

The news of Pierre Galliardin's death left Barbo empty inside. Cardinal Galliardin had been Barbo's close personal and professional friend for many years. Galliardin had handpicked Barbo to be his successor at the secretariat of state. If only the two of them could have spoken just one more time. Barbo had so many questions to ask him—about corruption in the Sacred College, about Calvaux's election, about the Mafia. But that conversation was not meant to be.

Chapter XXVI

AN EXHIBIT IN THE VATICAN

THE PRIME MINISTER stormed out of the cabinet meeting. Erika Wasserstein, his chief of staff, knew there would be fireworks.

"Erika, you'd better have a goddamned good reason for calling me out of the meeting. Those sons of bitches in Likud are threatening to pull out of the coalition."

"It's about the pope, Mr. Prime Minister."

"The pope! You call me out of a meeting about my political survival to speak to me about the pope!"

"Yes. That's what. . . ."

The prime minister seethed. "Go ahead, but it had better be good. First of all, which pope are you talking about—the new one or the old one?"

"The old one. There's just been an announcement on Vatican Radio. He's coming here." Wasserstein ran her hand nervously through her short-cropped hair.

The prime minister slammed his fist on Wasserstein's desk. "No he's not. This is not the time for a visit from a senile old man. Tell the Vatican ... we are, of course, honored, but the timing for such a visit is not opportune."

"It's not a visit, Shimon." Wasserstein knew that there was no way to sugarcoat the information.

"Well, what the hell is it then? I don't have time for this, Erika."

"He's coming to live in Jerusalem—permanently."

The prime minister slammed his fist on Wasserstein's desk again. "You must be joking! He'd be dead in a week. Some Palestinian would shoot him, and Israel would be blamed for it. The answer is 'No!' Now I've got to go back to the cabinet meeting.

The Vatican is just as out of touch with reality as these Likud ministers are."

Wasserstein stood blocking the door to the room. "Mr. Prime Minister, we have been receiving dozens of calls since the announcement was made. The White House even called. The president wants to speak with you before you release any statement on the matter."

"God damn it! Erika, I don't need to get into a pissing match with the United States over this sort of thing. Get the president on the phone."

Minutes later, Erika Wasserstein stuck her head into the prime minister's office. "He's on line two."

The prime minister picked up the receiver and pressed button two. "Mr. President, good to hear your voice. I'm returning your call."

"Thanks, Shimon. I guess you've got a problem with this decision by Pope Benedict to come to Jerusalem to live. The old pope was much loved in the Catholic Church. Catholics you know make up about thirty-five percent of the U.S. electorate. In the last election they backed me three to one."

"So you want me to allow this old man to live here. If he get's shot, it'll worsen the situation here dramatically."

"There is a story told about an early pope—I think his name was Gregory. When a barbarian army surrounded Rome, he rode out to the enemy camp unarmed and asked them to spare the city. And they did. No one could explain why."

"I'm still not convinced, Mr. President. It's only a story."

"Shimon, did I ever tell you my wife's a Catholic? She is terribly fond of Pope Benedict. By the way, before I forget—the shipment of the T-1 tanks Israel requested seems to have gotten tangled up in DOD bureaucracy. I'll try to move things along, but you know how slow a government bureaucracy can be."

"Mr. President, Pope Benedict can come to live in Jerusalem. We will, of course, protect him."

"Could you hold for a minute, Shimon? Someone is waving a message at me.... You won't believe the coincidence. The DOD now tells me the T-1 tanks can be shipped next week."

The prime minister smiled. "Thank you, Mr. President."

"Thank you as well, Shimon. Pope Benedict may turn out to be a blessing in disguise—like his predecessor Gregory, he may accomplish the unexpected."

When Pope Paul walked onto the stage, the audience broke into enthusiastic applause. Accompanying the Holy Father were Cardinal Francesco Barbo, former Vatican Secretary of State and now Director of the Center for Interreligious Studies in Jerusalem, and Archbishop Michael Finnergan, the newly appointed director of the Vatican Library. When the applause subsided, Cardinal Barbo walked to the podium.

"On behalf of the Holy See, I wish to welcome all of you to the formal opening of the Vatican Library's exhibit entitled "Parchments from the Apocrypha: The Life and Legend of the Magdalene." Although the exhibit contains many important manuscripts, the centerpiece of the exhibit, of course, is the newly discovered Magdalene parchment. Not since the discovery of the Dead Sea Scrolls has a manuscript so excited the scholarly imagination. We are honored today to have in the audience the Chief Rabbi of Jerusalem, Dr. Have Mendellson, as well as the First Lady of the United States. The governments of Israel and the United States have both been extremely generous in supporting this exhibit. Finally I must single out for special mention two men—Professor Victor Baldini from the University of Rome and Martin Fellows, Curator of Hebrew Manuscripts at the Vatican Library. Without their invaluable assistance in authenticating the manuscript and in organizing this exhibit, we would not be here tonight."

When Cardinal Barbo had finished his prepared remarks, Pope Paul rose from his chair and walked to the podium. The papal chamberlain looked startled. The pope had been scheduled to cut the ribbon opening the exhibit, but was not expected to speak.

"My Sisters and Brothers, the manuscripts that you are about to see this evening will deepen your understanding of this woman we call the Magdalene. You will see her as the partner of John the Baptizer and the mother of his children. You will see her as a woman for whom Jesus risks his own life. These documents will help you understand why the Magdalene stood bravely with Jesus at the foot of the cross. God has his reasons for things. It is not a coincidence that this Magdalene parchment has been discovered in the twenty-first century. Others down through history have kept it safe so that it could be shown to us today. It is for us to learn its message.

"Before we proceed to the ribbon-cutting, however, I wish to attend to one matter of unfinished business. Before Pope Benedict abdicated, he had appointed a cardinal *in pectore.* That person was Archbishop Michael Finnergan, who has recently been appointed director of the Vatican Library. I have decided to follow my predecessor's wishes and name Archbishop Finnergan a prince of the Church. He will be given his red hat at the next consistory."

Pope Paul's announcement was met with wild applause. The Holy Father smiled at the Irish archbishop. "I would ask our new cardinal-elect and director of the library to join me in cutting the ribbon to open the exhibit."

As the invited guests followed Pope Pul and Archbishop Finnergan into the exhibit rooms, Father Alessandri walked over to an elegantly attired man who was quietly waiting his turn to enter the exhibit rooms. "Mr. Chiaramonte, Cardinal Barbo has told me how generous you were in helping to fund this exhibit."

"It was nothing. My clients are always willing to help the Church when they can. By the way, I understand your name is on the list of newly appointed monsignori."

Alessandri nodded. "To celebrate, I hope you would join me for a glass of Tignanello after the exhibit."

"It would be my pleasure."

The two men walked together into the exhibit gallery.

About the Author

Gerald T. McLaughlin was born on September 16, 1941, in New York City. He earned his BA degree summa cum laude from Fordham College in 1963. In 1966, he graduated from New York University Law School, where he was managing editor of the *Law Review* and a member of the Order of the Coif. After graduating from law school, McLaughlin became a legal writing instructor at Boalt Hall (University of California at Berkeley Law School) and later an associate in the New York office of Cleary, Gottlieb, Steen & Hamilton. Following teaching stints at the University of Connecticut, Fordham, and Brooklyn Law Schools, in 1991 he became Dean of Loyola Law School in Los Angeles, where he currently serves as dean emeritus and a professor of law. He has lectured and written extensively in the field of commercial law, with particular emphasis on letters of credit. *The Parchment* is his first novel.

Printed in the United States
25878LVS00001B/279